ACCLAIM FOR *THE GIRL FROM THE TRAIN*

"Richly imagined and masterfully told, a love story so moving it will leave you breathless. And deeply satisfied."

—TAMERA ALEXANDER, *USA TODAY* BESTSELLING AUTHOR OF
TO WIN HER FAVOR AND *THE INHERITANCE*

"A riveting read with an endearing, courageous protagonist . . . takes us from war-torn Poland to the veldt of South Africa in a story rich in love, loss, and the survival of the human spirit."

—ANNE EASTER SMITH, AUTHOR OF *A ROSE FOR THE CROWN*

"Captivating. Emotional and heart-stirring. Joubert masterfully crafts every scene with tenderness and hauntingly accurate detail. It's a stunning coming-of-age novel that packs emotion in a delicate weave of hope, faith—and the very best of love."

—KRISTY CAMBRON, AUTHOR OF *THE BUTTERFLY AND
THE VIOLIN* AND *A SPARROW IN TEREZIN*

"A fresh voice and a masterpiece I could not put down—one I will long remember."

—CATHY GOHLKE, CHRISTY AWARD WINNING AUTHOR OF
SECRETS SHE KEPT AND *SAVING AMELIE*

"*The Girl From the Train* is an eloquent, moving testament to love and its power to illuminate our authentic selves."

—SHERRY JONES, AUTHOR OF *THE SHARP HOOK OF LOVE*

Dear Target Guest,

I am a retired teacher from South Africa, and I love writing historical novels in my native language, Afrikaans. I could never have dreamed that my books would one day be published in America. And now, I have the honor of having *The Girl From the Train* selected for the Target Book Club!

The Girl From the Train lies close to my heart, as it is based on true stories that I have encountered in my own lifetime. The first part of the story, where little Gretl Schmidt escapes from the train in the Polish countryside before it reaches Auschwitz, is based on Sarah's story.

I do not know Sarah's last name. I met her in the Caribbean while on vacation. On the first night of our cruise, a lady in her late seventies with a German-sounding accent sat next to me at dinner. Her answer to my polite enquiry was a firm, "I am certainly not German."

Initially, Sarah was reluctant to share her story with me. But the next day, she unexpectedly joined me on deck. I learned that Sarah was a Jewess, the youngest of three children, her parents German-speaking Poles. When Germany invaded Poland on September 1, 1939, Sarah was eight years old. Her father and brother were conscripted into the army, and their suburb was transformed into a ghetto. In early 1940, she was sent to Auschwitz with her mother and sister.

I knew that I would one day share this story. Sarah ended up in America in 1960, but I had to bring my little character to South Africa, to my readers. So I combined Sarah's story with another true bit of history that was part of my childhood—the German orphans who had been sent to South Africa after the Second World War.

In 1948, during the aftermath of World War II, the South African government welcomed eighty-three German war orphans who then were raised by Afrikaans families. Those individuals are now in their eighties and older. I spoke to many of them and listened to their heart-wrenching stories, realizing anew the devastation that war causes for children.

This is how little Gretl Schmidt became one of the German orphans who traveled all the way to South Africa.

Jakób Kowalski, the rebellious Polish student who finds Gretl, is also based on a true tale. Tommy Finés is a Hungarian whom I met in 1970. He studied in Czechoslovakia, became involved in the 1968 revolution, and had to flee the Communist regime. He ended up in England and eventually in South Africa where he worked for a steel company. His story became Jakób's story.

I hope, dear reader, that you will enjoy experiencing these combinations of true stories and my imagination as much as I enjoyed creating them.

With gratitude,

Irma Joubert

The Girl From the Train

Irma Joubert

Translation by Elsa Silke

Thomas Nelson
Since 1798

The Girl From the Train © 2015 by Irma Joubert

Irma Joubert, Tussen Stasies © 2007 by LAPA Uitgewers (Edms.) Bpk, Pretoria, South Africa

Published in Nashville, Tennessee, by Thomas Nelson. Thomas Nelson is a registered trademark of HarperCollins Christian Publishing, Inc.

Thomas Nelson titles may be purchased in bulk for educational, business, fundraising, or sales promotional use. For information, please e-mail SpecialMarkets@ ThomasNelson.com.

Scripture quotations are from the Holy Bible, New International Version®, NIV®. Copyright © 1973, 1978, 1984, 2011 by Biblica, Inc.™ Used by permission of Zondervan. All rights reserved worldwide. www.zondervan.com. The "NIV" and "New International Version" are trademarks registered in the United States Patent and Trademark Office by Biblica, Inc.™

Publisher's Note: This novel is a work of fiction. Names, characters, places, and incidents are either products of the author's imagination or used fictitiously. All characters are fictional, and any similarity to people living or dead is purely coincidental.

Translation: Elsa Silke

ISBN: 978-0-7180-9985-5 (Custom edition)
ISBN: 978-0-7180-9982-4 (Autograph edition)

Library of Congress Cataloging-in-Publication Data

Joubert, Irma, author.
[Meisje uit de trein. English]
The girl from the train / Irma Joubert; Translation by Elsa Silke.
pages cm
ISBN 978-0-529-10237-9 (paperback)
1. Afrikaans fiction—21st century. I. Silke, Elsa, translator. II. Title.
PT6592.2.O795V4713 2015
839.3636—dc23 2014047546

Printed in the United States of America

15 16 17 18 19 20 RRD 6 5 4 3 2 1

To my son Jan-Jan

CONTENTS

Glossary

biltong—a dish of jerked meat

Bloedsap—a staunch supporter of the United Party, South Africa's ruling political party between 1934 and 1948

Boer War/Anglo-Boer War—The Second Boer War was fought from October 1899 to May 1902 by the United Kingdom against the South African Republic (Transvaal Republic) and the Orange Free State. The war ended in victory for Britain and the annexation of both republics.

Brandwag, Die (The Sentinel)—a weekly Afrikaans magazine, discontinued in 1965

eisteddfod—a competitive festival of music and poetry

Great Trek—an eastward and northeastward emigration away from British control in the Cape Colony during the 1830s and 1840s by Boers

Huisgenoot, Die (House Companion)—a weekly Afrikaans-language general-interest family magazine; SA's biggest and oldest family magazine (est. 1916)

Jan van Riebeeck—Dutch colonial administrator and founder of Cape Town

kraal—an enclosure for cattle or other livestock surrounded by a stone wall or other fencing, roughly circular in form

kugeln—ninepins/cones

lametta—tinsel

matric (matriculation)—the final year of high school and the qualification received on graduating from high school

oom—uncle

ouma—grandmother

rag—for "raise and give"; university-level, student-run charity fundraising organization

rusk—a hard, dry biscuit

sakkie-sakkie—a simple, rhythmical style of Afrikaner music and dance

Slagtersnek—an early nineteenth-century rebellion in the Eastern Cape that played a role in the Great Trek

tannie—aunt

tickey—On February 14, 1961, South Africa adopted a decimal currency, replacing the pound with the rand. The term *tickey* is applied to both the 3d and 2½c coins.

volkspele—South African folk dances

weinachtskerzen—Christmas candles

1

"Let go!" her grandmother said.

She held on for dear life. The metal edge bit into her fingers. Her frantic feet searched for a foothold in the air. The dragon swayed dangerously from side to side.

"Gretl, let go!" Her grandmother's shrill voice cut through the huffing noise of the dragon. "We're nearly at the top, you must let go *now*!"

The child looked down. The ground was a long way below. Strewn with sharp stones, it sloped down into a deep gully.

Her arms were aching.

Her fingers were losing their grip.

Then her grandmother pried her fingers loose.

Gretl hit the ground. Shock jolted through her skinny little body.

She fell, slid, rolled down the embankment, stones grazing her face and legs. She clenched her jaw to stop herself from screaming.

At the bottom she slid to a stop. For a moment she lay panting, her heart pounding in her ears. It was so loud that she was afraid the guards might hear.

"Roll into a ball. Tuck in your head and lie very still," her grandmother had told her. "And don't move until Elza comes to find you."

She rolled into a ball. The earth trembled. Beside her, around her, she felt sand and stones shifting. She kept her head down. Above her the long dragon was still groaning and puffing up the hill, spitting smoke and pumping steam. She could smell its rancid breath, but she didn't look.

It was at the top now. She heard it panting, the iron wheels *clickety-clacking* faster and faster on the track.

She was very thirsty.

It was dead quiet.

Slowly she opened her eyes to the pitch-black night. There were no stars.

"What if we're afraid?" Elza had asked.

"Then you think about other things," Oma had said.

Mutti had just cried, without tears, because she had no more water in her body for tears. *I'm not afraid*, Gretl thought. *I escaped from the dragon. First Elza, then me. I'm brave. So is Elza.*

Carefully, painfully, she rolled onto her back and straightened her legs. They were still working, but her knee burned.

At the next uphill, Mutti and Oma would jump out as well. Then they would all go back to Oma's little house at the edge of the forest. *Not* to the ghetto.

There was sand in her mouth. No saliva. If only she could have just a sip of water.

Gingerly she rubbed her smarting knee. It felt sticky and clammy.

The water had run out yesterday, before the sun was even up. At the station the grown-ups put their arms through the railings of the cars and pleaded for water. But the guards with their rifles made sure that no one gave them any. The dogs with the teeth and the drooling jaws barked endlessly. And drank sloppily from large bowls.

The train had filled its belly with water.

"Don't look, think about other things," Oma had said. Oma's face looked strange, blistered by the sun. She had lost her hat.

Her voice had been strange as well. Dry.

Later Mutti stopped crying. Just sat.

It was hard to think about other things.

Gretl wasn't afraid of the dark. "Darkness is your best friend," Oma had said. "Get as far away from the railroad as possible while it's still dark. And hide during the day."

But now there were no stars at all, and the moon appeared only briefly from behind the clouds. Now and again there was a flash of lightning.

She wasn't afraid of lightning. Maybe it would rain soon. Then she would roll onto her back, open her mouth, and let the rain fill her up until she overflowed.

She had to think about other things.

Oma had a little house at the edge of the forest. Like Hansel and Gretel's, but without the witch. In the forest they picked berries. She knew there was no wolf, but she always stayed close to Mutti or Elza just the same.

Maybe she should sit up and softly call Elza's name. The guards and their dogs were gone, over the hill. She no longer heard the *choo-choo* and *clickety-clack*. Elza would never find her in this blackness.

She sat up slowly. Her head ached a little. She peered into the curtain of fog that surrounded her, trying hard to focus. She could see nothing.

"Elza?" Her voice was thin.

She took a deep breath. "Elza!" Much better. "Elza! El-zaa-a!"

Not even a cricket replied.

Jakób Kowalski moved the heavy bag to his other shoulder. Flashes of lightning played sporadically among the dense clouds. It was their only source of light. The terrain was reasonably even underfoot, but as soon as they started the descent toward the river they would need to see where they were going. He ran his fingers through his black hair and screwed up his eyes.

"I can barely see a thing," said Zygmund behind him. At odd intervals his voice still cracked. He was barely fifteen.

"And the rain is going to catch us," Andrei complained. "Why do we have to do it tonight?"

"The coded message said the troop train will pass here just before daybreak, on its way back to Germany." Jakób felt his patience wearing thin. The Home Army had given him two adolescents to help with this dangerous mission. "We must plant the bombs under the bridge before then."

"And you're sure there are no guards on the bridge?" asked Andrei.

"I'm not sure of anything," Jakób replied brusquely, "except that we've got to blow up the bridge tonight."

In silence they progressed slowly under the weight of their cargo through the tall grass and bushes. When the moon appeared for a moment from behind the clouds, Jakób said, "Let's go down here."

"Will we have to swim downstream?" Andrei asked. "Or clamber over the rocks?"

"It's going to be hard with the bags," said Zygmund.

"Are you in or are you out?" Jakób asked, exasperated. "If you're in, shut your traps."

They struggled down the steep slope, slipping in places, clinging to their dangerous load. The clouds seemed to be lifting somewhat, and once or twice the moon showed its face. Dislodged stones rolled down the slope, splashing into the water.

The final trek to the bridge took them more than half an hour. The water rushed past, glimmering in the faint moonlight. They tried to stay at the water's edge, but the pebbles were round and smooth and the bank was steep. The heavy bags dragged at their shoulders. The darkness provided good cover, but it also made the going tough. After every few steps Jakób stopped to listen, trying to figure out where they were. Then the clouds lit up faintly in the distance, there was a crash of thunder, and Jakób saw the bridge about ten yards ahead.

We're here, he motioned.

The other two showed him a thumbs-up.

At the bridge, Jakób placed their bags at the foot of the second column. Zygmund took off his boots, then his coat. Jakób tied two ropes around his waist. *I'm going up*, Zyg motioned, and he began to climb.

His progress was painfully slow. He found an occasional foothold on the crossbars of the smooth, steel column, but for the most part he had to hoist his wiry body up by his own strength. Fortunately the clouds seemed to be receding. Jakób stared upward, tension tightening between his shoulder blades, but all he could see was an occasional vague movement. Next to him Andrei stood waiting to catch the ropes. It was dead quiet.

After what seemed like an eternity, they saw both ends of one rope dangling in front of them, swinging beside the steel column. They attached the first bag to one end, then Jakób and Andrei pulled on the opposite end while Zyg worked at the top, all three of them lifting the shells together, inch by inch, careful not to let the bag swing.

After the bag with its hazardous contents arrived safely at the top, they transported the second load, a landmine acquired after the Home Army regaled a Russian battalion with homemade vodka, then relieved them of an entire consignment of light weaponry.

The third load was more difficult. It was an unexploded two-hundred-pound bomb left behind when the Nazis had passed through Poland in 1940. The slightest jolt might set it off. It took all Jakób's and Andrei's strength to hoist the bag.

When it was at the top, Jakób said, "Hold it steady. I'll tie the rope to the base of the column."

"Okay, but hurry," Andrei answered, panting.

When the rope was firmly secured, Zyg sent down the second rope for Jakób to climb. He removed his shoes and tested it before he began his ascent. He hauled his lithe body up the rough cord without too much difficulty, his muscles honed since boyhood by farm labor, his hands toughened over the past three years at the steelworks. A moment later he sat on the crossbar next to Zygmund.

Zyg clung to the bag containing the bomb. Together they found a good position for it under the track. It was a pity they had to sacrifice the sturdy bag, but removing the heavy bomb was too dangerous. Next they planted the landmine, took a final look around to make sure everything was ready, and began their careful descent.

The return journey was a lot easier. They were rid of their heavy load, and the clouds that had been obscuring the moon were dispersing. The two boys were frantic to get away, as if they had only just realized the adventure was real.

Jakób looked at the sky. In less than an hour, he reckoned, the moon would set. It would be about another three hours before daybreak.

Zygmund said, "I hear a train."

"Impossible," said Jakób.

"It's a train," Zygmund insisted.

They turned and looked downriver in the direction of the bridge, which was no more than two hundred yards from their present position.

Then Jakób heard it as well. "Find shelter!" he shouted. "Behind this rock! Quick!"

They scurried over the loose stones, then threw themselves down behind a low, flat rock. "Will this be enough cover?" asked Zygmund.

"It'll have to do," said Jakób.

He saw a light drilling a tunnel through the darkness and felt shock shoot through his body. "The train is coming from the wrong direction!" he exclaimed. "It can't be the—"

A brilliant flash lit up the sky, the horizon exploded with an incredible boom, and a blinding light shot upward, as if an enormous thunderstorm had been let loose over the bridge.

"God help us!" said Andrei, covering his head with both hands.

There were the sounds of steel ripping apart, of people screaming.

A second blast followed, louder than the first. Zygmund drew his head into the shell of his body. "Mother Mary!" he sobbed.

Andrei cursed and crossed his broad chest twice.

"That was the boiler exploding," said Jakób.

But where had this train come from? From the wrong side? On its way to . . .

In a flash he knew. Nausea pushed up in his throat, bitter as gall. "Come," he said. "Let's go."

Gretl jumped. She recognized the sound of bombs, knew she had to find shelter. The clouds on the horizon had a red glow. The explosion came from the other side of the hill.

It was far away, but the enemy could move fast.

In the gloom she crawled up the embankment and struggled to her feet. She could just make out the shapes of the bushes and tall trees flanking the railroad.

At the edge of a forest she stopped. She wasn't afraid, but there was always a wolf or a witch in a forest. Or a cruel stepmother, she knew. So she crawled under a shrub at the edge of the big forest and lay very still. She could smell the wet leaves, and the cold crawled under the shrub with her.

No planes.

No more bombs.

Just quiet. And terrible thirst.

After a while she fell asleep.

When she woke up, the sun was shining. Something had awakened her.

Thirst overwhelmed her entire body.

She had to find Elza. They should have got away from the railroad while it was still dark. That's what Oma had said.

She crawled out of her hiding place and cautiously looked around. Then she heard it—a whistle. That was how Mutti had always called them in the forest at Oma's house. Mutti was here!

She tried to whistle in reply, but her mouth was too dry, so she walked in the direction of the whistle.

"Gretl!" Elza called from the left. "*Gott sei dank, du bist heil.* Thank God you're safe."

"Elza? I heard Mutti whistle."

"It was me." Elza's voice sounded strange. Maybe she needed water too.

"Do you have any water?" asked Gretl.

"No, we'll go and find some."

"Shouldn't we wait for Mutti and Oma?"

"No." Elza set off, heading straight into the forest. Gretl stayed by her side.

"Elza? Did you hear the bombs?"

Elza glanced down at her. "It wasn't bombs," she said. "It was thunder." She looked straight ahead and quickened her pace.

Maybe Elza was afraid and had changed the bombs to thunder in her mind, Gretl thought. Elza was afraid of everything, even though she was fourteen. Gretl was hardly ever afraid, and she was only six and a half.

The tall trees made a roof over their heads. They walked through dense ferns, pushed branches out of their way, climbed over fallen tree trunks. "When are we going to find water?" asked Gretl.

"I don't know."

"Elza, are you crying?"

"No."

She knew Elza was crying because she was afraid. "Don't worry, we'll be out of the forest soon."

Elza said nothing, just kept walking.

"And then we'll find Mutti and Oma." She tried to comfort her.

Elza walked on.

After a while Gretl was tired. Her legs were aching, and she was very, very thirsty. Her tummy cramped, her throat couldn't swallow. "I have to find water now," she said.

"There's probably water down there," said Elza. Her face was red, her dark hair clung to her forehead. "There must be a river."

Gretl heard the water before she saw it. She forgot all about the wolf and the witch, ran ahead, fell on her tummy, and drank greedily.

Elza washed her flushed face. "Don't drink too much, you'll throw up," she warned.

Gretl rolled onto her back in the damp grass and looked up at the leaves overhead. The sun was glittering like gold through the trees. Now that she was no longer thirsty, hunger took over. "Elza, have you got anything to eat?"

"No."

She sat up. "Where will we find Mutti and Oma?"

"I don't know. Come, we must keep walking."

Reluctantly Gretl got up. "I'm still tired," she complained. "Where are we going?"

"To Switzerland, to find Onkel Hans," said Elza.

"Who's Onkel Hans?"

"Oma's brother."

"Is Switzerland far?"

"Yes, very far."

"Elza, how will we get there?"

Elza began to cry. "I don't know, I don't know!" she cried. "Stop asking so many questions. My head hurts!"

Gretl kept quiet. After a while she said, "Never mind, Elza. Oma will know what to do. We must just find her."

But Elza just cried harder. "Don't speak about Mutti and Oma," she said between sobs.

"All right." She would think about other things. Then the hunger would go away.

Switzerland was where Heidi and Peter lived, in the mountains, with a herd of goats. "Do you think Onkel Hans is as cross as Alm U?" She forgot she wasn't supposed to ask questions.

"Gretl, what are you talking about?"

"Switzerland, of course."

"Oh." But Elza didn't answer her question.

When they came out of the forest, there was a farm with a fence, and behind the fence an orchard. "Wait here," said Elza.

Gretl waited a long time. She looked at her shoes. They were very dirty. So were her socks.

Elza came back with her sweater full of apples. "Don't eat too many, your tummy will ache," she warned.

The apple crunched as she bit into it. It was a big, sour apple. "Why don't you eat an apple too?" she asked Elza.

"I'll eat one later. Give me your sweater. I want to tie two more apples in it, for our supper."

"What if I'm cold?" asked Gretl.

"Then we'll eat the apples. Come, there must be a road nearby. Maybe there's a signpost to show us where we are."

She wanted to ask about Mutti and Oma, but she was afraid Elza would cry again.

When they were near the road, Elza said, "Listen, Gretl, we're in Poland now. They don't like Germans here."

"Aren't we in Germany?" asked Gretl. She knew Oma's little house in the forest was in Germany. So was the ghetto.

"No, Poland. You mustn't speak German at all."

"What must I say?"

"We must speak Polish. Oma's language, remember? She used to speak it to us. And to Mutti."

Gretl nodded. "It's hard." She frowned.

"Yes, but you're clever."

Gretl nodded again. She was clever, she knew. "Don't they like Jews either?" she asked.

"I don't know," answered Elza. "I think they like Germans even less than they like Jews, but no one really likes Jews. I don't think we should mention Jews either."

"Oma is Jewish, I know," said Gretl.

"Forget about it." Elza looked as if she was about to start crying again. "Forget about Jews and Germans and everything else. You and I are two Polish children from the north, understand?"

She didn't understand, but she nodded gravely. "Papa was a German soldier," she said.

"Gretl, stop it now!" Elza said angrily.

So she stopped.

They walked all day. After a while her feet were hot and her shoes hurt her feet and her legs felt heavy. But Elza said they had to walk as far as they could. Not in the road, but in the bushes next to the road, where they could hide if they saw someone coming. Sometimes they rested. Elza complained that her head hurt. *It's from crying too much*, Gretl thought.

When it got dark, Gretl asked, "Where will we sleep?"

"Under the bushes. Until we get to Onkel Hans we're going to be sleeping under bushes and we won't be eating very often. Do you understand?"

She nodded.

"Once we're in Switzerland, it will be better."

She just had to ask: "Elza, where will we find Mutti and Oma?"

"They're not coming," Elza said brusquely.

In the night Elza curled up and trembled like a reed. She felt hot to Gretl's touch, and she was sweating, but she kept shivering. And she kept asking for water. Just before the sun came up, she spoke to Mutti in her sleep.

Gretl was cold as well. But the cold was more inside her, because the earth smelled so wet. She didn't rattle like Elza did.

When the sun was up, Elza got to her feet. "We must go on," she said.

"I think you're sick," said Gretl.

"Yes," said Elza. "Let's just find water."

There was plenty of water in Poland. They drank at streams and ate another apple each. But after a while Elza couldn't go on. She fell asleep in the shade of a tree.

Gretl lay on her back, gazing at the leaves. She missed Mutti. And Oma, especially Oma. Why weren't they coming along?

The branches and leaves closed in around her, almost like Sleeping Beauty's castle. Maybe she could sleep for a hundred years as well. No, that was a bad idea—she would carry on walking until she found Mutti and Oma. They'd be with Onkel Hans, she knew it, and they'd eat bread dipped in melted cheese. Just like Heidi.

I mustn't think about bread and cheese, she thought.

She sat up and looked around her. After a while she got up and wandered a short distance. She found a place where she could sit and watch the road. It was a quiet road. Occasionally a horse-drawn wagon came by. Sometimes someone on foot. Only one truck rattled past, but with pigs in the back, not soldiers.

She spotted a strange figure in the distance, clanging as he walked. On his back was a big bag. Jugs and a kettle hung from a belt around his waist, making the noise. In his hand he carried another bag. In the other hand he held a stick.

He walked slowly. Very close to her hiding place he sat down on the grass at the side of the road and removed the big bag from his back. It was full of things, but she couldn't see what they were. Then he opened the other bag and took out a piece of bread.

Gretl felt her tummy heave. It had been days since she last tasted bread. When he took some cheese out of his bag, her mouth filled with saliva.

The man cut off a thick chunk of bread with his pocketknife and picked up the cheese.

Gretl leaned forward to see better.

He turned. She knew he had seen her but she sat without moving.

He narrowed his eyes to see better. "*Dziewczynko, czy nie chcialabys troche chleba?*" he asked.

He was asking whether she wanted some bread.

Mutti had told her never to speak to strangers. But she had never been so hungry before. She nodded.

Come, he motioned. But she stayed in her hiding place. He shoved his stick into the ground and slowly pushed himself up. One shoe was broken, exposing a toe in a sock. He came up to her, leaned over, and handed her a piece of bread and cheese. His hands were dirty, the nails broken.

Her teeth sank into the bread. It was hard and tough, so she had to clamp her teeth together to tear off a piece. The cheese was also hard and dry, but it was the most delicious bread and cheese she had ever eaten.

"Gdzie jest twoja mama?" he asked. She understood what he was saying, but she didn't want to speak. She nodded.

The man got up and peered into the forest. Gretl stayed where she was. Though she hadn't told him about Elza, he walked straight toward her. Slowly Gretl got up and followed. The man stood looking down at Elza. Then he bent down and felt her forehead.

"She's very ill," said the man.

Gretl nodded.

"She can't stay here. I'm going to take her to a house where there are people who can look after her," he said. He looked up at Gretl and frowned. "Where are you going?"

"In der Schweiz." She had forgotten she was not supposed to speak German.

"Schweiz? Switzerland?" he said, astonished. He shook his head. "Switzerland?" he repeated.

"Yes, Switzerland."

He fetched his bags and hid them under some shrubs near the spot where Elza was lying. Then he bent down and picked up Elza. She groaned and her eyelids fluttered, but she didn't wake up. The man didn't look strong. He was very thin. But Elza was thin as well, and probably not heavy.

"Come," he said and set off down the road.

Uncertain what else to do, Gretl followed.

———

"What's this I hear about you blowing up the wrong train?" Stanislaw asked when Jakób arrived home two days later.

Jakób glanced around him quickly.

"There's no one here, little brother, relax," Stanislaw sneered.

"We didn't blow up a train, Stan," Jakób said, exhausted. "We blew up a bridge—the right bridge at the right time. But the information we were given wasn't right."

He went to the kitchen in search of coffee. Stan followed. The coffee pot had been rinsed out, and the cloth bag hung on the hook. The stove was cold.

Jakób looked around the kitchen. It was the heart of the home, especially during the cold winter months. Leading out of it on one side was his parents' bedroom. The bedroom on the other side belonged to his oldest brother and sister-in-law. There was a porch at the front, where they sat in the summer when it was too hot in the kitchen, and where he and Stan were presently sleeping. Too many people were living under this roof.

The kitchen itself was sparsely furnished. The stove was black and shiny, pots gleamed on a shelf, and on the floor next to the stove was a box filled with firewood. In the middle of the kitchen stood a rough wooden table and six wooden chairs. Against one wall was a painted cabinet for tableware and provisions. Because of the war, the metal chest that usually contained their flour and sugar was almost empty. Against the opposite wall stood an upright wooden bench. The stables were a few yards from the back door.

He heard his father working outside.

"Where's Mother?"

Stan shrugged. "Attending afternoon mass, I suppose. I've just woken up, I'm on night shift." He took a big homemade loaf out of the cupboard. "Hungry?" he asked.

Jakób nodded. He was ravenous.

"Get the cheese," said Stan, cutting thick slices of bread.

Jakób went out to fetch goat's-milk cheese and a piece of ham covered with a moist cloth from the cooler. He dipped a mug into a pitcher filled with cold water and sat down on a wooden chair beside the rough kitchen table.

"Meeting tomorrow night, same place," Stan said around a mouthful.

The members of the Polish resistance movement that met in Częstochowa were few but valiant, though their efforts had grown more desperate as the German occupation endured.

"We must improve our communication channels," said Jakób. "It's no good getting partial information."

"We're doing our best."

"Our best isn't good enough," Jakób said. A helpless fury took hold of him again. "How many Jewish refugees has the Home Army saved from the Nazis? And here we go and blow up an entire train with—"

"It was unfortunate," Stan interrupted. "But the train was unscheduled."

They ate in silence.

"London has asked us to collaborate with the Soviets," Stan eventually said.

"I refuse to help the Red Army," Jakób said firmly. "I don't trust the Communists."

"They'll give us the weapons we need."

"And as soon as we've played our role they'll disarm us and take us prisoner. Or force us to join the Polish Armed Forces in Russia. You know it as well as I do!"

"Without the help of the Red Army we won't make headway against the Nazis. Listen to what I'm telling you."

Jakób did not want to listen. He rinsed his plate in the basin and went out onto the porch.

A green field stretched downhill to the outskirts of the city. Częstochowa was a beautiful place, a historic landmark. From the porch he could see the Aleja Najświętszej Maryi Panny, a wide street running all the way through Częstochowa to the foot of the Jasna Góra monastery. From where he was standing, Jakób could see only the thick walls surrounding the monastery and the top of the bell tower. Far to the left lay the industrial quarter, where he and Stan were employed at the steelworks.

Jakób ran his hand over his face. He felt the stubble under his fingers. Maybe he'd feel better after he had washed and shaved. And he still craved a coffee.

———

First Gretl saw two little boys wrestling on the grass. Then she saw three goats grazing—like Peter's goats from the Heidi story. "Mamo! Mamo!" shouted one of the boys and ran on ahead. "*Idzie Mejcio!* Here's Mejcio!"

When she rounded the corner with the man who carried Elza, she saw a low building, like a stable. It had a sloping roof and there was only one door. A woman came out with a baby in her arms. A small girl peered out from behind her skirt.

The man and woman spoke too fast. Gretl couldn't understand what they were saying. They all went into the house. It was dim inside, and there was a bad smell.

The man laid Elza on the only bed. The woman felt her forehead. "She's very ill," she said.

"Yes," said the man. He spoke some more, but Gretl didn't understand.

The woman shook her head, spoke fervently, nodded again. "Yes, she looks Jewish," said the woman. "But the little one"—and she pointed disapprovingly at Gretl—"is definitely German."

Gretl took awhile to work out what she wanted to say. "*To jest moja siostra,*" she said. *She's my sister.*

The woman turned to her and spoke so fast that Gretl didn't understand a word. She fetched a moist cloth and gave it to Gretl. Gretl understood: she had to wipe Elza's brow.

"I'm going now," the man said after a while. "You're to stay until your sister is well."

"Okay," she said.

The woman—her name was Rigena, she'd heard—said something

about plants and motioned that Gretl should look after the two little ones. She thrust the baby into Gretl's arms and left.

Gretl looked at the baby. It was an ugly little creature, too pink. And it gave off a sour smell. There was no crib to lay it in, so she put it on the floor. But the baby opened its mouth and bawled. She grabbed it, picking it up from the floor. The little girl watched with large brown eyes from under the table.

"Mutti?" Elza murmured from the bed.

Gretl rocked the baby and replied, "No, it's me, Gretl. Are you better now?"

Slowly Elza opened her eyes. They were very red. "Why are you bouncing that baby?" she asked in a hoarse voice.

"It's the only way it will stop screaming," said Gretl.

"Oh." Elza closed her eyes again. "Water," she said softly.

Gretl looked around. There was a pitcher and a tin mug on the table, but she couldn't bounce the baby and get water at the same time. She put the infant back on the floor.

The baby screamed. She grabbed the mug and dipped it into the water. Under the table the little girl also began to cry. Gretl lifted Elza's head and held the water to her lips. It dribbled out, but Elza managed to drink some of it.

"My head hurts," said Elza. "Make the children stop crying."

Gretl picked up the baby and jiggled her. It helped, but the little girl was still crying. She saw a bowl with honey on a shelf. She dipped her finger into the honey and popped it into the little girl's mouth. She instantly stopped crying.

"Where are we?" whispered Elza.

"In a house," said Gretl. "But I don't know where Mutti and Oma are."

It was quiet for a long time. The little girl came out from under the table and motioned with a dirty finger that she wanted more honey. Gretl struggled to give her the honey while jiggling the baby at the same time.

When Elza spoke again, her voice was so soft that Gretl could hardly hear. "Mutti and Oma couldn't have escaped from the train," she said. "The gap was too small."

"But they said they would!" Gretl cried.

Elza's eyes were closed. "Just to make us feel better," she whispered.

"Where did they go, then?" Gretl asked.

But Elza didn't answer. Her breathing was shallow and rasping, her cheeks were blood-red, and her sweaty black hair clung to her scalp. *I must wipe her face again*, Gretl thought. But it was simply too much. She couldn't jiggle the baby, feed the little one honey, and wipe Elza's face all at the same time. So she left it.

After a while Rigena came back with the two little boys, who were making a great deal of noise. The baby began to scream again, and so did the little girl. Rigena rocked the baby and shouted at the boys to go outside to play. She fed some wood into the stove, put a pot with a little water on top, threw in a handful of leaves, and motioned to Gretl to wipe Elza's face. Gretl hoped Rigena wasn't a witch.

She wiped and wiped Elza's face. Rigena allowed the leaves to cool and tried to feed Elza the leafy water. But Elza couldn't seem to wake up and kept choking.

When darkness began to fall, Gretl went outside. She sat down and leaned against the wall of the house. Three goats were chewing their cud, and a few ducks were waddling toward the house.

Elza was very sick, she knew. Mutti and Oma were gone, she didn't know where.

She tried to think about other things, such as Oma's Hansel-and-Gretel house in the forest, but then she missed Oma and Mutti even more. She thought about Switzerland and Peter and Heidi, but now that Elza was sick, she didn't know how they would get to Switzerland. She tried to think about the story of the wolf and the seven little goats, and the one about the ugly duckling who became a swan, but nothing helped.

She wasn't usually afraid, but now she was. Not of the darkness or the bombs that might fall or of Rigena, who might be a witch.

She was afraid because she had never been so alone.

For the first time she began to cry.

2

When the Nazis had closed down the University of Krakow and interned most of the professors, Professor Sobieski and his wife fled just in time. A former student, now a metallurgical engineer at the steelworks, took them into his home, where Jakób and two others were secretly continuing their studies. Jakób hoped he would be able to complete his final year at the university when the war was over and qualify for his degree.

Tonight the professor and Jakób sat on a hard bench at a narrow wooden table in a candlelit kitchen. They had finished with the complicated mathematical formulas and the analysis of chemical compounds. The other two students had already disappeared into the dark.

"I have to go to Krakow next week," said Jakób, "but I'll be back the week after."

Never one to ask unnecessary questions, the professor nodded.

"I'll try to bring back that book you're looking for."

"You probably won't find it." The candle flickered, throwing dim shadows on the stone wall. "Nietzsche's words . . ." Professor Sobieski took off his wire-rimmed spectacles and polished them carefully. "Nietzsche's words about blood and horror being at the bottom of all 'good things' have come true. No nation has ever experienced the kind of oppression that Poland is undergoing now."

"True, Professor," said Jakób. He felt exactly the same about his country's suffering.

The professor carefully hooked his spectacles around his ears. A crack ran through the middle of one lens. "First Germany invaded Poland from the west, then the Soviet Union from the east, then they divided Poland between them as if we haven't existed as a sovereign nation for the past thousand years."

"True, Professor." Sometimes the professor took a long time to make his point.

"But what the Nazis did in the south is even worse," said Professor Sobieski.

The closing of the university was still an open wound.

"The University of Krakow is all of six hundred years old, one of the oldest universities in Europe."

It was quiet for a while. Jakób also understood what the professor was not saying. "I agree, Professor," he said.

"To close the university! It's disgraceful!"

The elderly man didn't mention his colleagues who had disappeared. Jakób nodded.

"You know, Jakób, I believe the Nazis aim to eradicate the word *Polak* from the vocabulary. Poland will become a colony and the Poles will be the Russians' slaves. The country will be a reservation, nothing but a labor camp for the Third Reich."

So that was what was bothering the old man. "We won't allow it, Professor," said Jakób. "The Home Army has a lot of support—we estimate around two hundred thousand men—who will rise up to fight when the time is ripe."

"What are you waiting for, then? When will the time be ripe? Has our nation not suffered enough already?"

"We don't have the means, Professor," Jakób tried to explain. "We have a reasonable supply of small arms, but not enough heavy armament. We don't want to act prematurely. In Operation Tempest, through sabotage—"

"Is it true," Professor Sobieski interrupted, peering past the crack in his lens, "that you're considering collaborating with the Soviets?"

Jakób chose his words carefully. "Some people are talking about it, yes, Professor, but I don't trust the Communists."

"I fought in Russia in the Great War of 1914. I don't trust them either."

"I fear the Russians even more than I fear the Nazis." Jakób leaned forward, speaking earnestly. The professor was the one person who would understand what he was saying. "I believe after the war Russia is going to emerge as one of the great world powers, possibly the greatest. I believe the Western nations who are presently bending over backward to accommodate their ally in the East are going to cry bitter tears one day."

The professor nodded. "We must restore the Soviet-Polish borders established during the Treaty of Riga in 1921," he said thoughtfully. "Remember the words of the great patriot and poet Mickiewicz . . ."

Later, when Jakób was walking home in the dark, he knew that Professor Sobieski hadn't understood his fear. Maybe he had just not listened. The full moon lit up the silent landscape and bathed him in a great loneliness.

———

The streets of Krakow were deserted. The Jewish quarters were quiet as the grave, the centuries-old synagogue in ruins. The clip-clop of horses' hooves on the cobblestones was silent, the brightly colored flowers and jumble of stalls on the market square gone. Even the bugler at the church with its twin towers had been silenced. Only the wide, deep waters of the Vistula continued to flow unhindered.

But at least Krakow was still there, Jakób thought, with its ancient buildings and its castle and the Church of St. Andrews. If the Home Army hadn't found out about the landmines and defused them in time, the face of the city would have been completely changed.

Twice along the way he was stopped and ordered to produce his papers. He felt the tension between his shoulder blades. He knew his documents were in order, but the Gestapo could always find something wrong if they wished. After each confrontation he walked on as calmly as possible.

A black swastika on a huge red banner was on display at the university. Jakób did not stop to enter. Professor Sobieski's book would have to wait until the war was over.

He had dropped off pamphlets at the home of Andrei Kiernik's parents the night before. His father would print more and continue to distribute them. When Andrei had walked him out, he had said, "You should visit that woman on whose farm you buried the ammunition."

"Why? Is there a problem?" Jakób had asked.

"No. But she asked me to tell you to come."

Jakób had sensed that Andrei was hiding something. It was probably nothing serious, or Andrei would have warned him, he reassured himself as he took a shortcut through a field. He walked at a fast pace. It was a two-day journey on foot back to Częstochowa, and he wanted to be home before dark the next evening. He had tucked a packet containing secret information and documents into the front of his shirt, where he could feel it rubbing against his chest.

The farmhouse looked even more run-down than it had a year ago, when he had come here to bury the ammunition. In one place the roof had caved in completely and a beam stuck up in the air at an odd angle.

"There's a child here you must take," said Rigena as soon as he appeared.

"Good afternoon, Rigena," said Jakób.

"Yes, good afternoon. She's Jewish, she can't stay here," Rigena said, tucking a strand of black hair behind her ear.

"A little girl?" Jakób didn't understand what Rigena was trying to tell him.

"I can barely care for my own children. I can't keep her here."

Jakób felt a heaviness inside him. Where would he go with a Jewish child? He asked the first question that came to him.

"Where did she come from?"

"I suppose she was on the train full of Jews you blew up," said Rigena and jiggled the little one on her hip.

Jakób closed his eyes. He couldn't get that picture out of his mind. "No," he said, "no one could have come out of it alive."

"Then I don't know. But you've got to take her."

"Rigena, I . . ."

A child appeared in the dilapidated doorway. She was small and dirty and terribly skinny. Her face was ashen, her blonde hair thin and matted. But her eyes were big and blue, and she looked at Jakób fearlessly.

He felt a strange tenderness stir in him and looked at Rigena. "Why do you think she's Jewish?" he asked.

"Her sister was dark, you know. And there was the nose."

He looked at the child again. She was still staring at him. She was fair, with a pert, turned-up nose. "Where's the sister now?"

From Rigena's gesture he understood he shouldn't mention it again.

Jakób shook his head. It didn't seem possible. "Rigena," he said desperately, "where could I take her?"

Rigena shrugged and turned to the child. "Get your bag," she said.

"Does she speak Polish?" asked Jakób, at a loss. He felt as if a strong current were sweeping him along. He was used to being in control.

"She doesn't speak. She understands," said Rigena.

The child reappeared in the doorway. She pressed a small, flat bag to her chest, holding it like a shield.

"Is this all she's got?" asked Jakób. "Doesn't she have . . . clothes?"

"No, just that," said Rigena. "You must go now, it'll be dark in an hour. I don't have any bread to give you, only apples."

"I have enough food, thanks, Rigena." He turned to the scrawny, blue-eyed girl. "Come," he said, making his voice as friendly as possible.

When they had been walking for almost an hour, he took out his water bottle and unscrewed the cap. "Water?" he asked, sitting down to rest.

The child nodded. She took a few sips, then wiped the bottle carefully with her dirty dress before handing it back to him.

He was surprised by her endurance. He had been walking at a much slower pace than usual, often looking over his shoulder for her, but he had never stopped. She had not uttered a sound and stayed with him every step of the way. He didn't know what he was going to do with her, though. "Are you German, or are you Jewish?" he asked.

"*Jestem Polka*," she said. *I'm Polish*. Her voice was strong for such a young child, but her accent gave her away.

"I see." He switched to German. "What's your name?"

She did not reply.

"I'm Jakób," he said. "Jakób Kowalski."

When she remained silent, he got up. "We must keep walking while we can still see," he said. "Are you tired?"

She shook her head and got up at once, still clinging to her bag.

Jakób swung his backpack over his shoulder and walked on. He kept to the road. He knew these parts. Hardly anyone except the local farmers ever used the road. He would hear any approaching trucks from a distance. There would be plenty of time to hide in the bushes.

Soon it became too dark to see. "We'll stop here," he said, still in German. "We'll eat and sleep. The moon will be up at two; it might be possible to carry on then." He didn't know why he was explaining. Surely she was too young to understand.

He opened his bag and took out the bread and ham Andrei's mother had packed for him. He would save the goat's-milk cheese for the next day. He broke the bread, carefully sliced the ham into thin strips, and put it on the bread. "Here," he said.

Wordlessly she took the bread. Her hands were small, the fingers incredibly thin and fragile looking.

He knew nothing about children, especially girls, Jakób realized. He didn't know anyone with a little girl. The neighbors had two unruly boys.

"Help yourself to the water," he said. He felt awkward, inadequate.

"Thank you." So she did understand German after all.

When they had eaten, he unrolled his thin blanket. "We must sleep," he said, lying down.

She lay down next to him on the blanket, turned her back to him, and fell asleep almost at once.

For Jakób, sleep didn't come. What was he going to do with this child? She could never keep up until they reached Częstochowa. It was much too far. Besides, it was unlikely that they would get home the next day. Their progress was too slow.

He would have to carry her. He just didn't know how.

Little girls cry a lot, he thought. He hoped she wouldn't start crying.

Around them the land lay dark and quiet. Peaceful.

Where would he go with her? He couldn't take a German child home with him—Germans were hated in Poland. Neither could he show up with a Jewish child—his parents, especially his mother, were diehard Catholics.

He couldn't think of anyone who would take her.

It was late when he finally fell asleep.

Something woke him. He felt the tense little body against him. Then he heard it, the distant rattle of gunfire. Instinctively he held out his hand. The bony little hand slipped into his own. "It's far away," he said.

"I'm not afraid," she said. But the small, icy hand clung to him.

———

By the time the sun came up, they had covered a considerable distance. They had rested twice, drunk all the water in the bottle, and walked on. "We must fill the water bottle," Jakób said.

She washed her hands and face at a stream. They each had a slice of bread and washed it down with water. "Please tell me your name," he said.

"Gretl."

"Gretl who?"

She said nothing more.

"Gretl Whatever, I don't really know where to take you."

"To Onkel Hans."

"I beg your pardon?"

"Take me to Onkel Hans, Jakób Kowalski."

He was flooded with relief. "Eureka!" he said thankfully. "Where does Onkel Hans live?"

"Switzerland."

"Switzerland?" The relief subsided.

"Yes, Switzerland." She sounded certain.

"All right. Where in Switzerland?"

"Just Switzerland."

Any remaining relief vanished completely. "Gretl, Switzerland is a very big country. We'll have to find out where in Switzerland Onkel Hans lives."

She looked at him with those big, blue eyes.

"Who is Onkel Hans?" He tried a different angle.

"Oma's brother, don't you know?"

"Fine. What is Onkel Hans's last name?"

She shrugged.

"What's your last name?"

"Schmidt."

"Right, Gretl Schmidt. This Oma of yours, was she your father's mother or your mother's?"

"Mutti's mother. I think."

The Onkel Hans option seemed even more remote. "Let's go," he said and got up.

———

By ten o'clock he knew they would never reach Częstochowa by nightfall. He had carried her for long distances at a time. He couldn't believe how thin she was, almost like the ducklings his family caught on cold evenings so they could sleep in a box in the kitchen. And as light as a feather. But they hadn't made good progress.

Jakób heard a wagon approach. When he saw that it was a farmer on his way to market, he stepped out from behind some trees and held up his hand.

"*Czy moge pomóc?*" asked the man. *Can I help you?*

"My little sister and I are on our way to Częstochowa," Jakób explained. "How far are you going?"

"Koziegłowy," said the man. "Częstochowa is on the way, so get on the back if you wish."

Jakób lifted Gretl onto the wagon and got up himself. She sat with her thin legs dangling over the back, still clinging to her little bag.

As they set off, she said. "You lied, Jakób Kowalski. I'm not your sister."

"Just Jakób will do."

"Okay."

"You understand Polish?"

"I am Polish." Her lips were drawn into a stubborn line, making her look very German.

He considered his next words carefully. She might look small and vulnerable, he thought, but inside was a core of steel. "Sometimes one has to lie," he explained. "Like you—telling me you're Polish. I understand why you're saying it, but I know you're German."

She sat very still and looked straight ahead.

"But you and I can't lie to each other."

His words seemed to make no impression.

He tried again. "I'm going to be honest with you: I can't take you to Switzerland now." The lips made a straight line again. "Not before I know exactly where in Switzerland Onkel Hans lives."

She turned to face him. She understood, he realized. "How will you find out?" she asked.

"I don't know," he admitted. "That's why you must be honest with me."

The blue eyes took on the fearless expression again. "Okay," she said.

He'd have to watch his step. "Gretl, how did you get to Rigena's house?"

She thought about her answer. "I walked. With Mejcio."

He had no idea who Mejcio was, but it was probably not important right now. "You and your sister?"

She was closing up again. He took her hand. "Gretl, what was your sister's name?"

She stuck out her chin. "Elza," she said.

"Good. Where did Mejcio find you and Elza?"

"I don't know." She withdrew her hand.

"Was it close to Rigena's house?"

"I don't know."

"I can't help you if you won't tell me," he said, slightly annoyed.

"In the road, near her house."

"Good. How did you get to the road?"

"Walked. Through the forest."

"Where from?" His patience was wearing thin.

"From the . . ." She shut her mouth.

Impatience would get him nowhere. "Don't be afraid to tell me."

The blue eyes looked straight into his. "I'm not afraid."

"You can trust me, Gretl. Where did you walk from?"

She narrowed her eyes slightly, and he saw her come to a decision. "From the railroad. Oma told us to jump out when it was dark and the train was going up the hill."

A cold hand closed around his heart. He had suspected it. The puzzle pieces fitted together. "You're Jewish," he said.

"No!" she said firmly.

"Gretl!"

"I'm not Jewish!"

"Your mother?"

"No." She hesitated a moment. "Oma."

"Good. And your father?"

"No. He was a German soldier."

It was not what he had wanted to hear. "Where is he now?"

"Shot dead," she said, loudly and clearly. The picture became darker. He sighed. He would have to take her home with him for a day or two, at least until he could find a place for her.

He thought for a long time before he spoke. "Gretl, listen carefully. We'll have to say you're Polish, from the north, on the German border."

"I know," she said.

"And you'll have to speak as little as possible. And when you do speak, you must speak only Polish."

Her blue eyes regarded him earnestly. "That's what I've been doing," she said.

"I suppose you're right," he said. She had indeed been doing exactly that, and it hadn't worked. "How old are you?"

"Almost seven."

One of the neighbors' sons was seven. "Aren't you small for seven?"

"No," she said firmly, "I'm just thin. How old are you?"

"Twenty-one," he answered, surprised. "Why?"

"You're old!" she said. "What's in that bag?"

He concealed the bag under his shirt. "Oh, just papers. What's in your bag?"

"Just papers."

Just before they arrived at Częstochowa, Gretl spoke: "Jakób Kowalski, are you a pirate?"

"A what?"

"A pirate. You look like one. Only, you don't have that patch thing"—she gestured with her hand—"over your eye."

He ran his hand over his black stubble and laughed, amused. "No," he said, "I'm not a pirate."

"Oh."

They climbed down from the wagon.

<hr />

It was warm when he carried her. It felt nice; she was tired and cold and her entire body was aching. It felt strange as well, because he was big and his body was hard. Oma's and Mutti's bodies were soft, even after they'd got so thin in the ghetto.

Don't think about the ghetto, she told herself.

He was solid, like a horse, and he was going to take her to a castle where maidservants were going to wash her with hot water and sweet-smelling soap. Then she was going to sleep in a big, soft bed.

It was morning when she woke up. She looked around her. She was lying in a bed, but not in a castle. She was in a room with wooden walls. There was no window or door, just a curtain. The bed next to hers had been slept in.

She had no idea where Jakób Kowalski was.

She pushed the blanket off her. She had slept with her shoes on. The bedding was probably muddy. Oma never would have allowed it.

Gretl brushed off the bed as best she could and shook out the blanket. It wasn't easy. She fared better with the pillows. She straightened the crumpled bedding. Then she tugged at her dress and opened the curtain.

She stood on a porch with an uneven stone floor. On one side was a door flanked by low windows. On the other side were fields, and a city in the distance. Goats just like Peter's were grazing in the fields.

She heard voices inside. There was a rumbling voice—she thought it might be Jakób's. She couldn't hear what he was saying. The woman sounded angry.

"Where do you want her to stay?"

Gretl couldn't hear Jakób's reply.

"Where will she sleep?"

They were talking about her.

"Take her to the convent. The nuns can look after her."

The woman didn't want her here, just like Alm U didn't want Heidi. But she had to stay with Jakób Kowalski, because he was going to take her to Onkel Hans. It was the only way she would ever find Mutti and Oma again.

She thought hard. She would be good and help in the house, just like Heidi. Then the woman would keep her until Jakób could take her to Switzerland.

The woman looked up and saw her on the porch. "She's terribly skinny."

Jakób turned and looked at her. "Come inside, Gretz," he said in Polish. "Have some porridge."

She stepped carefully into the Polish home. She had to remember: Gretz.

———

Later the woman said, "We must wash you. And your clothes."

"Yes," she said.

Jakób gave her one of his shirts. "Put it on until your clothes are dry," he said.

"Yes," she said as Jakób left.

The woman poured warm water into a tin basin. "Take off your clothes and give them to me," she said.

The water was nice. The woman washed her with soap that didn't smell very good and didn't foam at all. She washed Gretl's hair three times.

Gretl thought carefully before she spoke. "What's your name?"

"You can call me Aunt Anastarja," said the woman.

"Anastarja," Gretl repeated uncertainly. She said it four more times in her head: *Anastarja, Anastarja* . . . It was a difficult name.

Aunt Anastarja had pushed up her sleeves. She had strong hands and thick arms. She wore a black dress and a black scarf covered her hair.

A young woman carrying a bucket entered through the back door. She put the bucket on the table with a thump. "What's this?" she asked, pointing at Gretl.

"Jakób brought her. He's going to take her to the convent."

"Oh," said the young woman as she poured the milk into a pot. "I'm going to the factory."

Gretl put on Jakób's shirt. It nearly reached the floor. Aunt Anastarja washed her clothes and hung them in the sun to dry. After a while Gretl put them back on.

She sat on the grass alone. She tried not to think, because if she did, a lump pushed up through her chest, past her throat. And crying wouldn't help, Oma had taught her. It just made your head ache. Elza and Mutti were weepers, not Oma and her.

Don't think about Elza, she told herself.

She wondered where Mutti and Oma were.

Elza said they couldn't have jumped out of the train. But they must have gotten off somewhere. They would be heading for Switzerland, and she had to get there as well.

She got up and walked to the goats. They were fat, friendly goats with gentle eyes. She stroked their heads. Only the one with the little beard looked cross.

Aunt Anastarja and a big man were hoeing the garden, like the people around Oma's forest home. The man beckoned for her to come over. "Take this to the kitchen and wash it," he said. He had a deep, tired voice.

The basket was heavy and filled with potatoes, beets, and carrots smelling of soil. Gretl left the basket outside, entered through the back door, and fetched water from the pitcher. First she washed the carrots, then the potatoes and the beets. When the man returned, he looked at the vegetables. "Give the leaves to the pigs," he said.

It was almost dark by the time Jakób came home. "You look different," he said.

"I had a bath," she said in Polish.

"Good," he said. She didn't know whether he meant it was good that she had taken a bath or that her Polish was good.

"We must find a place for you to sleep," he said. "Stan is no longer on night shift, so he'll be sleeping in his bed tonight."

Gretl didn't know who Stan was. "I'll sleep on a bed of hay, like Heidi," she suggested.

"Who's Heidi?"

She looked at him, amazed. "She lives in Switzerland. With Alm U."

He shrugged and shook his head. She followed him to the stables where he stood regarding the haystack.

"We can put some in the box where you keep the firewood and stack the wood on the floor," she proposed in German. "Or there'll be hay all over the kitchen."

He looked at her for a long time. His eyes were black. "You're very clever for a little girl, you know?"

"Yes, I know."

"But you'll have to remember to speak Polish."

"Yes. I forgot. Who's the other woman?"

"Monicka. She's my brother Turek's wife."

"Oh. And the old man?"

"My father. You can call him Uncle Janusz."

"Okay. Who's Stan?"

"He's my other brother."

She understood then that they had no room for her. "You'll have to take me to Switzerland."

"Yes," said Jakób. "Just as soon as we know where Onkel Hans lives."

———

In time the days fell into their own pattern. The convent couldn't take her just yet. They were bursting at the seams with war orphans. Gretl was glad.

At first she didn't sleep well in the box. It was too short and it smelled of grass. But she soon learned to pull up her knees to fit inside. The hay was soft under the knit blanket.

Jakób and Stan left early in the mornings. Sometimes Jakób came back earlier, then he sat at the kitchen table doing sums. Or he would write. Monicka milked the goats because Aunt Anastarja's knees were stiff. Then she went to work at the factory. It was a clothing factory, but they made uniforms for the Nazis, not dresses.

Aunt Anastarja and Uncle Janusz worked on the farm. Sometimes the Gestapo came to see that they were doing their work properly and took food away with them: vegetables and pigs and sometimes ducks. Also goats' milk and cheese and ham that Aunt Anastarja had made. Twice a week Uncle Janusz loaded the wooden cart and pushed it to the city, where he sold his produce. On his way back in the afternoon he had to push the cart uphill. He was old, so he mostly waited until Stan or Jakób or sometimes Monicka could help him.

Gretl didn't know what Turek did. He left early and came back late. He was angry about the work he had to do. She heard him in the evenings where she lay in her box with her eyes closed. "I'm a farmer," he said, "not a farrier for the military!"

When Aunt Anastarja went to mass in the afternoons, Uncle Janusz had to work alone. On Sundays everyone went to church, except Gretl, who stayed behind because she didn't have the right clothes. In the mornings Aunt Anastarja baked bread, and when she came home in the afternoons, she sometimes made onion or potato soup, or mostly borsch, which was beet soup. Sometimes she made dumplings, but they didn't taste like Mutti's spaetzle. At times like those she missed Mutti very much. And Oma and Elza.

She tried to help around the house. She swept and washed dishes and laid the table. Twice she picked wildflowers, but Monicka said the table was too crowded and threw them away.

Gretl didn't like Monicka. She always seemed cross. Monicka made her a dress, but only because Aunt Anastarja had told her to. Monicka unpicked an old black dress that was too tight for Aunt Anastarja and used the fabric. She made the dress big so that Gretl could wear it for a long time.

When the Gestapo came, Gretl hid under the hay in the stable. The hay was nice and warm but itchy, like her bed. *The Gestapo could smell*

Jewish blood, Oma had said. Almost like the giant who could smell Jack on the beanstalk.

Once she crawled under the hay and knocked her head against something hard. When the Gestapo left, she saw it was a kind of machine with a handle you could turn, like the handle some cars had at the front. She thought someone must have hidden it there, so she carefully covered it with hay again.

Most evenings when Jakób went out, he told her to go to bed. But one evening all the others were gone as well. "You'll have to come with me," Jakób said. "But you must promise to be quiet as a mouse while we're busy."

They walked to the city through the moonlit landscape. "The moon is pretty," she said.

"Yes."

"Jakób, the Gestapo caught all the Jews, didn't they?"

"Yes."

"And they want to catch the Poles as well?"

"You might say so, yes."

She walked on for a while, thinking. "Jakób, are the Gestapo and the Nazis the same?"

"Yes."

"My father was a Nazi," she said.

"I'm sure he was a good Nazi who was just a soldier and didn't catch people," he said. "From now on you must be very quiet and walk in my shadow. Or wait, let me carry you instead."

It felt good. They walked through narrow alleys, keeping close to the buildings in the dark. She snuggled against his strong body. Finally they reached a house on the outskirts of the city. A woman opened the door. "This is Gretz," was all Jakób said. He put her down, and she followed him up a steep, narrow staircase.

At the top was a small room with a table, four chairs, and a bench. On a dresser stood a Primus stove and two mugs. There was a bed in one corner. A black drape covered the window.

An old man was sitting on a chair at the table, an old lady on the bed. Jakób sat down on the bench. "Sit here." He motioned to Gretl. She sat on the floor at his feet. Now she saw nothing but shoes. And Jakób's legs. They were hard and covered with black hairs and mud stains. Later two other men with dirty shoes and legs arrived.

They talked and talked. She was very tired, but she couldn't sleep because Jakób had told her to sit quietly.

Then the woman gave her a storybook with pictures. It was hard to read because it was Polish. She struggled, yet managed to understand. It was the story of a man, Maslok, who was too lazy to work. But just as Maslok began to talk to a ghost called Skarbink, Jakób said, "Come, Gretz, we're done."

She looked up, disturbed. She couldn't just leave the story.

"Take the book with you," said the woman. "Jakób can return it later."

She held the book close to her chest. When they had left the city behind, Jakób said, "Can you read?"

"Do you think I'm stupid, Jakób Kowalski?"

"No, but the story is in Polish. What's it about?"

"About Maslok, who had to work in a mine but was lazy. But just as Maslok began to speak to Skarbink, you said we must go. Skarbink is a ghost," she added, to make it clear.

He shook his head slowly. "You're a remarkable little girl," he said.

—•—

The radio whistled shrilly, then crackled to life. Jakób's Home Army companions had found an English transmission. The circle of faces turned to Jakób, who was the only one who understood English.

"They speak too fast," he said. "Look for a Russian broadcast."

Stan sat with one hand on the dial, his ear close to the set. He turned the knob slowly, the sound leaping over the whistling airwaves but returning time and again to the English transmission. He looked up, shaking his head.

"You'll have to translate," Francis Rzepecki told Jakób.

Jakób listened carefully. "It's something about D-Day," he said. "I don't know." Frowning, he listened some more. "Normandy, in France. I think the Allied Forces have landed in Normandy."

Everyone spoke at once.

"It means they've begun with the second front at last," someone said excitedly.

"Did they cross the English Channel?"

"Did they break through the German lines?"

"Quiet," said Jakób, a deep frown between his dark brows, "I can't hear."

But somewhere between the Polish countryside and the towering ruins of London the voice got lost. Stan turned the dial, Francis smacked the side of the radio set with his hand, someone cursed, but the set refused to give up anything more. After a while Stan said, "It's no good," and switched it off.

"Are you sure they've crossed the English Channel?" asked Jerzy Tatar.

"I'm not sure about anything," said Jakób.

"What's today's date?" asked Jerzy.

"June 8," Jakób answered slowly. He believed he had it right. "It must have taken place yesterday or the day before," he added, stunned. What Poland had been hoping for for years was finally happening.

———

It was like Christmas. The woman who lived at Professor Sobieski's house gave Gretl clothes her own daughter, Sonja, had outgrown. The clothes were tied inside a coat.

Gretl sat on the kitchen floor, carefully undoing the sleeves while Jakób's family sat around the table. She unfolded the coat and took out a dress. It was blue with a white collar. She stood and held it in front of her. It was a little long.

"It's true, Father," said Jakób. "The Allied Forces have landed in France. They're on their way to Paris!"

"Look at this dress, Jakób," Gretl said.

He turned to her. "It's pretty," he said.

"General Eisenhower is in command," said Stan. "Apparently there are thousands of American soldiers."

"So you really think peace is within reach?" asked Turek.

"Before Christmas, listen to what I'm telling you," said Stan.

Gretl put the blue dress down and picked up a skirt. It was red with a floral border at the hem. "Just look at the beautiful skirt, Jakób," she said.

He turned again. "Lovely," he said. "I hear Britain and the US are planning to send in a million troops."

"I'll believe it when the tanks are driving down the streets of Częstochowa, wiping every German from the face of the earth," said Uncle Janusz.

Gretl shuddered and reminded herself never to speak German. She held up a blouse. It was white with puffed sleeves and buttons down the front.

"And every bloody Russian as well," Jakób added.

Jakób was swearing. It was just as well she couldn't speak Russian, she thought. "Look at the blouse, Jakób," she said.

He turned. "Yes, pretty," he said. "The time is ripe for the Home Army to make a bold move."

"You don't stand a chance against the Germans," said Aunt Anastarja. "You might as well wait for the British."

"No, Mother," said Jakób, "we must do it ourselves. We must prove to our enemies and to the free world—and ourselves—that the Polish spirit has not been quelled. It's the only way we can ensure complete autonomy for Poland."

Finally Gretl held up the coat. It smelled of mothballs, like Oma's trunk. It was bright red, with big red buttons down the front. She put it on. It was a little big but nice and warm. "Look at my beautiful coat, Jakób," she said.

He turned to her. "Yes, very nice," he said. "We must start in Warsaw."

"We mustn't even try without the help of the Red Army," said Stan.

"I heard there's not much left of Warsaw," said Uncle Janusz.

"There are at least fifty thousand men in Warsaw ready to take up arms," said Jakób.

Gretl folded her new clothes neatly. There were two pairs of underpants as well, but she didn't show them to Jakób. When he took her to Switzerland, she would wear all the clothes on top of each other. Like Heidi.

"You must teach the child to milk the goats, Jakób," said Monicka. "It's getting too much for me."

"Fine, I will," said Jakób.

Gretl was too excited about the new clothes to sleep, so she took the latest book the old lady had given her and read a story. Reading the Polish stories was easier now, but before she had finished, the lamp was put out and she lay in the dark, wondering, *Where is Warsaw? What if Jakób went there and they shot him dead too? How would she get to Switzerland then?*

The big lump was back in her tummy. It pushed up, into her throat.

I've got new clothes, she thought. It didn't help.

Cinderella also slept in front of the fire. The good fairy came and she found a prince, she thought. This didn't help either. She didn't want a prince.

She was cold. She wanted Mutti and Oma. And Elza, though she knew about Elza.

———

On Sunday Aunt Anastarja said, "The child has clothes now. She can come along to mass."

"Fine, Mother," said Jakób.

She put on the blue dress with the white collar and shoes and socks. Her feet felt strange, because she hadn't worn shoes for a long time. She looked at herself in the broken mirror in Aunt Anastarja's room. Her hair had grown long, and it curled around her head in an unruly mop. Oma would tie it with a ribbon when she got to Switzerland, Oma didn't like messy hair. In the ghetto Oma had cut her hair short because of the head lice. *Don't think about the ghetto*, she told herself.

They walked to the cathedral, everyone except Stan, because he had to work. After a while Monicka and Turek slowed down. Monicka was getting a baby soon, Jakób had said when he taught Gretl to milk the goats.

The cathedral was big inside, with high walls. It was different from the synagogue she used to go to with Oma when they lived in the ghetto. But it smelled the same, of furniture polish. And it felt the same, as if God lived here too. The windows were very pretty. She suddenly remembered how Mutti had taken Elza and her to church every Sunday before the ghetto. The windows looked the same. She hadn't really listened to the pastor, just stared at the beautiful windows and made up her own stories.

When Jakób's priest began to speak, she understood nothing, just like in the synagogue. He wasn't speaking Polish. Maybe it was Russian. Or Hebrew. The priest's voice sounded just like the rabbi's—a falling-asleep voice. She looked carefully at what the other people were doing so that she wouldn't make a mistake and made up her own stories to stay awake.

Sunday lunch was always good, with boiled potatoes, a green salad, and meat, if there was any. After lunch everyone lay down for a nap. Except Jakób, who sat up, doing sums.

"Those are difficult sums," she said.

"Yes."

"Can I do sums too?"

He looked at her with his stern black eyes. Then he picked up an exercise book and showed her the back cover. "Okay," he said. "But first you have to learn these multiplication tables."

She looked at the page for a long time. It made no sense to her. "Jakób, I don't understand," she said.

He sighed and got up to fetch a few carrots from the shelf. "Watch carefully," he said. He made two piles of three carrots each on the table. "How many carrots are there?"

"Six," she answered at once.

"Right. Two times three is six." Now he made three piles of four carrots each.

She counted. "Twelve," she said.

"Right. Look at the book, there." And he pointed with his finger. "Three times four is twelve."

She understood. A new world opened to her. She read and read the numbers. After that she worked everything out—the people's ears, the goats' legs, the squares in her knit blanket, the carrots and beets and potatoes she washed.

Two weeks later she said to Jakób, "Do you know you're three times my age? You're really very old."

His dark eyes looked straight at her, as if he really saw her. "And you're really very clever," he said.

"I'm joining the PPR," said Stan out of the blue a week later when he and Jakób were walking through the moonlit landscape after a Home Army meeting.

Jakób stopped. "You're doing what?"

"Joining the Polish Labor Party," Stan said loudly and clearly.

A choking disbelief grew inside him. "You want to get into bed with the Communists?" He did not disguise the loathing in his voice.

"Not get into bed, fight," said Stan, walking on.

His own brother couldn't possibly be so shortsighted to fall for the Labor Party's pious talk! He grabbed Stan's arm. "They're Communists!" He spat out the last word.

"The PPR isn't pro-Russian," Stan said firmly, removing Jakób's hand from his arm.

"The PPR is as Communist as the Soviet Union itself," Jakób argued, feeling despair. "You can't trust the Reds."

"I suppose you're referring to the Katyn massacre?"

"Yes, Stan, that's what I'm talking about!" Jakób was angry now. "Fifteen thousand Polish officers in a mass grave, buried by the Red Army. Don't tell me to let that go. That and all the other atrocities they've committed!"

"The PPR is at the forefront of anti-German resistance in Poland, Jakób. They're more successful than the Home Army, you know that."

"Because they've ingratiated themselves with Russia."

The two brothers stood facing each other, dark, broad-shouldered, of equal height and fire. Stan spoke in a measured voice. "The Soviet Union is presently the only liberator of smaller nations. Without their help, we're lost."

"The Soviet Union," said Jakób spitefully, "is the puppet master pulling the strings! And you want to let them pull yours!"

"It's the only way, Jakób," said Stan. "Listen to what I'm telling you—the *only* way."

"Step by step the Communist parties are taking over the political power in Poland," Jakób said to Professor Sobieski in July.

"And the Home Army is allowing it?"

"We're in a difficult position, Professor. We're not getting any real support from Britain or the US."

"What are you telling me, Jakób?"

"The way I see it, Professor, we don't have much of a choice. The first thing we have to do is shake off the German yoke once and for all. After that we'll have to see how we can get rid of the Russians as well."

"So the Home Army is going to collaborate with the Red Army?"

"To free Warsaw. Yes, Professor." As he spoke the words, he knew he had not made peace with the idea himself. "Rokossowski's tanks and infantry, and the Cossack cavalry are advancing on the city already."

"Very well then." The professor removed his spectacles and polished them carefully. "May God be with you, Jakób."

"Will you fix us some provisions to take along?" Jakób asked his mother.

"You're wasting your time," Anastarja grumbled. "You play war games while we work our fingers to the bone."

Nevertheless she baked extra bread and wrapped up some salted ham and cheese.

Gretl trailed after Jakób and Stan and Jerzy Tatar as they walked to the train station. The station evoked strange memories, vague images of a journey to a ghetto, and clearer memories of a journey during which her grandmother had pried loose her fingers so that she could escape.

"Will you come back, Jakób Kowalski?"

"Yes, Gretz, I will."

"And will you take me to Switzerland then?"

His black eyes looked into her blue ones. "As soon as there's peace, we'll try to find Onkel Hans. In the meantime I want you to look after the goats and read your stories."

The train disappeared along the track. All the way home she could taste the acrid blue smoke at the back of her throat.

3

When Gretl returned, Aunt Anastarja was annoyed. "When are you going to milk the goats?" she scolded.

"I'll go at once," said Gretl, picking up the wooden bucket.

"Wash your hands," said Anastarja crossly. She tied a scarf around her head and spoke to Monicka. "I'm going to light candles for Stan and Jakób. Are you coming?"

Monicka shook her head. "You go. I don't feel up to the long walk." Monicka no longer worked at the factory. She was waiting for the baby to come.

I really hope it's only one baby, Gretl thought as she walked across the damp grass. A few days earlier one of the sows had a litter. Gretl shuddered. She knew now where babies came from. But if Monicka had that many babies, the screaming would be simply awful.

"I don't want to have babies when I grow up," she told Bruni, the friendliest goat. "But you will have to, or we won't have any milk to make cheese."

Back at the house, she poured the milk into the pot and swept the kitchen floor. Then she went to Jakób and Stan's bedroom on the porch. Jakób had said she could sleep in his bed while he was away.

The room smelled of Jakób. There was a hollow in the pillow where his head had rested. She pressed the soft pillow to her chest. It was warm and comforting. She wished Jakób hadn't gone away. Her father had also gone away. What if . . .

Maybe she should also light a candle for Jakób. She didn't really know how it worked, but she knew it had something to do with God. She vaguely remembered the *Weinachtskerzen* at Christmas, in the time before her father was shot—the lovely candles and the silver *Lametta* and brightly colored *Kugeln* on the tree. They hadn't celebrated Christmas in the ghetto. *Jews don't believe in Christmas*, Mutti had said.

Gretl put on her blue dress with the white collar, combed her hair, and followed the footpath to the cathedral at the foot of Jasna Góra. She was about to climb the steps to the church door when she realized she had forgotten her shoes. She considered going back, but if she went home now, Uncle Janusz would tell her to wash the vegetables and feed the leaves to the pigs, as he did every day. She pushed open the big door and entered.

It was quiet inside. The sunlight fell through the windows and made colored blotches on the long rows of wooden benches. The ceiling was almost as high as the sky. She shut the door softly and tiptoed down the aisle. The red carpet was soft under her bare feet.

A man in a long white robe was kneeling at the front of the church. She knew he was praying. A few women were also kneeling at a kind of counter, on which there was a multitude of flickering candles. She didn't see Aunt Anastarja among them.

Gretl looked around but couldn't find a candle to light. Maybe she should have brought her own. She decided she would just pray.

That was a problem too, because she didn't know how. In the ghetto Oma had prayed to God in a strange language. She didn't know the language in which Aunt Anastarja and the priest prayed either.

After Gretl's father died Mutti had stopped praying, but long ago, when Gretl was very young, Mutti had taught her to kneel beside her bed at night.

She didn't go to the front. She was afraid someone would notice that she didn't know what to do, so she knelt behind the first bench and prayed, "*Lieber Herr Jesus, mach mich fromm, dass ich auch zu Dir in den Himmel komm.*" She opened her eyes but remained on her knees. She had prayed for herself, not for Jakób. She closed her eyes again: "Dear God, make Jakób good so that he can also get to be in heaven with You. Amen."

She got up, though she still had not said what she meant to say. If Jakób was in heaven, it would mean he was dead, and then he couldn't take her to Switzerland. Now that she thought about it, she didn't want to go to heaven either—not yet, anyway. So she knelt again and this time she prayed in her own words. "Lieber Herr Jesus, bring Jakób home so that we can go and look for Onkel Hans. Amen." Feeling happier, she got to her feet and tiptoed outside.

She heard children singing and followed the sound.

Behind the cathedral was a red-brick building that turned out to be a row of classrooms. She walked past the first one. A woman in a long black robe was leading a group of girls in a song. They looked a little older than Gretl. In the adjoining classroom the girls seemed younger. They were drawing on their slates with slate pencils. The third classroom was crowded. A woman in a black robe and black headscarf was reading her young pupils a story. Gretl stopped and listened. She knew the story. It was about a brave man, Daniel, who loved God so much that he walked into a lions' den. The teacher at the ghetto school had told them the same story.

The teacher looked up. She wore spectacles with thick frames. "Are you new?" she asked in a kind voice.

Gretl nodded.

"Come in, child, come to my table," said the teacher. "What's your name?"

"Gretz."

"And your last name?"

Gretl hesitated a moment. "Gretz Kowalski," she said.

"Well, Gretz Kowalski, how old are you?"

"Nearly seven."

The teacher seemed surprised. Behind the thick lenses her eyes looked very large, but their expression was gentle. "Are you sure you're nearly seven?" she asked.

"Yes," said Gretl. "I can read and do arithmetic. I'm just thin, that's all."

The teacher gave a slight smile. "Fine," she said, "but your mother will have to come and register you."

Gretl nodded. "I'll tell her." She didn't leave, but stood waiting.

"Um, all right, then. Starika, move up. Gretz can sit with you."

Gretl turned to face the class. A sea of inquisitive faces looked back at her. They had dark eyes, like Jakób's. Only the teacher had gray eyes, or maybe they just looked gray through her thick glasses. There was a shortage of desks, so that four girls shared the same one. The girls moved to make room for Gretl.

Starika was a little chubby, which was probably why there had been only three girls at her desk. Gretl sat down. It was a tight squeeze.

"Why are you so pale?" asked Starika.

"I'm from the north, near the German border," Gretl whispered in reply. "That's why."

"You're not German, are you?"

"No," said Gretl firmly. "I'm Polish."

During a break Starika gave Gretl a piece of her bread. "Tomorrow you must bring your own," she said.

"Okay," said Gretl.

"You sound funny."

"It's because I'm from the north," Gretl explained.

"Oh. We can be best friends if you like."

"Okay," said Gretl. When the bell rang, Starika put her arm around Gretl's shoulders and together they walked back to their classroom.

———

Jakób walked with Stan and Jerzy through the quiet streets, their footsteps hollow. They didn't speak. Around them rose the skeletons of buildings. In some places chunks of concrete had been ripped off. Twisted steel girders pointed at the sky like gnarled fingers.

Jakób was filled with shock and disbelief. Was this really Warsaw? Was this what the proud Polish capital had come to?

He stopped beside a large crater in the street. He realized he was looking at the foundation of a house. It was as if a tornado had come from the sky, uprooting and funneling the entire house away.

A skinny dog was digging in the rubble.

"Come, Jakób," said Jerzy.

They walked on. Jakób felt sick.

Ryszard Syrop was about forty, a teacher at a primary school, he told the young men. But it was getting harder every day—parents were afraid to send their children to school.

"Are there still children here?" Jakób asked. He had seen hardly anyone. And those he had seen seemed completely out of touch with reality, worn out, world weary.

Ryszard gave a mirthless laugh. "Yes," he said, "thousands. They're the ones we're fighting for."

"But where do they find food?" asked Jerzy.

"They don't. Everyone is hungry. But we believe liberation is in sight." Ryszard's voice was firm.

In Częstochowa we don't know anything about this profound kind of suffering, thought Jakób. *There's always food on our table—soup and goat's cheese, sometimes ham, and usually bread, except when flour is unavailable.* Maybe his mother was right. Maybe the Black Madonna was watching over her city.

Ryszard said, "I hear the PPR are calling up their members to fight with the Home Army."

"Yes," said Stan, "I belong to the PPR. Those have been my orders too."

"Oh," said Ryszard with a slight frown. "Aren't you and Jakób brothers?"

"We are," said Jakób, meeting Ryszard's gaze. He and Stan might disagree about politics in the privacy of their home, but here they were brothers.

"Good." Ryszard seemed to hesitate before continuing. "The three of you will act as group leaders. We want to run this uprising like a military operation. Your groups will be known as sections. You'll have the rank of corporal. We have very few experienced men; those who have been in the military are all fighting at the front."

"Do you have any formal military training yourself?" Jerzy asked.

"Yes," answered Ryszard, "I was honorably discharged from the army about ten years ago, after a back injury. You'll all be in my company. I'll be your captain."

"Right, Captain," said Jakób. Good, he thought, Ryszard seemed to know what he was talking about.

"There's a planning meeting tomorrow morning at six. We will show you maps and aerial photographs. Did you bring any weapons?"

"We each have a Sten, Captain," Jakób answered.

Stan opened his bag. The rifle had been taken apart and neatly stowed among his clothing. "We don't have much ammunition, I'm afraid," he said.

"Ammunition is a problem," said Captain Ryszard. "The Allies have dropped supplies a couple of times, but it's hard. The Americans drop their loads from such a height that the winds blow them out of reach."

"What weapons do we have?" Jakób asked.

"We have a number of Mausers and Schmeisser machine guns seized from the Nazis," the captain answered. "And mortar pipes and bombs supplied by the Allies. For the rest, we make do."

It was dark outside when the four of them walked through Warsaw's empty streets to a deserted metro station that served as the Home Army's temporary headquarters. They walked through street after street piled high with garbage and waste. Ryszard seemed oblivious to the rubble and decay and the rotting garbage heaps on the grimy sidewalks.

Jakób's initial shock changed to a deep, throbbing ache. *This is the heart of my country*, he thought, *ripped apart, broken, collapsed, filthy, and stinking.*

The metro entrance was half hidden behind a gigantic concrete block. The steps leading down were strewn with debris. The tracks had fallen into disrepair.

"It's safe, come on down," said Ryszard as he led the way.

A naked light bulb here and there cast dim light across the cavernous tunnel. The hundred or more men inside spoke in subdued voices.

When Jakób looked around him, his heart swelled with pride, which slowly replaced the pain. These people were ordinary Poles, men and even a few women prepared to give everything for the country of their birth. He was standing among his people, and he knew he would never be anything but a Pole.

General Bór-Komorowski entered from the side. His bearing was erect, his body lean, and his uniform immaculate. His face looked almost emaciated. His bald head glistened in the naked light, and his black eyes looked straight at the group in front of him. He inspired confidence. When he held up a big hand, the soft murmur of voices died down immediately.

"My brothers, my sisters, my fellow Poles," the general began in a strong voice, almost a drawl, "my heart swells with pride to see you gathered here today. A gathering like this is a rare occurrence. That is why I want to tell you—Poland is proud of you. You are holding Poland's centuries-old spirit of liberation in your hands."

A short silence followed before the general continued, more gravely, "After almost a year's planning, after almost five years' suffering under German tyranny, we are ready to rise up, ready to show the world Poland will not submit."

There was an audible murmur, but Komorowski held up his hand again. "We have about forty thousand men, counting the Home Army and the PPR. More than half our men are younger than twenty, with no formal training and very little experience. We have about forty-four thousand hand grenades, and we have rifles for only one in every six men."

A murmur of concern went up.

"We'll chiefly use guerilla tactics and our own initiative. You all have experience of underground activities. We'll attack, drop out of sight, attack from behind, exhaust the Germans, break their morale. Our greatest problem is the shortage of weapons."

Stan shook his head. "Our situation is dire," he told Jakób. "The Red Army will have to help right from the start, listen to what I'm telling you."

This time Stan was right, Jakób knew.

As if he had heard Stan, General Komorowski said, "The Soviet forces are ready to invade Warsaw. Marshal Rokossowski's troops are advancing from the south and the east in a front that is almost fifty miles wide. In a matter of days they'll be on the banks of the Vistula."

"Surely the Allied Forces will help too?" someone asked. "Britain and America? And what about the Polish army in Russia and Italy?"

"They have promised to send reinforcements as soon as possible, yes." The general nodded.

"And the Germans?" asked one of the other men. "What's their situation?"

"On paper it looks better than ours," said the general honestly. "They have an estimated twenty thousand well-trained SS troops with heavy arms. But the soldiers are showing signs of exhaustion. I expect the Wehrmacht to offer very little resistance on the Vistula front." He looked around him, then said, "We'll divide into smaller groups now. The company commanders will move to the operations room; the rest will stay here."

Slowly excitement began to take the place of Jakób's shock and pain. They stood bent over tables. At each table a colonel explained their battle strategy. They studied maps of roads, buildings, underground tunnels, sewers.

"Forget the Russians and their games," Jakób said to Stan. "With or without the help of the Red Army, we'll drive the Nazis out of Warsaw, then out of all of Poland."

———·———

"I'm at school now," Gretl told Bruni late that afternoon. "We read and do arithmetic. Jakób will be proud of me when he gets back."

The goat looked at her with large eyes almost as gentle as her teacher's. "We call my teacher Sister Zofia. She reads us stories from the Bible."

The next morning Sister Zofia asked, "Will your mother be coming to register you?"

Gretl nodded.

"Today?"

Gretl shook her head. "She's too busy."

"Well, all right, then." Sister Zofia looked doubtful. "But she'll have to come before the end of the week, is that clear?"

Gretl nodded.

There were many children in the classroom. The teacher couldn't help them all with their sums and also listen to each one read. And the children were rowdy.

Starika wasn't good at writing. She held her slate pencil awkwardly. Gretl noticed she was using the wrong hand. "Why don't you use your other hand?" she whispered.

"I can't, the other one is stupid."

"Oh."

Her sums were also wrong. "That should be a five, not a four," Gretl whispered.

"You don't know everything," Starika snapped.

"Be quiet and carry on working," said the teacher. "Starika, come and read for me."

Starika went to the front of the classroom. Her shoulders were slumped and she was dragging her feet. Ewunia, who sat across the aisle, said, "She'll probably get spanked."

After Starika it was Gretl's turn. "You read very well, Gretz," said the teacher. "Where did you learn to read?"

"My sister taught me, and my teacher," Gretl said cautiously.

"Where did you go to school?"

Gretl shrugged.

The teacher looked at her closely. "Your arithmetic is good too," she said. "I think you should move up to the next class. But first your mother must come and register you."

The teacher in the next class was strict, Gretl had heard. "I'd rather stay here and help you. I'm too small for the next class," she said firmly.

The teacher gave a slow smile. "All right then, we'll see how it goes."

———

For the first five days of the fighting, it seemed as if the Home Army stood a chance against the mighty German Wehrmacht. Street by street, block by block, the Home Army drove back the Germans, until almost three-quarters of the city was under Polish control. Of the Russians there was no sign.

"Not that I mind," Jakób told Jerzy one evening. "The less I see of them, the better."

On the morning of the sixth day Jakób was sitting on the roof of a once-graceful, double-story hotel on the outskirts of the city. He and Stan had taken the last shift of the night and were waiting for day to break. It had been drizzling all night, and they were wet and cold. *In another week it will all be over*, he thought, *and we'll go home.*

Jakób frowned and squinted. He reached for his field glasses. Adjusting them, he tried to make out what he was seeing in the dim light. "Stan?" he said without removing the field glasses from his eyes.

Stan moved closer to where Jakob sat. "Yes, what?"

Jakób pointed with his finger. His brother looked, adjusted his own field glasses, looked again, then whistled through his teeth. "Lord have mercy!" he said at last.

Jakób felt his muscles tense in a kind of anticipation, almost excitement, a hunger for the possibilities ahead. "Are those German tanks?"

"A sea of German tanks and trucks and troop carriers," said Stan.

Jakób bolted downstairs to where their men lay sleeping in an empty room. "The Germans are coming!" he shouted. "Get ready. Borecki and Alexander, see if you can get the radio to work."

"Yes, Corporal."

"Józef, send a Morse code message that a large German force is approaching from the northwest."

"Right, Corporal," said Józef, throwing off his blanket.

"You two, go upstairs to Stan and bring me reports every minute. I want to know how many tanks there are, how many trucks, heavy guns, how many of everything, the direction they're moving in, every detail you can think of."

"Yes, Corporal," said the two boys and raced up the stairs.

"I'm ready to fight as well, Corporal, until I'm needed elsewhere," said Haneczka. She was a young woman in her early twenties, but strongly built and clad in men's clothing.

"Fine," said Jakób. "Keep your medical equipment with you at all times."

He felt the blood rushing through his body, a burst of adrenaline reaching the ends of his nerves. He looked around him. A skinny boy of no more than fourteen stood in front of him, eager to help.

"Waldus, stay with me. I need a messenger. Stan's men, start making Molotov cocktails; we want to give the Germans a proper welcome. My own troops, check the barbed-wire barricades and come back at once."

He heard the planes, their engines screaming. The roar became louder as they approached. There was a burst of machine-gun fire no more than two hundred yards away.

"Take up your positions," shouted Jakób. "Leave the barricades for now! Felix, everyone in your group, go up, get behind your guns! Róman, go."

A second squadron of planes swooped down. Guns blazed, shattering the windows, blasting chunks of plaster from the wall.

"Stay calm, focus on your task," Jakób said calmly. Taking the stairs three at a time, he raced up to the roof with Waldus on his heels.

The planes were heading for the city center. Jakób followed them with his eyes, saw them release their bombs, saw building after building explode in a mass of flames. Thick, black smoke billowed and became one with the gray rain clouds. He felt an enormous rage bordering on hatred. Through his field glasses he watched the wall of German vehicles approach.

A boy sat against the rear wall, a row of empty bottles lined up in front of him. He was meticulously filling each bottle exactly halfway with petrol. His hands were trembling. He wiped up the drops he had spilled with a cloth, pushed the cloth into the neck of the bottle with the end protruding, and carefully sealed it with a cork stopper, then set it alongside the other finished bottles. "We don't have much petrol, Corporal," he said.

Jakób suppressed the sudden wave of affection that washed over him. "How many Molotovs have you made?" he asked.

"Thirteen, Corporal."

"Fine. Save the rest of the petrol for tomorrow. It looks as if the Germans are heading straight for us. You five without rifles will take up your positions at the windows and pelt them with the Molotovs and the hand grenades. One bomb per vehicle. Target the armored troop carriers, they're open at the top. Or the open trucks, or aim for the hatch of a tank. We can't afford to waste our chances, so you'll have to take good aim."

"Yes, Corporal," replied a chorus of voices.

They were facing the mighty German Wehrmacht with an army of children—what lay ahead?

At noon Józef signaled to headquarters: "Under heavy fire. Enemy still out of reach. At least twenty tanks, thirty armored vehicles. Send reinforcements. Radio still out of order."

Almost an hour later a message came back: "Under attack from the north and southwest. No reinforcements available. Order: Stop Germans at all costs."

The German tanks and troop carriers kept rolling in. The Poles stacked sandbags and used building rubble to build barricades until their muscles ached and their hands were blistered and raw. They threw Molotovs, sometimes hitting the mark, so that German soldiers tumbled from their vehicles, burning. They threw hand grenades. Two tanks veered sideways and soldiers spilled out, covered with blood. Jakób aimed the bazooka and blasted a tongue of fire in the direction of a tank.

German snipers picked off the men in their observation posts. German guns and machine guns blew apart their barricades.

A mortar bomb struck the top of their building. The roof caved in with an enormous crash, covering the staircase with debris. The second story collapsed, burying two boys from Stan's section under the concrete. "Abandon the building!" Jakób shouted. "Retreat!"

By evening row upon row of buildings were on fire. Overpowering smoke hung over their heads. The flames colored the clouds a dirty orange. But the gunfire had stopped for the moment.

Stan's and Jerzy's sections had taken up position in neighboring buildings. Jakób's men were gathered around him. They ate bread and tinned fish and drank hot black coffee. Only Haneczka was possibly older than he was; the rest of his men's soft cheeks were covered with acne instead of beards.

"This coffee is horrible without sugar," said Józef. "I can't wait to put four spoonfuls in again."

"Bitter coffee is better for your teeth," said Haneczka. "Go slow with the water, the taps don't work anymore."

Jakób said, "Tomorrow will be no better than today, everyone. Try and get a good night's sleep. We'll change the watch every two hours."

"Right, Corporal," said Haneczka.

"Before we go to bed, we must make some more Molotovs," he said. "And let's try and make some limpet mines."

"How, Corporal?" asked Waldus.

"Use your socks," said Jakób. "Put dynamite inside, with the fuse protruding slightly. Then cover the sock with grease. It should stick to a tank."

Day seven broke gray, the rain falling in sheets, and soon became a protracted nightmare. They retreated through dense clouds of smoke, through driving rain. Crouching, they ran through black mud and dived for cover behind the rubble that had once been Warsaw. They clambered up buildings to throw their Molotovs and hand grenades. They waited in ditches to ignite the short fuses of limpet mines and attach them to the bulldozer wheels that traveled in above their heads.

Row upon row of German tanks rolled in, climbed over rubble, broke through wire barricades.

Haneczka had stopped fighting. She was applying pressure to wounds, bandaging, injecting morphine. And she was running low on supplies.

They fell back and hurriedly erected new obstacles, laid sandbags, built a barricade of rubble, and lay behind it in a line, waiting for the next wave of Nazis. The German troop carriers and infantry pushed forward. Officers rode in motorcycle sidecars, the tanks rolling along behind them.

Jakób's and Stan's sections climbed into stinking sewers and pushed open manholes behind the German lines, attacked hastily, disappeared again. They planted landmines and cut communication cables, but their petrol was finished, and their hand grenades as well.

"I can't understand what's keeping the Red Army," said Stan. "Without them we're not going to survive."

A squadron of airplanes swooped low overhead. Jakób saw the bombs being released from their bellies. Black smoke billowed thickly from buildings. The nightmare closed in around him.

More planes thundered in; deafening gunfire blazed overhead.

From the corner of his eye Jakób saw Józef trying to draw his head even farther into his body. Then a rain of bullets struck the boy, his body jerked back, his eyes froze, and his chest split open.

Shock held Jakób's body in an iron grip. A hot rush of nausea and revulsion pushed up in his throat. Józef would never put four spoonfuls of sugar into his coffee again.

———

One afternoon when Gretl got home after school, she learned that Monicka had had her baby. Only one, thank heaven. It was very small, with tiny feet.

"He looks more like a baby pig than a baby goat," Gretl told Bruni that afternoon, "because he's very pink and has no hair. But luckily he doesn't scream. Well, not too much anyway."

She was eating at the table now, sitting in Jakób's chair. That night Monicka didn't join them at the table. She was in bed.

"The news from Warsaw isn't good," said Turek, glowering from under his dense eyebrows. Gretl felt the lump in her tummy tighten.

"I'm not surprised," said Uncle Janusz. "What was the Home Army thinking, taking on the Deutsche Wehrmacht?"

"The Black Madonna will watch over them," said Aunt Anastarja.

"Who's the Black Madonna?" Gretl asked.

All eyes turned to her. They seemed surprised that she didn't know. Or maybe they had simply forgotten she was there.

Aunt Anastarja answered, "It's a painting of the Blessed Virgin Mary. Her face is black. She watches over the people of Częstochowa."

Gretl wanted to ask more, but the conversation had already moved on.

That night she lay in bed, wondering. Should she pray to the Black Madonna? In the end she decided to stick to Lieber Herr Jesus. Her prayers were in German, and she wasn't sure whether the Black Madonna would understand. Maybe she could ask Sister Zofia, who knew everything about God.

She heard the baby softly crying but it didn't bother her.

It was good that Jakób was fighting the Nazis, the Gestapo, who could smell Jewish blood. But it was hard to understand. Her father had also been a Nazi, a good Nazi, Jakób had said.

If something happened to Jakób, what would become of her?

She would think about other things: Switzerland, where Oma and Mutti would be waiting with Onkel Hans. It was going to be so wonderful, maybe Jakób would agree to live there too.

When at last she fell asleep, she dreamed of the Gestapo and the bombs and Jakób in the ghetto. When a bomb struck the house, she sat up in bed.

Complete silence reigned. The moon shone through a chink in the curtain.

It was just a dream, she told herself. *I'm not afraid.*

She lay quietly, waiting for sleep to come.

4

Within a week the Germans had confined the Home Army to an area near the city center. They were an island surrounded by a sea of Nazi tanks. The Poles fought valiantly, desperately, defended street after street—and gave up street after street. Their rations had been reduced to almost nothing, their medical supplies exhausted, their ammunition finished. Jakób and Stan were finding it hard to motivate their troops. Jerzy spoke openly about going home. He had a farm, a wife, young children.

"Paris has been liberated," said Captain Ryszard early one morning. "The German tanks are retreating; the Allied Forces have pulled down every Nazi banner; the people are dancing in the streets. Tell the men, it will give them hope."

"Paris is far away, Captain," said Jerzy.

Ryszard continued, "It's our company's turn to pick up supplies. Pilots of the South African Air Force are flying in tonight. They'll come in low so we'll have a better chance of recovering the cargo they'll be dropping."

"My section will go, Captain," said Jakób immediately. "I might need a truck driver."

Haneczka said, "I can drive, Corporal. My dad is a truck driver. I've been driving trucks since childhood."

Jakób nodded. "Waldus, get another two or three men to help load."

At midnight they were waiting in a clearing Jakób had carefully selected. If their mission was successful and they could get their hands on a decent stash of ammunition and medical supplies, it would boost everyone's morale.

The planes came from the south, following the course of the Vistula. Jakób looked at his three assistants. They were mere boys, no more than fifteen years old, with children's underfed bodies and the eyes of old men. Judging from the noise of the engines, the planes couldn't be flying at more than two hundred feet. They made a left turn over the cathedral and came in even lower.

An unexpected burst of machine-gun fire erupted. Jakób swung his field glasses in that direction.

"Bloody Germans are on top of us," said Haneczka.

"You'll have to load quickly, men," said Jakób. To Haneczka he said, "Don't cut the engine. As soon as we've got everything, jump in and put your foot down."

She nodded. "I'll help load," she said.

The next moment the planes were overhead. Jakób flashed their signal steadfastly: *quick-quick-quick, wait, quick-quick-quick.*

The cargo was dropped, the parachutes opened simultaneously against the red night sky, and the crates drifted down. But the wind pushed them toward the gunfire, which intensified.

"Drive toward the crates," Jakób shouted over the noise, but Haneczka was already on her way.

A volley of bullets struck one of the planes. At once thick, black smoke billowed from the tail. A second plane exploded and fell from the sky in a torrent of flames.

"Drive!" Jakób shouted.

They sped toward the crates with the precious, long-awaited cargo of ammunition, hand grenades and radio equipment, vital rations and medical supplies. But as they approached, they saw the burning wreckage land among the crates. The first crate exploded, setting in motion a chain reaction, creating a wall of flames between the Germans and themselves. Only two crates escaped unscathed. Jakób ran his hand over his face and got out of the truck. "Let's load, men," he told the dismayed boys.

After the Bible story, Sister Zofia told Gretl to take five of the girls outside to read. They found the reading hard, because they read the letters instead of the words. They didn't like reading either. "If you read to me, I'll tell you a story," Gretl said.

"What do *you* know about stories?" Starika sneered.

"I know a lot of stories, because I can read," Gretl explained.

"Like what?" one of the other girls piped up.

"I'll tell you, but first you must read," said Gretl firmly.

They looked at the book they all shared. "Look at the whole word," said Gretl, "or it will take very long. Look, it says u-n-c-l-e."

"We know that," said Starika.

"Well, look for others that also say u-n-c-l-e," Gretl explained.

After a while they got tired of reading. "Tell us the story you promised," said Anya.

She couldn't tell them the story about Siegfried and the Nibelungen, Gretl thought, because she didn't know the Polish word for Nibelungen. And the story about the Mouse Tower was too awful. She decided to tell them about the Lorelei, who sat on a rock, singing and combing her golden hair. "It's not a proper story," Starika complained.

"I'll finish the story tomorrow," said Gretl. "Look, Sister Zofia is calling us back to class."

That afternoon she told Bruni, "Starika is right, you know, it's not a proper story. But luckily the Lorelei has golden hair and she can sing, so tomorrow I'll make up my own story."

When she stood at the table the next day, waiting to have her sums marked, she asked, "Sister Zofia, can the Black Madonna . . ." She almost said "understand German," but she remembered just in time.

"Can the Black Madonna do what, Gretz?"

"Can she protect people?"

Sister Zofia put down Gretl's slate and folded her hands. "The Black Madonna is just a picture in our chapel, Gretz. It's a very old picture, much more than a thousand years old, and the Poles attach a lot of value to it. But it's not the picture that protects us, it's the Holy Virgin herself, the Mother of God."

"Oh," said Gretl. "Why is the picture in our chapel?"

"I'll bring you a book tomorrow," Sister Zofia said, checking Gretl's sums. "Then you can read about it yourself."

"Okay," said Gretl. "Where is Warsaw?"

"I'll show you in another book. Go back to your desk, your sums are all correct. Ewunia, come show me your work."

Every day Gretl was sent outside with groups of children to teach them to read. And to tell them stories. She soon learned that the children wouldn't listen if her story wasn't very good. At night she lay in bed making up stories that would keep the children quiet when the teacher had to leave the classroom.

"My dad also tells stories," said Anya, "but your stories are better."

Almost every morning Anya wanted to tell them something her dad had said. Sometimes Gretl could tell that Anya was lying. But one morning Anya had a secret to tell: "Listen, everybody."

They all gathered around her. She spoke in a whisper. "My dad says the Gestapo are catching all the Jews and sending them to a camp."

"What kind of camp?" Starika asked.

"Just a camp. Then they put them all into an oven and burn them. Like when Daniel had to go into the oven. But the Jews burn, because the angel of God doesn't help them."

"You're lying," Gretl said firmly. "And Daniel didn't go into the oven, his friends did. And they were also Jews. And God sent His angel because they were Jews. God wouldn't let the Gestapo burn the Jews."

"Do you think you know more than my dad?" Anya asked crossly.

"You think you're so clever, just because you can read stories. My dad says you're so pale, you look like a German!"

All day long Gretl could think of nothing else. She tried to think about her stories, but all she could see in her mind was the picture of Shadrach, Meshach, and Abednego that Sister Zofia had shown them when she told them the story. And no matter how hard she tried, she just couldn't picture the angel that had been supposed to protect Oma and Mutti.

The next afternoon when she came home from school, Aunt Anastarja was taking a large loaf of bread from the oven. When she felt the heat on her skin, Gretl fled outside, to the goats.

She wished with all her heart that Jakób would come home. He would make everything right, she knew.

———

It was a short bridge, no more than thirty yards long, with a wide, tarred road leading across it and a tall, steel arch spanning it from end to end. The bridge was unimpressive, but they could cut off the Germans here, maybe even hold them off until reinforcements arrived. Still there was no sign of help from the Red Army, nor from the American or British liberators.

"I've lost track of what day it is," Jakób said. It was long before winter, but he felt cold to the bone, as if he would never be warm again.

"It's August 13," said Ryszard. Jakób noticed that the captain's hands were trembling. His house had been razed to the ground, and there was no sign of his wife and children. Jakób feared the man was losing hope.

"What will our strategy be, Captain?" he asked.

Ryszard looked up, making an obvious attempt to focus. "We'll position ourselves west of the bridge," he said. "We'll try to stop the Germans before they reach it. If we don't succeed, we'll withdraw and blow up the bridge before they can cross. Jakób, dig in on the left side of the road, where the bridge begins. Stan, you on the right," said Ryszard. "If we have to retreat, you'll be the last to leave before we blow up the bridge."

"Right, Captain."

Jakób heard the planes before he saw them. They were heading straight for the bridge. Part of a wall was blown into a thousand pieces right next to him, raining dust and gravel.

"Bloody hell!" said Waldus. "I think they already know we're here, Corporal."

Jakób looked at the dust-covered child next to him. "I guess you're right, Waldus," he said.

Like caged animals they waited for the onslaught.

As soon as the guns and tanks came within striking distance, they began to fire. The noise was deafening, and Jakób could give no further orders. He aimed the machine gun at the leading tank and waited. The tank spat fire and a tree down the road burst into flame. Dense clouds of smoke hid the approaching tanks from view.

A boy came running to them, ducking as he ran. "The captain says we must withdraw!"

He ducked out to deliver his message to Stan's section, but halfway across the road he was struck by a bullet. He managed to drag himself to cover behind a flat chunk of concrete.

"Stay there!" Jakób shouted. "We're coming!"

From across the road Stan aimed the bazooka at the tanks and tried to provide cover for Jakób. Crouching, he ran to the injured boy, picked him up, and began to make his way back amid a hail of bullets. The next moment he felt a burning sensation in his calf.

Jakób laid the boy down next to Haneczka and fell down at Waldus's side. Hot blood was pumping through his brain, through his whole body.

"There's blood on your leg, Corporal," said Waldus.

"Yes," said Jakób. "You carry the ammunition belt. We must provide cover for Captain Ryszard and the other sections."

The German wave rolled on, bombs exploding, guns rattling, people screaming.

"Fall back!" shouted Ryszard over the noise. "Provide cover and fall back!"

"We're going to blow up the bridge!" Jakób shouted at his men. "Fall back!" He looked around him. "Haneczka, come!"

She threw the wounded boy over her shoulder. His head hung limply down her back. She grabbed her case and began to run.

"No! Haneczka! Wait!" Jakób shouted.

But she kept running, strong, fast, with her patient and her case. Jakób threw his gun to his shoulder and tried to provide cover. Haneczka weaved in and out among the rubble on the bridge. Then she disappeared behind a wall on the other side. "She's made it, Corporal!" said Waldus.

Jakób kept firing.

Stan's section retreated over the bridge, followed by Jakób's.

"Blow it up!" motioned the captain. "Blow it up!"

One of the men pushed the lever down with all his strength and fell to the ground. Nothing happened. He got up and pushed it again and again. There was no response.

The first tanks began to roll across the bridge.

"Get cover!" shouted the captain. "Fall back!"

Total chaos erupted. Men fell to the ground, tried to shoot, crawled to find cover behind mounds of earth and bricks.

Jakób headed for a disused factory. The earth seemed to suck at his feet while bullets exploded around him. He ran with the heavy machine gun pressed to his chest. His leg was throbbing. Waldus kept up with him, running slightly behind him, the ammunition belt draped around his neck. Planes dived, bullets cracked around them, bombs exploded overhead. He felt a pain in his arm and his side. They reached the door, stumbled over the threshold, fell against a blackened brick wall.

"Help me over here!" shouted Haneczka.

Through a haze of smoke and pain Jakób saw her crouching over the boy. The child was writhing, grabbing at the air with his hands, screaming soundlessly, his mouth wide open. Jakób crawled across the room.

"Hold him down," said Haneczka. "I must get the bullet out and disinfect the wound."

But before he could, there was a creaking noise as the building was ripped apart and collapsed around them. A sharp pain stabbed through Jakób's belly.

Then a thick, black mist swallowed him completely.

———

The mornings were getting colder, so that Gretl sometimes wore her red coat to school. It was still dark when she got up to milk the goats.

At school Anya said, "My dad says there's no food left in Warsaw. He says when people get really hungry, they eat rats and mice!"

"I know something even better," said Starika.

Anya said nothing, just looked at her angrily.

"What do you know?" asked Gretl.

"I know about that camp where the Jews are. I know the name of the camp!"

Gretl felt the lump in her tummy again. "What is it?" she asked softly.

"Auschwitz!"

"Auschwitz? How do you know?"

"My granny lives in Oświęcim. She told me. It's near her home. She says she can see the smoke from the chimneys."

"My daddy says all the people in Warsaw are dead, every single one, and the Nazis have caught all the rest," Anya countered.

Gretl grew ice-cold. Everyone dead? And the Gestapo caught the rest?

The knot in her tummy was so tight that it ached.

She prayed more than she had ever prayed before.

———

Gretl saw Stan first. She was scolding Rosie because the goat wouldn't stand still to be milked when she saw Stan coming up the hill.

Slowly she got to her feet. She looked again. He was walking very slowly, his head bent.

Jakób wasn't with him.

She began to walk down the hill, her heart pounding. When she came closer, she broke into a run.

"Stan?"

He looked up. "Is Turek home?"

"No, he's at work. Stan, where's—?"

"Call my father," he said. "Tell him to bring the pushcart to the bottom of the hill."

"Stan—"

"Go! Hurry!" He turned and walked away.

Gretl ran home. Uncle Janusz was standing on the porch. "Stan says you must bring the pushcart to the bottom of the hill," she panted.

He turned to go to the stable. "Bring in the milk," he said over his shoulder.

She ran across the grass and grabbed the heavy bucket of milk. Then she put it down and untied Rosie. She walked to the kitchen as fast as she could without spilling the milk, carefully poured it into the pot, and covered it with the cloth. Then she ran down the hill.

There were three people at the turnoff to the farm: Uncle Janusz and Stan and a big woman in men's clothing. They were loading someone onto the pushcart. The woman was waving her hands. Gretl stopped at a distance.

It was Jakób, she knew.

She stood frozen to the spot.

They pushed him up the hill, Stan and Uncle Janusz and the woman. His feet dangled limply over the edge of the pushcart.

She knew what it meant. She knew, because she'd seen it before.

"We were lucky to get out," said Stan. He sat at the kitchen table next to the woman. He sounded tired, not cross like usual.

"Jakób is very weak," said the woman. "And the journey here didn't do him any good."

"If he didn't have the constitution of an ox he would never have survived."

Monicka set plates of buttered bread in front of them. "Why didn't you leave him at the hospital?"

"Because there is no hospital," said Stan. "Warsaw has been razed."

"I'll leave the medicine that I've got with you," said the woman. "It's Prontosil. It fights infection. I found it in a German field hospital. Give it to him regularly, and keep him quiet for at least another month."

"Where are you going?" asked Monicka.

"Back to Katowice."

Slowly Gretl walked across the porch and pushed the curtain aside. Jakób lay on his bed motionless, his eyes closed. His head made a deep dent in the soft pillow.

She went to his side. He looked strange. A black beard like a pirate's covered his square chin. His eyebrows were dense and black; his face, which had always been brown, was white. She wished he would open his eyes so that she could see whether he was still in there.

Carefully she reached out and laid her hand against his cheek.

His eyes opened.

They looked the same, those black-black eyes. He gave her a slight smile. "Hello, Gretz."

Her smile was broad. "Hello, Jakób Kowalski," she said.

The next week she didn't go to school at all. She remained at Jakób's bedside, giving him water when he was thirsty. Sometimes he was warm and she wiped his face with a moist cloth. She thought of Elza and was sad. Aunt Anastarja changed the dressings on his chest and leg and arm, cleaned the wounds, and gave him medicine. When she went to mass or had to feed the baby his bottle, Gretl gave Jakób his medicine.

He was too tired to eat by himself. "I'll feed him his soup," Gretl offered.

In the mornings she fed him his porridge. After three mouthfuls he shook his head. "You must eat, Jakób Kowalski," she said.

He opened his eyes. "Where did you learn to be so strict?"

"At school."

"Oh?"

"I go to school now, at the convent. I'm the brightest pupil in the class. Sister Zofia said so. It's because I read a lot. And because you showed me how to do those clever sums."

He didn't answer.

"Are you asleep?"

"No, I'm listening. Tell me more."

"I'll tell you more if you eat another spoonful of porridge."

He opened his mouth, but his eyes remained closed.

"I help the other children with their reading and I tell them stories. I make up the stories myself, because I ran out of stories to read, kaput. You must swallow, Jakób; don't just lie there with the porridge in your mouth."

———

A week later Stan went to Katowice to find work, because his job at the steelworks had been given away. Gretl went back to school. Jakób had told her to go.

In the afternoons he lay waiting for her. She ran home. When she pushed aside the curtain, her cheeks were red and her blonde curls formed a halo around her head. She always waited, as if she wasn't sure she was welcome. She waited for him to say, "Hello, Gretz."

"Hello, Jakób. Do you want some water?"

"If there's coffee in the pot, you can bring me some."

She was soon back with the coffee. "Shall I put Stan's pillow behind your back?" she asked.

His left shoulder was in pain, and his left hand remained dumb. He did the exercises the old Jewish doctor in Warsaw had prescribed, but he didn't notice any improvement.

"Does your arm hurt a lot?" Gretl asked.

"No, it's nothing. My hand is just dumb."

"Starika writes with her left hand, so you can imagine how dumb her right hand is! If the baby cries, I'll have to go and pick him up, because your mother is smoking a ham. His name is Czeslaw, but everyone calls him Czes."

"Yes, I know. Monicka brought him to me."

He tasted the coffee. She had added sugar. He had become used to drinking it bitter, but he enjoyed the sweetness.

She clambered onto Stan's bed. "He's a cute little baby," she said. "He knows me. When I stand next to his crib, he smiles at me, except when he's crying. He likes to hold my finger in his little fist. Like this." She took Jakób's right hand and folded her hand around his index finger. "He has a strong grip, you know," she said. "Shall I take the pillows away?"

It was new to him, this compassion. She was so young, yet she cared for him. He had never known anything like it. "No, I'll sit like this for a while," he said. "How was your day at school?"

"School is the same every day, Jakób. Sister Zofia tells us about God, then we do arithmetic, and we read and write. It's very easy, we don't even do multiplication tables yet. When Sister Zofia has time, she talks about God, because she loves Him so much. If she's busy, I tell the children stories. I prayed for you every day while you were gone, Jakób Kowalski."

In the more than two months he had been away he hadn't thought of her once, he realized. If he had to go away again, it would be different. This had to be how Jerzy Tatar had felt when he left his young daughter behind—Jerzy, who wouldn't be returning to his farm. Or Ryszard.

One night he awakened to find her sitting up beside him in Stan's bed, petrified. "Gretz?" he asked.

"Just a dream," she said, but her voice was shaking.

He waited, but she said nothing more. "Do you want to tell me about it?"

"No, I don't want it to stay in the room." But she asked, "Jakób, what is Auschwitz?"

A cold hand gripped his heart. "It's a place between Katowice and Kraków."

She was silent for a while, then she asked, "Is there a camp there?"

The hand began to squeeze. "I've heard so, yes."

"Where Jews are burned in an oven?"

He lay motionless. *Mother of God, give me strength and wisdom,* he prayed.

"Jakób?"

"Where did you hear that, Gretl?"

"At school. Anya says her daddy said so. And Starika's granny lives in . . . What's the name of the town close by?"

"Oświęcim?"

"Yes, Oświęcim. Her granny sees the smoke. And she says other things that I don't want to repeat."

Jakób had no idea how to answer.

"Jakób?"

"I don't know, Gretz. I've heard stories too," he said. "Is that what your dream was about?"

But she didn't answer. Just when he thought she had fallen asleep again, she asked, "Where does Rigena live?"

"I beg your pardon?"

"Rigena, the woman who gave me to you?"

He sighed, wishing he could end the conversation. But he knew her. Once she was on a trail, it wasn't easy to distract her. "Between Katowice and Kraków."

"Near Oświęcim?"

"Not too far from there, yes."

It was quiet again, but he knew what was coming.

"Jakób? Mutti and Oma's train, it was going to Auschwitz, wasn't it?"

"I don't know."

"But you know everything."

He didn't answer.

"That's what my dream is about," she said after a while.

"About the train?"

"No, about Mutti and Oma. The angel doesn't come."

He didn't understand, and yet he understood only too well. He reached out, folded her cold little hand in his. When she had finally fallen asleep, he lay awake for a long time, still wondering about her words.

Because the angel hadn't come for him either.

———

One afternoon when she came back from school, he was sitting on the porch, wrapped in a blanket. Happiness bubbled inside her. "You're up!" she said.

"My father helped me," he said. "It's cold. It's probably going to start snowing this week. Is your coat warm enough?"

"It's a very warm coat, nice and big." She sat down on the floor and took off her shoes.

"Why are you doing that? Your feet will be cold."

"Because my shoes are too tight, that's why. Look, they make my toes pink." She held up her bare feet for his inspection.

"I see, yes. You'll have to get new shoes and warm socks."

"Shall I fetch you some coffee?"

"Yes, then there's something I want you to do for me. I hope you'll agree."

When she returned with his drink she said, "I'll do anything. I'm not afraid."

"Do you remember where Professor Sobieski lives?"

She thought. "Sonja says he lives at her house."

"Sonja?"

"The girl whose coat I'm wearing. I suppose I could go home with her from school."

"I want you to fetch a book from him. While you're at school, I want to learn too. Or one of these days you'll be smarter than me."

She laughed out loud. "Jakób Kowalski, I'll never be smarter than you!"

———

The next afternoon she waited to go home with Sonja. Sister Zofia allowed Gretl to stay in the classroom and look at the atlas. Gretl's teacher opened the atlas for her at the right place before she sat down to work.

Gretl found Warsaw without any difficulty, then Kraków and Katowice, because they were printed in dark letters. It was hard to find Częstochowa, and she searched for Oświęcim for a long time. Auschwitz wasn't on the map, maybe because it was just a camp.

There were roads on the map and railroads. She followed the railroad from Katowice down to Oświęcim with her finger, but it was no good; she still didn't know what had happened. Then she traced the road from Częstochowa to Warsaw with her finger, the one Jakób had followed. But not the return journey, because they had come back in a horse and cart along back streets and farm roads, Stan had said. Because the Gestapo had been everywhere.

She spent a long time looking for Switzerland, but she couldn't find it anywhere.

"Sister Zofia?"

The teacher looked up. "Yes, Gretz?"

"Where is Switzerland?"

"Bring the book and I'll show you."

The teacher turned back three pages. "Look, this is Switzerland," she said.

Gretl felt her heart sink. "All of that page?"

"Yes. There's a piece of Austria over here, that's Italy, and this is France over here. Switzerland lies between them."

"Where's Poland?"

"Oh, far from Switzerland," said the teacher, closing the book. "The other classes are out now. You can look at the atlas again tomorrow."

———·———

After fetching Jakób's book and accepting a storybook from Mrs. Sobieski, Gretl ran home. She had to speak to Jakób. But when she opened the curtain, he was fast asleep.

"He's been sleeping all day," said Aunt Anastarja. "I think he sat in the chair too long yesterday."

Jakób woke up when Gretl came in with his soup. "Is it evening already?" he asked, surprised.

"Yes," she said and arranged the pillows behind his back. He could eat by himself now. "Jakób, Switzerland is very big and very far away."

He ate a spoonful of soup. "We can make a plan to deal with the very far away. It's the very big that worries me," he said.

She waited. He ate his soup. When he had almost finished, he asked, "Gretz, what do you have in that flat bag of yours? Documents?"

She dragged the trunk in which she kept her belongings out from under Stan's bed. At the bottom she found the bag and carefully took out the documents, one by one.

"This is a photo of my father in his Nazi uniform," she said. Jakób studied the photo and held out his hand.

"And this is a letter." She gave it to him. "It's written in German."

He gave a slight smile. "I see, yes." He read the letter carefully. "It's a letter the government sent your mother when your father died. They say he was a brave man who died for his country."

"I know."

He put the letter with the photograph on the bed. "What's the other document?"

"I don't know." She handed it to him.

"This is a certificate of baptism to say you were baptized Gretl Christina Schmidt by Pfarrer Helmut Friedrich at the Deutsche Luthersche Kirche on December 18, 1937." He turned the document over. "Nothing more. No place name."

"Does it help?"

"Do you have anything else in your little bag?"

She turned the bag inside out. "Just a dead moth," she said.

He shook his head. "I still don't know how we're going to find Onkel Hans."

———

During the night of the first snowfall he had the worst nightmare. He woke drenched in sweat, his entire being filled with horror. He lay motionless.

"Did you have a dream, Jakób?" He heard the concern in the small voice that came out of the dark.

"Yes, but don't worry, it's nothing."

"About the war?"

"Yes, Gretz." He was glad she was there, a live being among all the phantoms in his memory.

"You must think about other things, Oma told me. It helps. I know, I dream about Oma and Mutti every night."

"Tell me what you dream, please."

"That they are burning in the oven at Auschwitz. They scream, but the angel of God doesn't come."

He weighed the possibility of telling her what he had known for months. "Would it be easier if you knew that they couldn't have been in the oven?" he asked hesitantly.

In the feeble moonlight he saw her sit up. "They escaped? But Elza said they couldn't have escaped."

"No, not escaped. There's something I must tell you, Gretz."

He saw her lean back against the pillow, felt the cold little hand slip into his across the gap between their beds. He closed his hand around hers. "Yes?" she said.

Suddenly he couldn't tell her after all.

"Yes, Jakób?" she insisted.

"Your Mutti and Oma's train—the rail bridge exploded, the train fell into the ravine."

Silence.

How could he say it? "All the people died, Gretz."

Silence.

Mother of God, help me, please. "Do you understand what I'm saying?"

"How can a rail bridge just explode?" The small voice cut through him.

"Someone must have . . . I don't know . . . planted a bomb."

"But who would want to blow up a train full of people?" she asked.

Her words flooded his being, opening up what he had patched with difficulty. "People who didn't know what they were doing," he said honestly.

"Yes," she said after a while, "people who didn't know what they were doing."

It was quiet for a long time. He would give anything to take away her pain, to make everything undone.

"Could they have escaped from the train, Jakób?"

He heard the explosions again, saw the carnage. "No, it fell too far."

"How do you know?"

"I saw it," he said.

After a long while she said, "I heard the explosion. I thought it was bombs."

"But now you know they were never in Auschwitz. They couldn't have burned in the oven, could they?"

She didn't answer.

He wanted to comfort her. "I'm sorry, Gretz."

After a while she asked in a small voice, "Can I get into bed with you, Jakób Kowalski? I'll be careful of your wounds."

She got in under the blankets and nestled in the crook of his arm. He held the thin, cold figure against him. She was a little duckling, *his* little duckling—his responsibility.

At first she cried softly, lost in her grief. "There now, Gretz," he said.

Then sobs racked her body, coming from somewhere deep inside her.

"There now, Gretz, there now." He awkwardly tried to comfort her. At that moment he knew he would do anything for this little person. *Mother of God*, he prayed, *you gave her to me long before I was ready to take her. Help me always to do what's best for her.*

After a while she calmed down, though an occasional tremor still ran through her body. "It's no good trying to find Onkel Hans," she said. "I don't even know him."

Long after she had finally fallen asleep, he was still stroking her silken hair.

5

Gretl would never forget the Christmas after she turned ten. She had been looking forward to it for weeks. There was no money for gifts, because Poland was still poverty-stricken. But Jakób was coming home from Katowice with Stan and Haneczka and their new baby. Gretl still thought of Haneczka as the big woman in men's clothes. But Gretl liked her. Haneczka took no nonsense from anyone! Especially not from Monicka. And Stan was much friendlier now that he was married.

Haneczka had saved Jakób's life. Gretl would never forget it.

The morning before Christmas she helped Aunt Anastarja with the food. On Christmas Day the kitchen would be too crowded for Gretl. She'd wanted to put up a Christmas tree, like the one she had seen in Sonja's home, but Monicka said they didn't have glittery paper to make chains. And there was no room for a tree anyway.

Monicka came home from the factory earlier than usual to lend a hand. At the factory they were making Russian uniforms now instead of Nazi ones. "Same thing," Monicka muttered. "Khaki outfits for men out to shoot each other."

"Stan and Haneczka will have to sleep on the porch," said Aunt Anastarja.

"It'll be too cold for the baby," Monicka replied.

"It's better since Turek put in a door." Aunt Anastarja was rolling out cookie dough. The cookies probably wouldn't be very good, because there was hardly any sugar.

"It will still be too cold," Monicka argued. She turned to Gretl. "Fetch the cabbage from the cooler. I want to make bigos," she ordered.

At four, Gretl said, "I'm going to the station. I've already milked the goats."

It was a long wait for the train. She sat on a hard wooden bench, looking at the locomotive huffing and puffing and shunting cars on a sideline, at the tall water tower where the train filled its belly, at the tracks at her feet. The smoke burned her nose and the back of her throat. A station was usually a sad place. But today the station was a happy place, because the train would be bringing Jakób home.

Once, when she told Jakób how she felt about stations, he said, "A station is just the beginning or the end of a destination, Gretz. It's how you yourself feel at the station that makes it a happy or a sad place."

"It's almost always sad, because people go away," she persisted.

"But at the other end they arrive at a new destination, and that's good."

"Sometimes." She was thinking of the ghetto and of Auschwitz.

"Okay," he agreed, "sometimes."

At last the train steamed in, packed with people. Her eyes searched and searched. She climbed on top of the bench for a better view.

He came weaving through the crowd. She waved her arms wildly. He smiled, put down his bag, and opened his arms. She ran into his hard body.

They both laughed. "Your hair is long," he said. "Here, I brought you something. Take a look quickly, before Stan and Haneczka come."

Her fingers fumbled with the parcel. Inside were two ribbons for her hair, a white one and a red one. "Jakób, how lovely!" she said, overjoyed.

"I've brought shoes too, warm shoes. They're in my bag."

She didn't know how to thank him.

Then Stan and Haneczka were there. "I'll carry the baby," Gretl offered.

At home they had supper. Just borsch, the usual beet soup, and bread. The real meal would be eaten the next day. They didn't mention politics while they were eating. Gretl was glad, because it usually led to arguments. After supper she and Jakób carried in hay to sleep on. "Remember to clean up tomorrow morning," Monicka said crossly.

At ten they set off for the midnight mass. They all walked together—everyone except Monicka, because she was going to have another baby. She stayed home to look after the little ones. The fields were covered with snow, and the moon cast a soft glow over the landscape.

The cathedral was lit up by candles, even more than usual. The organ music was beautiful. At times the boys' choir sang along. At midnight they took communion, and then mass was over. *Everything is perfect*, Gretl thought. *It's impossible to be any happier.*

———

It was a beautiful service, but Jakób couldn't concentrate. *Mother of God, why this? Why now? Couldn't you have waited another year or two?* he thought over and over again.

Outside it was cold. Snowflakes sifted gently to the ground. Jakób and Gretl hurried ahead to get home.

"I remember something," she said, looking up at him with her blue eyes. "When I was very small Mutti made an Advent wreath and when we lit the candles, we sang a song. Can I sing it to you?"

"Yes," he said, "but softly."

"It goes like this: '*Advent, Advent, ein Lichtlein brennt, erst eins, dann zwei, dann drei, dann vier; dann steht das Christkind vor der Tür,*' because it's one, two, three, four Sundays and then the Christ child is standing at the door. I can't sing very well now, because I'm a little out of breath."

He nodded thoughtfully. "It's lovely."

When they had walked for a while, she said, "You're very quiet tonight, Jakób. Are you cross about something?"

"No," he said, "I have a problem that I'm thinking about."

"Can I help?" she asked.

"In time, yes, but not right now."

Earlier that evening, just after they'd had coffee, his mother had taken him aside. Ever since their arrival, he could sense there was something on her mind.

"The child can't stay here any longer, Jakób," she said without mincing words. "We can't afford to feed an extra mouth, not even with the money you send. Look at her. She doesn't have clothes to wear to school. The child must go. Especially now that Monicka is having a third baby."

"The child has a name," he said. "She's Gretz." Ever since Gretl had taken such tender care of him during his recovery, he had been disturbed by his mother's indifference toward her.

His mother ignored the remark, as if a name might turn "the child" into a human being. "Mrs. Jurski has agreed to take her in, to help in the bakery."

"And become their servant?" Jakób said. "I know the Jurskis. Under no circumstances will I allow her to go there."

"She'll have to go to work anyway. She's almost twelve."

"She's barely ten!" he exclaimed, outraged. "She's just a little girl! She's extremely bright. She needs to take her studies as far as she can! I won't allow—"

"Then why don't you come up with a solution?" His mother raised her voice. "The neighbors are talking. She looks more German every day."

Maybe he could take her along to Katowice. But the moment it entered his mind he knew that the idea was impractical. He shared a room with another engineer at the steelworks, as the Communist system decreed for an unmarried man of his age. And Stan and Haneczka didn't have room for her either. Besides, Gretl was not their responsibility.

As Jakób and Gretl walked home together he asked offhandedly, "Do you remember a lot of German things?"

"Not really, more Jewish things. But I'm not always sure of the difference. Please tell me why you're angry, Jakób."

He made up the first excuse he could think of. "Nothing is the same anymore."

"Like what?"

"The farm, for example." He walked on. "For more than a hundred years my forefathers have been on this farm. We've never been rich, but the farm was ours. We could do as we pleased. Now we're suddenly part of a big collective farm. We're told to produce beets, or carrots, nothing else, and the government decides how much we'll be paid for our produce. We can't keep pigs anymore. My mother can't smoke ham. The government decides when we need ham. They seem to be watching us all the time, even when we're going to mass."

"If they do, they'll have your mother to answer to!" she said. "She spends most of her time in the cathedral nowadays."

Jakób made no reply.

"Your father and Turek seem content. Turek says we have enough food on the table."

"Content? Life is about more than being content!" He suddenly realized what he was doing. He had no idea why he had gone off like that. "Oh, Gretz, forget it. Why am I spoiling a beautiful Christmas Eve for both of us?" he said with a smile.

"You must talk to me," she said earnestly. "I talk to you too."

"Yes," he said, "we must talk." But he couldn't find it in his heart to tell her what they had to talk about.

Two days later, just before he left for the station, Monicka asked, "Did your mother speak to you?"

"Yes, she did."

"And?"

"I'll be back at the end of May. I'll attend to the matter then," he promised.

Jakób was granted leave over Easter. He went home, knowing he had to break the news to Gretl. He knew what he had to do. He didn't want to, but it would be for her own good.

"You can't stay here any longer, Gretl," he told her. "I must take you to an orphanage in Germany."

She stood in front of him, gazing into his eyes. She looked fearless, just as he had seen her that first day in the doorway of Rigena's house. "Why?"

"I've told you. The house is too full, especially now with the new baby. You're growing up. Turek's sons are growing up. There's no money to send you to school."

"I don't understand why I can't come with you to Katowice."

He felt his patience wearing thin. "You know why not. You're just being difficult."

"I want to be the one to decide where I go," she said crossly.

"Fine," he challenged her. "Come up with a solution, then."

She grabbed the bucket from the table and stalked across the field. *Poor goats*, he thought, and poured himself a mug of coffee.

"But why Germany?" she asked when she returned. She slammed the bucket down on the table, angrily mopping up the drops that had spilled. "If I have to go to an orphanage, why not one in Poland? In Kraków or Warsaw, or wherever?"

"The orphanages here are state controlled. Conditions are shocking. As soon as you turn twelve, you'll be put to work. You're clever, Gretz. You must study! In Germany, most orphanages are controlled by the church. They get financial support."

She glared at him angrily.

He tried another angle. "Poland is under Communist rule. It's getting worse every day, especially now that the so-called democratic election has made the Communist parties even more powerful. I want to take you to the British or the American zone in Germany, your chances—"

"I like being under Communist rule."

He got up and left the room. *Typical little female*, he thought, irritated beyond measure. He walked toward where Turek and his father were putting up a fence.

———

She saw him sitting on the grass. She sat down next to him and slipped her small hand into his big one. They sat for a long time before he spoke.

"Gretz, I made a promise to the Holy Mother of God to do the best I can for you, to do what I believe is best for you."

"I want to stay with you," she pleaded. "Jakób, who am I going to tell when I've had a scary dream?"

"Gretz, don't."

"I know." She lowered her head.

"Please don't cry."

"I won't. I just don't want to go to a German orphanage."

"I know," he said, "but I don't see any other solution. I read in the paper that refugees from the old eastern provinces of Germany are flocking to Schleswig-Holstein. There's a refugee camp in Kiel."

She put her fingers in her ears. "I don't want to hear any more," she said. She felt her tears pushing past the stone in her stomach and the lump in her throat, pushing up until they almost reached her eyes.

———

When Jakób returned in May, they left immediately, just the two of them. In her bag were her documents and clothes. Jakób took along a blanket and some food.

At the beginning of their journey, she sat at the window, looking out at the towns on the banks of big rivers, at the tall cliffs with castles at the top, at the farmers in their vegetable plots. She looked at the stations, the big signposts with the strange names, where people got off and others got onto the train. "No one wants to stay where they are," she said.

"Just as well," he said. "It's no good being satisfied with everything."

When she grew tired, she lay down on the seat next to Jakób and made up stories about the castles and the tall cliffs. It helped ease the great sadness inside her. But not much.

They changed trains four times. They went through checkpoints where rude officials stared at their permits. "The Communists are just as bad as the Gestapo," she whispered to Jakób.

"Be quiet, or they'll throw you in jail," he warned.

She kept quiet.

Since crossing over into Germany, they had spoken nothing but German. "It feels strange not to speak Polish," she said. "I speak better Russian than German. We learned it at school."

When they changed trains for the last time in Hamburg, Gretl said, "I'm sleepy." She tried not to think, especially not of what lay ahead.

"Take a nap. It'll be another two or three hours before we reach Kiel," said Jakób.

On the seat next to him lay a newspaper someone had read and left behind. *A stroke of luck*, thought Jakób. Maybe it would distract him for a while. He read the headlines, the sports news on the back page, unfolded the paper, read about the serious food shortages and the suffering in East Berlin and the Americans' latest invention. Finding it impossible to concentrate, he was about to fold up the newspaper when he noticed a heading: *"Kinder wandern nach Südafrika."*

Frowning, he began to read, "Two South Africans, Mr. Schalk Botha and Dr. J. C. Kriek, are presently in Germany in search of Protestant orphans. They plan to relocate fifty boys and fifty girls to South Africa, where they will be legally adopted by selected parents

who can offer them a happy home and a bright future in a sunny country filled with possibilities."

He put the paper down.

He could never send her to Africa.

She lay on the seat beside him, asleep, her blonde curls spread over
his thigh.

... a country filled with possibilities...

Poland was under Communist rule, the population was hungry.
Germany was in ruins, its people faced starvation.

But Africa was too far away. And too dark.

... a happy home... selected parents...

Gretl had stopped being a Protestant a long time ago. She had been
confirmed in the Catholic Church, went to mass every Sunday, had
attended a Catholic school. But she had a document that said she had
been baptized Gretl Christina Schmidt by Pfarrer Helmut Friedrich in
the Deutsche Luthersche Kirche on 18 December 1937.

Holy Mother of God, help me, he prayed.

He picked up the paper again and continued to read the story. "The
two gentlemen seek German orphans with pure Aryan bloodlines."
That ruled Gretl out. On the other hand, she looked Aryan. And only
one of her grandmothers had been Jewish.

He read on: "The orphans of fallen SS soldiers will help to increase
the Afrikaner population." In his mind's eye he saw the photograph of
her father in his SS uniform. He remembered the words in the official
letter. The net seemed to be closing in around him.

It was probably an old paper. There were many orphans. Surely
fifty girls would have been selected by now, Jakób told himself.

He turned to the front page. It was the *Schleswig-Holsteinische
Volks-Zeitung* of May 22, just a week earlier.

Before the Warsaw hospital had been destroyed, a South African
pilot had occupied the bed next to Jakób's. Nick Groenewald's plane
had been shot down over Warsaw. He had parachuted to safety but suffered serious facial burns.

They had talked a lot; it was all they could do. "South Africa is a beautiful country, the best there is," Nick had said. "It has good weather, a strong government, beautiful natural scenery, a healthy economy. It's a land of milk and honey."

Nick had told him that the South African government was staunchly anti-Communist, intent upon warding off the "Red Danger."

He shook his head and picked up the paper again. "The children will have access to an excellent education, up to university level."

By the time Gretl woke up, he had made his decision.

They walked through the streets of Kiel. All the cities looked the same. The gaping wounds of war were evident everywhere.

"I don't even know where South Africa is," Gretl protested. Her voice was thin; she held her chin high.

"I'll find an atlas and show you." Jakób tried to quell his own misgivings.

"I don't even know what *Protestant* means."

"It means Christian, but without the pope," he said.

"I don't know whether they can speak German. Or Polish, or Russian."

"Certainly not Polish or Russian. We'll find out what language they speak." He felt slightly irritated. She wasn't making it easy.

"I don't want to learn another language."

She pursed her lips and walked on, her back straight and stiff.

They found a library and entered. Jakób told the lady with the severe glasses what they were looking for. She inclined her head and stared at Gretl. Gretl met her gaze. The lady walked ahead of them and selected a number of books from the shelves. "Sit here," she said, then returned to her desk.

Gretl knew how to use an atlas. South Africa was on the other side of the world, she saw. The map didn't show any tracks, so she couldn't reach it by train. Nor by bus or horse-drawn cart either, only by ship. And close to South Africa there was a picture of a round-faced wind blowing fiercely across the sea.

She closed the atlas and picked up a book about South Africa. There were many pictures in it, pretty, colored pictures of a mountain that looked like a box with a cloud covering its top and a blue ocean at its feet. Everything was bathed in bright sunlight. There were pictures of animals—lions and elephants and large bucks with long horns. And cute little monkeys. There were also pictures of dark-skinned people with painted faces. They were completely naked except for a few beads. She wanted to show Jakób the pictures, but she noticed just in time that the women were also nearly naked, so she quickly turned the page. When she found a picture of a black man wearing nothing but a skin, she showed it to Jakób. "Yes," he said, "those are Negroes. They live in Africa."

If the Polish children had thought she was too white, what would the people in Africa say?

She sat quietly, studying the picture. The man was fat. He was barefoot and in his hand was a long stick with a sharp point. He was sitting in front of a round grass hut. She didn't think she wanted to live in a grass hut.

"Look, Gretl, they say here that South Africa is a rich country, because it has a lot of gold."

She looked in Jakób's book. The men were wearing clothes, thank goodness, and round metal helmets. They were pouring liquid gold into a brick-shaped mold. Behind them flames were burning high.

"And there are farms. See how wide and how flat the land is." Jakób pointed with his finger.

There was a picture of women working in the fields with hoes, just like Uncle Janusz and Turek did, and Aunt Anastarja too, when she wasn't at the cathedral. They were wearing dresses and scarves around their heads. She laughed. "Look, they've got babies on their backs!"

"Hush, be quiet." Jakób motioned with his eyes toward the strict lady at the desk.

Gretl nodded and carried on looking through the book. But she didn't enjoy it. Not because she was afraid, just because everything looked so strange.

"They speak two languages," Jakób said after a while without looking up. "English and Afrikaans. I know a bit of English. It's not too hard. And Afrikaans, they say here, comes from Dutch, so it's not too different from German. I understood from the article that the orphans will probably be placed with Afrikaans people." He picked up the paper again and opened it at the article.

In Africa the people speak Afrikaans. It made sense. "I don't want to go," she said, resolutely closing her book.

He lowered the newspaper and looked at her despondently. "Why not, Gretl?"

"How would you like to live in a round grass hut?"

"I beg your pardon?"

He could pretend to be stupid all he wanted. She wouldn't go. "And besides, I'm too white."

"Gretl, what are you talking about?"

He wasn't just pretending to be stupid, he *was* stupid. She opened the book at the picture of the man wearing a skin and sitting in front of a grass hut. "See here!" she said and pressed her finger on the hut. She turned back three pages to the picture of the bare-chested women. "And here!"

He turned his head and began to laugh softly. "Gretl, you're not going to live there!" He laughed louder, and the woman at the desk gave them an irate look.

"Behave! The lady is looking at us!" she whispered sternly.

He closed the books and got up. "Come," he said, "we've done enough work for one day."

They walked past a bakery. A single cake was on display in the window. Immediately when they entered his stomach cramped at the smell of bread.

"Are you going to buy the cake?" Gretl asked eagerly.

He looked down at her. "Of course, Gretchen. For our last meal together we might as well have cake, what do you say?"

She smiled up at him. He had never used that endearment for her before, but the prospect of being separated from her made it seem right. "Of course."

He took out the money. There wouldn't be enough to get him home again, but that was a problem for another day.

At the place he had chosen for the night, he spread the blanket on the floor and placed the cake in the center. "Can we eat it right away?" she asked. "My mouth is watering."

"I don't think we should waste any more time," he said, breaking off two pieces.

He drank in every movement she made, her thin hands around the chunk of cake, her pearly teeth sinking into it, her shiny eyes when she looked up at him. "It's the best cake I've ever had. Eat, Jakób," she said with her mouth full.

He bit into the soft cake, tasted the sweetness. *I wonder if I'll ever eat cake again without remembering this moment*, he thought.

"Lovely, isn't it?" she said. "May I have another piece?"

"Yes," he said, "let's finish it all tonight."

She laughed and took another piece. When she had finished, she said, "I'm full. And there's so much left."

"I'll eat another piece, maybe two, and we'll have the rest for breakfast tomorrow morning." He wiped the crumbs from her cheeks with his finger.

"Cake for breakfast! I've never heard of it!"

"Well, you learn something new every day, don't you? Lie down now," he said, "let's try to sleep."

"Okay," she said and nestled against him.

But he didn't really want her to sleep. "There are so many things I want to tell you, Gretchen."

"You've already told me."

He shook his head. "Other things."

"Like what?"

"Like . . . I don't know. Like . . . always remember you're Gretl."

"I like Gretchen too."

"Yes. But I mean more than your name. If you don't allow others to influence who you are, you'll have something no one can take away from you. It doesn't matter what other people are like, or even what they call you. You must continue to be Gretl. Gretchen. Do you understand what I'm telling you?"

"I think so."

"And . . ." He shook his head. "I don't know what else." He sat up and took a small package from his pocket. "I bought this for you. See whether you like it."

She sat up quickly. "For me?" Carefully she unwrapped it. Inside was a small wooden cross on a leather string. "Oh, Jakób, it's so pretty. Is it mine?"

"Yes," he said. "Let me put it around your neck."

She fell asleep with the little cross clasped tightly in her fist.

He didn't sleep. His thoughts went round and round, unable to escape from the vortex.

He sensed that she was awake. "Gretchen?"

"I woke up and I thought you were gone."

"I'm here."

"Will you hold me, Jakób?"

He wrapped his arms around the skinny little figure.

"Who's going to teach me things if you're not there?" she asked against his chest.

"You'll go to school in your new country."

"School can't teach you everything," she said.

"No, you're right. But you'll be part of a family. You'll have a new mommy and daddy to teach you. But you must teach yourself things too. That's what I still wanted to tell you. Look and listen carefully and make up your own mind. Decide what's right and what's good and do it, even if it's not what you want to do. It's the best way to learn."

"Will my new family hold me like this?"

"Yes, they'll hold you."

When he thought she had gone back to sleep, she asked, "Jakób, will you visit me in South Africa? Even if it takes a long time, will you promise to come one day?"

"I can't promise that, Gretchen. I'm Polish. I'll betray myself if I leave Poland."

"Just to visit?"

"Relations between the East and the West are getting worse. I live in a Communist country; the South African government probably won't allow me to come."

"Will you write to me, then?"

"No, I can't. No one must know you have any ties to Poland."

He felt the small figure tremble. "Jakób?"

"I'll never forget you, Gretchen, if I live to be a hundred. Always remember that."

"How will I know?"

Mother of God, help me.

At that moment the moon broke through the clouds. "Do you see the full moon?"

"Yes?"

"That same moon shines down on South Africa. At this moment it's shining down on South Africa and on Poland, on Częstochowa and Katowice. When you look at the moon, remember I am seeing it too."

"If there are no clouds in Poland," she said.

"Yes," he said, "if there are no clouds."

The first orphanage where they called the next day knew nothing about the relocation program. Neither did the second. But at the third orphanage a woman said, "I've heard of something like that. Try the Jugendbehörde, they should know more."

"I'm very glad I don't have to live in any of those places," Gretl said as they continued on their way. "They don't smell good. What's the Jugendbehörde, Jakób?"

"The youth welfare organization. They look after orphaned children and people who have fallen on hard times."

They walked through the streets of Kiel. Though they walked far, they arrived much too soon. Gretl stopped in front of the red-brick building.

"Here it is," she said.

He couldn't bear to look at the sign. "Yes, I know. Let's just sit here and talk for a while."

He sat down under a tree. It was cold. The rain had stopped, but the sun wasn't out.

"Gretl, listen carefully. We'll have to say you come from East Prussia, close to the Polish border."

"I know," she said.

"And you'll have to pretend you don't really know how you got there."

"I know."

"We'll have to say you're one of the Findelkinder."

"What's that?"

"A foundling."

"An unwanted child?" she asked.

"You're not unwanted. You're beautiful, clever Gretl Schmidt."

"Okay."

"And you must remember that you speak only German."

She regarded him earnestly. "And that I know nothing about the Catholic Church and don't have any Jewish blood. I know, Jakób. But I'm sick of all the lies."

He knew exactly how she felt. He wanted to pick her up and hold her and catch the first train back to Poland. Instead, he held out his hand and said, "I know, Gretchen, I know. Let's go inside."

After a long search they found an official who knew that the Jugendamt in Kiel had undertaken to find at least fifty orphans for possible selection by mid-June. "Are you a relative?" he asked.

"She's a Findelkind," said Jakób.

The man looked at them skeptically. "Does she have documents?"

"Only a certificate of baptism." Jakób held out his hand. Gretl gave him her papers.

The man studied the documents carefully, peered over his spectacles at Gretl, and said, "Take her to the Red Cross orphanage." He gave Jakób the address.

Back outside, Jakób said as cheerfully as possible, "Well, Gretl Schmidt, we've passed the first test! Let's find the Red Cross orphanage." His heart was weeping.

They found it without any difficulty. A kind, maternal woman opened the door and introduced herself as Frau Schumann. Another of the Findelkinder? She clicked her tongue sympathetically. Yes, she knew about the program. Was Gretl a Protestant? Gretl showed the certificate of baptism. Pure Aryan? Gretl produced her father's photograph and the official letter. A full orphan? "My father was shot dead," said Gretl.

"And your mother?" the woman asked, glancing apologetically at Jakób. "I'm sorry, I have to ask."

Gretl looked straight at her. "My mother died in an explosion. I heard it. And I saw it, the red glow."

"No other family?"

"My sister also died. She was very sick."

"I suspect it was tuberculosis," said Jakób. "You know what a problem it has become."

Frau Schumann nodded. She filled out a form and stamped it in blue ink. "I hope you're selected," she said. "You're a brave little girl. Come, I'll take you to your room." She turned to Jakób. "Thank you for bringing her, sir."

"I'm going outside with him first," said Gretl, "then I'll come back in."

On the sidewalk he looked down at her. "I'm going to be in Kiel for two or three more days, just to make sure you're all right. But we can't speak again, because they think I don't know you."

She nodded. Her blue eyes were unnaturally shiny.

He gave her a stamped, addressed envelope. "Write me a letter, Gretchen. Just once, if you're selected, so that I'll know. Never again."

She nodded, her lips trembling.

He felt his resolve begin to crumble, so he cupped her face in his big hands and stroked her cheek with his thumb. She gave him a brave little smile.

"Go in now," he said hoarsely.

She turned and went up the two steps, her back straight. She opened the big door, walked in, and closed it behind her without looking back.

———

As she was walking to church with the other children on Sunday morning, she saw him on the opposite sidewalk. She knew if she ran to him, he would open his arms wide and hold her tightly. But she also knew it wasn't part of the plan, so she gave him a brave smile and walked on.

On the steps of the church she turned and looked back down the street. He was still there. He smiled and waved. She knew then that he was going back to Poland. She reached up with both hands and waved wildly. She couldn't smile, her throat was too tight. Tears welled up from deep inside her and poured from her eyes so that his image blurred. Then the girls swept her along into the church.

6

Gretl was given a place to sleep in a room with eighteen other girls. There were only ten beds, which meant that they slept two to a mattress, their heads pointing in opposite directions. Only Elke had her own bed, because she was the oldest and the room captain. Except for her bad skin, she reminded Gretl of Sonja.

I mustn't think about Sonja, she told herself, *or other thoughts will creep in.*

The lump in Gretl's stomach remained rock hard.

Gretl shared a bed with Gisela. The memory of the bombs gave Gisela nightmares, but at least she didn't wet the bed. She was eight years old and coughed a lot.

The older girls had to help in the kitchen. No one considered Gretl old enough until she told them she was nearly eleven. "You look eight. You're really skinny," Elke said disapprovingly. Gretl helped clear the table, wash dishes, and clean vegetables. In the afternoons she made sandwiches with syrup for the little ones.

In the mornings they lined up and trooped to school. The teachers were strict and the children obedient. The arithmetic was easy and so was the German reading, but Gretl found it strange to write in German.

After the first week Gretl asked the teacher for a Dutch book.

"A Dutch book?" the teacher replied. "What do you want with a Dutch book?"

"I like reading other languages," said Gretl.

The teacher frowned and said, "No, I definitely don't have a Dutch book." But the next day she brought Gretl one.

The *Deutsche Luthersche Kirche*, where they worshipped on Sundays, was beautiful inside. Some of the windows were broken, because there wasn't enough money to repair everything that had been damaged during the war. The music was lovely, and the pastor spoke a German Gretl could understand.

She wasn't allowed to wear her cross to church, Frau Schumann said, because the cross was Catholic.

The nights were a dark, dark tunnel with no end. The moon didn't come out even once. In her dreams she sometimes believed she was back in Częstochowa, with Jakób. She shouldn't think about Jakób. But at night, while she was sleeping, she clasped the little cross in her closed fist.

One evening Frau Schumann said to the group, "Tomorrow two people from Südafrika will be coming to speak to you. They will be selecting children to take back with them. Wash yourselves with soap this evening, your hair as well. But use the soap sparingly, and bring what's left back to me. Elke, you're in charge of the soap."

The girls washed first. When it was Gretl's turn, she struggled to get her feet clean. She washed and washed her hair until Elke exclaimed, "Enough now! Give me the soap, you heard what Frau Schumann said!"

She tried to remove the stain from the front of her dress, but it was hard without soap. She would put her shoes on at the last moment, she decided, because they really hurt her feet. And she would tie the red ribbon Jakób had given her for Christmas in her hair and try to tame her unruly curls.

She wasn't a crybaby, but her throat grew thick at the thought of him, and the lump in her tummy grew harder.

The next morning the children were so excited that they could hardly eat their porridge. "Don't come running to me when you get hungry," Frau Schumann warned.

No one went to school. Everyone waited.

After a while two people arrived. Frau Schumann introduced them to the children. Onkel Schalk Botha wore smart clothes and round glasses, and Dr. Vera Bührmann was there to make certain they were healthy. Frau Schumann explained that Onkel Schalk was the secretary of the German Children's Fund, which was supplying the money for the children's transportation. It was obvious to Gretl that Onkel Schalk had a lot of money. His black suit was very stylish.

Onkel Schalk's German wasn't very good, and the smaller children soon grew restless. Twice Frau Schumann had to speak sharply. Gretl understood that the children were to be taken to a fine country where a kind new mommy and daddy would be waiting for them. They would have a very good life—"*sehr gut*," said Onkel Schalk, struggling with the pronunciation. But they had to understand that they would never return to Germany again.

Only children of eight years and younger were to be considered.

Elke lay on her bed for the rest of the day, crying. "Don't cry." Gretl tried to console her. "Crying makes your head hurt, and it doesn't make anything better."

"It's easy for you to talk," Elke sobbed and sat up. Her spotty face was even redder than usual, and her stringy hair had escaped from the white ribbon Gretl had let her borrow. "I'm fourteen. If they don't choose me, I'll have to go and work next year." She began to cry again. "Probably in a factory or a laundry or somewhere."

When Elke refused to be comforted, Gretl went to the kitchen. Her tummy ached.

The next day everyone who was older than eight was sent back to school.

Two days later Gretl decided to take matters into her own hands. After school she resolutely walked to Dr. Vera Bührmann's office.

The door was closed. Inside she heard voices: Frau Schumann's, the doctor's, and another person's. Then a child began to wail. The door opened and a young woman hurried out. She shut the door behind her and burst into tears. Inside, the child cried more loudly.

Gretl tried to comfort her. "Don't cry. Crying doesn't help, it—"

"I signed off my little boy," the woman sobbed, "for adoption in Africa." She ran out through the front door.

Gretl looked at the fleeing woman and remembered Jakób's words: *I made a promise to the Holy Mother of God to do the best I can for you, to do what I believe is best for you.* She understood now.

The child had stopped crying. Frau Schumann had probably taken him to the toddlers' section. Gretl knocked on the door, pushed it open, and went in.

The doctor sat writing at a desk. She looked up and said, "Yes?"

"I must be examined to go to Südafrika," said Gretl.

The lady had a slight frown between her eyes. She reached for a stack of files. "Your name?"

"Gretl Schmidt."

She looked through the files and said, "Your file isn't here. Where have you come from?"

"I'm here, at the Red Cross orphanage. I'm—"

"I don't have your file." She peered at Gretl through her spectacles. Her eyes looked kind but tired. "How old are you?" she asked.

Gretl lifted her chin and looked Dr. Bührmann in the eye. "I'm ten, but I look eight. I'm a Protestant orphan. I have a certificate of baptism that says Pfarrer Helmut Friedrich baptized me Gretl Christina Schmidt in the Deutsche Luthersche Kirche on 18 December 1937. It's in my file. Frau Schumann has it. My father was Herr Peter Schmidt, a fallen SS soldier. Here is a photo of him in his SS uniform." She took the photograph from her little bag and put it on the desk. "I'm a full orphan, because my mother died in an explosion, my mother and my grandmother. My sister also died, so I became a Findelkind. I'm Aryan," she added the most important detail.

"I see," the doctor said slowly.

"And I'm reading a Dutch book so that I'll understand when my new family talks to me," said Gretl. She had decided to keep that bit of information for last, to show the lady how keen she was.

The doctor got up and walked around the big desk. "You're ten, you say?"

"Yes, but I look eight," Gretl repeated.

"You're a truly remarkable little girl," said the doctor. "Sit here, let me examine you."

Gretl took off her dress and clambered onto the bed. Her heart beat wildly. She hoped the doctor wouldn't think there was something wrong with it. "My heart doesn't always beat this fast," she said.

"There's no need to be afraid," Dr. Bührmann said kindly.

"I'm not afraid."

The doctor pressed the cold listening thing against her ribs. "My, you're just skin and bones," she said.

"I can eat a lot and get fat," Gretl suggested, adding with a laugh, "Like Hansel and Gretel at the witch's house."

The doctor laughed. "No, that won't be necessary."

When they were sitting at the big desk again, the doctor said, "Gretl Schmidt, you're exactly the kind of child we're looking for. But you're two years older than our cut-off date."

Gretl felt her heart sink. "I have no one," she said. "If you don't take me to Südafrika, I'll have to go to work in a factory or a laundry. And I'm clever; I must study, that's why I must go." It was hard to look into the lady's eyes and not cry.

The lady took off her glasses and rubbed her eyes. "I promise, Gretl, if we don't find enough suitable children under the age of eight and we're given permission to push up the age limit, you'll be one of the first children I'll include."

"Why do they want only young children?" Gretl asked.

The lady put her glasses back on. "The new mommies and daddies prefer them," she said without looking at Gretl.

Gretl understood.

"Go back to your room now."

That evening she took the paper and envelope Jakób had given her from her bag.

"Lieber Jakób," she began to write. But she put the pencil down, because she still didn't know what would happen to her.

———•———

The next day Onkel Schalk and the lady doctor left to look for children in other places. For more than three weeks the children went to school and to church as if no one from South Africa were looking for orphaned children.

Then one rainy day when the sheets wouldn't dry, Frau Schumann called Gretl and eight other children to her office. "Fetch your things," she said. "You've been chosen to go to South Africa."

Gretl froze to the spot. Was it really happening, or was it just another story in her head? "Really?" she asked.

"Yes, Gretl, really."

She couldn't believe it. She looked at the other children, who were jumping up and down, creating a commotion.

She returned to her room in a daze. The other girls were helping in the kitchen. She and two of the younger girls were the only ones from their room to be chosen. They rolled their possessions into bundles.

"Lieber Jakób," Gretl wrote before she went downstairs, "I've been chosen to go to Südafrika. We're on our way to the Red Cross orphanage in Lübeck-Brandenbaum by bus." She put the letter back in her bag. She wouldn't mail it yet, because she could write only one letter to Jakób. She had just wanted to tell someone.

When they drove away, she did not look at the place where Jakób had stood.

———•———

The Red Cross orphanage in Lübeck-Brandenbaum was another red-brick building with many rooms where other selected orphans also gathered. Here Gretl had her own bed and received new clothes that Onkel Schalk had bought in London at Marks and Spencer. Gretl was given new shoes and socks, two pairs of underpants, a dress with yellow flowers that was a little too big for her, a navy blue skirt that was the right size, and a red blouse that was much too big. There weren't enough sweaters, so she didn't get one, but it didn't matter. She told the helper lady, Tante Hildegard, she still had the one Mrs. Sobieski had made for her two years earlier. And she had her red coat as well, even though the sleeves were way too short.

In her room she laid out her new clothes on the bed and took the letter to Jakób out of her bag. She tried to describe the clothes, so that he would know how fine she looked.

But she wasn't ready to mail the letter yet.

———•———

Two days later thirty-five children from Schleswig-Holstein were taken to Maschsee in Hannover. Before they departed they were addressed by a very important man, Schleswig-Holstein's minister of the interior, Wilhelm Käber. "You're about to go to a new country," he told them. "Remember that we Germans are a proud nation. You'll always have German blood in your veins. Be proud of it. And behave like true Germans!"

Because the minister made such a long speech, they had to leave without eating breakfast. But the helper ladies had packed sandwiches for the bus ride. It turned into a disaster, because the boys didn't behave like true Germans and got syrup all over themselves. Everything was sticky and the ladies were quite despondent.

Gretl hoped there would be no brother in her new family. Boys were undisciplined and silly.

"What's today's date?" she asked Tante Hildegard.

"August the twentieth," she answered. "Here, take this facecloth and wipe Ingeborg's face."

The head of the Jugendamt in Kiel, Dr. Walter Blaser, accompanied them to Hannover. On the bus he spoke to the older children. They took turns sitting with him in the front seat. After a while Tante Hildegard took Gretl to the front. "This could be the one you're looking for," she said to Dr. Blaser.

"She's very young," said the man.

"Exactly," said the lady, then she returned to the back of the bus, where two boys were fighting.

The man asked a lot of questions. What was her name? Where was she from? Gretl got all the answers out in a single breath, so that he wouldn't ask unnecessary questions.

"I see," he said. "And you're ten?"

"Yes." She looked him in the eye. "I know the new parents want younger children, but I'm going to be very good. I'll help them work, so that they'll want me."

He nodded. "I'm sure they'll want you," he said. "I want you to do something for me."

"Yes?"

"Say 'yes, sir' when you speak to a grown-up."

"Yes, sir."

"In Hannover there will be many journalists and people from the radio stations."

"I don't know what journalists are, sir."

"They write for the newspapers."

"Okay, sir."

"They want to speak to the children before they leave the Heimat."

"Where's the Heimat, sir?"

"The Heimat is Germany. I want you to speak to the journalists."

"Just me?" She realized too late that she had forgotten to say "sir," but he didn't seem to have noticed.

"No, you and a few others. Ask Tante Hildegard to tie a ribbon in your hair. The journalists might already be there when we arrive."

———

The journalists came after lunch. The children selected by Dr. Blaser sat around them on the lawn.

"What will you do in South Africa?" one of them asked.

"Chase the monkeys out of the tobacco fields," said one little boy.

"See that the lions don't catch the goats," said a second one.

What a dumb answer, Gretl thought, frowning. Did he think he was Daniel in the lions' den? He probably didn't even have Jewish blood. "I'm going to get a home and a family who wants me," she said, lifting her chin.

"That's a very good answer," said the journalist. "What do you know about South Africa?"

"The sun always shines, and there are lions and lots of bananas and oranges," said one little girl.

"And Negroes. I want to see a Negro," said a little boy.

"Black people," Onkel Schalk interrupted. "We shouldn't say Negroes."

"We'll have to learn a new language, Afrikaans," said Gretl. "It's a lot like Dutch, which is almost like German, so it shouldn't be too hard."

The journalist laughed. "You're a little sweetheart, aren't you?" he said. "Can you say a few words in the new language?"

"Yes," said Gretl. "One of the helper ladies taught me how to say good morning, good night, and sleep well. You say, '*Goeiemôre,*' '*goeienag,*' '*lekker slaap.*' It means '*guten Morgen,*' '*gute Nacht,*' '*schlaf gut.*' See, it's almost the same."

"You're right," said the journalist. "Teach me a few words too? Here, Gustave"—he called to a man with a big camera—"take a photo of this little one teaching me to speak Africa."

Gretl was on the verge of telling him it was Afrikaans, but she smiled at the camera instead, so that it would be a nice photo.

That night she finished her letter to Jakób. They would be leaving Germany the next day for the Netherlands, and she had to mail the letter in Germany because Jakób had put German stamps on the envelope. She told him everything, because she longed with all her heart to talk to him.

When she finished, she looked through the window. The clouds were gone and for the first time she saw the moon again. It wasn't a full moon, but it didn't matter, because Jakób would be seeing the same broken moon if there were no clouds in the Polish sky.

The next morning the journalists returned to photograph the children's last breakfast on German soil. They ate their porridge at a long table. They wore name tags, so that the helper ladies would know who they were.

The man with the camera gave Gretl a newspaper cutting. "Look," he said, "it was in this morning's paper. Who's that little girl?"

She couldn't believe it. She, Gretl Kowalski—no, Gretl Schmidt—was in the newspaper! In the caption below the photo she read her name and the answers she had given. "Keep it," said the man. "One day you can show your grandchildren what a sweet little thing their grandmother was."

"Thank you, sir," she said.

She looked at the photo for a long time. She read the words three times, memorizing them. Then she folded the cutting and put it in the envelope so that Jakób could read her clever answers and see how pretty she looked with the ribbon in her hair.

She licked the flap, sealed the envelope, and walked to the mailbox at the gate.

On her way back she could taste the glue on her tongue.

The station at Hannover smelled like stations everywhere: smoky and acrid. The odors made her tummy ache.

The station was crowded with people who wanted to see the German orphans. The children were wild with excitement, especially the boys. Some of the younger children were afraid and were crying.

Besides the helper ladies, Mr. Theodor Haenert and Mr. and Mrs. Johannes were also traveling with them. Mr. Johannes was a schoolteacher. Of course there was also Onkel Schalk Botha, their leader. The ladies and the men were Afrikaners, but they spoke German, because they had all once been Germans, Onkel Schalk explained. Just as they—and he waved his hand to include all the children—were on the verge of becoming Afrikaners.

Gretl was in Tante Hildegard's group, which included many little ones. Some refused to walk and had to be carried. Others were unmanageable and wanted to run away and play. "Gretl, will you please carry Horst and hold Ingeborg's hand?" asked Tante Hildegard.

It was hard to carry Horst, because he kept wriggling and squirming. When Gretl called him to order, he began to cry. At least Ingeborg behaved.

At last they were all on the train. People were crying, journalists were taking photographs, officials were inspecting their documents. A man in uniform gave a loud blast on a whistle.

The train huffed and puffed and blew out steam, and slowly the wheels began to turn. Children hung out of the windows, waving excitedly. Cameras flashed, people held up their handkerchiefs, a band played the German anthem. Gretl couldn't decide whether the station was a happy or sad place.

Then Gretl saw a woman running after the train. "No! No!" the lady screamed. "I made a mistake! Bring her back!"

A little girl of about four hung out of the window, screaming, "Mommy! Mommy!"

The train picked up speed, leaving behind it the last German station on their route.

It was hard to keep Horst quiet. He wanted to run up and down the corridor. He was too young to listen to a story. "Never mind, I'll take him," Tante Hildegard said after a while.

Ingeborg was a lot easier. She was scared and clung to Gretl's hand. "Look at the lovely cows," said Gretl, pointing out the window.

When Ingeborg fell asleep, Gretl sat looking at the landscape. She felt quite empty, as if she had lost something.

"Are you going to cry?" asked a girl from the opposite seat.

Gretl looked up. "No, I'm not a crybaby."

"Neither am I," said the girl. "What's your name?"

"Gretl."

"My name is Rita. I'm ten. How old are you?"

"Also ten."

"Oh? I thought you were younger."

"I'm just thin."

"Yes, you are." Rita looked through the window for a while, then asked, "Are you hungry?"

"No."

"I am. I'm going to ask for a sandwich."

When she came back, she brought one for Gretl as well. "We can be friends," she said.

"Yes," said Gretl, "then we won't be so lonely."

After a while Ingeborg woke up. Gretl told her a story, and when the younger child lost interest, Gretl pointed out things through the window. "Look at the pretty flowers," she said. "See the windmills? They go round and round when the wind blows." They were already in Holland, headed to Hoek van Holland, where the ferryboat was waiting to take them across the sea to Harwich in England.

———•———

There were many sick children and grown-ups on the ferry to England. The wind kept blowing, the rain fell in sheets, and the sea was gray and angry. Wave upon wave came rushing along, tilting and rolling the boat so that Gretl had to hold on or be tossed around.

Now I know how the disciples felt on the Sea of Galilee, Gretl thought. She tried not to be scared and to have faith, but the fury of the storm was increasing.

The children threw up on the blankets, on their clothes, and on the floor. It was a terrible mess. *To think we have to spend three more weeks on a ship to South Africa,* Gretl thought.

She clung to her little wooden cross and did her best to clean up before she fell asleep.

In England there were more train stations, more journalists, gifts of new toothbrushes and soft facecloths, and a brief stay at a smart hotel with shiny floors and carpeted stairs. It was smarter than a palace, Gretl thought.

The *Winchester Castle* was docked in Southampton. It was a big ship, bigger than Gretl ever could have imagined. If this had been the size of Noah's ark, she thought, she could understand how there had been space for the elephants and lions and the big antelope with their long horns.

They were shown to their rooms—cabins, they were called—deep in the ship's belly. The toddlers stayed separately, like at the Red Cross orphanage, and the helper ladies slept with them. Tante Irmgard Zemke slept with the older children. Some of the ladies spoke a strange German, but Tante Irmgard spoke exactly the way Gretl did. "It's Low German," she told Gretl. "It's the way people speak in the north."

Gretl realized then that her family must have lived in the north of Germany.

She and Rita shared a cabin with four other girls. They each had a bed, called a berth, but they argued about who would sleep in the upper berths. Herma, one of the bigger girls, suggested that they take turns.

Afterward they stood on the deck at the back of the ship, gazing at the people on shore. Sunlight glittered like diamonds on the water and wavelets lapped against the vessel. From the blue sky white birds dived into the water, making loud squawking sounds. The girls were very high up, and down below the people were bustling like ants. The ship was tied to the land—the quay, she heard people say—with paper streamers. There were balloons everywhere and a band was making loud music.

The ship's horn let out a deep blast—*boom! boom!* Slowly the ship began to move away from the quay. The people on land waved their handkerchiefs in the air. The streamers broke.

"So, we're on our way to South Africa. Finally!" Onkel Schalk said beside her. He had spoken Afrikaans, but she had understood.

———

Supper was quite good. They ate strange-looking spaetzle, not like Aunt Anastarja or Mutti had made it—thicker, with a long hole in the middle, like a limp tube. Gretl hadn't thought of Mutti for a long time, nor of Oma and Elza.

But Jakób was in her thoughts every day. Not because she wanted him to be. Her thoughts went there by themselves. Like right now.

"I like this spaetzle," she said to Rita, just to get her mind off Jakób.

That night when they were in bed, Tante Irmgard came to their cabin and played *"Guten Abend, gute Nacht"* on her accordion. When she left, one of the girls said from the lower berth, "I feel sad now. My mother used to sing that song."

"My mother too, before she died," Gretl remembered.

"My mother didn't die," the girl said.

———

The following morning after breakfast they were called to the games room, but not for games. Mr. Johannes read from the Bible and prayed.

Then he said, "I'm going to give you Afrikaans lessons every day so that you'll know a little of the language by the time you meet your new families."

Gretl was pleased, though she worried about English, which had posed some difficulty for her in England. If someone spoke English to her, she wouldn't understand a word.

"You're going to Afrikaner homes. The people won't speak English," Mr. Johannes reassured her. "Right. If you all work hard for an hour, you can go on deck to play."

An hour later the children could say good morning to their new father (*Goeiemôre, Vader*), good afternoon to their new mother (*Goeiemiddag, Moeder*), and good night to their new brother and sister (*Goeienag, Broer, Suster*). The g and the r sounds were hard to pronounce. Gretl thought it sounded as if there were a grater at the back of the throat, or as if the speaker had taken foul-tasting medicine. They could also say yes and no (*ja* and *nee*), please (*asseblief*), and thank you very much (*baie dankie*).

It was windy and cold on deck, but two crew members played games with the children and soon they no longer felt the cold. Mr. Johannes and Onkel Schalk and one of the helper ladies, Fräulein Ingrid Brocke, played along. They had to toss a flat ring into painted squares on the deck, they had to run with a beanbag and toss it into a basket, they had to push a thin wheel to the other side of the deck and back without letting it topple over. If it toppled, they had to start over. They played in teams and when a team won, each member was given a sweet. Gretl did her best because the sweets were delicious.

"Not very good for their teeth," said Dr. Vera Bührmann.

When it was time for soft drinks, Gretl went to the doctor. "Thank you for choosing me," she said.

The doctor smiled. "Actually, you chose yourself," she said. "I'm trying to figure out which child to place with which family."

"Do you know where I'll be going?"

"I think so, yes."

"What's their last name?"

"I can't tell you yet, Gretl. They have to agree to take you first."

Gretl knew then that they had actually wanted a younger girl, like Ingeborg.

———

One morning while they were playing games on deck, Gretl saw the moon in bright daylight. It wasn't full, but shaped like a fuzzy *c*.

"Can they see the same moon in South Africa at this moment?" she asked Mr. Johannes. "Or in another country, like . . ." She didn't dare say Poland. "Like Switzerland?"

"Yes," he said, "in all the countries on the same degree of longitude."

"What's that?"

"What's that, *sir*."

She kept forgetting. "What's that, sir?"

"Do you know how an atlas works?"

"Yes, sir."

"Good, let's see if we can find one."

She followed him to a part of the ship where she had never been. He took her to a room full of books, where people were reading in deep armchairs. "Is it a library?" she asked, amazed. A library on the ship?

"Yes, you must be as quiet as a mouse."

"I know," she whispered.

He found an atlas and paged through it until he found a map of the world. "Look, there's Germany," he said.

"Yes," she said, "and there's East Prussia." That was where Poland was.

"That's right. Do you know where South Africa is?"

She put her finger on the right spot.

"You're very clever. This is where we are now." He pointed.

"We're right next to Africa," she said, amazed yet again.

"Yes," he said. "In another two days we should be crossing the equator. See, there's the equator. On the other side lies the Southern Hemisphere."

She nodded.

"These are the degrees of longitude." He looked around. "Wait, let me show you on the globe."

When he had explained everything, she understood perfectly. Jakób had been right. South Africa and Poland lay on the same degree of longitude. They would see the moon at the same time.

"Does this library have Afrikaans storybooks?" she asked.

"No, but I have two you can read."

"Thank you."

"Remember to say 'thank you, *sir*,'" he said.

———

After the first week they could say a few Afrikaans words and sing a few songs. But the boys and some of the girls were unruly. The British passengers emigrating to the Union of South Africa gave them disapproving looks. When the English ladies were having tea and Horst Bremer's football—big Horst, not the little one—landed in the cake, one of the ladies tossed the ball over the railing, into the sea. Horst was furious. "Bloody English cow!" he said.

"Stay away from the other passengers," Onkel Schalk cautioned.

Then Horst was furious with Onkel Schalk as well.

On rainy days it was worse. They had to stay in the games room. Their classes were longer and the children became impossible. They played games like snakes and ladders or Monopoly, but soon they were arguing. They learned Afrikaans folk dances—*volkspele*—but the children twirled so fast that they fell over.

Gretl tried to read the Afrikaans books, but it was difficult. The ladies and Mr. Johannes didn't have time to help her because there were too many children to look after.

The nights were hard. What if she screamed and woke the other girls when her nightmares came? What would they think?

Her longing for Jakób returned every night. She would take out her little cross and press it to her heart. One morning one of the ladies found the cross in her bed.

"What's this?" she asked, frowning.

"It was a gift," said Gretl. If they took her cross and threw it into the sea, like Horst's ball, she would jump overboard.

"Get rid of it," said the lady. "Wearing a cross is a sin."

All day Gretl was troubled—how could wearing a cross be a sin? The nuns loved God so much that they did everything He said. They wore big crosses around their necks every day. But there was no one she could ask.

And there was another thing she was worried about—what if the people the doctor chose for her didn't want her? What if they took her only because they had to and they didn't like her at all? What if she was too old, too pale, too thin?

"They'll like you," Tante Irmgard said. "You'll see. Everyone likes you."

But Gretl knew it wasn't true. Monicka hadn't liked her at all. Neither had Aunt Anastarja, or she wouldn't have said there was no room for her in the house.

These thoughts gave way to other worries. *I must remember I'm not Catholic*, Gretl thought. *I am German-Lutheran. The people in South Africa must never know I once lived in southern Poland, because they will want to know how I got there. And no one must ever ever know I have Jewish blood, that I'm not pure Aryan. And I mustn't say I learned Russian at school, because the Afrikaners hate the Russians, just as the Poles hate the Germans and the Germans hate the English.*

The lump was back in her tummy, and it was hard as a stone.

Jakób loved her, though he had never said so. He wanted what was best for her. That was why she was on her way to South Africa now. She wished she had stayed with Jakób instead.

On September 8 the *Winchester Castle* docked in Cape Town at last.

Early in the morning they had to put all their belongings on their berths. Gretl pushed the cross deep into the pocket of her red coat, where no one would find it. The helper ladies wrapped their things in brown paper parcels and tied them up with string.

Their hair had been washed and they were all wearing clean clothes. The girls wore ribbons and looked very pretty. When they disembarked, more journalists would be waiting for them.

Onkel Schalk spoke to them one last time. "You are Afrikaners now, no longer Germans. The Afrikaners are a proud nation. Be proud of your new nation. Behave like true Afrikaners!"

But when they came on deck, there was no sunshine, only clouds and a light drizzle. The Union of South Africa looked gray and cold and wet. There were no lions or elephants, only people with umbrellas gazing up at the ship. Even the mountain Onkel Schalk had told them about was hidden behind thick clouds.

One of the older boys came running, shouting that he had seen a black man. *"Onkel Botha, ich habe einen Schwarzen gesehen!"*

Gretl got off the ship with the other children and stepped onto the soil of her new home.

7

Gretl listened to the *clickety-clack* of the wheels on the track. The train was heading deeper and deeper into Africa. She lay facedown in the middle bunk, the little wooden cross in her clenched fist. Lying on her tummy stopped it from aching so much. She looked through the train window. The full moon lit up the bare landscape. It was wide and open and dry and empty.

She was exhausted, yet she couldn't sleep. Something bigger than herself seemed to be growing inside her. Not fear, but a great uncertainty.

Tomorrow was the tenth of September, her birthday, but no one knew. She would be eleven, but she wouldn't tell anyone. On her eleventh birthday she would get off at the last station, meet her new parents, and go to bed in a new home. It was more than three months since she and Jakób had left the station at Częstochowa.

Jakób. He would know it was her birthday. He would think of her tomorrow, even if clouds hid the moon.

Yesterday many of the children had met their new parents. The rest of them were on their way to a place called Pretoria. All over South

Africa people were interested in the German orphans. Even the country's leader had taken a child, four-year-old Hermine Sönnichsen. Gretl
thought the man looked more like a grandpa than a daddy.

She had overheard someone who had come to see if he wanted a
German orphan telling another man, "I want to be quite certain the
child isn't Polish or Jewish or Russian. I won't allow a bad seed in my
household."

Gretl smelled the acrid smoke of the train. It burned the back of
her throat, burned paths into her memory, burned until her head ached.

The younger children immediately found homes. They were taken
away in the arms of men and ladies. On Gretl's third day in Pretoria,
Dr. Bührmann told her that the people who might take her would come
in the afternoon.

Might take her.

Just before teatime one of the helper ladies told Gretl to go to the
office. After lunch she had washed and not gone back out to play, in case
she soiled her dress or the ribbon in her hair came undone.

For a long time she sat on a hard chair in front of the office, her
feet swinging above the floor. The door remained shut. Inside, Dr.
Bührmann and a gentleman were talking to a mommy and daddy
who . . . Gretl told herself to think about other things.

The door finally opened. "Come inside, Gretl," said Dr. Bührmann
in German. "Meet your new parents."

She saw her new daddy first. He was very, very big. She looked up
into his blue eyes.

"This is your daddy, Oom Bernard Neethling," said Dr. Bührmann
in Afrikaans, "and this is young Gretl Schmidt."

She looked him in the eye and held out her hand. She greeted him
in Afrikaans. "Good afternoon, Father."

He bent down low. Her hand disappeared completely in his. His hands were hard, but his eyes were gentle and shining. "Good afternoon, Gretl." He said something else that she didn't understand, so she just smiled.

"And here's your mommy, Tannie Kate Neethling."

"*Guten Mittag*, Gretl."

The lady spoke German. Gretl felt happiness engulf her like a warm wave.

She looked up at the most beautiful lady she had ever seen, much more beautiful than any of the other new mommies. She had dark hair and her eyes were dark too, but not black like Jakób's. Her hands were soft. "Good afternoon, Mother," Gretl said, the way she had been taught.

The lady stroked Gretl's hair and said, "Thank you, Dr. Bührmann. She's perfect."

They walked along the path to the car, Gretl and her big new daddy and her pretty new mommy. Her entire body felt as if it were twisted up in her tummy. She couldn't think of anything to say, not even in German, so she just clutched the brown-paper parcel with her possessions to her chest, the little cross hidden in the pocket of her red coat.

They drove and drove in a big car. She sat in the backseat, alone. The man's big hands were on the steering wheel, and the hair on his fingers glinted gold in the sunlight. His hair was blond, like hers, and he had blue eyes, like her own. Maybe people would think she was his real daughter. When he looked at her in the rearview mirror and smiled, his teeth were shiny and white.

The lady's gleaming black hair was fixed in a bun. She wore pretty white beads around her neck. She turned to look at Gretl and said in German, "We're on our way to Johannesburg. We'll be spending two nights there before going home." She struggled a bit, as if she hadn't spoken the language for a long time. "We're going to see my father, Grandpa John. He's English."

Gretl nodded. "I don't understand English," she said.

The lady smiled. "You'll soon learn. Dr. Bührmann told us you're very clever. But let's just deal with Afrikaans first."

They drove along a road with very few houses. The land was flat and bare. The trees were few and far between. The sun blazed down on everything.

"Did you live in Germany before?" Gretl asked.

The lady turned again. "Only for a year. I was in a kind of school, not actually in Germany, in Switzerland," she said.

"In Switzerland?" Gretl asked, surprised. Onkel Hans lived in Switzerland, but she couldn't mention Onkel Hans, because he was Oma's brother and he was Jewish.

"Yes, what do you know about Switzerland?"

"Heidi and Peter live there, with the goats," Gretl said.

The lady smiled. "You're right. And Alm U. He was strict, wasn't he?" Gretl nodded. "But later he became kind."

"Yes," the lady said, "later he became kind."

She faced forward again. Occasionally she and the man talked, but Gretl didn't understand much. The lady did most of the talking. The man mostly said, "Mm." The painful lump was still in Gretl's tummy.

The lady turned once more and said, "Gretl, we'd like to give you an Afrikaans name, if it's all right with you."

"*Onkel Schalk hat das gesagt, auf dem Schiff, damit wir Afrikaner werden können, deshalb,*" she said.

The lady smiled and turned to the man. "She says Schalk Botha told them so, on the ship, so that they can become Afrikaners."

The man looked at Gretl in the mirror and smiled. "We're going to turn you into a real little Afrikaner," he said. "We just have to put some color in those pale cheeks and some fat on that skinny little body."

She understood a little of what he said. She thought carefully and said in Afrikaans, "Like the witch did with Hansel and Gretel?"

The man and the lady both laughed. "Where we live there's no witch," said the man.

"That's good," said Gretl. She wanted to say more, but she didn't know how.

"In Afrikaans their names are Hansie and Grietjie," said the lady. "That's what we'd like to call you: Griet. Or the smaller form: Grietjie."

"I like it," said Gretl. "Grietjie Neethling." The *g* and *r* would take a lot of practice for her to pronounce properly.

It was almost dark by the time they stopped at a tall iron gate ornamented with scrolls and twirls. Behind the gate she saw a big stone house covered almost to the roof with green ivy.

"It looks like Sleeping Beauty's palace," said Gretl.

The lady seemed surprised. "That's exactly what I used to think when I was a little girl," she said.

A tall man wearing spectacles opened the door. "Daddy, this is Gretl. We call her Griet."

"Grietjie," her new father said from behind. "She's too small to be Griet."

"Hello, Grietjie," said the tall man with the thick, gray hair. "I'm Grandpa John."

Gretl held out her hand. "Good evening, Grandpa John," she said. She had noticed that he also struggled to pronounce the *g* and the *r* in Grietjie.

The house looked like a palace inside too. Gretl was introduced to Aunt Nellie, who looked after Grandpa John, and to Elias, the cook.

They ate like kings at a table under a light dripping with diamonds. There was a lot of food, but she found it hard to swallow. Even the dessert.

"Never mind," the lady comforted her in German. "It's all new to you. You'll soon feel at home."

Upstairs, the lady ran her a bath. There was foam in the water and the soap smelled of flowers. The lady washed her hair and combed it. "I've always wanted a little girl with blonde curls and blue eyes," she said.

The lady was kind, but Gretl wished she would go now. She felt confused and wanted to be alone for a while.

The bed was big and very soft, like the bed of the princess who slept on a pea. The man came in to say good night. "Good night," said Gretl.

The man bent down. "Good night, little princess," he said, stroking her hair. "Sleep tight."

"I'll stay until she's asleep," said the lady.

The man stroked the lady's hair too and said, "Isn't she lovely?"

The lady touched Gretl's cheek. "She's perfect."

When the man had left, the lady spoke in German. "If you're afraid to sleep alone, I'll sleep here with you. See, the bed is big enough."

"I'm not afraid," said Gretl, closing her eyes, "just tired." And lonely, and longing with all her heart for the hard, narrow bed on the porch of a farmer's cottage in Poland.

She closed her eyes and breathed regularly so that the lady would think she was asleep. *They think I'm lovely, even though I'm pale and skinny*, she told herself. No one had ever called her lovely. Jakób had told her to remember she was his beautiful Gretl Schmidt, but that was just so that she wouldn't feel unwanted. The man and the lady had said she was lovely and perfect for no reason she could think of.

After a while the lady got up quietly and tiptoed out. Gretl opened her eyes and looked around her. In the soft glow of the bedside lamp it looked even more like the room of a princess. She got out of bed and crossed to the window. The city lights glittered like hundreds of stars in the dark night.

She saw the moon above the trees. *I have a new mommy and daddy who really want me*, she told Jakób. *They have a car and nice clothes, so they should have enough money to send me to school.*

But Poland was very far from South Africa.

She heard music from somewhere below. On her bare feet she went down the thickly carpeted stairs. She held on to the turned wooden banister and went down slowly, step by step, until she reached the shiny marble floor. She followed the chink of light that fell across the floor of the entrance hall. The door of the study was ajar, so she gently pushed it.

Grandpa John was sitting on the soft leather couch, his legs stretched in front of him, his eyes closed, a slight smile on his lips. Sweat had formed on his drinking glass on the table next to him, and the sweet smell of his cigar hung in the air.

He looked lonely.

Then he opened his eyes and smiled at her. He didn't look so lonely anymore.

"Come, sit with me for a while," he said, patting the couch beside him.

She sat very straight. Her feet didn't touch the floor. She sat quietly, listening to the beautiful music.

"Did you like it?" asked Grandpa John when the last notes faded away.

She thought she knew what he meant. She had found it beautiful, almost like the music in the cathedral, only more so. She nodded. "*Sehr schön,*" she said.

Grandpa John got up and took another record off the shelf. He bent down to the turntable and carefully lowered the needle. Then he sat down again and gave Gretl a smile.

A man began to sing "*Das Zauberlied.*"

"*Das ist Deutsch,*" Gretl said, surprised.

Grandpa John smiled and nodded. "Josef Schmidt," he said.

"*Mein Nachname ist auch Schmidt,*" said Gretl, "*aber jetzt heisse ich Neethling.*"

Grandpa John nodded and opened his arm. Gretl nestled against him. He held her tightly. Together they sat listening to the German music.

For the first time in months the lump in her tummy began to melt. Warmth flooded her, merging with the beautiful music and the sweet smell of Grandpa John's cigar and his unfamiliar arm keeping her safe and the dreamy knowledge that she was among people who cared. Later she felt him pick her up and carry her up the stairs. She didn't open her eyes, because it was lovely; it reminded her of the times Jakób used to carry her. Grandpa John put her down on the big soft bed, tucked the blankets around her, and carefully shut the door.

"I don't know what to call you," Gretl said when her new mommy came to see whether she was awake. She had already made her bed and put on a clean dress. She would have to wash the dress she had worn yesterday in order to wear it again tomorrow.

"You may call us Oom Bernard and Tannie Kate, or Daddy and Mommy, just as you wish."

The lady struggled with Gretl's hair ribbon. "I've never had a little girl, so I don't really know how," she admitted.

"Do you have a little boy?" asked Gretl.

"Yes, but he's a big boy now. He's fourteen and his name is Kobus. We live on a farm. He's waiting there to meet you, because today is Friday. During the week he goes to boarding school."

Gretl hoped he would be disciplined, not like some of the boys on the ship. "You smell nice," she said.

"Thank you, sweetheart." The lady stepped back and looked at Gretl in the mirror. "You look lovely, Grietjie. Come, let's put a little perfume on you as well."

It sounded strange, the name Grietjie.

In the grown-ups' bedroom the lady selected a small bottle from the big dressing table. "*Vier sieben eins eins,*" Gretl read.

"It's the name of the perfume," the lady explained in German. "But in English you say, 'Four seven eleven.'"

"Four seven eleven," Gretl repeated. She was proud to say her first English words.

While they were having breakfast, she kept breathing deeply, savoring the perfume the lady had dabbed behind her ears. She smelled like a real princess.

After breakfast they drove into Johannesburg, she, the lady, and the man. She and the lady were going to shop for clothes. The man had work to do. He ruffled Gretl's hair when he dropped them off.

The name of the store was John Orr's, she read on the big sign.

"That's English too," the lady said.

Her new mommy bought and bought: frilly panties Gretl had never seen the likes of, white socks with lace at the top, shiny black shoes that fastened with a strap, white shoes decorated with a bow for church, and sandals with red, yellow, and green straps.

"Why don't you keep them on?" said the lady. The sandals were so pretty that Gretl couldn't stop looking at her feet.

They took the escalator to the top floor, where the dresses were. Gretl grabbed hold of the lady's hand. It was her first time on an escalator, but she wasn't afraid, just careful. At the top she took an enormous leap. She didn't want the escalator to suck in her new sandals.

Walking by the lady's side, holding her hand, Gretl thought that they looked like a real mother and daughter. "I'm going to call you Mommy," she said.

The lady stopped in the middle of the shop floor, knelt, and hugged Gretl tightly. "It would be wonderful if you would call me Mommy, Grietjie, because you're my little girl now." She kissed Gretl on both eyelids.

They bought so many dresses that Gretl became confused: strappy dresses, because it was very hot on the farm, dresses that tied with a big bow at the back for church, dresses with puffed sleeves, fly-away sleeves, and long sleeves for when it was cold. Also shorts like the ones boys wore and blouses. They bought nightgowns and a robe and bedroom slippers, they bought ribbons and hairpins and two small hats for church. How they laughed at some of those hats! They even bought white gloves and a little handbag. When they had finished, they were exhausted.

Gretl wore her new red dress because it went with the sandals. They went to a tearoom in the store, and Mommy read the menu out loud so that Gretl could choose what she wanted to eat. But she was too excited to eat. She was just very thirsty.

A black man came to fetch them in Grandpa John's big black car. Gretl and Mommy sat together in the back. At Grandpa John's house they took all their parcels to Gretl's bedroom. Aunt Nellie came to look at everything they'd bought and clapped her hands together. After a while Grandpa John came too. He put his arm around Mommy's shoulders and asked, "Are you happy, Kate?"

"Very happy." She laid her cheek against his.

They all love each other, Gretl thought, amazed. *They don't argue.* It seemed so strange.

They were speaking about her. "What is Grandpa John saying?" Gretl asked.

The two grown-ups laughed. "He said you look like my mother," said Mommy. "Her name was Ouma Susan. She also had curly blonde hair and blue eyes. And she was small, just like you."

"Where is she?" Gretl asked.

"She died, Grietjie. A few months ago."

Gretl nodded. Now she knew why Grandpa John listened to music at night. *Nights are when you miss someone most*, she thought.

They put all the clothes away in the new suitcase, everything except the nightclothes and an outfit for the next day. The red coat with the little cross in its pocket went into the suitcase as well.

When they tucked the blankets around her late that evening, Gretl said in Afrikaans, "Good night, Daddy. Good night, Mommy. Sleep tight."

"Good night, Grietjie, sleep tight," said Daddy and kissed her forehead.

But in the night she took her cross out of the suitcase and held it in her hand. She was afraid her nightmares would return, and Jakób was very far away.

——•——

They set off early the next morning because it was a long way to the farm. Aunt Nellie had packed a picnic basket, and they stopped under a tree to eat. The land was completely flat and parched and hot. "This is called the Springbok Flats," said Mommy. "Once we've crossed it, we'll be in the bushveld, where we live."

Gretl sat up straight in the backseat, trying to take in everything she saw. South Africa wasn't a bit like the pictures in the library book she and Jakób had looked at.

It was almost noon when Mommy said, "Here we are in our hometown. Look, Grietjie, this is our church." She pointed at a white building with a tall spire. "This is our store." Gretl read the sign: *Cohen Crown General Dealer.* Farther along, she read *Northern Transvaal Co-op* and on the corner *Boere Koffiehuis*, which her mommy told her meant Farmers' Coffee Shop.

One street block farther Mommy said, "This is the school."

Gretl took a good look at the red-brick building with the long veranda and row of classrooms, much like the ghetto school before it burned down, and the convent school in Poland, and the German school she had briefly attended. But around this school there was no green grass, only bare earth. In front of the building grew a single gray tree with unhappy leaves.

"That's a pepper tree," Daddy said.

She tried to think of the Afrikaans words, but it was too hard, so she asked in German, "Does the brother also go to this school?"

"No," said Mommy, "Kobus is in standard six. The high school where he's a boarder is in a bigger town."

She didn't understand all of it, but she didn't want to seem stupid, so she said nothing further.

On the outskirts of the town Daddy pointed to the left. "There's the station." They stopped at the tracks to see if there were any trains, then drove *bumpity-bump* across. She didn't look at the station. There was a three-week ocean between her and Poland now.

A short distance out of town they turned onto a gravel road and drove through a gate and across an iron grille in the road. "This is where our farm begins, Grietjie," said Daddy.

The farm looked completely different from Jakób's. It was dry and the grass was brown. She couldn't imagine what the poor goats and ducks were supposed to eat. They crossed a bridge, but the river had no water. She saw a circular stone wall with cattle inside. She still hadn't seen any goats. On one side of the property was a rough mountain with big rocks instead of familiar rolling hills. The school was very far away. She would never be able to walk there. She felt her tummy contract again.

"How will I get to school?" she asked.

"I'll take you, my sweetheart, in the car," said Mommy. "But we'll wait until you understand a little more Afrikaans before we take you to school."

"Almost there," said Daddy. She understood what he was saying. "Look, there's the house. Over there, on the mountainside."

Gretl looked. She saw a big stone house with a wide veranda. "It's *sehr schön*," she said.

"Very lovely," said Mommy.

"Very lovely." Her lips and tongue wrapped around the strange words.

They stopped in front of the veranda. A big boy jumped over all the steps, landing at the bottom. He looked just like Daddy. Gretl opened the door to get out, and two large dogs came bounding around the corner—dogs that could bite, like the ghetto's guard dogs. She went ice-cold with fear.

Mommy went to the big boy and hugged him tightly. Daddy saw Gretl was afraid. He picked her up in his strong arms and held her out of the dogs' reach. She clung to him, drawing up her feet.

"Kobus, hold the dogs," he said. "I don't think Grietjie likes dogs."

He carried her inside, but when she still clung to him, he didn't put her down. "Never mind them, Grietjie," he said. "They're big, but they won't do anything. Close the door, Kobus."

Daddy carried her through a room with armchairs and a sofa, a low table, and a cabinet full of pretty things. They entered a room with a long table and many chairs. Against the wall was a cupboard with a big mirror, and in the corner stood a piano.

Only then did Daddy put her down.

Mommy put an arm around Gretl's shoulders. "Kobus, this is your sister, Grietjie," she said.

"Yes, Mom. Mom, she's tiny, Mom," said her new brother.

Their parents laughed. "You'll have to mind what you say," said Daddy. "She understands every word."

Gretl looked her brother in the eye, held out her hand, and said, "Good afternoon, Kobus."

He looked surprised, but he shook her hand and said, "Afternoon." To their daddy he said, "Dad, she's funny, Dad."

Daddy's eyes twinkled. "She's precious—just lovely," he said. "I don't think much will get her down."

"*Nur der Hund*," said Gretl.

Surprised, her daddy laughed again. "See?" he said. He turned to her. "You'll soon make friends with the dogs, wait and see."

A black woman entered. She wore a long black dress and a white headscarf. Gretl thought she looked like the Black Madonna in the monastery at Częstochowa. She was happy to know there was someone watching over this house as well.

"Grietjie, this is Maria," said Mommy.

"I know," said Gretl. "She is *ein Engel*."

Her mommy looked surprised. "Ye-es, I suppose so," she said with a slow smile. "Look, she's brought us some cold ginger beer."

The black madonna put the tray on the table.

"Good afternoon, Maria," said Gretl.

"Shame, the little creature is just skin and bones." The madonna clicked her tongue. "She looks sick." She turned to Gretl. "I'll call you Missy."

"She won't understand everything you say, Maria," said Mommy. "Bring some orange squash as well. I don't know whether she'll like the ginger beer."

"We must feed her milk," said the madonna and went back to the kitchen.

Kobus was furtively watching Gretl, but she gazed at him openly.

His feet were big and dusty, his clothes too. He didn't sit on a chair but stood as he sipped his ginger beer. His eyes were blue. He could have been her real brother, except for his size. "Come, I'll show you the calves," he said.

"I think we should show her her bedroom first," Mommy said hesitantly. "Maybe she'd like to—"

"I think she'll enjoy seeing the calves," Daddy decided. "I'll shut the dogs in."

Gretl walked across the farmyard with her new brother. "Do you know what calves are?" Kobus asked.

She shook her head.

"They're baby cattle."

"Oh," she said.

He opened a gate but stopped her. "Take off your sandals," he said, pointing at her feet, "they'll get dirty."

She took off her new shoes and he closed the gate behind her. The calves came trotting up to them.

"*Ach, sie sind* very pretty!" She stroked their heads. They had gentle eyes and wet noses.

"Here, hold out your hand and they'll suck on it," he said. He took her hand and held it out to a calf.

She laughed when the calf licked her with his rough tongue. The calves pushed and shoved to get to her.

"You can help feed them later this afternoon," Kobus said. "It's too early now."

"Wipe your feet on the grass," he said when they left. "There's dung between your toes."

As they walked back to the house, she was dying to tell him about Bruni with the lovely eyes and Rosie, who refused to stand still to be milked.

"Here's the pantry," said Kobus. "Look, that's the fridge." He opened the door of a cabinet that was cold inside and filled with jugs of milk. The pantry shelves were stocked with bottles and tins. There was a lot of food, honey as well, and an entire bag of sugar.

"It's nice," she said.

The front room was filled with people. Gretl stopped in the entryway.

"Come to me, Grietjie," said Mommy in German. "These people have all come to see you."

"My feet are dirty," she protested.

Mommy reached for Gretl's hand and smiled. "Come, say hello," she said. "This is Auntie Lovey. She and her family live on the farm as well."

A sweaty lady stepped forward, picked up Gretl, and hugged her tightly. Then she kissed her on the lips. "Shame, poor little orphan," she said, sniffing loudly. She turned to the thin man beside her. "This is Oom Doorsie. Say hello to Oom Doorsie."

Oom Doorsie was an old man with a prickly beard and yellow fingers. He hugged Gretl and kissed her on the lips. "She's very pale, isn't she?"

Gretl felt shivers go down her spine. She tried to pull away. If only she could stand on her feet, she would look them in the eye and hold out her hand to greet them. But the man was clutching her too tightly.

"I think she'd prefer to stand on her own, Doorsie," said Mommy, saving her from the man. Gretl clung to her mother's hand. "These are Oom Doorsie and Auntie Lovey's children: Boetie"—smack on her lips—"and Doorsie"—smack—"and Sis"—another wet kiss—"and Mattie . . ."

"I don't want to kiss them!" she protested in German.

"Turn your cheek," said Mommy, also in German. "Kissing is an Afrikaner custom that I also found strange at first."

Gretl realized that she and her mommy could speak German and the people wouldn't understand. It made her feel smart.

She raised her chin. "Good afternoon, Mattie," she said and held out her hand.

Mattie was a bit taller than she. He looked at her with vacant eyes. "Say hello to the girl, where are your manners?" Auntie Lovey scolded him.

"Afternoon," mumbled Mattie.

She met the rest of the Pypers family—Baby and Susie and Tiny— but she didn't kiss any of them. She fled to the kitchen.

"*Sie haben mich geküßt!*" she told Kobus, who had been drinking milk and had a white moustache on his upper lip.

"I can't stand being kissed!" he declared. "Want some milk?"

———

Her room had a big bed with a blue bedspread scattered with butter-flies. There were butterflies on the curtains too. She had her own closet with lots of space for her clothes. There was also a dressing table with ruffles around it in the same butterfly fabric and a little stool to sit on.

On the night table next to the bed was a Bible. She picked it up and ran her hand across the cover. "It's German!" She was so surprised that she cried out in German.

Next to the Bible she saw a candle and a box of matches. "Do you know how a candle works?" asked her mommy.

"Yes."

"You have to say, 'Yes, Mommy.' Do you understand, Grietjie?"

"Okay." She kept forgetting.

"We have a generator that gives us light in the evenings, but when we go to bed, Daddy turns it off. During the night you must light a can-dle. Are you afraid of the dark?"

"No, I'm not afraid of anything, except the dogs," she said.

"The dogs sleep outside. They look after us," Mommy said.

A blanket soft as a baby goat's skin lay on her bed. "It's your com-fort blanket," said Mommy. "When I was small I also had one. When you're alone or feel cold during the night, you can hug the blanky in your arms."

"Thank you," she said in Afrikaans.

They put all her things away in the closet, set the pink facecloth Onkel Schalk had given her in the bathroom, put her toothbrush in a mug, and hung each of her dresses on an individual clothes hanger. She couldn't believe she had so many things of her own.

When Mommy wasn't looking, she put her little wooden cross under her pillow. She would have to find a safe place for it so that Mommy and Daddy wouldn't be angry if they discovered it.

After supper Daddy said, "Grietjie, fetch the Bible."

Mommy showed her where the Bible lay in the cabinet under the big mirror. She placed it in front of her daddy. He opened the heavy Bible and looked at her. "Is there a passage you would like us to read, Grietjie?" he asked.

She understood what he was asking and thought for a moment. She remembered Sister Margaret reading about Ruth and Naomi. Sister Margaret hadn't always lived in Poland. She had come from Ireland because God had told her the children and the church in Poland needed her. She had shown Gretl in the atlas where Ireland was. Like Ruth, Sister Margaret had said, "Your people will be my people."

That day Gretl had known that God sent her to Poland as well, that Jakób's country had become her country, Sister Margaret's God her God. She realized then that Sister Margaret's God was sometimes the same God as Oma's, but not always. And she had to choose. If she wanted to speak to Lieber Herr Jesus or the Holy Mother of God, it was a different God from the one who lived in the synagogue. It was confusing. She couldn't ask Sister Margaret about the Jewish God, and she couldn't ask Jakób either, because at the time he had been working in Katowice. That day she had decided to choose the convent sisters' God as her God.

Now God had sent her to South Africa because there was milk and honey. The country was hard and strange, the language was rough and different, and the church called different things sinful, but Gretl thought that God was still the same.

She spoke to her mommy in German. "The part where Ruth says, 'Your people are my people.' That story."

Her father's eyes grew shiny and he said in a thick voice, "Grietjie, come and sit on Daddy's knee."

She climbed onto his knee. One big hand encircled her waist, the other lay on the table next to the Bible. He read. She didn't know the words, but she could hear that the story in the Afrikaans Bible was the same one Sister Margaret had read to them in the Polish convent.

"Let us pray," said Daddy when the story came to an end. He held his hands out to Mommy and to Kobus. Gretl leaned forward and placed her hands on his big hands, and Mommy and Kobus held hands across the table. They were all holding on to one another, making a circle.

Daddy prayed for a long time, but she understood very little. He didn't pray to Lieber Herr Jesus or the Holy Virgin, she could tell. Maybe he was praying to Oma's God, because he said Almighty God, but she doubted it, because the Afrikaners didn't like the Jews.

When he finished, Mommy said in German, "Daddy prayed for you too, Grietjie. He thanked God for sending you to us and he asked that you'd be happy with us."

"Thank you," she said to Daddy. She put the Bible away in its special place. She now had her own little task to perform in her new Afrikaans home every night.

———

"I won't take her to church today," Mommy said the next morning. "You and Kobus go; we need a little time alone."

When Daddy and Kobus had left in the car, Mommy took Gretl's hand. "Let me show you all the rooms in the house," she said in German.

In the dining room Gretl ran her hand over the piano. "Do you know how to play?" she asked.

Mommy smiled and opened the lid. The white and black notes were lined up in neat rows. She sat down on the piano stool. "Sit next to me, Gretl."

They sat together, she and her new mommy. Her mommy played German songs she knew. She sang along in German, Mommy sang in Afrikaans. "*Sah ein Knab' ein Röslein stehn*" and "*Komm, lieber Mai*" and "*Bruder Jakób.*"

"Give me your hand," Mommy said and put Gretl's fingers on

the notes. "That's right, lift here, press down like this." She patiently showed her.

When Daddy and Kobus came back from church, she could play the first two lines of "*Bruder Jakób*" and sing it in Afrikaans. They listened and clapped their hands. If they had known about her Jakób, Mommy would have chosen another song. Gretl wished with all her heart that Jakób could hear her sing and play that song.

Shortly afterward the neighbors descended on the farm to see the German child. Mommy made coffee and served cake. Gretl held out her hand to greet them, but the strangers drew her closer and kissed her. She turned her cheek, but they grasped her face and planted their wet kisses on her lips. The lump in her tummy threatened to push up into her mouth. She tried to look them in the eye and lift her chin and smile, but the nightmare went on and on. They clicked their tongues and said, "Poor little mite," and "Ag, shame," and wiped tears and sweat with big handkerchiefs. They drank cups and cups of coffee and tall glasses of ginger beer and ate cake.

Gretl sought shelter with the madonna in the kitchen, but a fat lady with beads of sweat on her nose and forehead found her there and carried her back to the living room. She clung to her mommy's hand, but a big girl pulled her away and picked her up as if she were no older than Ingeborg.

The cake stuck in her throat. After a while she sneaked out through the back door and hid behind the trunk of a big tree. A feeling of desolation overwhelmed her. These people wanted her, but she didn't want to be here. She was too pale, her accent was too strange, and it was too hot here, with too much dust and sun and not enough green grass. There were cattle but no goats, and chickens but no ducks. There were dogs and a strange mommy and daddy and an older brother. There were Oom Doorsie and Auntie Lovey and their many children in a small house on the farm, and a big stone house in which only the four of them lived, and in which she got lost. And there was a strange bedroom with a strange bed that was hers. There was a holy Black Madonna who stoked a hot oven.

But Jakób wasn't here, and he could never, never come.

She got up and began to walk, heading nowhere, just into the veld. Tears were streaming down her face.

———

She didn't hear the horse's hooves, so she got a fright when the big animal suddenly stopped beside her.

"I've come to look for you," said Kobus. "My mother is worried."

She didn't know the right words to explain. "They kiss me," she said.

"I know," he said and got off the big horse. "It's horrible. Disgusting."

"Hobbirel," she said. "Disgustible."

"Horrible," he said, "disgusting."

"Dishorribling," she said with feeling.

"Dishorribling," he agreed. "Come, I'll put you in front of me on the horse and take you home."

She shook her head.

"Are you afraid of the horse?"

She shook her head again. "I'm not afraid."

"You don't want to go home because of those people?"

She nodded.

"Okay, I'll show you something. But first I have to tell my mother you're safe."

"*My* mother *auch*," she said firmly.

He picked her up and put her on the horse, then got up himself. She sat in front of him, and they rode until they were close to the house. She waited with the horse while he ran inside. He soon returned with a floppy cloth hat. "Mom says you must wear this so that the sun doesn't burn you. You're very pale," he said.

The big horse carefully picked his way up the mountainside. She looked at her new brother's arms. They were brown compared to her own, and much thicker, with hairs that glinted gold in the sunlight, like their father's. She felt the loneliness of a moment ago dissolve in the sunlight. *Mom says you must wear this*, her brother had said. Because Mom cared.

At the top of the mountain he lifted her off the horse. Below them lay the scrubby veld as far as the eye could see. In the distance lay a blue mountain range, and the road to town snaked over the bridge and disappeared behind some trees.

"Look, Grietjie, you can see the whole farm from here," he said. "See, there's our house, behind the trees. And there, next to it, is the old homestead, where my great-grandfather lived. One day, when I'm grown up, I'm going to live there and run the farm with my father. See, there's the kraal with the calves, can you see?"

"Yes," she said.

"And there's the reservoir and the wind pump for the house, do you see?"

"I see, very nice," she said.

"Now look up the gorge. Do you see that dam wall?"

"Yes?"

"My dad built it himself. Now he catches all the water that used to flow to the sea. That's why we have such good fields. We put them under irrigation. Do you understand?"

"I understand," she said. She wished she could tell him it wasn't just *his* dad, but *her* dad too. But he kept talking and explaining.

He showed her the fields, the new citrus orchards, the camps for the cattle, more wind pumps with water troughs. He even pointed out the family graveyard. She struggled a little with the idea of a family graveyard, but he was good at explaining.

She said, "I see," and "I understand," and "That's nice," because they were the only words she knew.

It was almost lunchtime when he lifted her back on the horse and rode home.

After lunch Kobus packed his clothes in a suitcase.

"Will you help me, please, Grietjie?" said her mother. "Put the cookies in this tin and the rusks in that one."

There was a picture of a horse on the lid of the cookie tin. She arranged the cookies neatly. The rusk tin wasn't round, like the cookie tin, and it was old. The flower on the lid was scratched and faded. She packed the rusks in rows. Now Kobus wouldn't be hungry at school.

"We must put in some butter too," Gretl said. She knew that syrup without butter didn't taste very good on bread.

"They get all their food at the hostel, butter as well," her mother assured her. "The cookies and rusks are extra."

He won't be hungry then, Gretl thought. *That's good.*

"Would you like to come along for the drive, Grietjie?" her father asked.

She nodded and went to the car with him.

On their way to the bigger town where Kobus went to school she sat in the backseat. Kobus and their father talked nonstop, but she didn't understand much of what they were saying. One day she, too, would speak to their father like that, she thought. She'd ask Mommy for Afrikaans books to read, and she would learn the language in no time. And their mommy would have time to help her, because there were no other children at home.

They dropped Kobus off at the hostel. It looked like an orphanage, but Kobus didn't mind staying, because they would be fetching him again on Friday. On the way back she sat in the front seat, next to her daddy. They couldn't talk much, but she sat next to him and breathed in his smell and looked at his big hands. Sometimes he would turn to her and smile. In bed that evening she asked her new mommy, "Are you very sorry that I'm not younger?"

"Grietjie!" her mother said, shocked. "Why would you think that? You're perfect. You're exactly what we wanted. We asked for a little girl of any age."

"Why?" She wanted to be quite certain.

"We don't have a little girl and we really wanted one."

"Why didn't you have one yourselves?" Monicka and Haneczka had no trouble having babies.

Her mother gave a sad smile. "Daddy wanted more children, and so did I," she said, "but sometimes God has a different plan. Now I know why—so that you could be our little girl."

Gretl brought her hand—the one that wasn't holding the cross—out from under the covers and gently touched her mother's cheek. It was soft and warm. "Then why were you in the office for such a long time before you agreed to take me?" she asked.

Her mommy hugged her tightly. "My dearest Grietjie," she said, "*you* weren't the problem. It was me. You see, the selection board had decided that the adoptive parents should be pure Afrikaners who would promote the ideals of the Afrikaner nation. But I have an English background. My mother was Afrikaans, but Grandpa John is completely British. They had to decide whether I was good enough to be your mommy."

"You are," Gretl assured her. "You're the best."

That night she slept without waking up even once.

8

At the beginning of October Kobus came home for the week-long school vacation.

"Dad, may I drive the tractor when you start plowing, Dad?" asked Kobus. He kept saying Dad while Gretl had trouble remembering to say it even once.

"We'll wait for the first rains before we start plowing," said her father. "In the meantime you can take the Little Gray Fergie and the trailer and dump the salt licks in the cattle camps. And on Tuesday we'll start spraying the citrus orchards."

Kobus looked pleased. He liked driving the tractor. "Right, Dad, I'll do it, Dad. But, Dad, I want to teach Grietjie to swim, Dad, or one of these days she'll drown, Dad."

"I don't want to learn to swim," Gretl protested. She wasn't quite afraid of the big round reservoir with its brown water and frogs, just cautious.

"You have to swim. Everybody swims," Kobus insisted.

Gretl lifted her chin. "Then Daddy must teach me," she said.

Her dad smiled. "Daddy will, Grietjie."

After supper her father connected the flat-faced brown radio to a big battery and searched for a station. Not a train station, but a radio station. First they listened to the news and weather forecast, then to a story. On Saturday nights they listened to *Your Own Choice*—music like she'd heard in the cathedral, and like the music Grandpa John loved.

Before bedtime they sat on the veranda, where it was cool. In order to keep the bugs and mosquitoes away they kept the lights off.

Sometimes they played Monopoly. She knew the game, because they had played it on the ship. It was a clever game. You had to look out for someone who might land on your property. She kept her eye on Kobus, because boys like to cheat.

When she landed on Liverpool Station, her mother, who was also the banker, asked, "Wouldn't you like to buy it?"

"No, thanks," she said firmly. "I don't want to own a station!"

Some nights they sat reading. Her daddy read *The Farmer's Weekly* or sometimes *Die Huisgenoot* or *Die Brandwag*. Her mommy read English books while Gretl read Afrikaans storybooks. Her mommy had given her a book with stories she already knew, but now she could read them in Afrikaans. If there was an unfamiliar word, her mommy helped her. She was keen to learn because she wanted to go to school after the vacation was over. She loved it when they all sat reading together.

One evening Kobus entered the living room with a rifle in his hand.

Gretl felt her tummy contract. "What's he doing with that gun?" she asked her mommy in German.

"I'm going to clean it," Kobus answered in Afrikaans. "Tomorrow I want to ambush the mousebirds in the orchard."

"You're going to shoot little birds?" Gretl asked.

"Mousebirds, yes," he answered without looking up.

"Birds?" She still couldn't believe it.

"Yes, Grietjie," he said impatiently, "birds and buck. What else does one shoot with a rifle?"

"People," she said.

The three of them—her daddy, mommy, and Kobus—looked up quickly. She saw them glance at one another. She had said something wrong. "I didn't know you shot birds," she said self-consciously.

"Don't worry, Grietjie," said her father. "Come to Daddy." He wrapped his strong arms around her and held her close. She didn't really know why, but it was nice, except that it made her miss Jakób.

That night her nightmares returned. This time it was about the Gestapo with their dogs and their rifles at the station. Fiery tongues shot out of their rifles and the station went up in flames.

———

Saturday afternoon she put on her new swimsuit. It was made of a stretchy fabric. Her mommy plastered Nivea Creme all over her face so that the sun wouldn't burn her and told her to keep her hat on all the time, even if it got wet. Gretl felt paler than usual. Her mommy's skin was golden brown. She wore a big hat and dark glasses, and she didn't put Nivea Creme on her face. Kobus and her daddy had golden skins as well, even though their hair was blond like hers. Maybe she would look like them one day and not be so thin, and people would think she was their real daughter.

She clung to her daddy in the water. It wasn't cold, but it was brown and deep. Her feet didn't touch the bottom at all. Her daddy held her and didn't let her go. After a while she held on to his back while he swam. He was a very good swimmer. Kobus somersaulted into the water and jumped in with his legs drawn up to his chin. He did this right next to their daddy and splashed water all over the two of them, so that she gasped for breath and Daddy scolded Kobus. When their mommy came in too, the four of them went round and round and made a whirlpool. They laughed and floated in the current. Safe in her daddy's arms, she slowly began to relax and enjoy the water.

When they'd had enough, they sat in the shade on the grass beside the dam. Her daddy cut open a large fruit called a watermelon. He held a long knife by the hilt and sliced round and round the melon. Then he pressed on either side with his big hands and the watermelon broke open into slices. He cut the middle part, which he called the crown, into discs and removed a piece for her mommy. "A princess deserves the best crown," he said. Then he gave a piece to her, because she was the little princess. "Taste it, Grietjie."

She bit into the red flesh. It was crisp and sweet. *"Lekker,"* she said, licking the juice from her fingers.

Lekker was a new Afrikaans word she had learned, a nice word. Everything that was good was *lekker*—whether it was something she ate or smelled or felt or read, it didn't matter. *Lekker* was *lekker*. It was also the Afrikaans word for the sweets they had been given on the ship as prizes for winning at their games.

When they finished, Kobus took a piece of watermelon rind and sneaked up on their mommy from behind. He held her down and rubbed her face with the sticky rind.

"Don't, Kobus, no!" she scolded, trying to stop him. Kobus and their daddy doubled over with laughter.

Gretl saw Kobus sizing her up and knew what was coming. She jumped up and ran as fast as her thin legs could go, but he caught up with her, tucked her under his arm, and rubbed the watermelon rind all over her face.

"Don't, Kobus, no!" she scolded, too, but it made him laugh even harder. She and her mommy had to get back into the water to wash off the sticky juice. This time she held on for dear life to her mommy. Then her daddy and Kobus dived back in. One day she would also swim like a fish, she vowed.

Kobus took the remaining watermelon to Auntie Lovey's house. Her family lived in the small house behind the old farmstead, and Oom Doorsie helped her father on the farm.

"Why don't Auntie Lovey and Oom Doorsie live in the old farmstead?" she asked. They had a great many kids for one small house.

"They can't, because I'm going to live there one day," Kobus answered as if she were stupid. "And when Grandpa John comes to visit, he lives there."

Kobus told her a beautiful story. Grandpa John, who had been a British soldier in the Boer War, had fallen ill. Ouma Susan, who was dead now, had nursed him in the outside room of the farmhouse. But when she wanted to marry him, her father was furious because the Afrikaners didn't like the British then. They had to flee and only many years later, when their mother, Kate, was already grown up, did the great-grandfather forgive Grandpa John and Ouma Susan.

"I didn't know there was a war in the Union of South Africa as well," she said.

"Yes," he said, "but it was long, long ago. Don't say the Union of South Africa every time, just say South Africa."

"Okay," she said.

Kobus taught her to skip stones in the reservoir. He selected a handful of flat pebbles, drew back his arm, leaned back with his body, picked up his front foot, and launched a stone across the water. If it bounced on the water once, it was a cow. Every additional bounce was a calf. Kobus sometimes threw a cow and five calves. "Did you see, Grietjie, did you see?" he would shout.

At first her stones simply plonked into the water, but before they went back home she could throw a cow.

During the day her mommy taught her Afrikaans and told her about Jan van Riebeeck and Slagtersnek and the Great Trek and the Boer War because Gretl had to know about these things before she went to the Afrikaans school. She learned music as well. She could read some of the notes on the sheet music and play them on the piano.

On the Tuesday of Kobus's vacation, when her father was attending an emergency meeting of the Farmers' Agricultural Union, and Kobus had hitched the wooden water-cart behind the Fergie to spray the citrus trees, Gretl and her mother went to Cohen Crown General Dealer to buy school supplies. They bought black lace-up shoes and more white socks, this time without frills. They bought white shirts with short sleeves and two black school dresses with belts, called gyms.

They also bought a white hat with a hatband and elastic under the chin, called a Panama hat. In another part of the store they bought a satchel, pencils, a box with twenty-four colored crayons, an eraser, and a sharpener. The pencils, eraser, and sharpener went into a wooden pencil case with a sliding lid.

Her mommy allowed her to pick out her own lunchbox. They were all so pretty that she didn't know which one to choose. At last she chose a tin with a picture of two kittens on the lid, because they looked so warm and sleepy.

At home she laid out everything on the dining room table for her father and Kobus to inspect when they came home. She could hardly wait to go to school.

"Let me know if the children give you any trouble," Kobus said that evening. "They know me. I'll give them hell."

"Kobus!" their mommy scolded. "Watch your language!"

"Sorry, Mom. But, Mom, I just want Grietjie to know, Mom."

"Thanks," said Grietjie. She had noticed at church that Kobus was much taller than his friends. But she would rather not tell him if the children were nasty to her.

Alone in bed that night, she didn't know whether she was looking forward to school quite as much anymore. She clutched her wooden cross and her blanky for comfort.

On the Sunday before she had to go to school she was baptized Magrieta Katharina Neethling in the Afrikaans church. Magrieta was the Afrikaans name for Gretl, Mommy explained, and Katharina was her mother's full name. Kobus had been baptized Jakobus Johannes Neethling, after his grandpa Grootkoos, who had been dead for a long time.

It was sweltering and not at all beautiful inside the church. There were no colored pictures in the windows, no candles, not a picture of the Holy Virgin with the Child in sight, not even one of Lieber Herr

Jesus on the cross. In fact, there wasn't a single cross to be seen. A lady with thick calves pumped the organ, extracting a series of bleating noises that dripped from the walls and ceiling like thick syrup. The people didn't sing well either. The organ seemed to drag the notes from their throats. Some of the ladies were especially bad. She wished they could hear the nuns' choir just once, or the boys' choir at evening mass.

As she stood between her mother and father in front of the congregation in her white dress, she wondered if God didn't feel a bit despondent at having to receive her yet again. She couldn't remember being baptized Gretl Christina Schmidt in the *Deutsche Luthersche Kirche*, but she vaguely remembered Oma taking her and Elza to the rabbi in the synagogue. And she remembered very well how the priest had blessed her and the other girls in the cathedral on the green foothills of Jasna Góra.

After church everyone wanted to kiss and hug her yet again. The men crowded round her daddy, as they did every Sunday after church, discussing things like cattle and tractors and the price of corn. Her mommy held her hand tightly, but Gretl knew by now that Mommy couldn't save her from the sweaty ladies.

———

Gretl woke up early Monday morning. She couldn't eat Maria's maize porridge. Her father prayed that the Lord would watch over her at school. Her mother struggled to tie the white ribbon in her hair. She wanted Gretl to look pretty on her first school day.

Her mother got out of the car and went with her to the principal's office, where Gretl had to be registered. This time she had a mommy to do it for her. All the children on the playground stopped what they were doing and looked at them. She heard them talk as she and her mommy walked past.

"We'll try her in standard three and see how it goes," said the principal. "Standards two and three share a classroom, so if she finds the work too hard, she can join the standard twos."

A bell rang and all the children from grade one to standard five formed five neat lines in front of the veranda. In the last line were the children of the special class, where younger and older children shared the same classroom. The principal read a passage from the Bible and prayed. The sun blazed down from a cloudless sky. Then the children filed into the classrooms.

There were four female teachers and the principal, who was in charge of the combined standard four and five class. Gretl and her mommy went to a door that said *Standard 2 and Standard 3, Miss Grobler.*

Gretl's mouth was bone-dry, and the lump in her tummy had moved up to her throat.

"Come inside," said the teacher.

They entered the stuffy classroom. Twenty pairs of eyes stared at them, following their every movement.

"Ag, shame, is this our little orphan?" asked Miss Grobler. She had a big bosom and a broad face covered with beads of perspiration.

Gretl braced herself for the customary hug and kiss. She lifted her chin, looked the teacher in the eye, held out her hand, and said, "Good morning, Miss Grobler. I'm Grietjie Neethling." She had practiced it last night, when she was tossing and turning in her warm bed and sleep refused to come.

She heard someone snort. From the corner of her eye she saw children dive behind their desks. Others stared at her. For a moment she wondered whether she had mispronounced her *g*'s and *r*'s.

The teacher showed her to a seat in the second row, next to a boy with chubby bare feet. The standard twos sat on the side of the classroom, closest to the door, while the standard threes sat next to the window. Auntie Lovey's Mattie sat alone, right next to the teacher's desk.

After they had listened to a Bible story, it was time for arithmetic. Gretl began to relax. The sums were easy. She was first to show her book to the teacher. "Have you finished?" the teacher asked, surprised.

"Yes," said Gretl.

"Yes, Miss," said Miss Grobler while she checked Gretl's sums.

"I beg your pardon?" Gretl asked politely.

"Say 'Yes, Miss,'" said the teacher.

She kept forgetting. "Oh. Okay, I will," she said.

When she looked up, she saw a few children laughing behind their hands. "Behave!" said the teacher in a stern voice.

Gretl returned to her desk and sat straight. Her tummy ached. She opened the reading book the teacher had given her. It was easy, she saw. On the first page she read the title. *Janet and John* and *Grade 2*. The teacher probably thought she couldn't read.

Her heart was racing.

Then she felt a tug at her hair. She turned her head. The two boys behind her were pretending to write, but she knew one of them had pulled her hair. She returned to her reading book and tried to tilt her head out of reach.

Someone yanked the ribbon her mother had taken so much trouble to tie right out of her hair. White-hot anger boiled up inside her. She turned around in her desk. "Behave!" she said sternly.

The children laughed.

"Enough! You're behaving like hooligans!" the teacher warned. "Have you never seen a new pupil before?"

"Never such a pale one," said a boy at the back of the class.

The teacher picked up a thick, round stick and shouted, "Gert, Krisjan, Pietman, come forward! Bend over!"

Gretl froze. The first boy bent over. The teacher raised the cane high, and brought it down on his backside with such force that he jumped. "Bend!" the teacher roared.

Bile pushed up in Gretl's throat. She saw the Gestapo . . .

She swallowed hard and closed her eyes, but the dull thumping echoed in her ears. One of the boys burst into tears.

"Be quiet and sit down!" the teacher ordered. "The next one who misbehaves gets three of the best! Is that clear?"

"Yes, Miss," the class chanted.

"Mattie, come and read your lesson."

There was complete silence in the classroom. Everyone kept their eyes on their books. Gretl was still feeling nauseated.

"Grietjie, come and read your lesson."

She had forgotten that she was Grietjie. The boy with the chubby feet nudged her. "It's your turn to read," he said.

She grabbed her book, got to her feet, and went to the teacher's table, but her eyes were misty and she couldn't make out the words.

The queasiness pushed up, past her throat. She made a run for it, but she didn't know where to go. On the veranda outside the classroom her nausea caught up with her.

The teacher came out to help, but at the smelly outhouse, Gretl threw up again. She was mortified and wondered how she could ever show her face in the classroom again. She rinsed her face, wiped her new uniform with a damp cloth, and drank a little water. At playtime the teacher gave her and the two other girls in her class permission to stay inside because Grietjie was not feeling well.

The girls kept touching her and asking questions. Gretl answered as best she could. They ate their sandwiches, but Gretl couldn't eat the sandwich or the sweet her mommy had put in her lunchbox that morning. Her pretty white ribbon was missing.

After playtime the teacher gave them sentences to write. They were in English, and Gretl didn't understand them at all. She copied the sentences exactly, too afraid to ask what she was supposed to do.

She tried to focus on the words when the teacher told them a story about Bushmen, but she had no idea who Bushmen were. They were told to draw a picture of their rock paintings. At a complete loss, she drew a picture of a ship at sea.

At last the final bell sounded and they were allowed to go home. Stiffly she crossed the school grounds to the gate, where her mommy was waiting in her big boxy car. Gretl opened the door, got in, held her head high, and didn't look at her mommy. Mommy started the car and pulled away. She didn't ask Gretl any questions.

When they had left the town behind them, her mommy reached

out and drew Gretl close. Gretl couldn't stop the tears. Mommy stopped under a tree and held Gretl tightly. She was crying too.

"Never mind, my angel," she said, "you're with Mommy now. There now, Mommy's here."

When Gretl stopped crying, her mommy told her in German that she had felt very strange as well when she had first come to these parts, because she had grown up in the city, in Grandpa John's beautiful English home with carpets on the floors and diamonds in the lights. She had attended an English school and church. She had never even seen an outhouse before. But she loved Gretl's daddy so much that she came to live with him here on the farm, where he could work in the open air.

"I'm glad you came to live with Daddy," Gretl said, "or Kobus and I wouldn't have had a home."

"And I'm glad you came to live with us, or Daddy and I wouldn't have had a little girl," said her mommy, in Afrikaans now. "You'll see, once you get to know the people and they know you, school will be much easier."

Gretl nodded earnestly. "At least the children didn't try to kiss me," she said.

———

Two weeks later Mommy stopped taking her to school by car, and Gretl waited for the school bus at the side of the road with Mattie and his brother and sisters. They never had handkerchiefs, so Gretl gave them hers, but they still didn't use them.

Her heart went out to Mattie. He couldn't read, so he got a hiding every day. Gretl wanted to help him in the afternoons, as she had helped Starika when they had gone to school together. But Mattie smelled really bad, so she gave up on the idea.

———

One of the best things in the whole world was driving to town with her father. They drove in the big truck her father had bought from the Defence Force after the war. She had seen many trucks like that in Poland, usually with German soldiers in the back. But she didn't tell her father this, because she didn't know if there had been similar trucks in Germany.

When she and her father drove to town, they talked all the way. Actually, she would chatter and he would say "Mm," but she knew he was listening. In town they went to the Northern Transvaal Co-op to buy farm supplies and sometimes, if her mother had given them a list, to Cohen Crown General Dealer. Wherever they went, she got out of the truck and went inside with her father. Everyone knew her father and everyone wanted to talk to him, because he knew everything. He was chairman of the Farmers' Agricultural Union, Kobus had said, and he even talked to the minister.

Sometimes they went to the station to send oranges or other produce to market. At first she didn't want to get out at the station at all. But one day, when her father stayed away for a long time, she clambered out of the high truck and went through the small building to the platform. There were only two rows of tracks. To the left was the big water tank that filled the trains' bellies, and to the right a single track ran straight as an arrow toward the horizon.

She stood looking at the tracks for a long time, but when a locomotive began to let off steam and the acrid smoke burned the back of her throat, she turned and fled to the safety of her father's truck.

———·———

Sunday school was almost like school, but different. She had a little book with Bible texts she had to learn by heart and recite to the teacher. It was easy. The teacher told the children Bible stories but, unlike the stories the nuns used to tell them at the convent school, they were not about God's love. The Sunday school teacher told them scary stories.

If they weren't very, very good and didn't do everything God wanted, they would burn forever in the great fires of hell. God had a big eye that could see them, no matter where they were.

One night she dreamed of the devil and the great fire. She thought Mutti and Oma might be in the fire. She couldn't be sure, because their faces were turned away from her. But she did recognize Jakób.

"Jakób! Jakób!" she shouted. "Look out for the fire!"

But he was too far away. He couldn't hear her.

He would burn, the lady on the ship explained, because he was a Catholic, and being Catholic was a sin. *Beware of the Catholic Threat*, she warned. The big eye in the picture on Auntie Lovey's wall kept following her. Then a storm came from the English Channel and washed everyone overboard into a brown sea filled with frogs. Gretl looked in vain for her father to hold her head above water and keep her safe.

She woke up, drenched in sweat. She clung to her blanky and desperately tried to go back to sleep.

A week later she found her daddy outside the barn with a piece of iron and a white-hot flame. He was wearing special glasses to protect his eyes and he had taken off his shirt. She could see the muscles in his strong back.

From a distance she watched as sparks flew from the iron her father was heating and beating into a shape that would fit the horse's hoof. When it had cooled down, he tacked the shoe onto the hoof with small nails. The horse stood quite still, so she guessed it wasn't painful.

When they were sitting on the veranda later that afternoon, she asked, "Doesn't the fire scare you, Daddy?"

He shook his head. "No, I control the fire. I get worried sometimes, when the wind suddenly changes direction during a bush fire. But being afraid doesn't help. You just have to be careful."

"I'm not afraid either, except maybe a little of hellfire."

Her father frowned. "Who told you about that, Grietjie?"

"My Sunday school teacher. She says the eye of God sees everything, and if we don't do as God tells us, we'll burn eternally in the great fires of hell."

"Mm," her father said. "Some people stress the punishment of a jealous God, who will visit the sins of the fathers on the third and fourth generations of those who hate Him. They live in fear of Almighty God." She nodded earnestly. She didn't understand all the words, but she grasped what he was saying.

"But I believe in a loving God, who, through grace, forgives us when we ask for forgiveness. What do you think, Grietjie?"

"I think God loves me," she said without hesitation.

"Then you don't have to fear the fire," said her daddy.

After supper that evening her father said, "Grietjie, tonight I'm going to read from the book of Malachi, from the third chapter. You must listen carefully."

She nodded and listened attentively to her father's deep voice. "'He will sit as a refiner and purifier of silver; he will purify the Levites and refine them like gold and silver. Then the Lord will have men who will bring offerings in righteousness.'"

He closed the big Bible and explained. To purify silver, in other words to clean it, the silversmith has to hold it at the center of the fire, where the flames are hottest, so that the fire can burn away every trace of impurity. But the silversmith has to sit beside the fire and hold on to the silver. He has to keep his eyes on the silver all the time, for if it remains in the fire a moment too long, it will be destroyed.

"How does the silversmith know when the silver has been burned clean?" she asked.

He smiled at her. "When he can see his own image reflected in the silver."

"It's a nice story." She smiled back at him.

"It's not just a story, Grietjie, it's the truth. Just remember, when you suffer and feel the heat of the flames, that's when God is there. He watches carefully, until He can see His own image in you. He'll never leave you in the flames too long."

———————

At Christmastime, when schools closed for the summer vacation, Grandpa John came to stay with them. He and Kobus planned to sleep at the old homestead.

After supper Grandpa John told Gretl he had something to show her. From behind his back he produced a flat parcel. She tore it open carefully and gasped—it was an Advent calendar he had ordered from Germany. She touched the beautiful calendar. She couldn't believe the Advent calendar had come all that way.

It was already the sixth of December, so she opened the first six windows. Everyone watched and exclaimed each time they saw the beautiful picture behind the little flap. On the twenty-fourth there would be a picture of Mary and Joseph and the Christ Child in the *Weihnachtskrippe*, she knew. But they would all have to wait until *Heiligabend* to see it.

Grandpa John had also brought *Weihnachtsstollen* and *Lebkuchen* he had bought at a German shop in Johannesburg. The family ate these with their coffee.

Two days before Christmas Gretl and her mommy decorated the *Weihnachtsbaum*. A *Tannenbaum* didn't grow in the bushveld, because it was too hot and dry, but Kobus chopped a wild plum from the mountain and planted it in a tin. Her mommy took out the pretty balls and shiny stars from the tissue paper they were wrapped in, and Gretl hung them on the tree. Grandpa John and Kobus helped hang the decorations on the topmost branches. Finally they added the candles, and the tree was lovely. She couldn't wait for Christmas.

On the morning of Christmas Eve her mommy and Grandpa John put the presents under the tree. Grandpa John had brought a bag full of gifts, almost like Father Christmas. But there was to be no Father

Christmas, because her father said it was the celebration of Christ's birth, not a circus.

The sun kept shining and wouldn't go down. They had to wait for darkness to light the candles. They read from the Bible and sang "*Stille Nacht, heilige Nacht*," and only then did they get their presents.

Gretl didn't even know what the others got, because she was too excited about her own presents. Her mother and father bought her two gifts: a book of true stories in Afrikaans and a soft woolen bear to sleep with at night. Kobus gave her hairpins and ribbons. She suspected their mommy had bought them, because Kobus knew nothing about girly things.

The best, best present came from Grandpa John. It was a wristwatch! A real watch she had to wind every morning and take off when she went swimming. She held out her arm and he clasped it around her wrist.

"Thank you, thank you, Grandpa John!" she said.

———

When everyone was asleep, she went outside. She couldn't help it, her heart was aching. The quiet bushveld lay stretched out around her, and the dogs rubbed sleepily against her legs. She wasn't afraid, because the veld was asleep. *This has to be what Bethlehem's open fields had looked like, when the shepherds heard the angels sing and the* Drei Heilige Könige *saw the star*, she thought.

The moon was almost full, and the garden path and the grass and the yellow flowers of the sweet-thorn trees were bathed in its soft light. Since she had first looked in the early evening, the moon had traveled a long way through the starry sky.

Her memory chose its own painful path—to where the fields were covered with snow and the moon cast its soft glow over a world that was entirely white. To red and white hair ribbons. To a cathedral full of candles. To a walk home in the moonlight.

She knew she should think about something else, but she didn't want to.

———

When she walked up the steps of the old homestead's veranda that night, Grandpa John opened his arms. She checked her new watch. It was almost eleven. He sat down on the wicker chair, and she sat in his lap with her arms around his neck. His face was wet from crying for a long time. She understood. Ouma Susan, whom she resembled, had still been here last Christmas. She stroked his gray hair, and he stroked and stroked her curls. They didn't speak; there was no need.

———

When the school reopened in 1949, the principal declared Gretl too advanced for standard four and suggested that they promote her to standard five. At first her father refused, because he thought she was too young. But her mother thought it was a good idea, and so did she, and so she ended up in standard five. Standard four and standard five shared a classroom and did the same history, geography, and nature studies anyway. Only the arithmetic was different. She found the standard five sums easy, because Jakób had already taught her most of the work.

She had nearly forgotten what Jakób looked like.

The only subject she found really hard was English. "I could speak English to you if you want," her mommy suggested.

"Okay, but only when we're alone," said Gretl. She knew that no one liked English, not even the teachers, who were forced by law to teach it to the children. "And I must read English books."

"Once you discover English literature, a new world will be open to you," said her mommy. *She should know*, Gretl thought. Mommy was always reading English books.

In May Gretl took part in her first *eisteddfod*. She recited a poem called *"Amakeia."* It was the most beautiful poem she had ever heard, about a black housemaid murdered by her own people for protecting a white infant. When Gretl reached the part where the black warriors say, "Die, or give us the white child!" she put on a fierce expression and spoke in a booming voice. She spoke her favorite part clearly, with her chin raised: "'Over my dead body,' Amakeia answered proudly!" She was awarded a gold certificate, and the newspaper published a photo of the little German girl who had done so well in the Afrikaans *eisteddfod*. She also received a silver certificate for a duet she sang with a standard-four boy.

"We should have won the gold," she told her mother and father, who had both been in the audience. "But he sang off-key on purpose, because he didn't want to hold the basket with the plastic roses the teacher had brought!" She would never sing with a boy again, she fumed. They couldn't be trusted.

"Mm," said her father.

"Why, Daddy?"

He smiled. "Because I don't blame him," he said.

"Never mind," her mother consoled her. "You've got your gold certificate. We'll hang it on your wall. And just think how happy you've made the two who were placed first."

"That's true," said Gretl. "They were pleased, weren't they?"

Jakób would be proud of her if she could tell him, she thought before she fell asleep that night.

At the end of 1949, Gretl's father fixed the old ox-wagon in the barn and put up a new white canvas tent, then he took the family to Pretoria to celebrate South Africa's pioneers. They camped at the base of the new Voortrekker Monument with other Afrikaners. Everyone lived in tents and cooked on open fires, just like the old Voortrekkers. They sang Afrikaans songs, and the children played old-fashioned games and did *volkspele*.

Her father grew a beard, which was bristly when he kissed her and her mommy. They complained, but secretly Gretl liked it. Kobus wasn't allowed to grow a beard, because he was still at school. "But I could if I wanted to!" he assured her, rubbing his chin.

Kobus had secretly packed a jar of Brylcreem for his hair, in case there was a pretty girl around. As it turned out, there were many pretty girls, and Gretl thought it looked as if a cow had licked his head. When their father noticed, he ordered Kobus to wash his hair and threw the Brylcreem away. Kobus was upset. Gretl thought he looked much better without the Brylcreem, but she felt it would be better not to say so.

Gretl and her mommy wore long gathered dresses with lace neckerchiefs and bonnets. They looked beautiful, Gretl thought. Her daddy and Kobus wore leather breeches and hats with the brims rolled up on one side. Daddy was the leader of the people from their district. She felt as if her heart would burst with pride.

As the people laughed and danced together, Daddy told Gretl she was his sweetheart.

I'm no longer a German orphan, Gretl thought. *I have a home and a mommy and daddy who love me, and a birth certificate stating I was born in the bushveld. My certificate of baptism says I am Magrieta Katharina Neethling, baptized in the* Nederduitsche Gereformeerde Kerk.

I stopped being Gretl Schmidt a long time ago, she realized. *I'm Grietjie Neethling, Afrikaner, only daughter of big, strong Bernard Neethling and beautiful, gracious Kate Neethling, only sister of Kobus Neethling, headboy of the high school and captain of the first rugby team.*

I am Grietjie Neethling, and I'm proud of it.

9

KATOWICE, POLAND, 1956

"Have supper with us on Saturday," Haneczka said one cold winter's evening toward the end of January. Jakób, Stan, and Haneczka were huddled around the stove in the apartment's small kitchen. Stan's three boys had gone to bed.

Jakób was immediately wary. In a country where three meals a day in the communal dining hall had more value than the cash the workers earned, Haneczka didn't cook unless there was a reason.

"What are you planning?"

She gave him an innocent look. "Supper, Jakób, with soup, bread, cheese, and ham, if I can find some."

"Who else will be coming?" he asked. He knew his sister-in-law too well.

She sighed. "Fine," she admitted, "I've invited a doctor who started with us just after Christmas."

"And?"

"And nothing. Just the four of us, if the kids behave. We might—"

"Does the doctor have a name?" He couldn't help smiling. Her schemes were so transparent.

"Yes, Dr. Bòdis."

He frowned slightly."From Czechoslovakia?"

"Hungary."

"I see." He looked at Stan, but his brother was immersed in his paper, and no help would come from him. "Does the doctor have a first name?" he asked after a while.

"Of course she has a first name," Haneczka said.

"Aha!" he said triumphantly. From the corner of his eye he saw Stan smile. "Are you part of this conspiracy?"

"I'm just reading the paper," Stan said.

"Her name is Mischka. I've invited her because she doesn't know anyone in Katowice," Haneczka protested. "And if you and Stan could refrain from arguing about politics, we might have a pleasant evening. She's a competent, intelligent woman."

"Bun, spectacles, stethoscope, white coat?" Jakób played along. His sister-in-law usually got her way with him and Stan, he had to admit.

"Totally." She nodded earnestly.

"I see," said Jakób and drank the last of his coffee. "Han, when are you going to accept the fact that I'm a confirmed bachelor?"

"At thirty-three no one doubts it anymore." She got up to rinse out the coffee cups. "Forget that she's a woman. Treat her like one of the guys. It worked with me." She hung the dishcloth on the hook. "And now you must go home, please. It's past our bedtime."

———

When Jakób arrived at his brother's apartment the next Saturday evening and Haneczka introduced him to the new doctor, he instantly knew it wouldn't be possible to treat her like one of the guys. She was attractive, probably in her mid-thirties—tall, dark, and olive-skinned, with a straight nose, high cheekbones, and full lips. She looked at Jakób, her head tilted slightly, her dark eyes inscrutable, though not unfriendly.

"Good evening," she said and held out her hand. She spoke Polish with a strange rounded accent, rolling the words in her mouth before uttering them.

"Good evening, Mischka," Jakób answered. Her handshake was firm, her hands surprisingly soft.

Stan poured the wine Jakób had brought and a shot of vodka for himself. It was bitterly cold outside, so they gathered around the stove. The apartment was warm and cozy—so different from his own place in the single-men's quarters, Jakób thought with a touch of envy.

When they sat down to eat, Mischka smiled, surprised. "You've made *gulyashus*," she said. She was even more attractive when she smiled. Her face softened, and the sadness momentarily disappeared from her eyes. But her mouth still looked vulnerable.

"I *tried* to make goulash," Haneczka said. "I'm certainly no chef!"

The conversation was halting at first as Jakób and Mischka took stock of one another. They discussed the icy weather, the food they were eating, and the widespread food shortages even now, eleven years after the end of the war.

"You can make goulash anytime, Han, it's delicious," Stan said.

"If I can get my hands on meat," said Haneczka. "It's ridiculous to have to stand in line for everything. People are unhappy! Poland is like a simmering pot; one of these days it's going to boil over."

"For centuries Poland fed its people without trouble," Jakób said. "Then the Russians moved in."

"The same thing is happening in Hungary," said Mischka. "In the end it's the people who suffer. I wonder if the government realizes how hard it is for them."

"The government has no idea what the people want," said Haneczka.

"There's only one way forward," Stan said firmly, "cooperation with Russia, but without Russia prescribing to us. Poland can't stand alone."

"You promised not to discuss politics!" Haneczka scolded her husband as she dished up second helpings for the men.

"Communism is the only thing that will work for industry and agriculture," Stan continued, unruffled. "The time when a subsistence farmer could eke out a living on a small patch of land is over, worldwide. There are too many people who have to eat; listen to what I'm telling you."

"You may be right," Mischka said thoughtfully.

"The same goes for the industries. Production at the steelworks where Jakób and I work has dramatically increased since the plant was nationalized," said Stan. "Ask Jakób."

"I think the main purpose of increased industrialization is to bolster the Soviet army," Jakób said. He looked at Haneczka. Her eyes clearly said she'd like to throttle the two of them.

"You can't argue with the fact that Poland is doing better every year!" Stan challenged.

"Our industries may be thriving, but the ordinary man doesn't have food on the table. No one can eat steel!"

Mischka gave a slight smile and looked from one brother to the other. "So the two of you don't agree on how Poland should be governed?" she asked calmly.

"They're like day and night," Haneczka sighed, "and it's no use arguing. They'll never agree."

Mischka turned to Jakób. "What do you think the solution is for Poland, Jakób?" His name sounded like poetry on her lips, he thought.

"Unbelievable!" Haneczka said and got to her feet. "I'll put water on for coffee."

"I think we should move away from Communism completely," Jakób answered, "return to democracy, where our traditions and religion are respected."

"Democracy won't work here," Stan said. He turned to Mischka. "In fact, Polish Communism wants to preserve our traditions, and it won't interfere with the Catholic Church. It's not a mindless imitation of the Russian model."

Jakób felt his patience wear thin.

"I happened to read in yesterday's paper," Mischka said, "that there's a name for people who share Stan's sentiments: radishes. They're red on the outside and white inside. True Communists are beets or tomatoes."

"Then Jakób must be a potato, or a turnip, with absolutely no red anywhere," Haneczka said, trying to keep the conversation light.

"What's your contribution to this vegetable broth?" Jakób asked Mischka. He was eager to know.

She thought for a moment. "I don't know enough about Polish politics to have an opinion." She smiled. "And I really don't want to end up in the soup so soon."

"A smart answer," Haneczka said.

Very smart, Jakób thought when they were each sitting with a steaming mug of coffee in their hands. He studied her discretely. She was beautiful.

And seductively neutral.

Jakób and Stan were both employed by Stalinogród Steelworks, the flagship company of the industrialization program, but they saw little of each other at work. Stan was a floor manager in one of the workshops. Jakób was one of the engineers responsible for the complicated process through which the ore from the mines at Wrocław was processed to supply the never-ending demand for iron.

Early one Sunday morning at the beginning of March, after a long shift, Jakób's manager, a staunch Communist named Mr. Drobner, called him to his office.

Jakób combed his hair with his fingers. He was exhausted—not only from a lack of sleep, but also from the intense concentration it had required to solve the complicated problem. Jakób came into the office like a sleepwalker.

Mr. Drobner opened the top drawer of his desk, took out an envelope, and handed it to Jakób. "For you," he said. "Tickets to a music recital. They were given to me when Workshop Three reached an output of a thousand tons last week. It's for the extra hours you put in."

"Thanks, Mr. Drobner." But at the moment all Jakób wanted was a hot shower and his bed. He put the envelope in his pocket and walked back to his apartment through the quiet, cold streets, past sparse trees and emaciated cats and rows and rows of gray apartment buildings marked with soot. Home was a bleak room with a bed and a sofa and a cold Primus stove. And a radio he never listened to, because the broadcasts were chiefly Communist propaganda, and they hardly ever played Chopin anymore.

———

Two days later, when he was putting his clothes in the basin to soak, he remembered the tickets. The recital would take place Saturday night. Jakób was unfamiliar with the composers whose works were being performed, and he had never heard of the two Russian pianists either. He sighed and returned the tickets to his pocket. He'd offer them to Stan and Haneczka.

"A piano recital?" Stan exclaimed that evening. "You mean you and me at a piano recital?"

"No, Stan!" Jakób protested. "You and Haneczka!"

"Not for me, thanks!" said Haneczka firmly. "Why don't you ask Mischka? The two of you should go. It would do her good to get out. She works hard."

"I don't know if she likes classical music," said Jakób. He had toyed with the idea of contacting her, but, remembering the effect she'd had on him that first night, he had decided against it. He had absolutely no plan to get involved with anyone.

"Hungarians love music, as far as I know," said Haneczka.

"Why did she leave Hungary?"

"Who? Mischka?" Haneczka shrugged. "Who knows, some or other sad story, if you listen to the rumors. Anyway, we're glad to have her. It's hard to find doctors of her caliber."

"I see." Maybe he should ask Mischka after all. "Will you find out whether she's free?" he asked on the spur of the moment.

Saturday night Jakób and Mischka sat beside each other in the theater. His eyes took in her neat figure in the stylish black dress— she looked elegant, sophisticated, lovely. Her hair was piled on top of her head, and there was a single strand of pearls around her slender neck. A strange feeling took hold of him. He was proud to be her partner.

"I'm really looking forward to the concert," she said. "I don't know how you got the tickets. They're very hard to come by," she said.

"I worked myself to a standstill," he said with a wry smile. He no longer had any misgivings about spending the evening in her company. But he was annoyed with himself for not having learned about the composers or performers.

She laughed softly. "Then I hope you'll enjoy it too. Do you like the works of Tchaikovsky and Mozart?"

He shrugged. "I don't know much about music," he admitted. "I listen to the organ and the choir in the cathedral and I sing in the shower. That's as far as my knowledge goes."

The lights dimmed. "You'll enjoy it. It's going to be wonderful," she said.

To Jakób's surprise, there was an entire orchestra at the back of the stage. He had expected a sole piano. At the center of the stage were two pianos and the conductor's rostrum. The orchestra members were already seated. The conductor entered, and Jakób applauded with the rest of the audience.

The orchestra struck up, and Jakób glanced at the program. He leaned toward Mischka and whispered, "Is this Tchaikovsky's *Concerto number 1, opus 23*?"

She chuckled. "No, Jakób," she whispered back, "the orchestra members are tuning their instruments. *Opus 23* sounds slightly different."

"Oh," he said, embarrassed. *Thank goodness*, he thought. He certainly couldn't have endured this cacophony for long.

The two pianists entered, took their bows with flapping coattails, and were rewarded with fervent applause.

The concert began.

The conductor waved his baton, and the two bow-tied gentlemen at the pianos played with such fervor that they were soon perspiring. It sounded good after all, Jakób decided.

The applause was deafening, the conductor was skilled, the pianists behaved with suitable humility.

Jakób glanced at the program again. Only one more piece before the end. Maybe they'd still find a pub open where they could have a nightcap. "Are they going to start with Mozart's *Concerto number 9 in E flat* now?" he asked.

"No, they've just finished the *Allegro* part of *Opus 23*, that's the lively part," Mischka explained. "Now it's the *Andante*, the slower part. Mozart comes after the intermission."

"Oh." He smiled apologetically. "As I said, I don't know much about music."

"Jakób, you know nothing at all about music." She laughed.

"I know who Chopin is," he said in his own defense.

"Every Pole knows who Chopin is," she answered.

When the intermission came, Jakób was grateful to stretch his legs. He had enjoyed the music so far, but it certainly went on for a long time. How he was going to stay awake until the end he didn't know. And he doubted whether they would find any pub fit for a lady open after midnight.

During the second half he already knew he could deal with the *Allegro*, but the *Andante* would do its best to put him to sleep. He leaned back and looked at Mischka in the dim light. She sat erect with her eyes closed. She had surrendered herself to the music. At times her hands, shoulders, or head moved almost imperceptibly. She was obviously familiar with the music. Sometimes she smiled contentedly or gave a slight nod when the orchestra came to a part she had been waiting for.

She was gorgeous.

Jakób felt an overwhelming urge to reach out and touch her cheek, but he controlled the impulse. He didn't want to spoil a hallowed moment.

He closed his eyes and tried to immerse himself in the music, allowing it to sweep him along.

I could easily fall in love with this woman, he thought dreamily, *though it was certainly not my plan.*

The music lifted him and dropped him back on earth. *It might not be such a bad idea after all,* he thought as the music faded serenely into the background—*this falling-in-love business.*

"Wake up, it's almost over," Mischka whispered in his ear.

Jakób sat up, mortified. "I surrendered to the music," he tried to explain.

When they were walking back through the quiet streets, she asked, "Was it very hard for you?" He saw the smile on her lips.

"No, the music was very good."

She raised her eyebrows and looked amused.

"All right, fine," he admitted. "Next time I'll give you both tickets and you can take a friend."

For the first time since they met he saw her laugh. It wasn't an exuberant laugh, the way Haneczka sometimes laughed, or a happy little chortle, the way he remembered Gretl laughing. It was an amused laugh, he thought, the way one would laugh at a private joke.

"Poor Jakób," she said, "now I appreciate the outing even more. I found it absolutely marvelous. Thank you very much!"

"I'm glad." He drew her hand through his arm. He felt her presence by his side. He felt her every movement, the swing of her hip against his own, the early spring air fresh on their faces, their breath in small clouds ahead of them.

Never before had Jakób found the street so beautiful.

———•———

During the week that followed it was impossible to arrange a meeting with Mischka, and after that Jakób became so busy that he didn't have time to think about her again. When a fortnight had passed, he knocked on her door one late afternoon. There was no reply. "She left about half an hour ago," said a nurse, poking her head out of the room next door. "I think she's on night shift."

Well, that's it then, he thought as he returned to his own apartment.

He saw Mischka at Stan and Haneczka's apartment a few times during the following months. And despite Haneczka's warning that it was a turnoff, politics reared its head in almost every conversation where Mischka was present.

Sometimes Jakób walked her back to her quarters. During their walks they talked, mostly about politics. He wished he could talk to her about other topics, but he simply couldn't think of any. Their conversations were mostly a continuation of what had been discussed at the apartment.

One evening she stopped and turned to him. "I wish you wouldn't get so upset about the political situation, Jakób," she said. "It's beyond your control."

"We can all do something," he answered passionately. "Just by talking we're already doing something. Revolution starts with the intellectuals. Think of the French Revolution; their writers didn't remain silent. When Poland is silent, I'll know the Polish spirit has been broken."

She walked on without reacting. When they reached her quarters, she didn't invite him in.

Jakób walked back to his own place through the quiet streets, the bright moon propelling his long-legged shadow ahead of him.

———

On a warm Friday evening in the middle of June, Jakób and Mr. Drobner were standing at a drawing board.

Jakób slowly shook his head. "We must be making a mistake somewhere," he said. "No problem is unsolvable."

"Jakób, you're just tired. Catch some sleep. Tomorrow, when we're both fresh, we'll continue to search for a solution."

"I think I will, thank you," said Jakób and stretched.

"Before you go, listen: I would like you to accompany me somewhere later this month."

"Not another piano recital, please," Jakób pleaded.

"Piano recital? What are you talking about?"

"Never mind. You were saying?"

"The steelworks can send two delegates to the Poznań International Fair. All the latest products and technology will be exhibited. I want you to come with me."

"The International Fair? In Poznań?" Jakób asked, surprised. "I'd love to go, but surely there are more senior people who would jump at the chance."

"I've decided you should go. You're the type of young man the Party likes to invest in. We'll reap the rewards."

The steelworks might, Jakób thought, *but definitely not the Party.*

Mischka walked to the station with Jakób. It was a sultry afternoon. He had stopped at her place on the spur of the moment to say goodbye. "I'll walk with you," she had said. "I could do with the exercise and some fresh air."

The sun was bright in the lush green treetops. Jakób was intensely aware of her presence next to him, the slender line of her neck, the golden skin of her bare arms, the graceful swing of her hips in the flared skirt. She walked easily, as if she was used to walking long distances. *As soon as I'm back,* he thought, *I'll ask her out, to the theater, maybe.*

"Enjoy your few days away, Jakób." He couldn't get enough of her accent.

"Actually, I'm going for work," he said.

"I know. But it will be stimulating, with the whole world exhibiting there. Not all of us get an opportunity to see what's happening in the West."

Jan Drobner was waiting at the station when they arrived. His wife and two teenage daughters had come to see him off. When the train pulled away, they waved excitedly. "Bring us something from Poznań!" the daughters cried. "Remember to take your medication!" his wife called out.

Mischka wasn't on the platform.

Jakób leaned his head against the seat and stared through the window. Buildings and factories flashed past, then houses, then small farms, fir plantations, blue rivers, tall cliffs. It grew dark. He stretched his long legs in front of him and surrendered to the train's rocking motion.

He wondered about the woman called Mischka Bòdis. How did he really feel about her? Was he more than just physically attracted to her? One thing was certain: every time he saw her, every time he was in her presence, he felt his body respond. He found her company stimulating, interesting.

At times he longed to be with her, but when he saw her, she always kept her distance.

At Poznań station he and Mr. Drobner got a horse and buggy, a *droshka*, to take them to the hotel. "It's chock-full of foreigners," the old cab driver said, trying his best to get the two tired horses to step lively. "They're from all over—Germany, England, Japan, America, and of course Russia!"

It was very late before Jakób fell asleep at last in the strange bed. But it was a restless sleep, because he dreamed of a tall woman with long dark hair who kept turning her face away.

———

Monday morning Jakób and Mr. Drobner visited the factory of Zispo, the largest in Poznań, before the exhibition opened.

"Impressive," said Mr. Drobner in the hearing of their guide, and "Take note, Jakób!" But privately he said to Jakób, "Our own systems work better, don't you think?"

At ten the manager excused himself. An important matter required his attention. The chief engineer would accompany them on the rest of their tour.

"There's been an unexpected development," the chief engineer explained. "Last Saturday the workers demanded that a delegation of thirty men be sent to Warsaw to negotiate with the Central Union Council. I suspect it's what this call is about."

"What are they unhappy about?" asked Jakób.

"Not unhappy, really," the chief engineer said hastily. "They want to discuss the usual stuff—working hours, wages. Nothing serious, I assure you."

But the afternoon newspapers told a different story. The *Przegląd Kulturalny* carried a report on the country's serious economic dilemmas: enormous problems in agriculture, chaotic conditions in factories resulting from bad management, discrepancies in the supply of materials. The people at ground level were suffering, the paper said.

Jakób turned to the center spread, dedicated to the Lenin Steelworks, which was established in the late forties near Kraków as part of the industrialization program. On the surface it was just another propaganda piece: see how well the Party looks after the people of Poland? *Long live Communism*, Jakób thought cynically.

But the last paragraph grabbed his attention. "The decision to build an enormous industrial complex near the country's most historic and conservative city seems suspect," the journalist wrote. "Could it be that the Party wants to create a strong socialist working class that will eventually transform the structures and relationships of an established, conservative society like that of Kraków?"

Jakób felt the words echo in his heart, felt them growing in his mind. *I agree*, he thought. *How wonderful that a newspaper has the courage to say it.*

He opened a second newspaper. *Po Prostu* dedicated its entire front page to a conference that had taken place in Warsaw over the weekend. It had been attended by seven hundred Polish economists.

Bull's-eye! Jakób thought. The Poles were fed up. The sooner these Communist leaders realized it, the better. He considered taking the article home to show it to Mischka but decided against it. His plan was to talk to her about other things.

At dinner that evening Mr. Drobner said, "The Party will have to jack up the media censorship. The papers are getting bold."

They spent all of Tuesday and Wednesday at the trade fair. Jakób found it enormously interesting—the innovative ideas, the new technology, the revolutionary approach to certain products. He had a long conversation with a British engineer, a Mr. Wilson, who was from the steelworks in Liverpool.

"Tomorrow I'd like to spend some time at the Japanese exhibition," Jakób told Drobner as they walked back to their hotel late that evening. "Mr. Wilson says it's very interesting."

"Spend some time at the Russian exhibition instead," his employer advised. "It will look better."

But on Thursday morning, when they were trying to get a *droshka* to take them to the trade fair, the city was in turmoil.

"What's going on?" Mr. Drobner asked a group of bystanders.

"The delegation members who negotiated with the Central Union Council in Warsaw were arrested and thrown in jail!" said a woman with a nose as sharp as a wedge of cheese.

"No," said a thin man next to her, "some of them are on their way back, but the negotiations have failed."

"The workers are furious," a third person said breathlessly. "They're marching to the square in a 'peaceful and orderly' way. What a joke! Chaos is going to break loose!"

"I'm going to the Zispo factory," said Mr. Drobner. He looked worried.

"I'll walk to the fair," said Jakób. "I'm sure it'll be open."

But his feet took him to the square instead, where he joined a crowd of disgruntled compatriots fed up with the struggle to survive. As he walked along, he listened to their frustrations, their dashed hopes, and their suffering. He shared their conviction that things had to change.

A sense of pride grew inside him, a confidence that Poland would not succumb to Russian domination.

The stream of people grew, became wider and thicker, pressed forward. They were joined by workers from factories and offices, some carrying banners, most of them hastily assembled: "Give us bread." "We demand lower prices and higher wages." "Freedom and bread—now."

Jakób was swept along, part of the crowd, one with the crowd. He saw overalls and heavy boots, rough hands. He heard voices, women's voices as well, some with a child on the hip or one by each hand. *All we want is a decent life*, they were saying, *the same as our people for centuries before us*. He smelled the people around him—his people. Adrenaline rushed through his veins. It might be a peaceful march, but it was the first stab, the first instance of public rebellion against Russian domination since the war had ended.

The Polish sun blazed down from above, from below the street reflected the heat, around him he felt the press of warm human bodies. He was glowing, but not because of the hot day; there was a heat inside him he had almost forgotten existed.

On the square in front of the city hall the stream dammed up. By ten o'clock a great mass of people filled the square. They had been joined by students singing patriotic songs and waving banners that read: "Away with the Russians! We want freedom!" "Away with false Communism!" "Away with dictatorship!" "Away with Soviet domination!"

The events were beginning to take on a revolutionary color, Jakób realized. A hot wave of excitement washed over him.

A middle-aged woman stood next to Jakób, clad in the overalls of a factory worker. The scarf covering her graying hair had become undone; the soles of her shoes were worn thin. In her hand she held a Polish flag.

"I'm glad the Poles have begun to stand up for their rights," she said to Jakób. "I just hope the children won't get hurt."

"Attack the prison! Free the prisoners!" shouted one of the ring-leaders who had clambered up a pillar in front of the city hall.

"Take the guards' weapons!" shouted a second one from the top-most step.

Matters are getting violent, Jakób thought. *Maybe it's a good thing; maybe the Soviets will realize how strongly the people feel.*

Momentum was building, pushing against the breakwater.

A group of people overturned a car. Others joined in and more cars were overturned. Emotions were churned up to a breaking point. The march turned into a riot.

In front of the radio station, where Western broadcasts were outlawed, a tram was ablaze.

Then the first shots rang out.

Someone shouted, "The secret police are firing at us! From their building!"

Out of nowhere Molotov cocktails appeared. Bottles containing petrol bombs flew through the air, shattered against closed windows. Within minutes thick black smoke was billowing from the broken windows. More shots were fired. People ducked, screamed, fell over each other to get away. The crowd surged.

Jakób watched with a sick feeling of helplessness.

Two army trucks with infantrymen in the back pushed their way through the sea of people, followed by three tanks. The protesters shouted, "Poles don't shoot fellow Poles!" The students shouted, "Away with the Russians!" The crowd shouted, "Away with Communism!" "Away with dictatorship!" "Away with Soviet occupation!"

Next to him, the woman who had lost her scarf was struck by a bullet.

She collapsed at Jakób's feet, the Polish flag still in her hands. He knelt next to her and turned her over. Her eyes were wide, glazed, fixed in an expression of surprise. She stared past him, already gone.

A boy of no older than fourteen took the Polish flag out of her hands and waved it wildly. "You shot her! You pigs! You shot her!" he screamed.

Two big hands grabbed the boy from behind, lifting him up. The hands belonged to a red-faced man in the uniform of the secret police.

"Who are you calling a pig?" he roared.

They took the child away. But before they clamped their hands over his mouth to silence him, the boy shouted to Jakób, "Take my mother to hospital, please! I think she's badly hurt."

Workers climbed up on the trucks, engaged in hand-to-hand fighting with the soldiers, took command of the tanks. They sang patriotic songs, planted Polish flags on the trucks and tanks, waved Polish flags above their heads. They attacked more buildings, including the police station, and began to loot shops. They used overturned cars to build barricades.

Reinforcements arrived, possibly in the form of Soviet soldiers. Jakób couldn't be sure.

In the late afternoon Jakób made his way back to the hotel. He saw no sign of Mr. Drobner. Hastily he threw his things into his bag and slung it over his shoulder. He walked the few miles to the station at a brisk pace, as if he could exorcize the horrors. The station smelled of smoke and urine. He bought a ticket on the first train back to Katowice.

Jakób didn't remember how he got to Mischka's apartment. He wasn't aware of having knocked on the door. But she had opened it a crack.

"Jakób?" Her voice was thick with sleep; her dark hair tumbled over her shoulders.

He shouldn't have come. What was he thinking?

She opened the door wider. "Come in," she said, stepping aside.

He hesitated on the threshold. "I shouldn't have come."

"Come in, Jakób, you'll wake the neighbors." He couldn't get enough of the way she said his name.

He went in and closed the door behind him.

He stood, taking in his surroundings. There was a dresser, much like the one in his mother's house. On a shelf stood a Primus stove and a kettle. Three cups hung on hooks. The sugar and the coffee were on top of the dresser in labeled tins. A two-seater couch stood in front of the window, and next to it a deep armchair. Against the other wall was a table containing several books, a pile of records, and a gramophone. A curtain separated her sleeping quarters from her living space. Her home was cozy, comforting.

"Sit, I'll make coffee," she said and began to pump the Primus stove. Over her shoulder she asked, "Is everything okay?"

He made a declining motion with his hand. "Just tired," he said.

"You've just come back from Poznań?"

"I'm sorry, I don't know why I disturbed you in the middle of the night."

"Sit," she said firmly. "You came because you didn't want to be alone right now."

He sank into the deep armchair and felt an immense exhaustion take hold of him. He watched her, the graceful movements of her hands, the silky black hair cascading over her shoulders, the soft curve of her hips under the thin robe. Along with the weariness he felt an unfamiliar sensation, a kind of tenderness, a pleasant strangeness, as if he were treading on sacred ground.

You're losing it, Jakób Kowalski, he told himself and deliberately closed his eyes.

She put the kettle on the stove and sat down on the two-seater. "Do you want to talk?"

He shook his head.

She got up and put on soft music. He didn't recognize the melody, but it was soothing. She came to stand behind him and put her hands on his shoulders.

"Okay if I rub your shoulders?"

Wordlessly he nodded.

Her touch jolted his body. He leaned back and felt her fingers softly kneading his stiff muscles, rolling them under her fingertips. Gradually he felt himself relax.

"I heard about the riot in Poznań, Jakób." Her words were round, like pebbles, her voice the water of a deep, quiet river.

When he spoke, his voice sounded hoarse and distant in his ears. "It began peacefully."

She said nothing, just kept up the rhythmic massaging.

"They were just people, workers, wanting bread and freedom."

Her fingers kept kneading, sending painful spasms into his head. He lowered his head when she began to massage his neck. He felt her calmness.

"Then they began to shoot." There was no need to explain—she would know.

She followed the muscles of his neck to his scalp. Her fingers were in his thick, dark hair.

"They say it was a policewoman who lost control and fired the first shots."

He tried to focus on her strong fingers.

"A woman and a child were shot dead."

She worked methodically, almost professionally. He didn't want to say more, didn't want to bring the images into the room. But he didn't want to stop talking either. "Many people fell—men, women, children. They shot a soft-spoken woman with a flag right next to me. And threw her young son, just a child, into a police van."

He was drained, couldn't say anything more.

He tipped his head back, kept his eyes closed. She began to massage his face, her fingers circling his mouth, his eyes, his temples. No one had ever touched him like that before. Life flowed slowly back into his body. He tried to focus on nothing but the moment, tried to ignore the effect her closeness had on him.

He had been with women before, beautiful women, but he had never felt this way.

She tenderly rested her lips on his forehead. Slowly he opened his eyes. "The kettle is boiling." She smiled.

He sat up. The room, the two-seater, the steaming kettle came into focus. "Do you have anything stronger than coffee?"

"Vodka? Wine?" She bent down and took a bottle of red wine and two tall, slim glasses from the dresser.

He got up, opened the wine, and poured. She put another record on the turntable. The beautiful, tranquil music filled his mind.

He looked at her as she sat on the sofa, her long legs stretched in front of her, the slender ankles crossed, her eyes closed, her face relaxed, almost serene. He stared blatantly at her sublime beauty.

She gave him an amused smile. "Why are you looking at me like that?" she asked.

She had caught him unawares. He changed the subject.

"You could actually see it coming. I should have brought you one of the papers I bought in Poznań."

She looked at the ruby-red wine in her glass, reflecting the soft light, then up into his eyes. "Try to stay out of politics, Jakób," she said. "It's not worth it. I know."

Something in her voice got through to him. He felt the urge to wrap his arms around her, to protect her from the hardships she had evidently experienced. With a great effort he controlled his feelings. He gave her a searching look. She said nothing more.

"Will you tell me?" he asked softly.

"Maybe someday," she replied. She took a last sip of wine, got up, and took the glasses to the basin. When she opened the tap, he saw that her hands were quaking.

He got up as well. She opened the door for him.

In the doorway he turned. For a brief moment he put his arms around her, held her. He felt her tremble, was aware of his own desire.

"Thank you for tonight, Mischka," he said into her hair before he turned and left.

When he arrived at his own place just before sunrise, he realized he hadn't told her he had offered to testify at the boy's trial.

10

"Where can I find tickets for a show or something?" Jakób asked Mr. Drobner the next week.

His boss gave him a surprised look. "A show? You? Oh, I see, you want to impress a lady."

"She's rather sophisticated," he admitted.

"Well, well, how the mighty fall," said Drobner, amiably patting him on the back. "I'll ask my wife. She's good at that kind of thing."

"Czech black theater!" exclaimed Mischka the next evening. They were standing in her small living room, and he had just showed her the tickets. "Jakób, you surprise me more every day!" Spontaneously she threw her arms around his neck and hugged him.

He wrapped his arms around her. "Mm, we can do it every week if you promise to thank me like this every time."

She laughed softly. "It's been five years since I last saw a black-theater performance," she said, smiling and stepping away from his embrace. "Wine, vodka, or coffee?"

"Red wine, thanks. Here, I'll open the bottle. I've brought bread and cheese. It's in the brown-paper packet."

———

After mass on Sunday Jakób visited his brother's family. The conversation turned to Black Thursday, which had ended with fifty-four dead, more than three hundred wounded, and three hundred twenty-three people still detained three weeks after the event.

"Do you think the trials will be of a political nature?" Stan asked.

"I hope they'll focus on crime," Jakób answered. "There was a lot of looting and random vandalism."

Stan absentmindedly scratched his cheek. "I'm afraid you're too optimistic," he said. "The Russians have something to prove."

"At least the workers also proved that they're a power to be reckoned with. I was proud to be Polish."

"Watch out," Stan warned. "Your name is on the witness list; the secret police will take note of you."

Jakób cut off that worry and turned to Haneczka. "What's Czech black theater?"

"Czech what?"

"Czech black theater."

"Jakób, how on earth should I know?"

"You're a woman—women know these things."

"You, Jakób Kowalski, have no idea what women know."

I fully agree, he thought, *but I still have no idea what Czech black theater is.* "Will you find out for me?" he asked.

She sighed, "Yes, Jakób, I will. Please help the boys with their math, won't you? I'm out of my depth. I'll see to the food on the Primus, that's a big enough problem for me."

———

By the time Saturday came around, Jakób knew what Czech black theater was. Nonetheless, he was amazed at the sight of the miniature stage. When the show began, it was pitch-dark. Violet fluorescent light turned white-gloved hands into people walking on tiny feet, performing intricate dance steps, climbing ropes, falling in love, leaning over, kissing.

Completely unbidden, little Gretl Schmidt was back in his thoughts. She had believed in fairy-tale worlds of castles and princesses, of Sleeping Beauty and Hansel and Gretel and a little Swiss girl called Heidi.

He sighed and closed his eyes.

He wondered whether his skinny little duckling with the silky-soft hair still liked to escape into her imaginary world. His Gretchen, so delicate, so brave. Whom he had taken on a train ride. And left on the steps of a ruined church in Germany.

She had taught him to think about other things when life got tough. Sometimes it worked, sometimes it didn't.

He opened his eyes and leaned toward Mischka. "They're very good, aren't they?"

"They're incredible, Jakób! It's hard to believe people are doing this with their hands."

He smiled in the dark. She was beautiful when she was so animated. He put his arm around her bare shoulders. She leaned against him, and he felt her relax.

It was hard to concentrate on the rest of the performance.

———

"There's a big Polish-Catholic festival in Częstochowa at the end of August," Haneczka said one Sunday afternoon.

"Where Grandpa and Grandma live?" her oldest boy asked excitedly.

"I don't think the steelworks will give me leave," said Stan.

"It's on the weekend. The hospital will just have to give me leave," Haneczka said firmly. "They owe it to me!"

"Tell me more about the festival," said Mischka.

"This is the year of the Madonna," Jakób explained. "I understand the culmination of the celebration is a pilgrimage to Częstochowa."

"That's right," Haneczka added. "It coincides with the three-hundred-year commemoration of the crowning of the Black Madonna as 'queen of Poland.' Thousands of people will attend."

"The cathedral at Częstochowa is where the painting of the Black Madonna is?" Mischka asked.

"That's right," said Stan. He turned to his brother. "Why don't you speak to Drobner, Jakób? Maybe you can arrange something for us."

"I can try," Jakób hesitantly agreed, "but I don't know. He's a hard-bitten Communist. I doubt whether he sets much store by religious-patriotic gatherings."

"I didn't mean you should ask the man along!" Stan protested.

Jakób laughed. "It never crossed my mind!"

When they were walking back to the hospital's residences, Jakób asked Mischka if she would join them at the festival.

She was silent for a while. When she spoke, she sounded distant. "Why, Jakób?"

He stopped, gently held her back by the arm, and turned her so that she was looking at him. "It would mean a lot to me if you came."

Her gaze was inscrutable. She turned and walked on. "I don't know if I could get leave."

He nodded. She had been at the hospital for barely eight months. They walked slowly. A tram rumbled past. Boys chased one another down the street. A horse-drawn cart clip-clopped past them.

Everything looks so ordinary, so normal, Jakób thought, *but I don't feel the least bit normal. I have just started something that I want to see through.*

Or maybe he didn't want to. All of a sudden he didn't know.

"But would you like to come along?" he found himself asking.

She thought for a while before she spoke. "We have a good friendship, Jakób."

The words were like a blow to his stomach. "I understand," he said.

But when they reached her door, she said, "I'll see whether I can get the weekend free. It might not be a problem after all."

His heart lurched back in motion. *Calm down, Kowalski*, he told himself. "I'm glad. And I won't forget about the good friendship."

She smiled. "Thank you, Jakób."

When she didn't invite him in, he turned to leave. "I'll be going, then," he said.

When he had taken a few steps, he turned. She stood in the door-way and waved.

"You certainly don't make it easy for a man, Mischka Bòdis!"

She smiled. "I'm sorry!"

He took a few more steps and turned again. "Will you tell me about it someday?"

She was still smiling. "Go now," she said, but her voice was gentle.

The only thing that dampened his spirits that evening was a man leaning against a building across the street from Mischka's home, smoking. Jakób had caught glimpses of the shadowy stranger all week. This one wore worker's overalls, and he pretended not to watch Jakób, but Jakób knew better.

Haneczka packed a picnic for the train journey. Mischka brought sweets for the children. It was a jolly affair. Usually the kids saw their grandparents at Częstochowa only once a year, at Christmas.

The train was packed. Extra trains to Częstochowa had been arranged from all over Poland. "I don't know where all these people are going to stay," Haneczka said skeptically. "There isn't much accommo-dation in Częstochowa."

"I wonder where all of us are going to stay," Jakób said, suddenly anxious. Even with the room Turek had built on, their parents' house was hopelessly small for seven guests.

Haneczka shrugged. "Some of us can sleep in the stables, as we do at Christmas," she said.

I shouldn't have brought Mischka along, Jakób thought. *I can't expect her to sleep in the stables like a goat.*

"Sleeping in a stable would be kind of symbolic," Mischka said as if she read his mind.

"Stan, don't let that kid hang out of the window like that!" Haneczka said. "What if he falls?"

"Come," Jakób offered the boys. "I'll tell you the story of how the Blessed Virgin became queen of Poland."

"May I listen too?" asked Mischka. She looked cool and beautiful in her soft blue dress. She had tied a scarf around her hair for the journey, and her face was relaxed and open.

An overwhelming desire to touch her, to stroke her satiny skin, welled up in Jakób. He suppressed the urge with difficulty. "Only if you sit quietly and behave," he said, pretending to be strict.

The two older boys thought it was hilarious, but the youngest one frowned. "Don't speak to Aunt Mischka like that, Uncle Jakób."

Jakób laughed and began to tell the story. "Once upon a time, long ago"—he looked at Mischka—"in 1655, to be precise"—she nodded earnestly—"the king of Poland"—he looked at Mischka again—"more specifically King John Casimir"—she smiled slightly, nodding again—"waged war against the Russians and the Cossacks. Then the king of Sweden decided"—he looked at her—"more specifically King Charles the Tenth—"

"I'm listening, Jakób," she said, laughing.

"Who are you telling the story to, Uncle Jakób?" the oldest boy asked impatiently.

"Good question," Stan said from behind his newspaper.

Jakób went on, unfazed. "Then King Charles the Tenth of Sweden decided to attack Poland from the north. The Poles were totally outnumbered"—he waved his hands—"and within months all of Poland was under Swedish rule, except for a few cities that kept the invaders at bay. Among these cities was Częstochowa, where Grandpa and Grandma live. Behind the high ramparts of the Jasna Góra monastery, seventy monks and fewer than two hundred soldiers, led by Father Kordecki, fended off one attack after another for several weeks."

He looked at the three dark-eyed boys—the next generation of proud Poles. "Eventually their food ran out, their water ran out, and they had no more bandages or medicine. Still they didn't surrender. Every morning Father Kordecki knelt at the painting of the Black Madonna and asked the Blessed Virgin to protect them—not only them, but all of Poland. Then the men went back into battle!"

"And then, Uncle Jakób?" asked the middle boy, carried away.

"Later, when the tables were turned and the Polish soldiers had driven the Swedes and the Russians and Cossacks out of Polish territory, the heroic deeds of Father Kordecki and his group of monks became known all over the country. King John Casimir dedicated the country of Poland to the Virgin Mary, to thank her for returning Poland to the Polish people. Since then the Blessed Virgin has been our only queen." He looked at them earnestly. "That happened in August 1656, exactly three hundred years ago."

"I'm glad we're going to the festival," the oldest boy declared.

"Me too." Mischka smiled. "You're an excellent storyteller. Thank you, Jakób."

I had lots of practice and a very good little teacher, he thought. But he didn't say anything aloud.

————

The station at Częstochowa was crowded. People pushed and shoved and called out to one another. The streets were a teeming mass of people. In the wide Aleja Najświętszej Maryi Panny that ran through the heart of Częstochowa to the foot of Jasna Góra, not even a horse and buggy could make headway. There were hundreds of thousands of people—the newspaper estimated more than a million—in the streets and buildings, on the green hills, around the tall monastery walls. Everywhere people were pitching tents or erecting homemade shelters. The smoke of numerous fires was rising from the hills.

"This must be what Bethlehem looked like when there was no room at the inn for Joseph and the Holy Virgin," said the oldest boy. Jakób held his nephew's hand tightly. If a child got lost here, he'd never be found again. Jakób also carried Mischka's travel bag, while his own bag was slung over his shoulder. Mischka stayed close behind him. Stan and Haneczka were nowhere to be seen.

"Goodness, what a throng!" Mischka said. "I wonder where Haneczka and Stan are."

He shrugged. "They'll find their way home." Looking into her eyes, he said, "Mischka, my people are plain folk, small farmers. Our home . . ."

She put her finger to his lips. "Jakób, my parents are farmers, too, and I've slept in worse places than a stable. During the war I worked in the medical corps."

He let go of the boy's hand and put his arm around her shoulders. "You're amazing," he said.

From a distance he spotted his father and Turek in the vegetable plots. Monicka came out on the porch to greet them. "Mother is inside," she said.

Jakób stood back and allowed Mischka to enter first.

Each time he returned, the house seemed smaller, more dilapidated, more cluttered.

"Mother, this is my friend, Mischka Bòdis. This is my mother, Anastarja Kowalski."

Mischka held out her hand. "Good afternoon, Mrs. Kowalski."

His mother turned to him. "She's not Polish," she said.

Humiliation flooded him. "She's Hungarian, Mother. She lives and works in Poland now."

His mother turned back to Mischka. "What is your faith?"

Jakób felt himself grow cold. "Mother! Please!"

"I'm a Christian, Mrs. Kowalski," Mischka answered calmly. "A Protestant, but a Christian, just like you."

Jakób was furious. "Are you planning to make Mischka feel welcome, or should we return to Katowice straightaway?"

Mischka put her hand on his arm. "Don't, Jakób. Your mother wants what's best for you."

His anger abated somewhat. "Mischka is what's best for me," he said.

Anastarja didn't take Mischka's hand. "There's coffee on the stove. Help yourselves to bread and ham if you're hungry. I'm on my way to evening mass. There'll be soup for supper when I return."

On Sunday more than a million festivalgoers converged on Jasna Góra. Only invited guests, such as dignitaries of the Catholic Church, heads of state, important church officials from neighboring countries, even delegations from countries abroad, were allowed to pass through the monastery walls. Everyone else gathered on the surrounding hillsides.

With the children in mind, Monicka and Haneczka had packed picnic baskets. The men carried the baskets and blankets while the women tried to keep the children under control. Anastarja was the only family member absent from the group. She had left before sunrise to find herself a good place close to the wall.

"Shall we sit here?" Jakób asked Turek. "We'll have a good view of the proceedings."

"And we'll be able to hear!" said Stan. "Look at those huge amplifiers. The mass is going to be broadcast."

"It's as good a place as any other," Turek said indifferently.

Most festivalgoers, especially the women, were clad in the national costume: wide skirts trimmed with brightly colored embroidery or appliqué, matching vests, and white blouses with frills around the neck and sleeves. Many had flowers in their hair.

Monicka, Haneczka, and the children were all in costume, but the big Kowalski men had declined to wear the black gathered trousers, white shirts, and embroidered vests.

Mischka wore a simple white dress that set off her suntanned skin and gleaming black hair to perfection. Jakób couldn't keep his eyes off her.

"Jakób," she said with an embarrassed smile, "don't stare at me like that. You're making me uncomfortable."

"I apologize." For just a moment he averted his eyes. "I'm sorry, I've tried, but you're too beautiful."

"Thank you." She seemed to take him almost too seriously. Maybe he should be careful after all. Maybe the "good friendship" was more important to her than he had thought.

"I suggest you look at the wall now," she said, smiling, "or you'll miss the ceremony."

On top of the ancient ramparts an impressive procession was slowly moving toward them. The boys' choir led the way with their beautiful voices. They were followed by chanting nuns, rosaries strung through their fingers. Behind them came the important officials of the Catholic Church, clad in their ornate vestments. The Byzantine painting of the Black Madonna was held aloft as they paraded around the monastery so that everyone in the crowd could catch a glimpse of it.

The pilgrims sang one hymn after the other. The singing rippled over the green Polish hills and told the story of a nation anchored in its faith and its church, and of a people who would not allow strangers with foreign ideologies to sever the ropes that anchored them.

The people got to their feet and remained standing long after the procession had passed.

Jakób joined in the singing with his strong voice. He raised his face to the sky in praise of the Blessed Virgin who had protected Poland through the ages. He sent up a silent prayer that she would keep protecting them.

He felt Mischka's hand slip into his own. He looked down at her. Her eyes were shining with emotion. Suddenly he knew without a doubt that he wanted to share the rest of his life with her.

He drew her closer.

The procession came to a halt diagonally in front of Jakób and his party. Two priests placed the ancient painting on an altar. Beside the altar was an empty throne adorned with roses in red and white— Poland's national colors. It was a tacit allusion to the absence of the imprisoned archbishop, Cardinal Wyszynski.

The mass was broadcast over the huge speakers so that the sea of festivalgoers could feel themselves part of it.

Afterward, the archbishop of Łódź solemnly repeated King John Casimir's oath, dedicating every Polish heart and home to the Blessed Virgin. The pilgrims knelt and repeated his words: "O Queen of Poland! We renew the Pledge of our Fathers and promise that we will diligently strengthen and spread in our hearts and in the Polish Lands your honor and the worship of you, Mother of God."

After the proceedings ended, a hallowed atmosphere descended on the hills around Jasna Góra. People began to pack up, but the high spirits of the morning had vanished. It was as if each of those million people knew that Poland and the Polish Catholic Church were at a crossroads. Cardinal Wyszynski's sumptuous empty throne stayed behind on the wall when the procession departed.

"Does anybody here understand English? Does anyone speak English?"

Jakób turned. A thin, red-faced woman with tousled hair was looking around as if she was seeking help. "I speak a little English," he said. "Can I help you?"

She looked relieved. "Thank goodness!" she said. "I didn't know there was still a place anywhere in the world where people don't speak English!"

"How can I help you?" Jakób asked again.

"Could you explain to me what just happened here?" she asked.

In broken English Jakób explained to her the history behind the events and tried to answer her questions. "For centuries Poland has been trapped between Germany and Russia," he explained. "We've been trampled on, we've even been erased from the world map, but Polish nationalism breeds a quality of patriot who always gets up again to fight back."

The woman seemed interested. She wrote down every bit of information, asked his name, even wanted to take a photo of him.

"You have strong feelings about this," she said at the end of their conversation.

"Everyone here does, I'm sure you can see that. What happened here today is a testimony of the people's commitment to their faith. Poland won't bow to the Communists, you'll see."

When he joined the rest of his family for the walk back home, Mischka asked, "Who was that?"

"A British tourist," answered Jakób. "She was impressed by the proceedings but didn't have a clue what it was about."

"Then I'm glad you could help her," said Mischka.

"I hope she's just a tourist, brother," Stan said seriously.

———

The sun set behind the green hills and the clouds cast the golden glow back to earth. A cold breeze came up. Jakób noticed that Mischka was rubbing her arms. "Walk closer to me, I'll keep you warm," he said and opened his arm.

With his arm around her shoulder, he held her against him. Her slender body was soft against his own. "Better?" he asked.

"Much better."

They walked slowly, alone in the crowd as his brothers' families hurried back to the farm. The hills darkened, and the sun slipped over the horizon in a red blaze.

"Did you like it? The ceremony?"

"Very much," she answered. She looked up at him. "Thank you for bringing me."

He stopped. "Mischka?"

"Mm?"

He placed his hands around her face and raised it to his own. "I'm going to kiss you," he warned her.

"I know." She smiled.

He felt his heart beat faster. He tasted her mouth, shy at first, unsure. Then her lips parted slightly, and he felt his body react. Her breathing quickened, he smelled her delicate perfume, he tasted her lips. He felt her body begin to respond. It stirred up a strange mixture of emotions inside him: ecstasy, excitement . . .

Then he felt her withdraw. He released her at once, but he still held her face between his hands. "You're beautiful, Mischka," he said hoarsely. Then he let her go.

She leaned against him. "What's happening to us, Jakób?" she asked.

"We're cultivating our good friendship," he answered with a smile.

She laughed softly, happily.

———

The next Friday Drobner called Jakób to his office. He didn't welcome him or invite him to sit down as usual, but came straight to the point.

"Why are you being watched, Jakób?"

Jakób felt as if he had been doused with icy water. Drobner's expression was equally cold.

"I think I was watched for a while after we returned from Poznań, sir," he answered calmly. "I doubt whether it's still the case."

"Why were you being watched then?"

Jakób pushed his fingers through his black hair. "On my way to the trade fair I found myself in the workers' march to the city hall. I witnessed an incident involving a young boy. I offered to testify for him."

"For a boy? Against the secret police?" his chief asked. His voice was as chilly as his eyes.

"Yes, Mr. Drobner. I don't have a choice," Jakób answered resolutely.

"Is there no other reason why you're being watched?" asked Drobner. "Because I assure you, they have not stopped."

"None at all," said Jakób.

Drobner nodded and sat down behind his desk. He sounded worried now. "Take care. You don't want the Party to find anything against you. You're a brilliant young man; there's a bright future ahead of you."

"Thank you, sir," said Jakób. "I'll be careful."

A week later Stan came to his drawing board. "There's a problem at my plant I'd like you to take a look at. Later, when most of the men have gone home." He left without explaining.

Jakób frowned. A feeling of impending disaster took hold of him. Something was wrong. The correct procedure was for Stan to fill out an application form, after which a designated engineer would attend to his problem. Jakób couldn't think of any problem he could help Stan with. He had no expertise in Stan's field.

It was almost dark when Jakób set off for Stan's workshop.

"What's the problem?" he asked when he arrived.

"I'm not happy with this machine," said Stan, crossing to one of the big machines. "I'd appreciate it if you could open it up and take a look."

"I—" Jakób began.

"Open it," Stan ordered softly.

They knelt beside the machine. Jakób unscrewed a bolt. He had no idea what he was doing or how to operate the machine. "Now this one," Stan said brusquely.

Jakób loosened another bolt.

"The problem lies deeper inside—Francis Rzepecki contacted me—keep looking," said Stan.

A shock went through Jakób. Francis Rzepecki of the Home Army? He belonged to a different time, when they had fought the Russians just as hard as the Germans. "I didn't know he was still alive," he said softly.

"Can you see anything?" Stan asked loudly and got to his feet.

"What do you think is wrong here?" Jakób motioned for Stan to bend down again.

"He says there was an article in a British newspaper about the things you said at the festival. With your photo, large as life. And the same article has appeared in newspapers worldwide."

The British tourist with the wild hair. On the green hills outside Częstochowa.

Jakób got up slowly. He looked around. Here and there workers were standing around in groups. Nothing seemed out of the ordinary. "What are we going to do about this?" he asked.

"It won't just disappear," answered Stan. "I'm afraid to carry on with production. It could be dangerous."

"Do you really think so?" asked Jakób.

"I'm positive," said Stan.

Jakób bent beside the machine again. Stan crouched next to him. "Francis suggests that you get documents, in case you have to flee."

"I'll never run."

"He could get what you need." Stan got up. "Well, at least you know now what the problem is," he said. "You'll have to think of a solution."

Jakób got up too. "I will," he said. "I don't think there's any immediate danger. You can carry on with production."

Stan shrugged. "If you think so. But the responsibility is yours if something goes wrong. And things do go wrong, listen to what I'm telling you."

———

When he told Mischka that evening, she turned white.

"Jakób, you have no idea what these people are capable of!"

"The Communists?"

She nodded. "Don't do anything to antagonize them."

He folded her in his arms. She was rigid. "I have to testify at the boy's trial, Mischka."

"Don't, I beg you! You'll go up against the secret police!"

He stroked her hair, at a loss how to comfort her. If he, Jakób Kowalski, was to remain true to himself, he had to testify that the child was innocent, a victim of circumstances.

"Mischka, there's something else we have to discuss."

She stepped back, held up her hands. "Don't! Please, don't!"

"Someone from the Home Army has offered to arrange documents for me if I need them."

She lowered her head into her hands. "If you have to flee." Her voice sounded dead.

"It's premature. I didn't want to mention it now. But . . . I want to share my life with you, Mischka. I love you."

"Jakób—"

"I know it's too soon. It's probably quite unnecessary. I believe we're being paranoid, but I must know . . . in case . . . I'm not making much sense, am I?"

She smiled slightly. "I love you too, Jakób."

A strange happiness settled inside him. A wave of tenderness washed over him. He didn't speak, just held out his hands to her.

She took his hand and pressed it to her face.

When he could trust his voice again, he asked, "Can I arrange documents for you as well?"

"My documents are fine, Jakób. No one is looking for me."

The trials began at the end of September. Right from the start a distinction was made between the workers who had been simply protesting and those who had committed crimes. The criminal trials took place in Poznań, while the political trials were moved to Warsaw.

"I don't know how objective the media reports are with press censorship the way it is," Jakób remarked to Stan. They saw each other only at work these days. Jakób didn't want to expose Stan's family, especially the boys, to unnecessary danger. Even at work they had to find excuses to talk so that their encounters would not raise suspicion.

"Francis says your documents will be ready next week," said Stan.

"I'm not going anywhere," Jakób said firmly.

"One doesn't always have a choice."

"I believe one usually does. Anyway, if I'm forced to go, Mischka is coming as well."

Stan looked at him skeptically. "This is no time for a romantic interlude, brother."

"It isn't a romantic interlude." Jakób ran his hand through his hair. "If she doesn't come, I might as well rot in a Russian jail."

Stan gave a wry smile. "I never thought I'd live to hear you speak like this! You'll probably be taking her to the ballet next!"

He didn't tell Stan that the tickets had already been bought.

———

Professor Chalasinski of the University of Łódź, Jakób read, was one of the first expert witnesses at the trial. He told the court that the march had started as a peaceful protest. Initially an almost devout atmosphere had reigned, as proved by the singing of songs and the national anthem. Then the protesters were stirred up by rumors that the secret police had fired at children, and they were further provoked by the arrival of tanks. Feelings ran high—the fiery Polish patriotism took over, so that the initial protest turned into a violent uprising that spread like wildfire.

The professor said he doubted whether anyone could have defused the situation after that.

It shouldn't be too hard to prove that the boy was a victim of circumstances, Jakób thought. And when this was over, he'd make very certain that he didn't get himself involved in any further trouble.

———

"Our young people refuse to be crushed by the Russians," Jakób said to Mischka one evening. He folded the newspaper. "Come and sit with me on the sofa," he said.

She closed the shutters and turned away from the window. "Your friend is waiting out there under the tree," she said.

"It will all be over after the trial." He tried to reassure her. "And before you say anything else, Mischka, I'll be very careful. I have too much to lose."

She nestled under his arm. "I'm glad. I'm on night shift for the next two weeks. We won't see much of each other."

He groaned. "I might not survive," he complained.

She laughed happily.

"I'll probably have to go to Warsaw sometime during the next two weeks for the trial," Jakób said. "And when it's over, we'll put the past behind us and talk about our future. Together."

He felt that spring was in the air. *Kowalski*, he thought, *you're a sad case—it's October—autumn, the beginning of winter. Spring is a long way off.*

But his heart did not listen to his head.

Over the next month unrest in Poland grew. University students organized a revolution against Stalinism. Workers demanded that the dethroned Gomulka, a politician with ties to the old Polish Worker's Party, be reinstated as first secretary of the Politburo in hopes that he would break away from the Soviet bloc.

Gomulka is not our salvation, Jakób thought. *He's just another Communist who will keep Poland under the Communist yoke.*

Soviet troops were advancing on Warsaw. A Russian delegation arrived to oversee talks about the appointment of a Polish leader. Ships from the Soviet Baltic Fleet arrived near the Bay of Gdańsk.

When Jakób heard the news that Gomulka had been reinstated, he realized that the Soviets had turned Gomulka into a national hero. The Polish people were united behind him. They believed he had shown the Russians that the Poles would not be intimidated. Students and workers gathered to show their support for their leader.

Jakób was filled with an intense longing for Mischka. He wanted to speak to her, discuss the state of affairs, just be with her. But she was on night shift. He decided to drop in on Stan and Haneczka after all. He put on his coat and went outside. But when he saw the man under the tree, he took a walk around the block and returned to his room.

He was trapped, like a caged animal.

Because he was going to testify on behalf of an innocent boy.

Against the secret police.

And because he had spoken against the Communists to a British tourist.

———

In October Jakób was summoned to the trials in Warsaw. On the train he read more disturbing news. The Moscow paper *Pravda* launched a sharp attack against Poland, and the Sunday paper from Katowice reported that anti-Communist protests were on the increase, especially in Kraków. Gomulka's dilemma, the paper speculated, was how to take Poland forward without alienating Russia.

Poland's dilemma, Jakób thought, was that Gomulka wanted to replace one Communist regime with another.

It was impossible to relax in the train. If only all trains didn't smell the same. The pungent, smoky smell reminded him of other journeys he preferred to forget.

In Warsaw he found a cheap hotel within walking distance of the court building.

That evening Radio Warsaw reported, "It is spring in October, a spring of renewed hope and renewed national pride. Poland is inventing its own form of Polish Socialism. We have crossed our Rubicon. Nothing can stop the transformation of the Polish Socialist Revolution now."

———

On Monday Jakób spent the day on a hard, wooden bench outside the courtroom, waiting to testify. A large group of young people had destroyed the offices of the Polish-Soviet Friendship Society, someone said. They were looting shops, damaging buildings and posters, overturning vehicles, creating havoc.

Jakób waited patiently on his bench.

On Tuesday the trials progressed even more slowly. All those involved seemed more interested in the political landscape than in events in the courtroom.

Gomulka himself spoke on Radio Polski: "I'm calling on the workers and youths not to do anything that could possibly damage Soviet-Polish relationships. I assure the Polish people that it will be a priority of the new government to rectify the mistakes of the past. I ask all generals, officers, soldiers, every factory worker and hospital clerk, every student, tram driver, and farmer to respect our ties with the Soviet Union, and to reinforce them where possible."

An exceptional weariness washed over Jakób.

The local radio station at Gdańsk reported that a Soviet-minded group had compiled a blacklist of anti-Communists to be presented to Gomulka.

Jakób waited and waited on the hard bench outside the courtroom. At six he returned to the hotel.

That evening Radio Warsaw reported that the Hungarians in Budapest had begun to protest against the Russians in support of the Poles.

Shortly after dinner Jakób received a phone call from Mr. Drobner. He took the call at the reception desk.

"Have you testified yet?" asked his employer.

"No, but I'll definitely testify tomorrow, probably in the afternoon," Jakób answered. He tried to assess his boss's tone of voice but the line was unclear.

"Come straight back to Katowice afterward," said Drobner.

"I'll be on the evening train, sir."

———

Wednesday a fine drizzle trickled down Warsaw's buildings, forming puddles on the tarred streets and concrete sidewalks. Jakób didn't take the stand until late afternoon.

It took only five minutes for the judge to rule that the boy had been an innocent victim of circumstance. The court was adjourned. More interesting things were happening in the outside world.

Jakób walked back to his hotel through the wet streets. He felt stripped, completely drained.

He wanted to get back to Katowice as soon as possible. To be with his people. His family. Mischka.

He hastily packed his bag and settled his account with the homely hotel receptionist. "Are you on your way back to Katowice?" she asked.

"Yes," he replied, "on the evening train."

He walked down the main street to the station.

From a distance he saw the crowd that had gathered in front of the Palace of Culture, waiting to hear Gomulka speak.

Jakób looked straight ahead and continued on his way.

He heard the crowd cheer when their new leader appeared on the balcony.

Amplifiers carried Gomulka's voice across the square and into the surrounding streets.

"After our recent meeting with the Soviet delegation, we each have come to a better understanding of our respective situations," said the new Polish leader. His guiding principles were Communist, he explained, but they differed from those of Soviet Communism. He believed Poland should remain in the Soviet bloc and maintain strong ties with Russia. It was the only way Poland could survive.

"There must be no obstacles in the path of collaboration between Poland and Russia. All efforts to incite anti-Soviet feelings will be crushed," Gomulka said. "All persons with anti-Communist sentiments will be arrested and brought to trial."

Jakób's feet carried him away from the square.

He didn't buy a newspaper at the station. He didn't glance at the posters on the walls of the stations they were passing through.

He didn't think of anything. He tried to think of nothing. He just wanted to get home.

It was after eleven when the train stopped at a station outside of Katowice. A child, a young girl, got on and sat down opposite Jakób. What was a child doing alone on a train at this late hour? Jakób wondered absently.

As the train pulled out of the station, the child said, "Don't look at me, Uncle Jakób. Keep looking through the window."

Shock jolted through Jakób's body. The voice belonged to Stan's oldest boy.

With an enormous effort he managed to keep his eyes on the window.

"Daddy said to tell you not to get off in Katowice. They're waiting for you, the soldiers. Keep going. I'll leave this bag when I get off. Take it."

The child got up and stood waiting at the door to get off at the next station.

Anger rose up in Jakób. He found it hard to remain seated. Who had known he would be on that particular train? Mr. Drobner? The homely hotel receptionist? Someone who had been watching him?

As the train pulled out of the station, he resolved to get off in Katowice after all. He refused to be intimidated. He would not flee from the Communists.

He would get off and go to Mischka. They would speak about tomorrow, not about today or yesterday.

But Stan and Haneczka had risked the life of their son to warn him.

He opened the bag left behind by his nephew. Inside were his documents: a new passport in the name of Józef Nikolajzcski, with his own photograph. There was money as well, Czech korun and German marks. Not a lot, but enough to start him off. And a certificate dated 30 June 1946, confirming that a degree in metallurgical engineering had been conferred on Jakób Kowalski by the University of Kraków.

He gave a cynical smile. If anyone searched the bag, his name was in plain sight on this document. He would have to hide it well, along with his existing identity card.

The bag also contained a letter addressed to him.

My darling Jakób,

My heart is filled with sorrow, but there's no other way. I have to stop running, I know that now. I belong in Hungary—my parents are still there, my brothers too. It's where I'll be returning as soon as I have worked out my notice month at the hospital. I can't do anything else.

I fled from Hungary, just as you have to flee from Poland now. But there's a big difference. I know. My husband refused to flee, and he paid for it in the cruelest way imaginable.

Jakób, get as far away from these people as possible. Go to a place where you won't find any of them, and start a new life. Forget about someone called Mischka—consider our friendship an interlude to show us both that life can be worthwhile.

Don't contact your family, you'll be putting their lives in danger. The same goes for me.

I'm sorry, Jakób, I know you loved me. It has been a privilege for me to know you.

Your friend,
Mischka

That was all.

———◦———

Jakób walked. He walked in bright daylight, he walked in dim moonlight, he walked in rain, over cliffs, through valleys. His steel-hard body carried him in a westerly direction. Always west, toward the mountains between Poland and Czechoslovakia a hundred miles away.

He ate when he was hungry, he drank when he was thirsty, he seldom rested. He avoided all signs of people. He wasn't aware of when he left Poland and entered Czechoslovakia. He left everything behind. Everything but his credentials . . . including the yellowed newspaper cutting of a small girl with a broad smile and a ribbon in her hair. It was somewhere in one of his books.

Not even during the 1944 uprising in Warsaw had he felt so dead.

11

"Where are you off to now?" Karin asked from under the covers. "It's cold, you'll freeze!"

Grietjie laughed and put on her coat. "A person doesn't freeze that easily, roomie. My Polish lesson has been moved to today. Mrs. Bronski is going away for the weekend, so she won't be here Friday afternoon."

"I don't know why you insist on learning those pagan languages," Karin mumbled and snuggled deeper under the blankets. "Russian, Polish. The next thing you know, uniformed police will turn up to arrest you for being a Commie or something."

Grietjie stuffed her books into her shoulder bag and looked around the room. "Have you seen my gloves?"

"On the chair."

"One day I'm going to make lots of money as a translator. I'm off. See that there's coffee when I get back," Grietjie said over her shoulder.

"Oh, remind me to ask you something later. Francois wants me to ask," Karin called after her.

Grietjie hurried through the cold streets of Pretoria to the nearest bus stop. It was only six street blocks to the Bronskis' home. She usually walked, but today was exceptionally cold.

She was looking forward to her lesson. Mrs. Bronski was a lovely lady. She always spoiled her only student with some kind of Polish delicacy. She was very proud of Grietjie's rapid progress. "You wouldn't believe she's been taking lessons for only eighteen months," she liked to tell her Polish friends or her husband. "She speaks like a native."

"Don't forget, I used to speak Polish before I left Germany," Grietjie hastened to say.

"And, would you believe it, the child is learning Russian too, with Mr. Ulyanov." But Mrs. Bronski was careful who she told, because most of her friends didn't want to hear the word *Russian* mentioned. After all, the Russians were the ones who had driven them from their native country.

When Grietjie returned toward evening, Karin was still in bed, reading. "It's just about time for the supper gong. Are you coming?" asked Grietjie.

Karin groaned. "What do you think is worse, freezing or starving to death?"

"Don't talk like that!" Grietjie scolded. "There's the gong. Are you coming?"

On their way to the dining room, Grietjie asked, "What did Francois want you to ask me?"

"Oh yes. He's doing an honors degree in psychology this year, and they have to do a case study."

"So?"

"He wants to know if you'll be his case study."

Grietjie stopped in her tracks. "Me? A case study? Do I look like a nutcase?" she asked.

"Wait, roomie," Karin protested. "It's just . . . you've known hard times, during the war and so on, and your mother and your family died and all that. And you handled it so well. It's not a study of someone who has a screw loose—you came through it in one piece."

Grietjie lifted her chin. "I don't want to talk about things I've put behind me, Karin," she said firmly.

"He just needs you to talk—not about what happened, more about how—"

"No, definitely not. Tell your brother that's my final answer."

Behind them, the Dragon spoke. "When you two ladies have sorted out your personal affairs, would you allow me to pass, please?"

The Dragon was their residence head. Her name said it all.

———

On Friday evening a first-year knocked on their door. "A visitor for Miss Grietjie," she said.

"Where are your manners?" Karin asked crossly. They were second-years now and commanded respect.

"Good evening, Miss Karin, Miss Grietjie," said the girl before making herself scarce.

"The first-years are cheeky!" Karin grumbled. "Who's your date?"

"Gerrit. And he's not my date, we're just going for coffee. He has a test tomorrow."

"Poor science students. A test on a Saturday, I ask you!" Karin sighed and switched on the immersion element to boil water in the enamel jug. "Why didn't he bring Kobus along? We could all have gone out for coffee."

Poor Karin, Grietjie thought as she went downstairs to the foyer. She was in love with Kobus, but Grietjie knew her brother wasn't the least bit interested.

But it was Francois, not Gerrit, who was waiting in the foyer. "I've told Karin I won't talk to you," she said.

"Hello, Grietjie."

"Yes, hello to you too. I'm still not going to talk to you."

Francois nodded slowly. He seemed amused. "Okay, I get the message. But seeing that I'm here now, could we go out for coffee?"

"No."

"Oh?"

Grietjie shrugged. "I'm waiting for Gerrit. He'll be here any moment."

Francois nodded again. "I see."

"I'm not going out for coffee with you on any other day either, Francois. I won't be your guinea pig!"

—•—

On Sunday after church Grandpa John's big black car picked her and Kobus up and took them to lunch at his beautiful home. They knew they could expect a first-class Sunday lunch with the best wine and a selection of desserts—enough to take some back for their friends at their respective residences. In winter there was a fire in the fireplace, beautiful music, and lively conversation. Sometimes the conversations were deep, because Grandpa John was an excellent listener, and sometimes it was just idle chatter, because Grandpa John loved to laugh. Or they would ask his advice, because he knew everything.

"I hear you've broken up with Sandra," Grietjie ventured on their way to Grandpa John's house.

"Mm." Kobus's head almost touched the roof of the big car. He was as tall as their father.

"I thought the two of you were so close."

"She required too much E.M."

"E.M.?"

"Emotional maintenance."

"You men are all the same!" Grietjie said crossly.

"Mm."

It was no good being annoyed with him, she thought as the bare highveld landscape between Johannesburg and Pretoria flashed past the car window. She turned to him. "Do you have your eye on anyone else?"

"Mm. Quite a few."

Beast! She waited a few moments. "Why don't you ask Karin out? She's really very nice."

He looked at her with that expression a brother reserves for his dim-witted little sister. "Grietjie, your idea of very nice and my idea of super fine are poles apart."

"But if you—"

"Not my type, thank you very much."

Grietjie made no attempt to hide her irritation. "Men are animals! Morons!"

"Mm."

She didn't speak to him again until they stopped at Grandpa John's big gate. Kobus got out to open it.

Grandpa John stood waiting for them on the veranda. He stood up straight and walked briskly despite his eighty-six winters. His thick silver hair gleamed in the weak winter sun.

"Come inside where it's nice and warm. Grietjie, you're more striking every time I see you."

She laughed and put her arms around her grandpa. "And you're the most charming gentleman on the planet!" she said sincerely. "They don't make them like you anymore." She said it for Kobus to hear.

Grandpa John drew Grietjie closer while he held out his hand to Kobus. "Hello, my boy. How's the rugby coming along?"

Maybe Grandpa John was a little like other men after all, Grietjie thought as they went through to his study. Men talked about rugby first, then about their studies or work, then about girls.

At dinner Grandpa John was the perfect host. Grietjie sat to his left in what used to be Ouma Susan's place. She played hostess and rang the small silver bell for the plates to be cleared. She also served the dessert. Some Sundays they were joined by Uncle Peter and his English wife, Diana. And sometimes by their English cousins, Britney and Sarah, and their English husbands.

But today it was just the three of them and that was the best. They talked about the rugby season and the ensemble group Grietjie sang in and their studies and the approaching winter vacation. Grandpa John was preparing to visit the farm, where it was warmer. He had delayed his trip in order to have lunch with his two favorite youngsters today.

"This is a thousand times better than the food we get at res," Kobus said appreciatively, helping himself to a third serving of meat and baked potatoes.

"Our food isn't too bad, but the Dragon is unspeakable. Shall I tell you of her latest mission?"

"What's that?" her grandfather asked.

"She's forbidden us to wear sandals that expose our little toes. She says we're out to seduce men."

Grandpa John laughed.

"Kobus, do you find a girl's pinky toe seductive?" she asked.

He looked up. "What are you on about?"

"The Dragon. And our pinky toes. You haven't been listening. Do you go weak in the knees at the sight of a girl's pinky toe?"

He looked at her as if she had lost her marbles. "I can think of many other parts of the female anatomy a lot more seductive than pinky toes!"

"Kobus! Grandpa, tell Kobus a gentleman doesn't talk like that in the company of a lady!"

But Grandpa John was laughing too much. "You opened that door yourself, my dear."

Men, she decided—*deep down they're all the same.*

After lunch Kobus fell asleep on the sofa. "He was probably out until all hours last night," she told Grandpa John as they strolled through his beautiful garden, which he maintained exactly as Ouma Susan had laid it out more than forty years earlier.

He nodded, pretending to be serious. "He's a blot on the family name! You, on the other hand, stayed in to study, like the model student you are?"

She began to laugh. "Not quite, Grandpa John!"

"I'm relieved to hear that."

"But exams start next week. I'll have to work really hard. It's going to be disgustible."

"Disgustible, yes." They sat on a bench in the sun. "But after that you'll be on vacation?"

"Yes, and that's going to be wonderful." She remembered something. "Grandpa John, we have a history assignment to complete during the vacation, and we have to use primary sources. That's when someone actually lived through something and can tell you about it firsthand. Or we can use original, official documents of the time. Will you tell me about the Anglo-Boer War?"

He nodded slowly. "Or the miners' strike in 1922?" he suggested.

"Ye-es, but you were one of the mine bosses, and that probably wouldn't look so good."

He laughed. "I suppose not, especially to the University of Pretoria. But remember, in the Anglo-Boer War I fought on the wrong side."

"That's true," she said. "But you ended up marrying a Boer girl."

"Is this the historian speaking, or the novelist?"

"The historian for the time being, unfortunately. But one day I'll write a book, one day soon, you'll see."

"I know you will," he said. "I'll tell you about the war, but it's not a pleasant subject. There's never a winner, only losers."

She thought about his words. "That's true, Grandpa John. Maybe it should be the motto of my assignment."

"Your motto as a historian?"

She sighed. "You're right again. I must remain neutral and objective." On the spur of the moment she said, "Someone asked me to talk with him about my childhood, probably my experiences during the war as well. He wants to use me as a case study for a research paper in psychology."

Grandpa John looked thoughtful. "What did you say?"

"I refused. I don't want to talk about it, Grandpa."

"Why not, Grietjie?"

"There are some things only I know about."

He nodded. After a while he said, "You still have dreams. Nightmares."

It was a statement, not a question. She hadn't even realized he knew.

"Yes, Grandpa." Softly, because she was reluctant to admit to a weakness.

Karin also knew. It couldn't be helped. That had to be why Francois wanted to study her.

They sat in silence for a while. Then Grandpa John said, "In time buried hurt becomes an abscess. It must rupture and form a scab before it can heal. Or be carefully lanced by someone who knows what he's doing."

"But it always leaves a scab," she said. "And when the scab comes off, the scar remains."

"Not if it's treated right." He thought for a while. "Besides, sometimes a scar gives character."

She thought about his words. "The scar is already there, isn't it, Grandpa?"

He nodded slowly, earnestly. "And the strength of character." His voice was strong, certain.

She snuggled up to him and he put his arm around her. He was still big Grandpa John, even though he was so very old. "I don't want to be just another case study," she said later. "It sounds so . . . weak."

Grandpa John laughed softly. "Our beautiful little German," he said and held her closer.

That same evening she phoned Francois. "Come and talk if you want to," she said. "But not now, after the vacation. This week I have to cram."

He groaned. "I'd hoped we could start this term."

"Definitely not," she said firmly. "I'm going on vacation first."

And I need to plan, she thought as she went back to her room. Because she certainly couldn't tell him everything.

The vacation was a string of lukewarm, bushveld winter days in the big sandstone house with her mother and Grandpa John, or out in the open with her father and Kobus. It was a string of cool winter nights around the table with everyone she loved, playing games in front of the fireplace, listening to stories told by her father or Grandpa John, or anecdotes of student life told by Kobus and herself—the edited versions, of course.

Three weeks flew by like a dream. Grandpa John would be spending the rest of the winter on the farm, so Grietjie and Kobus caught the cold, bumpy milk train back to an icy Pretoria. Their parents took them to the station, where they said good-bye.

She hated the station, the good-byes. She hated the train. It was a dragon with foul breath that swallowed her and spat her out in a distant place.

"A train is a disgustible thing," she told Kobus, who was lounging on the opposite seat. "And you'll have a crick in your neck by the time we get there."

"Mm. You're in a foul mood, aren't you? Let's see what's in the basket."

"Can't you think of anything but your stomach?"

He sat up, put the basket in his lap, and opened the lid. "Mm!" he said.

"If you eat all the food now, you won't survive until we get to Pretoria. And remember, some of it is for supper, because the residence won't be serving meals yet."

"Mm." He took out a chicken drumstick, a sandwich, and a hard-boiled egg and tucked in with relish.

"And some of it is mine! For tonight as well!" she protested.

Men, she decided, were a strange, thick-skulled, ball-kicking species no one on earth could have a sensible conversation with. She was very, very glad her brother had no interest in dating her dear roommate. She must remember to tell Karin that.

On the first Saturday night after the vacation, Francois and Grietjie sat in the corner of a small café, eating toasted sandwiches. They would order coffee later. It promised to be a long evening. "I can't feed you every time, d'you hear?" he warned her. "Tomorrow it's French fries in the park."

"French fries are fine. On with the interrogation." The sooner they got it over with, the better. She should never have agreed to talk to him, but it was too late to back off now.

"First I need some basic information about your background," he said. "Then we'll get to what I'm really interested in. But just tell me as much as you're comfortable with."

It was the basic information that concerned her most. "You must understand, everything is rather fuzzy. I was really young when the war broke out. I can't remember a time before the war."

"You'd be surprised what young children can remember," he said, opening a notebook. "What was your name?"

"Gretl Schmidt." He wrote. "Schmidt ends in a *t*," she said.

"Thanks. How old were you when the war broke out?"

"I suppose . . ." She made a quick calculation. "Germany invaded Poland ten days before my second birthday."

He looked up and smiled. "You're exact, aren't you, Miss Historian?"

"Yes, I am. So you'd better get your facts straight, Mr. Psychologist."

"I've told you you can check everything I write," he reassured her. "Where did you live?"

"I have no idea. If I knew, we might be able to trace my family."

"Did you move away from your place of birth?"

"Yes. My father was an SS soldier who died on the battlefield in 1941. I have a letter the government sent my mother, if you need a primary source."

"I doubt it, but thanks. You're my primary source."

"I'm glad I'm no longer a case study!"

He smiled and looked at his notes. "And then? After your father's death?"

"We went to live with my grandmother. My mother's mother. I don't know where. And I don't know her name and surname. She was just Oma."

"And your grandfather?"

She shrugged. "He wasn't there. He might have died already. I never knew him."

"Who else lived there?"

"My grandmother, my mother, my sister, and me."

"Tell me about your sister."

"Elza. Her name was Elza. She was quite a bit older than I, maybe eight years or more."

"No other siblings?"

"No."

Something niggled at the back of her mind.

"Did you stay with your grandmother until the end of the war?"

This was where she had to take care with what she said. "No, we had to go away, to a town far from there. I don't know where."

"Why, Grietjie?"

"I don't know. They evacuated everyone from the place where Oma used to live."

"And then?"

"We lived in a house with other people. I don't know who they were."

The ghetto. Fortunately she remembered very little of the ghetto—only the lice. And details about a vermin plague in a Jewish ghetto during wartime had no bearing on how she had psychologically survived the war, she decided. So there was no point in mentioning it.

"Did you stay there until the end of the war?"

"Until my mother and grandmother died in an explosion."

He wrote for a while, as if he was wary of asking anything else. "Fire away," she said. "While I'm trapped here, you might as well make the best use of the opportunity."

He looked up. His face was very serious. "Tell me if you've had enough for the day, Grietjie."

"I will," she said.

"The explosion . . . How did it happen?"

"A kind of bomb, I think."

"And you weren't with them?"

"No. Elza and I were some distance away. But I heard the explosion, and I saw it."

"Did you know your mother and grandmother . . . I mean . . ."

"Only later." Much later. "In the beginning I thought we'd find them again."

"And Elza?"

"She knew, I think. She died shortly afterward. I think of tuberculosis; that's what someone said."

Jakób. Long, long ago.

She mustn't think about Jakób. He was stashed in a deep drawer for safekeeping. Along with her wooden cross.

"And then, Grietjie?" His voice sounded odd.

"Then someone found me. And took me to an orphanage. In Kiel."

And, just like that, she built a bridge that spanned four years.

"And did you stay there until the end of the war?"

"Until the German Children's Fund came to look for suitable orphans to place with South African parents."

Now it was easy. She told him about the selection process, the journey from Kiel to Pretoria, the meeting with her new parents, the school, church, everything. Also about Grandpa John and Kobus. Up to the present.

It was almost eleven when she glanced at her watch. "I must get back to my res at once!" she cried. "If I'm not there by eleven, the Dragon will lock me out!"

"Up you get!" he said.

She held on tightly while he pedaled his bike so fast that the wind whistled past her ears. They skidded to a halt at her residence with two minutes to spare. "That was fun!" She laughed.

"Great fun!" he said. "Especially the way you clung to me."

"No, you fool!" she protested. "I'm talking about the wind in my hair!"

He laughed. "See you tomorrow, about noon?"

"Remember the French fries! You promised!"

"Will you be coming inside, Miss Neethling, or do you plan to sleep on the porch tonight?" came the cold voice of the Dragon.

Grietjie slipped in. The big door was locked behind her.

The deception was easy, she thought as she lay awake in the small hours. Much easier than she had expected. Luckily Francois wasn't a history buff and had no clue about dates that didn't correlate.

But when she finally fell asleep, the nightmare returned. The fire blazed so high that she couldn't see a thing.

———

It was a lovely, warm winter afternoon. They lay on a blanket in Magnolia Park, sucking their fingers to make sure that they got every last bit of tastiness from the French fries. The sky was pale blue and a few fleecy clouds drifted by.

"This is the life," Francois said contentedly.

"We're actually here to work," Grietjie reminded him.

"You're right, I suppose." He sat up and took out his notebook. "Aren't you going to sit up?"

"No, I can talk while I'm lying down. *You* have to sit up to write."

"Okay. I'll start at the beginning and ask you how you felt when certain things happened. Right?"

"You're testing my memory!" she said.

He looked at his notes. "How did you feel when your father died?"

She thought for a moment. "I don't know. I doubt whether I understood what had happened. I barely knew him—I was two when he left for the front. No, I don't think it affected me."

"And the rest of your family?"

She thought. "My mother stopped laughing. And cried a lot, I remember. And we went to live with Oma."

"How did you feel about that?"

"I loved it." She lay on her back, watching the clouds. A small cloud was chasing a bigger one. "Her house was at the edge of a forest. We picked berries. Any moment now that small cloud is going to take a bite out of the big one."

"For crying out loud, Grietjie! I can't have an intelligent conversation with you while you're flat on your back."

"Not my problem," she said, but she rolled onto her side. "What else do you want to know?"

He sighed. "What was your grandmother like?"

"Strong. Not a crybaby. She was strict with my mother." She thought for a moment while he wrote. "I think my mother lost hope after a while."

"Why?"

"Because of the war."

"No, I mean, why do you think that?"

"I don't remember her doing anything but sitting and crying. Not so much while we were living with Oma, but later, when we had to go to the other place."

To the ghetto. Phantoms against a dark background.

"And your sister?"

"She was kind. We slept in the same bed. She held me when the planes with the bombs came over so that I wouldn't be afraid. But *I* wasn't afraid, *she* was."

"What else do you remember about the time in the other town?"

"We had to black out the windows at night. We all lived in one room. Oma struggled to get food. Sometimes I stood in a long line with her. I don't really remember much else."

Except the lice.

"Can you remember being hungry?"

"Oma taught me to think about other things. You can think away the hunger so that after a while you don't get hungry anymore. Thirst is a bigger problem."

The train. Filling its belly with water. The slurping dogs.

She mustn't think about the train.

"I'm not helping you much, Francois. If you like, I'll get you a book on the Second World War. It'll probably give you more information."

"We'll see," he answered vaguely. "The explosion—can you tell me about it?"

"There isn't much to tell, Francois. I thought I heard planes, maybe I was wrong. Then I heard the blast and saw the red glow. I looked for shelter; it was all I could think of."

"You didn't realize the explosion had taken your mother's and grandmother's lives?"

"No. I only realized it later, after my sister's death."

"How did you feel when your sister died?"

"Alone. Very alone. A man found me and took me to a woman who had four small children."

Rigena. The baby that wouldn't stop crying. The language she hadn't really understood.

"I felt very strange. Not really afraid, because I believed I would find Mutti and Oma again. Just strange. And alone. Very alone."

"And when you discovered your mother and grandma were gone?"

"Dead. You say *dead*, that's how final it is," she said.

"Grietjie?" he asked.

"I had to accept it. Carry on. What else?"

"You were very young. How old? Seven? Eight? How did you deal with it all at such a young age?"

Six, she thought. *I was six.* "I kept my thinking small. I thought closer, not wider, and especially not backward." She thought for a moment. "And when the backward thoughts threatened to creep in, I thought about other things—stories."

He sat motionless for a long while. Sometimes he wrote; sometimes he just stared at his notes.

Later he said, "I'm going to make that the focus of my research: 'I kept my thinking small, closer, not wider, not backward. When the backward thoughts threatened to creep in, I thought about other things . . .' It's perfect. Thanks, Grietjie."

"Have we finished?" she asked, relieved.

"No, this is just the beginning. But yes, for today, we've finished. Would you like some ice cream?"

———

Endless sessions followed. "How did you feel, Grietjie? What did you think of this? Can you remember that? Why didn't you . . . ? Don't you think you . . . ? Are you sure you . . . ?"

"If you keep asking and asking and you don't write anything down, you'll get nowhere," she told him.

He shook his head, deep in thought. "We're not getting to the heart of the matter, Grietjie," he said. "You see, you can't always think about other things. It's a short-term solution. In the long run it will catch up with you. We're not getting to the part that really matters."

Maybe she should tell him about the nightmares after all. But they made her seem pathetic.

"There's something else I've been wanting to ask you." Suddenly he looked different, less businesslike.

"Shoot. I surrendered a long time ago," she said.

"No, it has nothing to do with this. Are you going to the year-end ball with Gerrit?"

She looked at him, surprised. The year-end ball hadn't crossed her mind. "No, Gerrit and I aren't together. We're just friends." Not that Gerrit wanted it that way, but she wasn't ready for a steady relationship.

"Would you like to be my partner?"

She stared at him. "At the ball?"

He raised one eyebrow slightly, as he did when he was amused.

"Oh. Yes. I haven't given it any thought," she muddled on.

"Thanks," he said. "It's two weeks from Saturday."

"I haven't said yes," she protested.

"Well, I heard a yes. Come now, Griet, it'll be fun."

She might as well go with him. Maybe Gerrit would finally realize there was no future for the two of them.

"Fine." She had never thought of Francois as anything but Karin's brother who was using her as his case study.

Now she looked at him through fresh eyes. *Mm,* she thought, imitating Kobus, *he may be my type after all.* Tall, athletic, with dark-blond hair and sharp green eyes behind his glasses. A straight nose, an attractive mouth that smiled easily. Long fingers—he would be a good pianist.

"Do you play the piano?"

His smile lit up his face. "Is it a requirement?"

"No, I'm just asking."

"When I was young, my mom dragged me to piano lessons and forced me to practice in the evenings. I passed grade five, I think. I can play 'Chopsticks' and 'In the Mood.' Do I qualify?"

Maybe not her type after all. "Do you enjoy making fun of people?" she asked.

The smile was even broader. "Not people who happen to be a breathtaking beauty."

"Are you making fun of me now?"

"No, I'm dead serious."

Karin whooped when she heard the news. "Calm down!" Grietjie protested. "We're just going to the ball as pals."

"Will you wear your blue dress?"

"I don't have much of a choice, do I?" Grietjie laughed. "It's either the blue dress or the black one that I wore last time."

"We can try to do the blue one up a little," Karin suggested. "We could take out the sleeves or alter the neckline. Give me that dress, let me see."

"Aren't you writing criminology tomorrow?" Grietjie asked in a stern voice.

"It can wait," Karin answered. "Give me the dress."

———

The ball kicked off with some ballroom dancing. Graceful, old-worldly. *Kind of boring*, Grietjie thought.

The two of them danced well together, though Francois' hand on her back felt odd.

Then the band launched into the latest hits of Elvis Presley and Pat Boone and Buddy Holly. "Jailhouse Rock" and "Ain't That a Shame" and "That'll Be the Day" thumped through the ballroom.

The elegant waltzers were instantly transformed into students. They jived, they rocked, they danced the Madison and the cha-cha. Coats and ties came off, and stiletto heels were kicked under the table. They laughed and sang along and wiggled their lithe figures. The spring ball was a roaring success.

Later the music slowed down. The jivers changed into smitten couples swept up in the thrill of the evening. "Love me tender, love me sweet," the long-haired singer crooned into the mike.

Grietjie surrendered to the haunting melody. She felt content, lazy, pleasantly tired, and footsore. Francois' hand on her back no longer felt odd; her head rested comfortably on his shoulder.

The melody flowed into her fingertips, into the roots of her hair.

"I have dreams," she said, "almost every night." He probably knew anyway, she thought.

At first she thought he hadn't heard her. He danced on without missing a beat, carrying her along in the circle of swaying bodies.

"Do you want to tell me about it?" he asked.

She didn't know. "Not now," she said.

He laughed softly. "No, definitely not now," he said and drew her closer.

Just before midnight they walked back to her residence across the moonlit campus. She didn't look up at the moon. For years she had been avoiding the sight of it. Her hand in Francois' felt like the most natural thing on earth.

Just before they reached the door of her res he said, "May I fetch you tomorrow? For church?"

She nodded.

"We can talk afterward. French fries, I promise."

She smiled. They were still friends. Maybe something more, but definitely friends.

A pity they had to talk.

———

"Francois, that's everything, really," she said the next afternoon. "I dream about fire. I see the flames, I hear them and feel them, smell them, taste their bitterness at the back of my throat. But I don't know how they get there, where they come from. I don't think it's a bomb, I don't know. I just wish the dream would go away."

Today was different. His arm was behind her and she leaned against him. He didn't write at all, just sat, quietly listening. His voice was soft, calm.

"It could go away forever," he said. "But we'll have to find out what started it."

She shook her head hopelessly. "I've thought and thought. I think back, far back. I think more deeply and widely than I want to, but there's just a dark, empty tunnel. It's not that I don't remember anything—I remember lots of things."

"Such as?"

"The furniture and the outside of Oma's little house. The room where we stayed later. I remember Oma and Mutti and Elza—even some of the others in the house, vaguely."

"And? Tell me more, anything you remember."

"I remember the stations. And the train. At the head of the train there was a fire, too, you could see it when the locomotive steamed past. The smoke smelled acrid and sooty, different from any other fire's smoke. It's definitely not the fire of my dreams."

For a long time they sat motionless. Then he asked, "Do you remember the bombs?"

"Yes," she said, "I remember the droning of the planes and the sounds of the sirens and the bombs."

"You saw the bombs strike buildings?"

"Yes, I did. I saw the flames too, and the black smoke. But I know that's not my fire."

It was good talking to him. Maybe he could find out where the fire came from, maybe he could even find a way of putting it out.

"Did a bomb ever explode near your home?"

"Yes, sometimes closer, sometimes farther away. After a while you get used to it. When the people stood in line for their food rations, they didn't even seek shelter, because they might lose their place."

"And . . . Grietjie, you must tell me if I must back off."

"Ask away, you might even be helping me," she said. "Grandpa John always says you have to be cruel to be kind."

"The explosion in which your grandma and your mother died?"

She shook her head. "For a time I thought Oma and Mutti might be in the fire of my nightmares, but they're not. That's not what my dream is about, I know."

"Good." After a long silence he spoke again. "Grietjie, I don't have the right training to help you, not yet. Wouldn't you like to speak to someone who can be of more help? I can arrange with—"

"No, Francois," she said firmly. "I won't do it. Definitely not."

"Why not? If the person can help you? Can take away the dreams?"

"No. Besides, I can't tell him anything I haven't told you."

"Fine," he answered. "But if you ever get the chance to speak to someone, promise me you'll do it. Please?"

"I will." She realized it was most likely an empty promise.

"And if you want to talk to me, please tell me. It won't go any further, you know that."

"I know." And she did know. But she had already told him everything that might be relevant, and still nothing had come of it.

"I'm handing in my research paper on Wednesday. Would you like to read it first?"

"No," she answered. "I trust you with my dark past. Besides, I'm writing my last paper on Thursday. Kobus finishes on Friday, and then we're off to the farm!"

They sat in silence for a while. A comfortable silence. A contented silence. Then he said, "I'll miss you. It's going to be a long vacation."

"Yes." Strange, she didn't really know whether she would miss him as well. She only knew she was going to spend the vacation with her family in their lovely sandstone home. She, her mom and dad, and Grandpa John and Kobus.

She wrapped the knowledge around her like a comfort blanky.

———

Christmas that year was a huge family affair. Grandpa John was already there when she and Kobus arrived at the station—he had come to town with their mother to fetch them. In mid-December Uncle Peter and his attractive wife, Diana, arrived.

Grietjie liked to talk to her Uncle Peter. He was at the head of Grandpa John's big company, Rand Consolidated. Soon after the Anglo-Boer War, Grandpa John had established Rand Consolidated as a one-man business with one exhausted mine. Through hard work and inborn business acumen he had developed it into one of the most stable mining houses on the stock exchange.

Just before Christmas Britney and Sarah arrived with their husbands. Britney had two little boys, busy little imps. Sarah was expecting her first baby in April. She felt the summer heat to such a degree that she went swimming in the frog dam with Grietjie and Kobus. It wasn't long before everyone was in the water except Diana and Grandpa John.

The house was full, the old homestead as well. At breakfast they crowded around the long table. In the evenings they barbecued meat and ate outside. Grietjie wished they could live together all the time.

"It would never work," said Kobus. "A week is just long enough, after that Dad and I wouldn't be able to stand the Pommies anymore."

"Grandpa John stays for months and he's a Pommy," Grietjie reminded him. "You even speak English to him!"

"Grandpa John is an exception," said Kobus.

On Christmas Eve they sat in the living room around the Christmas tree. They sang carols, but this time in Afrikaans and English. The two little boys were so excited, they could hardly wait to open their gifts.

Late that night her yearning returned. Despite all the joy and the love and merriment, she longed for that distant country where snowfall reflected the moon and stars on Christmas Eve. And for Jakób, always for Jakób. She stroked the dog's head and gazed at the golden moon over the arid bushveld. Like every other Christmas Eve, she went to Grandpa John's room, because they were the only ones who knew how long the yearning for another person could last, long after everyone else had forgotten.

———

The year 1957 started weirdly. She drove back to the university in the big black car with Grandpa John and his chauffeur. Kobus had finished his studies, and her father didn't want her to take the milk train on her own. On the second night after her return Francois took her out for coffee. She was glad to see him, but when he began to tell her how he had missed her, she quickly changed the subject.

Classes were also weird. The lecturers and her peers were the same, but the classes were smaller and all of a sudden the students were treated like grown-ups. It was a pleasant change, but unexpected.

"You can't take four majors, Miss Neethling," the dean said one day early in the term. "Why don't you study French after hours, as an additional subject?"

"I'm already doing Polish and Russian after hours," said Grietjie. "It would be so much easier if I could just take French as one of my regular subjects. I'll work hard, Professor, I promise."

He studied her grades for a long time. *He can stare until he goes blind*, Grietjie thought. *I'm at the top of my class in all my subjects. I'm certainly not going to give in.*

The professor looked up. "Miss Neethling, your grades seem satisfactory. Let's try it for a term and see how it goes."

"Thank you, Professor." She gave him a relieved smile. "I won't disappoint you."

"Satisfactory!" Karin cried when Grietjie returned to their room. "What is his idea of brilliant, I wonder?"

Things became even weirder when she arrived at Mrs. Bronski's home for her Polish lesson.

"Grietjie, my girl," said the stylish lady in her charming accent, "I have a big shock for you. The police arrested Mr. Ulyanov just after New Year."

Mr. Ulyanov? The dignified gentleman who was her Russian lecturer? "But, Mrs. Bronski," she said, shocked, "what could he have done wrong?"

"Apparently he's a Communist," said Mrs. Bronski, fanning her face with her handkerchief. "I just can't get used to the heat in this country."

"A Communist? Impossible! Are they sure?"

"Seems like it, yes. Just goes to show you can't trust anyone," sighed

Mrs. Bronski. "Let's take a look at what we want to do this year. There's an anthology of poems by Mickiewicz I want us to start with."

When Grietjie returned to her residence in the late afternoon, Karin looked almost pleased by Mr. Ulyanov's news. "I told you Russian was a Communist language!" she cried triumphantly. "I hope you're not going to look for another teacher."

"No," said Grietjie. "I can read and write Russian reasonably well. I think I'll focus on my other subjects. Besides, French is quite hard this year."

Francois didn't look shocked or surprised either. "You can never trust those Commies, Griet," he said.

"But I can't imagine that he's a Communist," she said.

"They're all Communists, the people from those countries," he said decisively.

"Mrs. Bronski's family are definitely not Communists!"

He shrugged. "Possibly not. They came to South Africa after the war, didn't they?"

"Yes, they came here to get away from the Communists."

"Be careful anyway," he said. "You never know."

———

On the night of the rag dance Francois kissed her for the first time—a real kiss, not just a good-bye peck.

That felt weird too. She had been kissed before, but never like that. Not in a way that made her feel almost guilty because it was so good.

She had been in standard eight when a boy kissed her for the first time. He was one of Kobus's friends, and they were in the pantry on the farm of all places, where he had been supposed to help her fetch the ginger beer. She had slapped his face to make sure he wouldn't try the same trick again.

But the next day Kobus told her it wasn't exactly how she should have behaved. He said it took a lot of courage for a boy to kiss a girl, because how was a boy supposed to know if a girl wanted to be kissed or not? He couldn't very well ask, "Hey, do you feel like kissing me?"

"No, he can't," Grietjie agreed.

Next time, Kobus explained, she should just turn her head and politely say that she didn't feel like kissing right now, but she appreciated the fact that he wanted to kiss her.

"Has a girl ever done it to you?" she asked.

He gave her an astounded look. "Of course not!" he answered. "Girls always want to kiss me."

"You're such a windbag!" she said.

"But it's a good thing that you don't go around kissing boys left, right, and center," he continued. "Boys are bastards, they take chances."

"Kobus! What would Mommy say if she heard you swear like that!"

"Just so you know," he answered and walked away.

After the matric dance her partner had also kissed her. She quite enjoyed it, because they were all in high spirits. But then he opened his mouth and it turned into a messy affair, so she turned her head and said thanks, but no thanks. The boy was a bit cheesed off, but they managed to stay friends.

At university, men had also wanted to kiss her. "I don't understand it," she had complained to Karin. "When a guy takes you out for the evening, he thinks you're obliged to kiss him."

"It doesn't happen to me very often," Karin had said dejectedly.

She hadn't discussed it with Karin again.

But the night of the rag dance was different. It was late; the seniors were allowed to stay out until half past twelve. A few couples were saying a lingering good-bye in front of her residence.

Francois pulled her into the shadow of a tree. When he wrapped his arms around her, she could feel his heart beat through his white shirt.

When he lifted her chin, she knew what was coming. She also knew that she wanted to kiss him, really wanted to kiss Francois. His lips briefly touched hers, as if he didn't know whether she was willing. Her lips parted slightly, her fingers crept around the back of his neck. She felt his hands on her back as he drew her closer.

When the kiss became too intense, she pulled away. He let her go immediately.

"Grietjie?" he said.

She smiled. "Thanks for a wonderful, wonderful evening, Francois."

His eyes had a tender expression. "You're amazing, you know?"

"Thanks, Francois. Will I see you for church tomorrow?"

"Wild horses couldn't keep me away." He smiled back at her.

"What was your evening like?" Karin asked when she entered the room.

"Very nice, thanks," said Grietjie. She had no inclination to say anything more.

———

On a Sunday morning early in March, she went home with Francois and Karin for the first time. They caught a train from Hatfield to the main station, and from there another train to Lyttelton. Their home was within walking distance of the station.

Francois and Karin's mom was a charming lady with gentle blue eyes and a friendly smile. Grietjie had seen her at the residence a few times. Their dad was a lean, affable man with a military bearing. He was in the air force. They barbecued outside, but the day was hot, so they had coffee in the living room, where it was cooler.

After lunch Grietjie stood in the hallway, looking at a collection of photographs on the wall: a corseted great-grandmother with a severe expression standing beside her moustached husband, a fat baby in a christening gown like a wedding cake, a wedding photo of Karin's parents, Karin and Francois as toddlers, playing in a muddy puddle. *Our house has photos like these too*, she thought, *of weddings and great-grandparents and Kobus as a toddler and myself as a skinny eleven-year-old. And my German father in his SS uniform.*

She was soon joined by Karin's father. "Photos like these have a story to tell, don't they?"

She smiled and nodded. "Did you serve in the Second World War?" she asked, pointing at a group of airmen posing in front of a fighter plane.

"Yes, mainly in North Africa, but toward the end of the war in Europe as well. I wasn't involved in many battles myself, more in bombing targets like oil refineries and munitions depots and factories. And of course in the airlift, during which we dropped supplies for the Polish Home Army in Warsaw."

She felt her heart jump. She stared at the photograph. "Will you tell me about it?" she asked as casually as possible. "About the airlift?"

He gave a slight smile. "There's a lot to tell, but not much either, because every night was more or less the same."

"I'm really interested. I'd like to hear," she said.

He lit a cigarette. After a while she wondered whether he was going to tell her after all. Then he began to speak. "We took off from Italy, because the distance from Great Britain was too great and Stalin refused to allow the Allies to use Soviet airfields. They were night operations, but we were forced to take off and cross the enemy lines in broad daylight, because it gets dark so late in the European summer." He gave an embarrassed smile. "But you'll know that, you grew up there."

"I was very young. I don't remember much," she said quickly. "What route did you take?"

"We crossed the Adriatic Ocean, followed the course of the Danube, then headed north across the Carpathian Mountains. The weather was usually very bad. Have you ever heard of St. Elmo's fire?"

"No, I haven't."

"It's when lightning makes blue circles around the propellers, and blue flames form on the wingtips and are dragged along behind the aircraft."

"Sounds scary!" she said.

"It looks worse than it is," he said. "After we crossed the Carpathian Mountains we were in Poland. We had to avoid Kraków, because the

Luftwaffe had an airbase there. We flew to Warsaw. When we saw the first glow on the horizon, we had to start descending. We dropped the cargo at as low a level as possible."

"Glow?" she asked. "Didn't they black out the windows?" She remembered very clearly that not a glimmer of light was allowed to show or the Gestapo might see it.

"Warsaw was on fire at the time. Every building seemed to be in flames, street after street, block after block. The smoke was very dense, up to a thousand feet or more, lit up by the fires on the ground. Sometimes it was almost impossible to see where you were flying."

Jakób had been among those burning buildings, Grietjie thought. Surrounded by flames. Until the Nazis had shot him.

"We flew north along the Vistula," Karin's dad continued, "turned left above a cathedral, descended to less than a hundred feet, and flew south until we picked up that particular night's Morse code signal. Then we dropped all the crates at once—they were attached to parachutes—and got ourselves back to Italy as quickly as possible."

"What was inside the crates?" This man made her feel closer to Jakób. He must have seen the planes.

"Light machine guns, hand grenades, radio equipment, food, medical supplies. Most of it reached the people on the ground in one piece, I believe, because we flew at very low levels and at a very slow speed. It was incredibly dangerous, come to think of it. The Germans fired at us with rifles, machine guns, even pistols, that's how low we were!"

They stood side by side, looking at the photo of seven smiling young men in air force uniforms, a moment from the past trapped in an image for the next generation. "Only three of us survived the war." Karin's dad turned to leave and said, "But that was long ago, in another world."

On their way back Karin dozed off. Grietjie asked Francois, "Does your father vote for the United Party?"

"He does. He's a Bloedsap, as they say."

"My dad is a staunch Nationalist."

He frowned. "That could be a problem."

"Why?" Surely their fathers would never meet?

He smiled. "I'll tell you one day," he said.

Grietjie felt a lump in her throat. She couldn't explain why, but she didn't want to think about their parents meeting anytime soon.

———

In the early hours of the morning, the fighter planes thundered through her mind. St. Elmo's fire was dragging from the wingtips, a spectacular display. But the blue flames backtracked to the wings and the entire plane exploded in a fireball. The plane plummeted, setting the entire city alight, the city where Jakób was. The blaze singed her hair. Someone groaned dreadfully.

She woke with a jolt.

Fortunately she had not woken Karin.

———

The final three weeks of term were taken up with assignments and tests. Everything had to be finished before the short April vacation. "Lecturers don't know how to plan," Karin complained on Thursday evening. "I'll probably have to work all through the night on this assignment."

"You're not the only one, roomie," Grietjie assured her. "I have a test on this book tomorrow and I've read all of three pages."

"Let the studies begin!" Karin announced dramatically and sat down behind her desk.

Half an hour later there was a hesitant knock on the door. "Go away, we have work to do!" Karin shouted.

The first-year on front-door duty cautiously opened the door. "Good evening, Miss Karin. Good evening, Miss Grietjie."

"Yes?" Karin asked brusquely.

"Miss Karin, I'm sorry to bother you. Miss Grietjie, you have a visitor."

"Francois knows I have to study tonight," Grietjie said, annoyed. "Tell him I'm on my way," she told the first-year. "I'm just putting on my shoes."

"He's waiting in the sitting room, Miss Grietjie," said the first-year, then rushed off.

I didn't even comb my hair, thought Grietjie as she opened the door of the formal sitting room where they were supposed to receive their gentleman friends. Francois' timing was really bad. He knew she was snowed under with work.

She pushed open the door.

He was standing at the far end of the room. Dark. Large as life.

Just as she had so often seen him in her dreams.

Impossible, yet true.

For a second or two she was frozen to the spot.

"Gretz?" he asked uncertainly.

12

Shock jolted Grietjie's body. She retreated slowly until her back touched the wall. Her mouth was dry.

He was there. Tall figure, broad shoulders, black hair, smoldering pitch-black eyes. He looked exactly as she remembered him.

"Jakób?" she asked in a small voice. "Jakób Kowalski?"

She stood breathless, her heart in her mouth. Hot tears began pouring down her cheeks. She tasted their saltiness in her mouth.

Then her knees buckled and she slid to the floor, her back still pressed to the wall.

He knelt beside her, reached for her hand. "Gretchen?"

She laughed nervously, disbelievingly. Then she shook her head and wiped the tears from her cheeks. His other hand touched her arm. He was here. It wasn't a dream.

"It's really you, Jakób Kowalski." She spoke Polish. It came naturally. Time had made a backward leap of nine years. She held out her hand to him. She couldn't believe how little he had changed. Except for his eyes. His eyes were different, she just couldn't pinpoint how.

Slowly life flowed back into her limbs, but her mouth remained dry, so that she found it hard to speak.

He should have phoned ahead and warned her. The people of the German Children's Fund who gave him her details had suggested he should prepare her for his arrival.

And he should have prepared himself. Nothing about this girl reminded him of his little Gretchen.

The skinny little body now had soft curves, the frizzy blonde hair curled softly at her neck, the hands she had clapped to her cheeks were slender and delicate. It was a beautiful hand with manicured nails, not the bony little fingers that had clutched his as they walked together.

"You look different," he said.

Time had leaped ahead, leaving him behind.

A strange feeling began to grow inside him. It felt almost like . . . loss.

She got to her feet. "We can't sit on the floor like this," she said. She reached out and took his hand. He followed her to the sofa.

"Jakób, what are you doing here? How did you get out of Poland? Are you here on business? Will you be here for a while? When—"

"Whoa." He protested with a slight laugh. "Too many questions, Gretz."

She smiled. "I'm Grietjie now." The name was as strange to his ears as the sight of her was strange to his eyes.

"Grietjie." His tongue couldn't quite manage it.

Her familiar laughter bubbled up unexpectedly.

"*Grietjie,*" she stressed, "with a *g* and an *r*. Strange sounds, aren't they?"

He nodded slowly. "Everything is strange."

"Should I make some coffee?"

Make coffee. Just as she used to when she came back from school after he had spent the morning in bed, waiting for her. Or when he came back to Częstochowa from his work in Katowice. In those later years, she had always waited for him at the station.

"Could we go out for coffee somewhere? At a café or something?" he asked.

She looked at her watch. "Too late," she said. "The rules here are very strict."

He gave a slight smile. "Stricter than the nuns?"

"Yes. But, Jakób, please tell me now, how long will you be here?"

"I don't know." It was hard to say it in words. "I'm not going back, Gretz. Grietjie."

He saw the confusion in her face. "Not back to Poland?" she asked.

"I had to flee."

Her hand flew to her mouth. "From the Communists?"

"Yes."

In her eyes he saw that she had heard his words and was processing them, interpreting them, making sense of them.

Her eyes filled with tears again. She swallowed hard.

———

She knew what it was in his eyes. It was the flight, the finality of the journey. The country he had to leave behind. It was this strange country, the language that was not his own, the harsh, dry veld, the sun blazing down from the wrong direction, the unfamiliar stars.

She understood only too well.

"You've come to a good country." She didn't know what else to say.

"Are you happy here?"

Gradually her mind cleared. She didn't quite know how she felt—astounded, overwhelmed, happy, impossibly . . . what? She grabbed at a straw to comfort him.

"Jakób, I'm so glad I can tell you tonight: sending me here was the best thing you ever did."

"Did you find a good home?" he asked.

"I have the best parents any child could want." She shook her head in disbelief again, reached for him, touched his arm. "And now you are also here, really here. You'll stay, won't you?"

"I don't know. I'm considering it, yes. Maybe."

A bell rang in the corridor. "Visiting hours are over," she said.

He looked at her uncomprehendingly.

"It means you have to go." She got to her feet. "Jakób, where do you work? Where do you live? Here in Pretoria?"

"Yes, here in Pretoria. I work for Iscor. I'm getting a flat in Sunnyside next month. Do you know where that is?"

They walked to the front door. "Yes, I know. Listen, the vacation starts next week. I'll be going home on Wednesday. But I must see you again before I leave. You must tell me everything."

The Dragon stood at the door and rattled her keys. A couple said a passionate farewell. It was a long time until tomorrow.

"Come on Sunday afternoon, please?" she pleaded. "Will you, Jakób?"

"I will," he said.

Then the Dragon closed and locked the door.

Upstairs, Grietjie entered her room as quietly as possible. Karin didn't look up. She was immersed in her reading. Grietjie sat down at her desk, opened the book to page three, and stared at the pages.

Everything felt unreal. Jakób belonged to the past, like someone who was dead.

But no man could be dead for nine years and then reappear, large as life.

She felt completely bewildered.

When she stood in the shower an hour later, her book was open at page five.

Water splashed on her face and body, streamed down her legs. She washed and washed her hair, but her mind simply wouldn't clear.

Suddenly she wasn't sure whether she wanted him here or not.

He knew about the nuns, the Catholic school, all the childhood dragons in her life. He knew about her Jewish blood.

He had slipped out of the bottom drawer of the big closet in her bedroom on the farm.

She had never imagined he could escape from there.

Jakób walked from the bus stop to his boarding house through the quiet streets. His little Gretz had grown up. He hadn't foreseen that his skinny little duckling would turn into a graceful swan. Here, in a strange country, where there were no swans.

He felt dismayed, disillusioned.

He walked past his boarding house without realizing it.

His Gretchen was a big girl, he thought. All grown up.

But, he told himself, she had grown up beautifully; she had grown up well. She wasn't working in a factory or a laundry; she was a student at a university. That was what he had wanted, after all.

It was just . . . she had grown up.

He should have realized she would no longer be the ten-year-old he had known.

He walked and walked. And step by step, street block after street block, his dismay receded. The emptiness inside him was filled with amazement at the miracle of the duckling who had turned into a swan and with immense gratitude to the Blessed Virgin for the undeserved grace.

Mother of God, he prayed silently, *you showed me the right way.*

Late that night, unable to fall asleep, he realized that, for the first time in the weeks he had spent in this strange, southern country, he did not feel so completely alone. For the first time he would have a reason to get up on Sunday morning.

———•———

Sunday afternoon was unexpectedly cold. Winter was on its way. They sat at a café table in front of the window. "You should have come in September," Grietjie said. "You would have come from summer in Europe to summer in South Africa."

"In September I was still in Poland," said Jakób. He couldn't stop looking at her. She was exquisite. Today he was prepared for the fact that she looked different, that somewhere inside she was still his little Gretz, but that, since he last saw her, she had become Grietjie.

"Do you want to tell me about it, Jakób?"

It was a raw, gaping hole. "Someday, maybe," he replied. Not now, or it would stay in the room.

"You must talk about these things, you know, Jakób, when you're ready. At least tell me how you ended up in South Africa," she said.

"In June last year I attended the International Fair in Poznań," he said. His eyes were neutral, his voice even. "I met an Englishman there, a Mr. Wilson, from the steelworks in Liverpool. When I left Poland, I first went to Germany and from there to Liverpool."

"We got off the train at the Liverpool Station in London when I came to South Africa," she told him.

"This Liverpool is a bit farther north," he said with a straight face.

"Yes, I know. I know my geography! I'm just saying, that's all."

That's all . . . his little Gretz.

"For a few months I worked in Liverpool," he continued, "but when a South African delegation came to recruit professional people for Iscor, I decided to come."

"Because I'm here?"

She was truly lovely!

"Yes, Gretz . . . Grietjie. It was one of the reasons. I always wondered how you were. Actually, I was sick with worry. I always regretted sending you away."

He had never told this to anyone else.

"But now you know I was fine, right from the start." She smiled at him.

"Yes, I'm so glad. I also came because I knew South Africa is a country with a strong anti-Communist policy. It was a very strong consideration."

"And there are good opportunities here, especially for graduates," she added.

"You're smart, aren't you?"

"Jakób!" she said indignantly. "I'm nearly twenty! I'll be graduating at the end of the year. Then I'll start working as a fully qualified professional!"

He still couldn't believe it. He knew so little about her. "What do you want to do?" he asked.

"Write. Translate. My majors are Afrikaans, English, German, and French, and I've had private lessons in Polish and Russian." She didn't mention Mr. Ulyanov, who was no longer her teacher because he was a Communist.

"Impressive," he said, slightly disconcerted. "You've always been very clever."

"It's a lot of work," she said. "I read at the speed of lightning. My first choice would be to work for a newspaper, translate articles from abroad or something, I don't really know how it works. But next term I want to go to Johannesburg, to the head office of Voortrekker Press, they publish *Die Transvaler*. It's an Afrikaans newspaper. I want to take a look at how things work. And I'm going to write a book, as soon as possible."

She was much too young to make such important decisions.

"On Wednesday I'm going home for the vacation," she chattered on. "I'm going with my grandfather. I call him Grandpa John. He's very old and very rich, and he has a big black car and a chauffeur who wears a uniform and the most beautiful home you've ever seen. Grandpa John, I mean, not the chauffeur. And he's the best person in the entire world. He reads the papers every day and he reads his company's financial reports and he can talk about absolutely everything under the sun. But he's English, completely English."

The in-between years fell away. Jakób could forever listen to her stories, so uncomplicated, so animated.

At five o'clock she said, "I'll have to go back to my res, Jakób."

"Won't you have dinner with me?" he asked. He didn't want to let her go.

"I can't. I promised Francois I'd go to church with him tonight."

A cold hand closed around his heart. "Francois? Who's he?"

"Francois? Oh, he's kind of my boyfriend."

Jakób couldn't sleep. She was much too young for a boyfriend, even a kind-of boyfriend.

He rolled onto his other side and pulled the blankets up to his chin.

Loneliness closed in around him like a murky blanket of fog waiting to smother him.

If that so-called boyfriend lays a finger on her . . .

She's no more than a child: young, innocent . . .

He got up and drank a glass of water.

If that youngster dares . . .

Outside the city traffic died down. The streetlight lit up his room through the thin curtain.

Loneliness had become part of his fiber.

If that Francois, or any other . . .

On Monday he went to work with a splitting headache.

They left Johannesburg early. At first they talked, but as they made their way across the Springbok Flats, Grandpa John fell asleep.

Grietjie gazed through the window. For the first time she had a chance to think, to surrender to her thoughts without feeling guilty about her studies.

Last night with Francois was another fiasco. She didn't want to get serious just yet. All her friends were getting engaged, but she had no inclination to follow suit. Not that Francois had ever mentioned marriage—not at all. It was just—she didn't want to get serious.

"But why not, Grietjie?" he'd asked dejectedly. "All I'm asking is that we go steady. We're good together, I love you, and I believe you love me too. What more do you want?"

"I just don't feel . . . ready." She didn't know why she felt that way.

He was quiet for a while, then said earnestly, "Grietjie, I want you to realize one thing—if you don't extinguish those smoldering coals inside you, you'll never be a healthy person. You *must* talk to me. You can trust me. What you tell me will stay between us."

"Why do you keep nagging? I've told you everything; what more do you want me to say?"

"It's for your own good. Some things lie deep. You may have forgotten them because you were taught to think about other things. It's been your means of survival."

"I remember everything, Francois," she said glumly. "I've told you a hundred times, I remember everything very clearly. Keeping silent is still important for my survival. There are things I can't speak about at all. And that's more than I've ever told anyone, I'll have you know. You'll have to trust me as well. I *know*."

She could see he was considering her words. "Fine, I don't understand, but I'll accept it," he said at last. "As long as you know that sooner or later you'll have to speak to someone, and the sooner, the better. It doesn't have to be me. Sometimes it's better to speak to a total stranger. Maybe a minister or someone?"

A minister, she had thought, was the very last person she could speak to. Or maybe the second last—her parents could never know.

"Grietjie?"

"Please stop nagging me!" she had burst out. "I'm tired and I still have to pack. Grandpa John is fetching me at seven tomorrow morning. Can we please go back to res now?"

Today she was sorry she had argued with Francois. He meant well. It was just . . .

She sighed and picked up a book. Maybe thinking wasn't such a good idea after all.

But the thoughts kept returning.

Maybe she should talk, tell the whole story again. She could tell Jakób. He knew everything anyway. She just couldn't see how it would change anything.

But the dreams were driving her crazy. Sometimes she was afraid to go to sleep. They seemed to be getting worse.

She and Grandpa John arrived at the farm just after one, much more quickly than the milk train, which took the entire day.

Everyone was delighted to see her. The dogs wagged their tails exuberantly. Her mom cried happy tears at the sight of both her and Grandpa John. He was exhausted, so her mom took him off to rest. Her dad held her tightly. "The terms seem to be getting longer," he said. "I wish you'd come back for good next year."

"I can't, Daddy." She laughed. "I'll have a job next year! There's no work for me around here! But that's the only reason."

"Perhaps you could teach English? Or one of those foreign languages you know?"

She laughed. "I wouldn't be a good teacher! You know how strict I am."

Maria was in the kitchen. Her husband, Philemon, had died unexpectedly at the end of January. "She's heartbroken," said Grietjie's mother, "but she's been looking forward to your arrival."

Grietjie went to the kitchen. "Maria?" she said hesitantly.

Maria turned from the big coal stove and her face lit up. "Missy!" she said and held out her hands.

Grietjie pressed Maria's hands to her face. They were big and strong, and rough from hard work. "I'm so sorry about Philemon," Grietjie said sincerely. "I pray for you every night."

Maria nodded. She smiled bravely and said, "But you're home now."

"Yes," said Grietjie, "I'm home. And I can't wait for supper."

At four Kobus came in from outside. He looked as if he had been dragged backward through a mud hole.

"Goodness, Grietjie," he said, "you're getting prettier by the day. Do you have a boyfriend yet?"

She laughed. "And you're getting dirtier by the day. Don't you have a girlfriend to keep you clean yet?"

He advanced on her menacingly with his filthy hands. "Come, let me greet you properly," he threatened.

She jumped up and fled, screaming, "Kobus! No, I love this dress! Go away! Mommy! Tell Kobus—"

Their mother laughed. "Silly kids! Quiet, you'll wake Grandpa."

"Grandpa is awake," said a voice from the dining room door. "Is there any coffee in this house?"

One day I want to bring Jakób here so that he can see how wonderful my family is, Grietjie thought. But she knew it could never happen.

That evening when they were all sitting on the veranda Kobus said, "I do have a girlfriend, I'll have you know. You'll meet her on Sunday. She's coming for lunch after church."

"Where did she spring from?" Grietjie asked, surprised.

"Standerton."

"No, I mean, where did you find her in this backwater?"

"Oh. She's a teacher at the junior school in town. Her name is Salomé. She studied in Heidelberg, at the teachers' training college. She's . . . amazing."

Grietjie stared at her brother, astonished. "Kobus," she said, "you're in love!"

He nodded. "Head over heels," he said.

Well, she decided before she fell asleep in her own bed, *the year is only getting stranger.*

———

Thursday was a scorching day, a swim-in-the-frog-dam day. But first Kobus wanted to show her what he'd been doing.

"I've signed a contract with a bacon factory at Estcourt in Natal," he explained. "It's a leap into the unknown."

"I've never heard of a bacon factory before!" She laughed.

"Yes, they make bacon and smoke hams and that kind of thing, you know."

I know pigsties, she thought, *I know pigs eat vegetable leaves. I know how a sow gives birth and how a pig is slaughtered and how a ham is smoked. I just can't mention it.*

They walked past the old homestead and down the new road Kobus had graded. He told her about his plans to renovate the old house, adding modern amenities without spoiling the character of the place. But it would be costly, and he'd have to wait awhile.

"Do you have wedding plans yet, Kobus?" Grietjie teased.

"Well, ye-es. I definitely do, but I haven't mentioned them to Salomé yet."

She was about to make fun of him again, but something in his eyes made her change her mind. "I'm really happy for you," she said. "Salomé must be a very special girl."

"She is, Grietjie, she is. She's a lot like you, only completely different. If you know what I mean."

She had no idea what he meant, but it didn't matter—she understood. She walked in the blazing bushveld sun with her older brother to look at his new pigsties. She couldn't think of anything she'd rather do than admire his work.

The pigsties Kobus was building were poles apart from the lopsided wire pens she had known in Częstochowa. These began with a kind of kitchen where the pigs' food was prepared. There were smaller enclosures for the pregnant sows, weaner pens for the piglets, and fattening pens for the pigs due for slaughter. Kobus talked and pointed, explained how the hosing system would work, which health measures he had to put in place, and where he would build the loading ramp for the animals bound for the station.

"Will the pigs go to Estcourt by train?"

"Yes, it's by far the cheapest way of getting them there."

In an open car on a train bound for the slaughterhouse, she thought as they walked back—*in an open car on a train bound for the gas chambers.*

———

At home she put on her swimsuit and applied Nivea Creme to her face. "Are you coming for a swim?" she called down the hall to her mother.

"Daddy and I will come as soon as he's back from the fields," she answered. "Did you remember the Nivea?"

"Yes, Mommy."

"And don't go swimming on your own!"

"No, Mommy, Kobus is coming with me!" she called over her shoulder as she ran out through the back door.

A few yards from the back door she noticed Maria wrapped in a warm blanket. On this sizzling day? She hoped Maria wasn't sick. She was about to ask what was wrong when she heard Kobus softly calling her name.

Leave her alone, her brother gestured.

"Is she sick?" she asked as they headed for the dam.

"No," he answered, "just sitting."

After a while they were joined by their mom and dad. When they were tired of the water, her dad and Kobus hauled their big wet bodies onto the dam wall and sat there talking, while she and her mom floated on their backs, gazing up at the deep blue sky. Grandpa John was waiting at home, and in a while they'd all have coffee together. *This must be what King David had felt like,* Grietjie thought, *when his cup was overflowing.*

At six she wandered into the kitchen. "I'll lay the table, Maria," she offered.

"It's milk noodles tonight," said Maria. "Remember the cinnamon sugar."

When she had finished, Grietjie dawdled in the kitchen. "You must teach me how to make homemade noodles, will you, Maria?" She thought they reminded her of Oma's spaetzle, but she couldn't really remember.

"Yes, I will," Maria replied and moved the heavy cast-iron pot to a cooler part of the stove. "Your great-grandmother, Miss Hannetjie, taught me. She's been under the tall trees for many years, since before you came. But she knew how to cook."

"Maria," Grietjie ventured, "I saw you sitting in the boiling heat today wrapped in a blanket."

"Yes," Maria answered, "it's my mourning blanket."

"Mourning blanket?"

"Yes, Missy. In our culture you mourn, but not all day long. That's why my people use the mourning blanket. Once or twice or three times a day you get into your mourning blanket, along with the person who has died, and you grieve with your heart and your body and your mind. Then you put away the mourning blanket, stop mourning, and go back to work."

"It sounds like a wonderful strategy," Grietjie said, amazed. "I have a friend who's studying psychology. It's about helping people deal with their troubles. I'm going to tell him about your mourning blanket. It's so clever."

"It's the way of our forefathers, Missy."

On Friday afternoon, when Grandpa John was taking a nap after lunch, her mother said, "Grietjie, is anything bothering you? You're quieter than usual."

She wished she could tell her mom about Jakób, about how happy she was, how confused and scared. Her life had been perfect, except for that one small piece hidden away in the drawer. Now that piece had come out, and nothing seemed right anymore. No, that wasn't true, it was just that she was afraid everything would go wrong.

Still, she was no coward!

Her mother gave her a quizzical look.

"I have a friend, Mommy, Francois. He wants to get serious."

I have a friend, Mommy, Jakób. *He has dragged my past along with him all the way to South Africa.*

Her mother reached for her hand. "How do you feel about it?"

"I don't want to. I really like him, but I'm just not ready for a serious relationship."

I want to bring him to the farm, Mommy, just as he took me to his farm when I was lost. But I can't.

"Why not, Grietjie?"

"I don't exactly know. Maybe I'm afraid."

Afraid to disappoint you, afraid you'll learn about the Catholic Threat in my background, because it was in the Catholic Church that I first gave my heart to the Lord. Afraid you'll find out about my Jewish blood. Afraid Daddy will find out about my lies all these years—Daddy, who says honesty is the most important quality anyone can have. Afraid to take you into my confidence because you have always believed that you and I have no secrets from each other.

"How long have you known him?"

"Francois? He's Karin's brother, Mommy. He's the guy who used me as a primary source for his research paper. I've known him since my first year."

I've known him thirteen years. Since the day he fetched me at Rigena's and took me home with him.

Her mother nodded slowly. "You don't have to do anything you don't want to, Grietjie," she said. "You'll know when the time is right. And you'll know if it won't work."

"Yes, you're right, I probably will." She looked at her mother's calm face, at her gentle mouth, at her dark eyes radiating peace and serenity. "I wish I was your age," she said. "I feel as if I'm on a runaway train, as if the stations are flashing past and I *must* get off somewhere, *must* reach a destination, but I don't know where it is. It feels as if . . ." She stopped and looked up, confused.

"Grietjie?" her mother said worriedly. "Sweetheart, talk to Mommy."

Grietjie felt the tears coming. What was wrong with her? She was not a crybaby. She swallowed hard and tried to go on. "Mommy, I don't know what's wrong with me. I argued with Francois before I left, for no reason at all. And I . . ." She shrugged.

Her mother held her hands tightly. "When you told him about your experiences during the war for his research, did you mention . . . I mean, did you tell him about your nightmares, Grietjie?"

"Yes, Mommy. We spoke about it. I told him—he . . . we couldn't understand . . . Well, actually we couldn't find a solution."

"Did you tell him everything?"

"Not everything, just what he wanted to use. But, Mommy, I remember everything, clear as daylight. I have no problem with that. I'm just being silly."

I'm so sick and tired of hiding things. As I have to hide Jakób now.

"I wonder if you're working too hard," her mother said apprehensively. "Four majors! It's unheard of!"

"They're easy subjects, Mommy," Grietjie protested.

"They require an incredible amount of reading," said her mother. "Are you sleeping enough?"

I'm afraid to go to sleep, Grietjie thought. "I don't sleep any less than all the other students, Mommy. After the vacation things will go back to normal. It's wonderful to be home." After a moment she said, "You know, it feels as if the farm and the house have wrapped themselves around us, like Maria's mourning blanket. But in our case it's not a mourning blanket, but a comfort blanky, because we love each other so much."

"As long as you remember how much we love you, my darling," said her mother. "And as long as you remember you can talk to us about anything."

"I know," said Grietjie.

Anything.

But not everything.

———

Back in Pretoria she realized just how hot the bushveld had been. As she and Karin were walking to class in the early morning, she said, "I can't believe I was swimming just the day before yesterday! It's almost winter here."

"No," said Karin, who had grown up in Pretoria, "winter is still some way off. This is just a false alarm. In a few days we'll be back in our summer clothes."

Francois showed up during visiting hours that evening. He looked snug and warm in his dark-blue, cable-knit sweater. They went out for coffee and chatted effortlessly.

Two weeks passed before she heard from Jakób again. A first-year called her to the phone.

"I thought you'd vanished from the face of the earth," she said. "Have you moved into your apartment?"

"Ye-es, partly. But I don't have much furniture to speak of."

"It still sounds *lekker*," she said, using the Afrikaans word for "nice." No other language had such a word.

"*Lekker*?" he asked.

"Yes, it's Afrikaans. It's the best word you can think of. You'll have to learn to speak Afrikaans, Jakób. You can't live here and not speak Afrikaans."

"I've noticed, yes. But your Grandpa John doesn't speak Afrikaans, does he?"

"Not much, but he understands it. And besides, Grandpa John is Grandpa John, that's all. But I'll teach you to speak Afrikaans if—"

"Your three minutes are up," said the operator.

"You have to put in another tickey," Grietjie said quickly in Polish. She heard the coin drop. "Wow," she said, "she almost cut us off! When will I see you again? Hurry, three minutes is a very short time. And I—"

"That's why I phoned." She could hear the laughter in his voice. "But I can't get a word in edgeways. Would you like to go to mass with me on Sunday?"

"Oh, yes, Jakób, I'd really love to. And will you show me your apartment afterward? Maybe we could buy French fries for lunch. It's not expensive, and I know a place where they make wonderful French fries. And I can start teaching you Afrikaans, if you want me to. It's not too hard because you know German. But you haven't said when you'll pick me up."

He laughed. "I've been waiting for you to take a breath," he teased. "About nine?"

On Saturday she told Francois she wouldn't be spending Sunday with him. "Are you going to visit your grandpa?" he asked.

"No," she said vaguely, "I have other plans."

He gave her a strange look but left it there.

With Karin it was harder. "But where are you going?" asked Karin.

"I'm going to church with someone I knew at junior school," Grietjie answered. "I have to wash my hair now, or it will never get dry. Do you have a lemon I can use?"

Luckily Karin didn't ask any further questions.

On Sunday morning she waited outside so that there was no need for him to come into the foyer. She didn't feel like fielding anyone's questions.

They took the bus to the city center. "Second-hand cars are reasonably priced over here," said Jakób. "I'm considering buying a Volkswagen, but of course I don't have a driver's license. And it'll be weird driving on the left side of the road."

"I don't have a license either, but I know how to drive," she said. "My brother taught me, first in the tractor and then in the decrepit old Opel we keep in the barn. And was he strict! I know how to drive in loose sand and on bad farm roads and I know how to back up. I just can't drive on paved roads."

"I plan to drive chiefly on paved roads," Jakób said seriously, though his eyes were twinkling.

"Yes, I know. Maybe we could go for our licenses together. Maybe we could go in the town where I live, because my dad knows everyone . . ." She stopped. She couldn't take Jakób to her hometown.

"What were you saying about your dad?"

"Maybe we should rather get our licenses in Pretoria," she said.

He frowned and gave her an inquiring look, but she ignored it and changed the subject.

At Schoeman Street they got off the bus and walked the two street blocks to the cathedral.

The big stone building stood on a corner.

Suddenly Grietjie was filled with apprehension. Waiting inside were the beautiful music and the scent of candles and the tall, stained-glass windows. She remembered the tranquility and the sense that God was truly present, the solemn movements of the priests and the ancient sacred rituals. And she longed for them, for their familiarity, for the memories they held, especially for the peace they brought.

But inside there would also be a cross and images of the crucified Savior. The beautiful windows would have pictures of the Holy Virgin, of a baby with a halo, of a man with a cross on his shoulders and a crown of thorns on his head.

"Why is the Catholic Church wrong, Daddy?" she had asked her father years before. They were out in the veld, as they often were when they discussed serious matters.

"The Protestant churches believe the Catholics are on the wrong track, Grietjie," her father had explained. "You know about Martin Luther, the German monk who initiated the protest against the Catholic Church?"

"Yes, I do." But she'd also known from a young age about the battle the small monastery of Jasna Góra waged three hundred years ago against the Protestant king of Sweden to protect the Catholic faith. She knew this because she'd attended the convent school at Jasna Góra. Just as the Voortrekker leader Sarel Cilliers had recited the Covenant night after night, and God had helped the Voortrekkers, Jasna Góra's Father Kordecki had prayed every morning at the painting of the Black Madonna, and the great hand of God had helped the handful of Catholics to fend off the Protestant multitude.

Would God have helped them if they had been on the wrong track?

"I don't really know the Catholic rituals," her father had continued, "but we Protestants don't believe in graven images or any kind of portrayal of our Holy God. We also believe that the rituals are unnecessary. We don't need the Virgin Mary to intercede with God. We just have to bow our heads and He will hear us."

She understood. But what about the nuns? Dearest Sister Zofia, devoted Sister Margaret. The impressive cardinal of Łódź . . . Jakób—were they all on the wrong track?

"I suppose there are good Catholics as well," she had dared to say.

"Yes, of course, Grietjie. One of the best men I've ever known was Father James. At the time of the depression he did wonderful work among Johannesburg's poor."

"Then why is it called the Catholic Threat, Daddy?" That was what bothered her most. "Surely they're not dangerous?"

"Oh, but they are, Grietjie. They're false prophets, especially to people who don't know any better."

She didn't really remember the rest of the conversation. But she had great respect for her father. And she knew she could trust his judgment.

Now here she was standing in front of the Catholic Threat. And she knew God was waiting inside. Much more than in the sweltering bushveld church, where the sun beat mercilessly through the uncovered windows and the organ wailed out the glory of God.

Jakób must have felt her hesitation. He took her hand in his. "Come, Gretchen."

With Jakób by her side she stepped through the heavy door, back into the world of her childhood.

Bach's organ sounds filled the cathedral. It boomed from the organ pipes, shot up against the high ceiling, echoed through the building. The sounds enveloped the people in the sacred atmosphere.

She smelled the candles. The scent took her back to cold Christmas nights, to the midnight mass. It took her back to the time when Aunt Anastarja had lit candles for Jakób and Stan every day—when she, Gretz, had discovered the true meaning of prayer.

She saw how the stained-glass windows bathed the people in soft colors. She saw the images on which her entire childhood faith had been built—the manger, the Child in the temple, the sower, the fishermen, the Savior on the cross.

And she remembered her father's caution. St. Paul warned against being led astray from sincere and pure devotion to Christ.

She clung to Jakób's hand.

Because it felt to her as if everything—the music, the candles, the art all around her—was in fact leading her closer to a sincere and pure devotion to Christ.

As the service moved through the familiar rituals, she knew with greater certainty that she also felt at home here. This church, which *her* people regarded as a threat, this church was inextricably a part of her.

———

His apartment was sparsely furnished. There was a bedroom with a bed, a living room with a coffee table and three chairs, and a kitchen with a stove and a small fridge. No curtains, no rugs, pictures, or even a radio. "All in good time," Jakób apologized. "Most important are the curtains. A colleague has promised to help."

"Is she an engineer?" Grietjie asked, surprised.

Jakób laughed. "No, she's our human relations officer. She's helped me a lot."

"Oh." Grietjie felt slightly taken aback. *She* had wanted to help Jakób, just as he had helped her when she was new to his country.

"But the stove works, so you can make coffee," he said. "And you'll find bread, ham, and cheese in the fridge."

While she was buttering the bread, he sliced the ham thinly.

"Is she married?" she asked.

"Who?"

"Your human relations officer."

"No, divorced. I really must buy a sharper knife. This one is useless."

"My dad always says a blunt knife is an omen. Is she old?"

"Who?"

"Your human relations officer, dummy!"

"Oh. About my own age, I suppose. Tell me about the people who adopted you, Gretz."

"Grietjie. Remember, I'm Grietjie now."

"Grietjie."

"My dad is big and strong. He's a farmer, but the farm is very different from yours at Częstochowa. He's very religious, but we're Protestant, of course, not Catholic. And he's very Afrikaans. He won't speak English, not even to Grandpa John." She laughed softly. "You know, Jakób, I have an aunt who is completely English—Diana. You should hear her speak Afrikaans when they come to visit! She and my dad actually get along well."

"Well, it seems I'll have to learn Afrikaans then," he said. "Shall I slice more ham?"

He mustn't get it in his head to meet her father, Grietjie thought. *It will never work, even if he speaks perfect Afrikaans.*

"Is this enough ham?" he asked again.

"Oh, yes, I'm sure it'll be enough."

"And your new mother?"

"She's my only mother, Jakób. Mommy is a beautiful lady with a fine English upbringing. She's educated, with a master's degree in sociology. She and my dad are leaders in the community. I'm so proud of them."

They set out the food and coffee on the low table and sat in two of the chairs. He leaned back and stretched his long legs in front of him. "You don't know how grateful I am, Gretz."

"Grietjie," she corrected him. "Why?"

"Grietjie." He struggled to say her name. "Because you're happy. If the rest of the language is as difficult as your name, I'll never learn to speak it."

"Only the *g* and the *r* are hard to say. The rest is easy. You'll be happy here too, Jakób, I'm sure of it. Next time I'll bring you an Afrikaans reading book, an easy one. I'll help you read it. You'll soon pick up Afrikaans, you'll see."

They talked and talked. She told him about Kobus and his pigs, and her roommate, and her Polish tutor. He told her about Stan and Haneczka and the boys, about Turek and Monicka and the farm and his parents. And about little Czes, of course, who was thirteen now.

"I don't believe it!" Grietjie said, amazed. "I still think of him as an adorable little three-year-old."

"Yes, it's hard to believe how quickly a child grows up," Jakób agreed.

———

The apartment felt emptier after she left than before she had come. She still had the ability to flit into his life and brighten up his surroundings. Now that she was gone, he was painfully aware of the bare floors, the gray walls, the gaping windows.

Alice had promised to work on his curtains this weekend. She was another highlight in his life—an attractive, mature woman: efficient, friendly, at times even fun.

He made fresh coffee and stood at the living room window. An occasional car drove by in the street below. But late on a Sunday afternoon most people were at home with their families.

Alice had a family of her own. Two children at junior school, a boy and a girl. Jakób had taken her to the movies a few times, but it was hard for her, because she had to arrange for someone to look after the kids.

"Have supper with me one evening instead," she had proposed. "I make a wonderful pot roast."

But he wasn't quite ready for that yet.

Even the food here was different. Familiar food, like ham and cheese, tasted completely different, bland. And delicacies like biltong and rusks, which his colleagues were crazy about, were totally strange to his palate. Not to mention the barbecues!

But the country itself was good. And he was beginning to understand the people—strong and hard, but also hearty and warm, as Gretz had said.

Gretz. His thoughts always returned to her. She was happy, he could see it. But something wasn't quite right, he saw that as well.

Something rankled. He had to find out what it was, because at this point she was once again the most important person in his life—a safe, familiar harbor on a foreign shore.

———

After church on Sunday evening, Grietjie and Francois went out for coffee. The events of the day were dominating her thoughts.

"What's eating you?" asked Francois. "You're miles away."

He had said she should talk to him. She knew she could trust him. She looked him in the eye and said, "I attended mass at the Catholic cathedral this morning."

She registered the astonishment on his face. "You did what?"

"You heard." She shouldn't have said it. It was always better to say nothing.

"But why, Grietjie?"

She shrugged. "I wanted to."

"And how do you feel now?"

He's turning into a real psychologist, she thought, slightly irritated. "Still the same. It was interesting. This place has lovely coffee, don't you think?"

He laughed softly. "So you went to take a closer look at the Catholic Threat?" There was a grudging admiration in his voice. "Just don't let your folks find out or they'll skin you alive! My father would, and he's not even a Nationalist!"

———

The weeks flew past. Francois was working hard at his master's degree, and they seldom saw each other. *It's better this way*, Grietjie thought, *or he might just want to get serious again.*

On Wednesday evenings just before six, Jakób picked her up in the Volksie he'd finally purchased. Karin thought she was going to her Polish lesson. She waited for him outside. They went out for a bite to eat or bought French fries and ate them in the car. They talked, and she taught him Afrikaans.

"You're very clever!" she said. "Just look at the progress you're making!"

"How long did it take you to learn Afrikaans?" he asked.

"Not as long as it's taking you," she admitted. "But remember, I lived in a house where they spoke nothing but Afrikaans to me all day."

"I work among people who chiefly speak Afrikaans," he reminded her.

"Also true. What do they say about your progress?"

"I don't speak Afrikaans there."

"One of these days you will. And then you'll see how pleased they'll be."

He looked happier, she thought. He spoke about his job more often. He told her he was solving problems they'd been struggling with for a long time.

"I knew you were the best engineer!" she said proudly.

He laughed. "Not really, it was just something I happened to have come across in Poland."

He asked, but she refused to go to mass with him again.

Her studies took up a lot of her time. She spent hours doing research in the library, and she sat in the feeble winter sun reading one prescribed work after another.

"Your eyes will end up as square as those pages," Karin warned.

One Friday afternoon at the beginning of June, when Karin and Francois had gone home for the weekend, she phoned Jakób at work. She had never done it before. But she was lonely, she missed home, she'd had another terrible dream the night before, and she didn't want to be alone.

"Can I come over this evening?" she asked.

She hadn't been in his apartment since the first time. "I shouldn't really come to your place on my own," she had explained.

He was glad she'd been raised so well.

But now she was here, and he understood again.

"It looks brand-new!" she said, surprised. "The curtains, the rugs, you even have a sofa, Jakób. And a bookcase." She began to laugh. "But you've only got five books!"

He smiled. "It's five more than I had a month ago."

"And two of them are children's stories I gave you. You'll have to start buying books. You can't go through life without books."

"I have to buy many other things first," he said and opened the cabinet in the living room. "Are you old enough to have wine?"

"Jakób," she scolded, "I'm long past eighteen! And yes, thank you, I'd love a glass of wine. Dry red, just like Grandpa John taught me."

He took out a bottle of red wine and began to open it. "What if I didn't have dry red?" he teased her.

"Then I would have had to take you to Grandpa John for a lecture," she said.

"Will you introduce us one day?" he asked.

"Maybe," she said vaguely.

They talked about the usual things. He stole a glance at her—she looked paler than usual, and tired. She sat deep in the armchair, her legs tucked under her. She turned the stem of the wineglass round and round in her fingers. The last rays of the winter sun made the dark-red liquid sparkle like rubies. Her hair glinted gold in the last light.

She was indescribably beautiful. And . . .

"Do you still feel the cold?" he asked. "When you were a little girl, you were always scrunched up when the weather was cold."

She laughed. "Probably because I was so thin. When I look at photos from that time I realize I looked like one of those skeletal children from the Boer War concentration camps. At least I've put on some flesh." She thought for a moment. "And my family is wrapped around me like a comfort blanket. They warm me from the inside."

Usually she radiated happiness, he thought, but tonight she was different, maybe because he could see she was tired. Tonight she seemed calm. She exuded a kind of intimacy that washed over him. He drank it in now to savor it later.

"I'd like to meet your family," he said. "Your parents, your brother, your Grandpa John as well."

Her blue eyes gazed at him. "I haven't told them about you, Jakób."

He frowned slightly. "Why not?"

She kept her eyes on him. "Because they know nothing about my roots," she said evenly.

"You mean . . . ?"

"Yes, I mean they don't know about the convent school or the years I spent in Poland or my Jewish blood."

"Grietjie," he said, astounded, "you can't live like this."

She raised her chin. "I've been living like this for years, and it's been a good life," she said.

"But it's unnecessary. Just tell them."

"You knew it was quite necessary. We discussed it at the orphanage—do you remember? I know the Afrikaner people. The Roman Catholic Church is the Catholic Threat against which we have to protect our faith. Anything that comes from Poland is Communist and part of the Red Danger, against which we must protect our country. And the Jews are non-Aryans, against whom we must protect our blood." She was silent for a moment. "My parents are all I have."

He was shocked. Not by the unyielding stance on the Catholic Threat or the misconception about Poland—but by the utter loneliness of the young person in front of him.

"Grietjie?"

His eyes sought out hers. He knew she was battling not to cry, but he said nothing, because he also knew she hated being a crybaby.

Awhile later she said, "I still dream, Jakób. Much worse than when I was younger."

"About the fire?"

"Yes."

For hours they talked or sat in an easy silence. They forgot to eat the meat pies he had bought on their way over. Much later they had coffee.

He understood everything, yet he didn't know what advice to give her.

At ten he took her back to her residence. "You can bring your books and study at my apartment tomorrow," he suggested.

"I have research to do in the library, so it won't work. But thanks, Jakób."

He didn't ask about Sunday again.

Back in his flat he poured the last of the wine into his glass and returned to his window. A bus drove past. The rest of the street was deserted.

He had so badly wanted to take her in his arms and hold her, to protect her against the hurt she carried inside her.

But it was not the little girl he had wanted to protect—it was the beautiful young woman.

He sank down in the chair and lowered his head into his hands, tried to banish the feeling. *Jakób Kowalski*, he told himself, *pull yourself together! This is Gretz, the little girl you fetched from Rigena's tumbledown house and left on the steps of a ruined church in Kiel.*

But he knew she was more.

When the sun had bathed her in its rays in the late afternoon, when she had sat in the chair tonight with her legs tucked under her and the glass in her hand and her hair like a golden halo around her head, she had been more than beautiful.

She had been infinitely desirable.

13

Taking exams has its advantages, Grietjie thought one afternoon late in June after she had written her last paper. The biggest advantage was that she had no time to think. She was much too busy. And she was so tired that she just wanted to get back to res, take a shower—if there was hot water, mind you—and get into bed. Tomorrow she would tidy her room, pack her things, and start looking forward to the vacation.

Only then would she start wondering what had become of Jakób.

He had phoned her two or three times, asked how she was, asked how the exams were going and whether she was getting enough sleep. But he hadn't come to see her again.

She slept like a log that night, past her usual wake-up time and right through breakfast. When at last she surfaced from the vapors of sleep and looked at her watch, it was almost ten o'clock. She flew out of bed. Karin and she had plans to go into the city to look for fabric for new evening gowns.

When they came back just before five, she decided she didn't want to spend the entire vacation wondering what was wrong with Jakób. She found two tickeys and went down the stairs to the phone booth.

"Why haven't you come to see me again?"

"Hello, Grietjie."

"Hello, Jakób. I'm going home tomorrow for three weeks and I haven't seen you in a month."

"How are you?" he asked in Afrikaans.

"Very well, thank you." She reverted to Polish. "If you stop seeing me, you're going to forget all the Afrikaans I taught you."

"Doesn't my Afrikaans sound good?" he asked in Afrikaans.

For a moment she was taken aback.

"Your three minutes are up!" said the operator.

"Jakób, you're wasting my tickeys!" Grietjie scolded and dropped her last tickey into the slot.

He laughed. "You're a little firecracker, aren't you?"

"I'm not wasting my money arguing with you any longer. If you don't come to see me tonight, you'll have to wait another month. And by that time I might not recognize you anymore."

He laughed again. She liked it when he laughed. "We can't take that chance," he said. "I'll pick you up at six. We can go out for something to eat."

"French fries?"

"No, better than French fries."

She had just got back to her room when a voice called down the passage, "Grietjie Neethling! Telephone!"

She trotted back to the phone booth. If Jakób had changed his mind, she'd know he was angry with her. She just didn't know why. Maybe she bored him with her juvenile conversation. Maybe he'd rather spend time with the human resources officer. What was her name? Alice.

It was Francois calling.

"I'm really sorry," she said when he invited her out, "I would have loved to go. I haven't seen you for so long." She was truly sorry. Maybe Francois would think she didn't want to see him. "But I promise, the first evening I'm back we'll spend time together. Promise."

"It's going to be a very long vacation," he teased, but she heard the serious note behind the banter.

Long before six she was waiting outside for Jakób.

When his blue Volksie pulled up, she went to meet it. He got out and playfully opened his arms. She felt a surge of happiness, as always, when he did that. She laughed and walked into his embrace. It felt exactly the same—familiar, safe, happy. He hugged her for a moment. Then he let her go and opened the car door for her.

They went to Janina's, a fancy restaurant in the city. She looked at the menu while he studied the wine list.

"What would you like to drink?" he asked.

"Red wine would be nice, thank you."

"I don't think they serve alcohol to minors," he said.

"Jakób!"

He laughed.

When he had ordered the wine and the food, he turned to her. "So, are you done with all your exams?"

"Yes, all done. Jakób, don't ever stay away so long again! Why didn't you come?"

"How did it go?"

"It was fine. Why didn't you come?" she asked again.

"You had to study."

"You know very well I can't study all the time. I missed you."

"You did, did you?" he joked.

"To tell you the truth," she said with a twinkle in her eye, "I missed you so much that at times I couldn't study at all."

"If your grades are poor," he said with mock severity, "Father Jakób will have to give you a hiding."

"You're not my father!" She remembered something. "There's a song in Afrikaans called 'Vader Jakób.' It was the first tune my mother taught me to play on the piano."

"You play the piano?" he asked, surprised.

"Yes, I'll play for you one day. And after the vacation we must continue with your Afrikaans lessons. The way it's going, you'll never speak Afrikaans."

"Is that what you think, Miss Neethling?" he asked in Afrikaans.

She narrowed her eyes. "Jakób, who's teaching you?"

"Oh, it comes naturally. Whereas women may find it hard to come to grips with new—"

"Jakób!" she warned him.

He laughed. "A colleague."

"Alice?" That Alice creature seemed to be taking over completely!

"No, Alice is English. I'm learning from Jo."

"Is Jo also a human relations officer?"

"No, he's an engineer."

She was flooded with relief. She had no idea why.

They talked and ate and laughed and talked some more, because it was good to be together again.

When they had finished their meal, Jakób placed his knife and fork side by side on his plate and asked, "Would you like some dessert?"

After they ordered he said, "I have to learn Afrikaans as quickly as possible so that I can speak to your father."

Grietjie looked up, perturbed. "I've explained to you it's impossible," she said.

Jakób leaned forward. His big hands were folded on the table where his plate had been a moment ago. His black eyes regarded her earnestly.

"Yes, I know, Grietjie, and I understand. I've also given it a lot of thought. You'll have to—"

"No." She shook her head. "You don't understand."

"Yes, I do. I discussed the situation with some of my Afrikaans colleagues."

Anger rose up inside her. "You discussed my business with your colleagues?"

He kept looking at her earnestly. "Not specifically your business. I just asked what they thought of the Catholic faith, and of Jews. The people who work with me are reasonably open-minded, but the older generation, they say, is—"

"Well, if you know everything, why do you still want to speak to my father?" She couldn't believe he was spoiling a wonderful evening with this senseless conversation.

"Be quiet for a moment and let me have my say," he said.

"Don't speak to me as if I'm a child," she snapped.

"And don't take out your cranky German temper on me," he said firmly. "Listen to what I have to say like a grown-up person, and then we'll discuss it."

She clamped her mouth shut and stared at him. She would let him speak. Then he could take her back to her res.

But he didn't say anything. He leaned back, waiting.

"Why aren't you saying anything?" she asked.

"Because I've seen this attitude before," he said calmly.

She closed her eyes and took a deep breath. Then she opened her eyes and said wearily, "Fine, speak. I'll listen."

He held out his hand, but she kept her own hands in her lap. He withdrew his hand, leaned forward, and began.

"Grietjie, the more I speak to people, the more I realize the extent of your dilemma."

"Why speak about it then?" she asked dejectedly.

"Because you owe it to your parents to tell them—to your parents and yourself," he said seriously. "In the long run there's only one thing that works, Grietjie, and it's honesty. Absolute honesty."

She nodded slowly and sighed. "I know. That's what my dad also says."

"Your dad sounds like a wise man."

"He's also a typical Afrikaner."

He nodded. "Maybe you'll find it easier to speak to your mother?"

"Maybe." She didn't want to, though.

When he reached across the table again, she put her palm in his. His broad, strong fingers closed around her hand. She knew he wouldn't give her the wrong advice. He never had before.

"Promise me you'll start telling your parents the truth during this vacation?"

She felt stupid tears just under the surface. "I can't promise, Jakób."

His thumb stroked and stroked her hand. "Fine. Just promise you'll try."

She wanted to. Strange, but for the very first time she wanted to—it would be liberating. "I want to, yes," she said, "but I don't know whether I can."

———

When he pulled up in front of her residence, she turned to him.

"I don't want to go home anymore."

"Don't be silly, of course you do. Nothing has changed. And if the opportunity arises, you'll tell them."

"Ye-es."

"Or you'll try to create an opportunity to speak to at least one of them."

"Yes, Jakób." She didn't want to leave the safe space of the Volksie.

He got out and opened the door for her. "Come, Grietjie."

"Okay."

He walked her to the front door. "Enjoy the vacation and get a good rest."

"Yes, thanks."

He turned and walked away.

———

Back in their room Karin asked, "Who's the guy you went out with?"

"We didn't go out," Grietjie said quickly, "we just went for coffee."

"Same thing."

"Not really. 'Out' is—"

"Who's the guy?"

"Just . . . someone I've known since junior school." She tried to change the subject. "What are you going to do during the vacation?" she asked, preparing to boil water for coffee.

"Stay at home, sew," Karin answered. "He looks a bit old?"

He was thirty-three. She knew his exact age. "Yes, now that you mention it. Are you going to make that blue evening gown you designed?"

But Karin ignored her digressions. "How old?" she demanded.

"About thirty-ish, I don't really know. Stop pestering me."

"He's the guy who keeps phoning, the one you've been out with a few times. Right, roomie?"

Grietjie sighed. "We've been out for coffee, yes. But we haven't been *out*."

Karin shrugged. "He's handsome, that's for sure! But beware of older men."

"Good grief, Karin," Grietjie said, annoyed, "he's not an older man! He's just Jakób. I've known him for years!"

"Fine, if you say so," Karin gave in. "The water is boiling over the top of the jug. Shall I make the coffee?"

———·———

Jakób, handsome? Grietjie considered this as Grandpa John's chauffeur drove them across the Springbok Flats. Grandpa John had fallen asleep, as usual. She closed her eyes and tried to conjure Jakób's image. He was big and strong, with broad shoulders and solid muscles from the physical work he'd been doing since childhood. He had thick black hair and black eyes, lovely eyes, come to think of it. Did all those features make him a handsome man?

Girls always thought Kobus was attractive with his athletic build, blue eyes, and sandy hair. To her he was just an older brother whom she loved.

Francois might be attractive, but she didn't really know. He was her friend.

She opened her eyes and looked at Grandpa John next to her. *I love him*, she thought, *that's why he's one of the most attractive men I know.*

I don't want to tell Mom and Dad, the thought came to her out of the blue.

But she also knew she had to try.

———·———

Kobus's pigsties had been completed, the first pigs were in, and the first litters had arrived. He was planning to go to Estcourt at the end of July to sign the final contract with the bacon factory before taking her back to university.

She was astounded by the multitude of squirming piglets. "Look at all my hams, Grietjie," Kobus boasted.

"If you turn all these piglets into ham, you're going to make a stack of money!" she said. "Do you realize what you pay in the store for four thin slices of ham?"

"I have a lot of debt to pay off," he reminded her.

"A bank loan?"

"No, I borrowed money from Grandpa John. He charges me interest, but less than the Land Bank."

"If I get a job at *Die Transvaler* in Johannesburg next year, I'm going to live with Grandpa John," she said. "He said I could. For free, until I get my first salary."

"What are your chances?"

"A hundred percent. If you work, you earn a salary."

"No, stupid, of getting the job."

"Don't call me stupid!"

"Your chances?"

"Good," she answered. "I've already had an interview. I should hear in August."

————

Salomé came over often. Grietjie was used to getting most of Kobus's attention, but when Salomé was present, Kobus hardly noticed her. He only had eyes for Salomé. Grietjie didn't like it at all.

"I don't know whether I like Salomé much," she told her mother one evening when Kobus had gone to town to visit his girlfriend. "She's a bit wishy-washy, with her high-pitched voice and her mannerisms and stuff. She won't last on the farm."

Her mother laughed. "I felt the same way about Diana when your Uncle Peter married her. I thought he could do much better."

"I know Kobus can do better," Grietjie said firmly.

"I think all sisters feel that way about their brothers' wives," said her mother. "One day Kobus will feel the same about the man you marry."

"I doubt whether I'll ever get married," said Grietjie.

"Oh? And what about Francois?"

"He's just a friend. We don't see much of each other anymore."

Her mother nodded. "The right man will come along and sweep you off your feet," she said. "We must do our best to make Salomé feel at home in our family."

Up in the gorge, Grietjie's father told her of his latest plans. "The soil is sandy, it drains well. This is where I want to put in the first vines," he said.

"Are you going to make red wine?"

"No, you little tippler," he teased. "I'm going to grow table grapes. I'm going to put in just a handful of vines at first and see how it goes."

As they were walking back, Grietjie asked, "What's your opinion of Jews, Daddy?"

"Do you mean the Jews of the Bible, the modern Jews in Israel, or the local Jews here in South Africa?"

She didn't know what she meant. "The Jews here," she ventured.

"The Jews will always be foreigners trying to take advantage of the Boers," her father answered. "Grandpa John has many good Jewish friends, and I have known old Cohen Crown for years. But they'll always be neither fish nor fowl."

The lump so familiar to Grietjie during her childhood was back in her stomach. Yet she soldiered on. "And the Jews who were persecuted under Hitler, Daddy?"

"Grietjie, there are various theories about that. I agree with the people who believe that the so-called Holocaust never took place, that it was just a ploy by the Communists to vilify the Germans."

She couldn't believe what she was hearing. He must have noted the surprise in her face.

"Think about it for a moment—who reached the so-called concentration camps first? Russian soldiers. They said the Germans had burned most of the camps to destroy the evidence, but I believe it was just a story to cover up their own lack of evidence that the camps ever existed. And today Westerners are refused entry into Communist countries. In that way the lie is being perpetuated and the world continues to speak ill of Germany."

Surely her father, her wise daddy, couldn't really believe what he had just said? "Don't you believe that they sent the Jews to ghettos and later transported them to the camps in open cattle cars?" she asked, just to be sure.

"No, Grietjie, I don't believe it for a moment. You have German roots, you know the Germans. Do you believe that such a highly civilized, proud nation could descend to such depths?"

That night her safe bed in her safe room became a fire that almost consumed her. Fortunately her parents didn't wake up.

But three nights later her mother did wake up. She wiped Grietjie's drenched face with a damp facecloth. She soothed her and comforted her and spent the rest of the night in the big bed with her. The next day she took Grietjie to their family doctor, and they returned with a handful of pills.

"The doctor says she's completely overwrought," Grietjie overheard her mother tell her worried father and Grandpa John in the dining room. "She must get enough sleep and rest. She's in bed now."

"Maybe we should take her to Dr. Gertjies in Pretoria," she heard her father say. "I've heard his powders can do wonders."

Later her father sat down at her bedside and took her hand. She opened her eyes. "Grietjie . . . Daddy's little girl," he said tenderly and put his big hand on her forehead. "Daddy wishes he knew what to do."

She pressed her father's hard hand to her cheek. "I'm sorry I'm such a worry to you," she said. "I promise I'll be back to my old self soon, I just have to catch up on a little sleep."

But she stayed awake for as long as possible, because she was afraid to close her eyes.

———•———

During the day she made a point of getting as much exercise as possible. At night she was exhausted and fell into a deep sleep. The family processed meat and made beef biltong, and she and her mother talked nonstop. She drove to town with her father to try on the ball gown Aunt Bettie was making for her from the fabric she'd purchased in Pretoria. They talked all the way to town and back. She and Kobus went horse riding. She walked through the old homestead with Salomé, listening to all her plans. She sat talking to Grandpa John in the warm winter sun. These were her people, whom she loved.

In the last week of the vacation she was feeling almost well again. For an entire week she hadn't had a single dream.

By the time Kobus drove her back to university at the end of the vacation, she had spoken to her family about every topic under the sun. Every topic but Poland, and the convent school, and her Jewish blood. And Jakób.

———•———

On Wednesday and Thursday she phoned his work but he wasn't there. By the weekend she still had not heard from him.

Saturday dawned bitterly cold. The sky was full of dark clouds that hid the sun completely. Karin had a bad bout of flu and had gone home on Thursday. Grietjie missed the people and the places she loved.

Enough was enough. At nine she put on her warmest clothes and went down the stairs. She was going to walk until the dark cloud inside her had lifted.

There was a fine drizzle outside. *You're not getting me down, clouds,* she decided and went back inside to put on her raincoat.

She walked and walked, down Park Street, past Girls' High, past the big stone gates of the Eastern sports grounds, past the Arcadia Nursing Home. The rain was a gray blanket around her. The fine spray stung her face. The jacaranda trees were bare skeletons. She sidestepped the puddles on the sidewalk. She walked briskly, she breathed deeply, and slowly her mind cleared.

I'm almost in Sunnyside, she realized. *I might as well see if Jakób is home.*

She had to knock a few times before he opened. He was still in his pajamas, his hair tousled, day-old stubble dark on his chin.

"Don't kiss me, you'll be prickly!" she warned him.

"Good morning, Grietjie. What are you doing here?" he asked, surprised.

"You don't answer your phone, so I've come to see if you're still alive. May I come in and pour coffee?"

He stepped aside and closed the door behind her. "How did you get here?"

"I walked. Why isn't there any milk in your fridge?"

"In the rain?"

"Yes. Milk?"

"We'll have to drink it black. You'll get sick out in the cold like that."

"I'm wearing a raincoat, Jakób. You're not listening to what I'm asking!"

"I was away all week," he answered, pushing his fingers through his thick black hair. "You shouldn't—"

"Where were you?" she asked, carrying the black coffee to the living room.

"Thabazimbi, for my job."

"Thabazimbi?" she said, surprised. "It's in the bushveld, like our farm. But Thabazimbi isn't close to the farm. Did you cross the Springbok Flats and turn west at Warmbaths?"

"That's right. Where's the sugar?"

"I've already put some in and stirred. When we go to the farm, we head north past Warmbaths and Nylstroom and all those towns. Jakób, you were in my part of the country and you didn't even know it."

"I like your part of the country," he said. "But if it's that hot in winter, I don't know what the summers must be like!"

"There's a man who helps my dad on the farm," she said. "Oom Doorsie. He always says there's just a chicken-wire fence between the bushveld and hell, and that fence is broken in places."

Jakób laughed. "I think Oom Doorsie is right," he said. "Did you have a good time at home?"

She told him about Kobus's pigs and Salomé's mannerisms and her dad's plan to grow vines.

At last he asked, "Did you speak to them, Grietjie?"

She told Jakób what her father had said about the Holocaust. He shook his head. "I can't believe it!" he said, astounded.

"And my father isn't stupid!" Grietjie hastened to assure him. "It's just the way people think around here."

When they were on their third cup of black coffee, she told him about the dreams and all the pills she had to take. "But I'm better now," she assured him.

"You're better *for now*, Grietjie," he said. "We must find a solution."

She looked at him earnestly, at his familiar face, his big hands, his dark eyes. "Sometimes I think you're the only one who can help me," she said.

But no matter how they talked and deliberated, they couldn't come up with any ideas.

———

In mid-August she received a phone call. "Miss Neethling?" a female voice asked on the other end of the line.

"That's me," she answered uncertainly. She hoped it wasn't bad news.

"Can you come in to the head office of Voortrekker Press? We would like to finalize your appointment at *Die Transvaler.*"

Grietjie's heart began to race. "Did I get the post?" she asked.

"That's right. When can you come in?"

Her mouth was dry, her heart beat in her throat, she could hardly speak. *Professional Magrieta Katharina Neethling,* she told herself. "Saturday morning? Would Saturday morning be good?"

"Around ten?" asked the thoroughly professional voice on the other end.

After she had replaced the receiver, Grietjie quite unprofessionally charged up the stairs, taking them two at a time. Karin was not in their room. Grietjie grabbed her purse and rushed back downstairs.

Jakób took so long to come to the phone that she had to put in another coin. "Kowalski," said his familiar deep voice.

"Jakób, guess what? I got the job at *Die Transvaler* in Johannesburg, and you took an awfully long time to come to the phone, and I had to put in another tickey."

"Hello, Grietjie."

"Hello, Jakób. Can you believe I got the job? I, Grietjie Neethling, got the job. I'm a journalist now. Nearly."

"Yes, I can believe it. You said you were almost a hundred percent certain you'd get the job."

"Yes, but you don't understand—I've got it now!"

"It's wonderful, Grietjie. I'm very happy for you. Shall we celebrate tonight?"

"No, from now until tomorrow morning I have to study nonstop because I have two tests tomorrow. And then I'm going to Grandpa John's for the weekend to finalize my appointment. I'll probably have to sign a lot of papers, and I think I should take Grandpa John along to make sure they don't cheat me, because I don't know anything about that kind of thing. Jakób, I'm so excited I feel I could fall over backward."

"You're going to fall over backward if you don't stop to take a breath every now and again." He laughed.

"Three minutes!" the operator said.

"'Bye, Jakób! Enjoy the weekend!" Grietjie shouted before the connection was cut.

———

No one in the whole world has a more wonderful grandpa than I do, Grietjie thought on Friday afternoon as she sat in the luxurious backseat of his car. Her friends liked to take a peek when the chauffeur in his white gloves opened the back door of the big black Bentley for her and closed it softly behind her with a slight bow. When they pulled away, she always waved like the queen of England, who had come to South Africa in 1947, or Princess Elizabeth, who had become queen a few years afterward.

After dinner she and Grandpa John sat in his study. He had a new record of Tito Schipa he wanted her to listen to.

"Please smoke your cigar if you like," she said. "Can I get one ready for you?"

"A gentleman doesn't smoke a cigar in the company of a lady," he said, his eyes twinkling.

"And if the lady insists?" she played along. "If the lady says she thinks it's the loveliest smell in the world?"

"Then the gentleman would have to agree," said Grandpa John. "Your wish is my command."

She sat beside him on the soft leather couch. They talked about various things: her appointment at the paper, her meeting the next day with the human relations officer, her studies, the bus boycott by the workers in Alexandra.

"How does the boycott affect Rand Consolidated, Grandpa?" Grietjie asked.

"We're always adversely affected by miners who stay away from work," Grandpa John replied. "But usually it's not a long-term problem. At this point a shortage of technological expertise is a more serious problem."

"What kind of expertise?"

"We need professional people, specifically engineers. Keep your eyes peeled at university for a clever young engineer, one who is worth his salt."

"I know an engineer," she said without thinking. "A metallurgical engineer, named Jakób . . ." She swallowed his last name. Just in time.

Grandpa John didn't seem to have heard the name. "Yes, I suppose a metallurgical engineer could work, though I think Uncle Peter is actually looking for a mining engineer. I'll ask him."

"Actually, he has a very good job at Iscor," she said. "I don't know whether he'd be interested in moving."

When the music faded, Grandpa John did not change the record.

"What's your opinion of Jews, Grandpa?" Grietjie asked on the spur of the moment.

For a moment he looked at her keenly. Or maybe she'd imagined it, because he answered in his normal voice, "Some of my best friends are Jews, Grietjie. They're like any other nation. There are exceptional people among them, and there are those you would rather not associate with."

She nodded slowly. She didn't know why she had asked.

He looked at her earnestly. "My mother was Jewish, you know, Grietjie."

Her jaw dropped. Could it be true?

He smiled slowly and nodded. "She was the most wonderful mother I could ever have wished for."

Surely it couldn't be!

"And your father, Grandpa?"

"He was a cranky old Englishman," Grandpa John remembered.

"What faith did you grow up in?" she asked. "I mean, were you Christian or Jewish?"

"My parents set little store by religion," said Grandpa John. "It was only after I got to know Susan, bless her beautiful soul, that religion became important to me."

The knowledge sank in slowly. Grandpa John had Jewish blood. Even more than she.

"Then Mommy has Jewish blood too?" she said as the realization grew.

"Yes. Your mother's grandmother was one hundred percent Jewish," said Grandpa John. He puffed at his cigar.

Just like her own Oma.

She moved in under his arm. "Does Daddy know?" she asked.

"Yes, your father knows. He's known since the beginning." The fire burned slowly, languidly. Actually, the evening was too warm for a fire, but Grandpa John was always cold these days. "If people love each other, there's no need for secrets."

That was all he said. He would never pry. But she knew he saw and understood much more than he ever let on.

All weekend she brooded. Her darling mother, Kate, was just as Jewish as she was! And her Afrikaner daddy worshiped the earth beneath her half-Jewish mommy's feet. And they didn't have secrets from each other, because their love could bear all things.

She was the only one with secrets. An entire drawer full of skeletons.

She didn't want secrets anymore.

But when the chauffeur took her back to Pretoria on Sunday afternoon, she still had not said, "My grandmother was Jewish too."

She had wanted to, but she couldn't.

———

Jakób had a telephone in his apartment now, so she could phone him anytime outside office hours.

"But you should phone me," she told him, "because it's at least one tickey every time I call."

"And I call for free?" he asked.

"No, but you earn a big salary every month. There's something I must tell you, Jakób!"

"I already know you got the job."

"No, something even better. But I want to tell you in person, not on the phone. Can I come over on Saturday? Then I can see your phone as well."

"Oh, Grietjie," he sighed.

"Don't you want me there?" It was fun to tease him. He was always so serious.

"Shouldn't you be studying?"

"On a Saturday morning? Jakób, you're really terribly old, you know! Should I take the bus or will you fetch me?"

———

He knew he shouldn't fetch her. But if he didn't, she would simply get on the bus and come by herself. Or she would walk.

He loved having her at his apartment. Today she was wearing a yellow frock—his personal ray of sunshine. Her hair had been cut in a shorter style and the unruly curls framed her face.

In the car on their way over she told him, "Grandpa John's mother was Jewish, so my mother is just as Jewish as I am! And my dad knows this about her, and he worships the earth under her feet."

"Did you tell your grandpa you're also Jewish?" he asked.

"I'm not Jewish," she answered. "I'm a Christian-Afrikaner. And no, I didn't tell him, and don't be angry. I couldn't, that's why I didn't."

"You passed up a golden opportunity."

"I know. Next time I will."

Now she was walking through his flat, inspecting everything.

"Wow, you even have a radio and a gramophone now! Next time I'll bring a few of my records so that you can catch up with what the students are listening to."

He shouldn't have brought her. It was lovely that she was here, but unsettling. He sat down on the sofa.

"Do you like dancing, Jakób?"

Did he like dancing? He thought of Mischka in her elegant black frock in his arms on the dance floor.

"I don't think my kind of dancing and the way today's students jump about are remotely the same," he answered.

"I'll teach you," she said. "Not only students dance, you know. The Afrikaners also love dancing, especially in the barns on the farms at New Year or at weddings and special occasions. Do you want some cake?"

"Yes, thank you."

"You'll soon learn, you'll see."

"I said yes to cake, not to dancing lessons," he protested. "Anyway, I know how to waltz."

"The waltz is old-fashioned," she said from the kitchen. "But it's nice, you're right. I'll teach you all the modern moves." She handed him a slice of cake and sat down in the armchair, facing him. "Jakób, are you happy yet?"

He gave her question some thought. "Yes, I think I am," he said honestly. "I enjoy my job, definitely a lot more than I did in Poland. I like the people, especially my Afrikaner colleagues. They're a proud nation, good people. In a way, they remind me of the Poles."

She began to laugh. "When I first came, everyone wanted to kiss me! It's one of the typical Afrikaner traditions that I'll always find strange."

He smiled. "I haven't had such luck. And don't imagine that there aren't pretty Afrikaner girls working at Iscor!"

"And the country?" she asked. "It's harsh and dry when you compare it to Poland, don't you think?"

"Yes, it is, but it has its own charm. I've fallen in love with Africa," he admitted.

"Have you ever fallen in love with anything other than a country?" she asked out of the blue.

The question ripped the memory wide open.

To his surprise, he found that thinking of Mischka didn't hurt quite as much anymore. A scab had formed on the wound and it was hardly visible now.

When he didn't answer at once, she said, "I suppose I shouldn't have asked."

"I did love someone, yes, before I left Poland," he said.

"I'm sorry, I shouldn't—"

"We thought about getting married, but in the end she couldn't bring herself to leave the country with me."

"I'm really . . ." Her pale-blue eyes looked directly at him. "You should have told me. We don't have secrets, remember? You and I, we know everything about each other."

He nodded. "You're right," he said. "Her name was Mischka Bòdis."

She frowned slightly. "Polish?"

"No, Hungarian."

They sat facing each other without speaking, he on the sofa with his legs stretched out in front of him, she in the soft armchair with her legs tucked under her.

"What does it feel like to love someone, Jakób?" she asked. "I've gone out with a number of guys, I've kissed a few as well, I mean really kissed, but I don't know how to tell if you love someone enough to want to marry him."

This is turning into a difficult conversation, Jakób thought, *like so many of our conversations in the past, even when she was very small.* But he had to answer her honestly, that he also knew, because she wouldn't be satisfied with anything less.

"Jakób?"

He gave a slow smile. "I don't really know, Grietjie. I should think it's when you always want to be with the other person, when you'd rather be with him or her than anywhere else in the world."

She looked into his eyes. "Then I love you, do you know that, Jakób?"

Holy Mother, give me wisdom, he prayed softly. "You love your parents the same way, don't you? And your grandpa?"

"Yes, I do. Our home is the best place in the whole world. I really wish I could show it to you. But I just can't tell them."

"I think you should start with Grandpa John." Jakób was grateful to steer the conversation in a new direction.

"Yes, I should. The vacation starts in two weeks," she said seriously. Then her face brightened. "And next week it's my birthday."

"I know. I suppose you'll be celebrating with your friends?"

"On the weekend, yes. But on Thursday the tenth I'm going to celebrate it with you."

He couldn't refuse her anything.

It was becoming harder and harder to be close to her. He had to stop himself from wiping a strand of hair out of her face, from stroking her soft arm. He wanted to wrap his arms around her and hold her tight.

Those feelings filled him with indescribable guilt.

———

For the first time since Kobus had graduated she was going home by train. Not on her own—her dad would never allow it. She was traveling with a male first-year student from the neighboring town.

Jakób had picked them up at her residence in his Volksie and dropped them at the main station, but she had told him not to bother getting out of the car. She kept wishing Jakób could have come home with her, but she said nothing, because it was her own fault that he couldn't.

The station hadn't changed. She got the familiar smell even before she walked through the door. The sounds were the same—locomotives puffing and blowing, wheels screeching on the iron tracks, muted thumps as the cars banged against each other. She saw the white billows of steam and the black smoke of a departing train. She saw red flames where the fire was stoked in the locomotive.

But today the station was not an unhappy place. Today she was going home for all of ten days. It was just a pity about Jakób.

At the end of their journey her father was waiting at the station with the big truck. "I don't have that much luggage!" she teased him.

He laughed. "We'll have to put your luggage at your feet. I've had to load pigs for Kobus, so the back is dirty."

She was glad she hadn't witnessed it.

At home the dogs and her mother were waiting—in that order, because the dogs had to be calmed before she could get to her mother.

"Do you remember how scared I was of the dogs when I first came?" she asked as she patted their heads.

It was almost suppertime and a feast was waiting. And, after hours of talk, she went to sleep in her very own bed in her very own bedroom.

Saturday morning she rose early. Kobus was already in the kitchen, making coffee. He pumped and pumped the Primus stove.

"This thing is from Noah's ark," he muttered. "Mom should get a new one. Do you want coffee? And would you like to go down to the pigsties with me?"

Later that morning Salomé arrived. Her small Morris was chock-full of curtains—a few of the old ones that she had washed and a few new ones she had made. There was even a covered pelmet for the living room. They worked all morning to hang the curtains. Salomé and Kobus were getting married the week before Christmas, and the old homestead was almost ready for the new bride to move in.

"I've been wanting to ask you, Grietjie, will you be my bridesmaid?"

"Your bridesmaid!" Grietjie cried, surprised. "Salomé, thank you, I'd love to!"

"I'm glad you're going to be my sister. I only have brothers," Salomé said sincerely.

I once had a sister, Grietjie thought, but she didn't say it aloud.

That evening she said to her mother, "Salomé is actually a nice girl once you get to know her."

"Yes, she's lovely."

Well, I don't know whether I'd go that far, Grietjie thought. Aloud, she said, "What are we making for supper, Mommy?" Maria didn't come in on Saturday nights.

"I haven't given it any thought," answered her mom.

"I'll make pancakes," Grietjie suggested. "I know it isn't raining, but it's been a long time since we last had pancakes."

"Lovely," said her mother. "But let me find out what your dad wants. I hear him calling."

"Did I hear the word *pancakes*?" Kobus asked from the doorway. "And it isn't even raining!"

"If we have to wait for rain," Grietjie said as she measured out the ingredients, "we'll never have pancakes. Please get me two eggs from the pantry?"

When Kobus returned with the eggs, he said, "I'll help bake."

"No," said Grietjie, deftly mixing the batter with a wooden spoon, "I'll bake. Last time you baked, half the pancakes landed on the floor."

"I accidentally dropped one pancake," Kobus protested and sat down at the table.

"It was one too many," said Grietjie as she took the Primus stove down from the shelf. She shook it to see whether there was enough kerosene in the tank. "You can mix the cinnamon sugar," she said. She carefully poured methylated spirits into the spirit cup. "But don't put in too much cinnamon," she said as she set the spirits alight, "or the pancakes will be bitter."

"Where do I find the cinnamon?"

"In the pantry—in the basket with the herbs and spices."

When the spirits were hot enough, she began to pump the stove.

"Is this the cinnamon?" asked Kobus from the doorway.

She turned.

An explosion rocked the kitchen.

She felt the hammerblow of the scorching flames.

Someone pulled her away.

She smelled burning hair.

She smelled smoke.

The smoke was all around her and inside her.

Someone was screaming.

She saw the curtains catch fire, and the carpet, and the bed.

The big bed on which Jurgen lay sleeping.

The smoke made everything black.

Someone was screaming dreadfully.

Screaming and screaming and screaming.

Dreadfully.

14

On Monday morning just before nine, Alice walked into his office. "Jacob, someone inquired about you, a Mr. Woodroffe."

Jakób smiled politely. "Woodroffe? I don't know anyone by that name. Did he ask for me personally?"

"Not personally. He asked whether we had a metallurgical engineer named Jacob. But he pronounced it oddly, and not like the Afrikaans fellows either."

"Jakób?" he asked.

"Yes," she said, "like that."

"It's the Polish pronunciation of my name," he said, still frowning. A feeling of dread took hold of him. But what could they do if they traced him here? Besides, they would use his last name rather than his first name if they made inquiries. "This Mr. Woodroffe didn't mention my last name?" he asked.

"No, he just asked for a metallurgical engineer by your first name. He said it wasn't about business, it was a personal call. Here's the number if you want to return his call," said Alice.

Jakób took the note from her and looked at the number. It was a Johannesburg number. Woodroffe? In Johannesburg?

The realization struck him like an icy blast.

He looked up. Alice was still standing there. "Thanks," he said, "I'll phone him later."

The moment she had left, he picked up the receiver and told his secretary, "Get Johannesburg 30851 on the line. Mr. Woodroffe. It's urgent."

It could only be about Gretz . . . Grietjie.

The call came through at once. "Mr. Woodroffe? Jakób Kowalski speaking, from Iscor."

"Mr. Kowalski?" It was a strong voice. "Do you know a Grietjie Neethling?"

He felt the cold fear turn to ice.

"Yes, I do."

"I'm John Woodroffe, Grietjie's grandfather."

"Grandpa John," said Jakób. Something had happened to her. "What happened? Is she hurt?"

"No, she's fine," said the voice through the static in their connection. "But she's had a bad fright. She's asking for you."

Asking for him? She was with her family and she was asking for him? And her grandfather had found him? It didn't make sense.

"I don't understand, what happened?"

"There was an explosion, but she wasn't injured," Grandpa John said calmly. "I'm going to the farm this morning. I'd like to take you along, if possible. I know Frikkie Meyer. I could arrange it, if you're willing."

Mr. Meyer, the head of Iscor? It was probably not necessary. "I'll arrange it myself," Jakób hastened to reply. "Where shall I meet you?"

In the street below Jakób's apartment the big black car with the chauffeur was already waiting—exactly as Grietjie had always described it. He ducked his head and got into the backseat. The chauffeur closed the door behind him.

"Jakób Kowalski? I'm John Woodroffe," said the man with the snow-white hair.

"I'm pleased to meet you, Mr. Woodroffe. Grietjie has often spoken about you."

The chauffeur wound deftly through the traffic. When they left the city behind and the road lay open ahead of them, Grandpa John said, "Grietjie once mentioned your name during a conversation. I'm glad I was able to find you."

Jakób frowned. "She didn't tell her parents about me?" he asked.

Grandpa John gave him a serious look. "No. Should she have?"

He nodded slowly. "Yes, Mr. Woodroffe. She should have, long ago."

The old man kept looking at him. "Are you Russian, Hungarian?"

"Polish," answered Jakób. "I emigrated to South Africa at the beginning of the year."

"After the Polish revolution?"

"Yes, after the revolution."

"And you know Grietjie?"

"Yes, I've known her for a long time. But if you'll excuse me, Mr. Woodroffe, I can't say anything if she hasn't spoken to her parents yet."

The old man looked at him earnestly and nodded. "Yes, you're right."

"Just tell me what happened, please," asked Jakób.

"The Primus stove blew up," said Grandpa John. "Fortunately she'd averted her face or . . ." He shook his head at the thought of what might have happened.

A cold shiver ran down Jakób's spine. Her beautiful face.

"Kobus, her brother, pulled her away. Her hair caught fire at the back, but he put out the flames with his bare hands. In the end his injuries were worse than hers, but he managed to extinguish the fire before it could cause any real damage."

"And Grietjie?" Jakób asked, fear ice-cold inside him. Something was wrong, something serious, or he wouldn't be driving with Grandpa John in his big car to the farm on the other side of the Springbok Flats.

"I'm not quite sure myself." The old man shook his head. "Her mother—my daughter, Kate—phoned to say she's in shock. She was asking for Jakób. They didn't know who Jakób was. They phoned her roommate, Karin, but Karin was no help. It was only last night that I remembered a conversation I'd had with her, in which she mentioned that you were a metallurgical engineer at Iscor."

"You didn't get much sleep, did you?" said Jakób.

"No, Mr. Kowalski. She's my granddaughter. She has a very special place in my heart."

In mine too, Jakób thought—*in mine too.* "Please call me Jakób," he said.

They drove on in companionable silence. Jakób closed his eyes. *They would only have sent for me if it was really serious,* he thought, running his fingers through his thick black hair. He wished the imposing car would go a little faster.

After a while Grandpa John said, "Tell me about your work, Jakób."

He's not asking about my past, where I'm from, why I fled my own country, how I know Grietjie, Jakób realized. *He's asking about my work, because he knows it's something I'll be comfortable with.*

Jakób told him about his work at Iscor. He asked about Rand Consolidated. They discussed the government's labor policy and the possible extension of the pipeline at Iscor.

When they were approaching the farm, the old man said, "Call me John. Mr. Woodroffe is too formal."

I'll never be able to call this dignified gentleman by his name, Jakób thought. "Would you allow me to call you Grandpa John?" he asked. "That's how I've come to know you over the past months."

The old man smiled. "Yes," he said, "that's what everyone calls me."

At Grietjie's home, Jakób stood slightly apart while the family greeted one another. Then Grandpa John turned to him.

"This is Jakób," he said. "My daughter, Kate. My son-in-law, Bernard."

He didn't mention my last name, Jakób realized. *My foreign-sounding last name.*

The woman was beautiful. "I'm so glad my father found you," she said sincerely. "May I offer you something to drink?"

"He speaks English," said Grandpa John.

"I understand Afrikaans," said Jakób. "Coffee would be lovely, thank you."

The man looked him in the eye and gripped his hand. "How do you do, Mr. Neethling," Jakób said in Afrikaans.

"I'm grateful you're here," said Mr. Neethling. "Did you have a good trip?"

"We had a good trip," Jakób said cautiously. "Your farm looks good."

"Just dry, very hot and dry. We're urgently needing rain. Let's go in."

"I want to see Grietjie," said Jakób. He turned to Grietjie's mother. "Please tell me what's going on."

"We don't know," said the woman, and her eyes filled with tears. "I'm sorry, I . . ."

Jakób instinctively put his hand on her shoulder. "Take me to her," he said.

Grietjie lay curled up in bed. The day was hot, but she lay under a thick quilt, her head deep in the pillow.

The ice-blue eyes were open but showed no sign of recognition.

Jakób's heart shrank. He reached out and stroked her face. "Gretz? Gretchen?"

Slowly the eyes focused. "Jakób?" She struggled to get the word out. "I didn't know where you were," she whispered in Polish.

Gently he wiped the hair out of her face. He was afraid his heart would break. "I'm in Pretoria, you know that, at work, and at home in my apartment."

Her icy hand came out from under the covers and clung to his. "I thought you were gone."

"I'm here, Gretz, I'm here." He bent over the bed and put his other arm around the small figure bunched up under the quilt. His head was close to hers. "I'll stay here with you. I'll sit by your side. Sleep now."

"You won't go away?"

"I won't go away," he promised.

She gave a deep sigh and closed her eyes. Her hand was still clinging to his. Her mother drew up a chair for him. He sank into it slowly.

The striking woman watched her sleeping daughter with a sad expression in her eyes.

Once or twice the blue eyes flew open.

"I'm here," Jakób assured her.

The woman smiled. "Thank you," she said and left.

Long after Grietjie had fallen asleep, he continued to stroke her silky curls.

Later, Grietjie's mother quietly brought him coffee. He took the cup with his free hand.

"Thank you, Mrs. Neethling."

"Please call me Kate."

"Thank you, Kate."

They spoke softly, in whispers. "It's the first time she's been calm. I hope she'll sleep for a while. I'm sorry, but we didn't know who you were."

"I knew Grietjie when she was young," said Jakób.

"When she was at junior school, Karin said. When I tried to speak to Grietjie in German, she didn't react." She looked at him and asked, "What language were you talking?"

He hesitated for a moment. These people really knew nothing. "Polish," he answered. "My last name is Kowalski. I'm from Poland."

"Poland?" she asked, perplexed.

"Mrs. Neethling—Kate, there are things you don't know." He looked at the sleeping girl and pushed the hair back from her face. "I don't want to say anything. Grietjie should be the one to tell you. Do you agree?"

She nodded and sighed. "She never wanted to speak about her

experiences during the war or her time at the orphanage afterward," Kate said. She looked up at him with sorrowful eyes. "She has the most terrible dreams."

"Yes," he said, "she's been dreaming of the fire since she was very young."

"Do you think it's the explosion in which her mother and grand-mother died?" Kate asked.

It was never going to stop—his own nightmare about the train. "No," he said, "she didn't really see it. And it was only much later that she learned they were dead."

"Are you sure she didn't see it?" the woman inquired.

"She saw the glow and heard the blast," said Jakób, "but she didn't see any fire." *There had been no fire*, he thought, *just a train being ripped apart, and open cars plunging into a river far below.*

"How's she doing?" Grietjie's father asked softly from the doorway.

Kate's tears began to flow again. "She's sleeping peacefully," she said.

"Then you should go to bed as well." He put his arm around his wife's shoulders and drew her to him. "We'll call you as soon as she's awake."

When she had left, Mr. Neethling sat down and looked at Jakób across the bed. "Excuse me for being so direct, Jakób, but Grandpa John tells me you are from Poland."

Now I'll have to be careful, Jakób thought. *Not just to find the right words in Afrikaans, but also to tell the truth without letting Grietjie down.*

"I had to flee Poland because I didn't agree with the Communist regime."

The man looked at him. His eyes were almost as blue as Grietjie's.

"So you came to South Africa?"

Jakób switched to English. "I'm an engineer. Iscor was recruiting staff in England, so I decided to come."

"Why here?"

"It was a good opportunity. And I heard your government takes a strict anti-Communist line. And I knew Grietjie was here."

The man facing him frowned more deeply. "What exactly is your connection with Grietjie?" he asked.

Jakób rubbed his chin. "I knew her during and after the war." He tried to sidestep the question.

"In Germany?"

"No, in Poland, Mr. Neethling."

"Call me Bernard."

"Bernard, I've told your wife as well, there are things you don't know about. And I'm not the one who should be telling you."

Bernard closed his eyes for a moment. "We knew the child was bearing too great a burden," he said, "but she wouldn't confide in us."

Jakób hesitated, then decided against saying anything more. "I understand," he said. "Why don't you try to get some rest too? I'll stay with her."

———

It was late afternoon when she opened her eyes. "Jakób?"

"I'm here, Gretz."

"I don't know where Jurgen is."

He had no idea who Jurgen was. "Where was he before, Gretz?"

"On the bed."

"The bed in your room?"

She closed her eyes again. "The bed that burned," she said.

"The explosion was in the kitchen." He tried to make sense of the conversation.

"Everything was in the kitchen, the bed as well," she said.

He tried to think. "Who else was there?"

"Just Mutti and me. And Jurgen. He was asleep on the bed."

Something began to take shape. "How old is Jurgen?"

"Very young," she said. "I'm so tired."

He bent over her and tucked the quilt around her. It was hot outside, but she was bunched up with cold. "Go to sleep, I'll stay with you," he said softly.

She turned on her side, took his hand, and put it under her cheek. With both hands she held on to his arm. She did not relax her grip, even when she fell asleep again.

Awhile later a younger version of Mr. Neethling entered the room. "You must be Jakób," he said in English. "I'm Kobus."

Jakób came halfway to his feet. "How do you do?" he said in Afrikaans.

"Sit, sit, I see she's holding you down," Kobus protested. "Goodness, I'm glad she's asleep. It's the first time since the accident."

"How are your hands?" asked Jakób.

"I'll survive. It's just a nuisance. I have work to do."

"At the pigsties?"

Kobus laughed. "You clearly know more about us than we do about you," he said.

"You must put me to work," said Jakób. "We used to farm with pigs where I grew up."

"Your job is to get Grietjie better. That alone would be a miracle. The doctor even considered sending her to a clinic where patients are treated with electric shock therapy to get all their ducks back in a row."

Jakób didn't understand where the ducks came in, but he could almost feel an electric shock jolt through his own body. "I'd never allow it!" he said and placed his hand on Grietjie's forehead.

"Nor would I," said Bernard. He entered the room with his wife, who carried the family Bible.

"We're going to have our evening devotions in here tonight," Kate explained.

They sat in a circle around Grietjie's bed. Bernard opened the Bible. "I'll be reading in Afrikaans," he told Jakób.

"Don't worry, I'll understand," Jakób answered in Afrikaans.

He listened to the well-known words of Psalm 8: "'When I consider

your heavens, the work of your fingers, the moon and the stars . . .'"
Familiar words in an unfamiliar language. He listened to Bernard's
strong voice, looked at the big hands respectfully holding the Bible.

This faith was her anchor, he knew. These people, this home, this
Bible in a strange language had become her anchor.

Bernard's prayer was long and earnest. Jakób understood very little, yet he understood everything.

It was the simplicity that struck him, the big man's respect for
the Almighty Father, the humility of the beautiful woman and the
strong young man and the dignified old gentleman as they bowed to
their Creator. Here, in this bedroom, in this small domestic circle,
they were talking to God. It was strange to talk to God like this. But
it was good.

When Bernard said amen and they raised their heads, Grietjie said
in Polish, "Daddy prayed for you too, Jakób. He thanked God for sending you to us and he asked that you'd be happy with us."

Deep in the night he woke when he felt her stroke his hair.

"Jakób, are you still here?"

He had fallen asleep in the chair, with his head resting on her bed.
Pale moonlight was falling through the window.

"I won't leave, Grietjie."

"The moon is shining in Poland as well, isn't it?"

"Yes," he said, "if there are no clouds."

"If there are no clouds, yes."

Grietjie woke hungry. She ate porridge for breakfast. She spoke a few
words in Afrikaans to her mother but became distraught when Jakób
got up to leave the room.

"I just want to wash you and dress you in clean nightclothes," her mother soothed her. "Jakób can come straight back."

Bernard was waiting on the veranda. "Kate is washing her," said Jakób.

He nodded.

"It's hot so early in the day," Jakób said. He could manage short sentences in Afrikaans, but in a conversation he soon reverted to English.

"I'm driving to the fields if you want to come along," Bernard said.

"I'd love to see the farm," Jakób replied. "I grew up on a farm myself. But I'll have to convince Grietjie to be without me for a while."

"I can wait half an hour or so," said Bernard. "I'll be in the barn, with the tractor."

Convincing Grietjie turned out to be harder than Jakób had anticipated. Her blue eyes flew open. "Jakób, you can't go with Daddy. He doesn't know you!"

"He knows me now, Grietjie. He's often spoken to me. Don't you remember that he prayed for me last night?"

She nodded slowly. "You were with us, at devotions," she remembered. Her blue eyes looked vulnerable. "I don't know what's going on. I'm terribly confused."

Kate watched anxiously from the other side of the bed—she didn't understand a word they were saying. "She says she's very confused," he interpreted. To Grietjie he said, "I came to visit you here because you were asking for me. There's nothing to worry about."

"But, Jakób, I'm scared."

"If you're too scared, I'll stay with you. But I think your mommy wants to sit with you so that I can go with your daddy to take a look at the farm. I won't be long."

"Okay," she reluctantly agreed.

He leaned over and kissed her forehead. "I'm going with Bernard," he told Kate and left.

His body walked to the barn, but his heart stayed behind in the bedroom.

They drove in the pickup truck along the bumpy farm road to where Bernard had planted his new vines. They inspected the cattle licks and made certain that the troughs were filled with water. They wound along a narrow road up the rough mountainside until they could see the entire farm. Bernard pointed out the house and the kraal, Kobus's pig farming units, the fields, the enclosures for the cattle, the dam higher up in the gorge.

"The people in this country are blessed to have farms like these," said Jakób. "In Europe the farms are the size of a postage stamp compared to these vast open spaces."

"Water is our big problem," said Bernard.

"Which influences the capacity of the pastures, I presume."

Bernard nodded.

On their way back they came across a place where the fence was broken. They got out and fixed it.

"The last time I put up a fence," said Jakób, "must have been about ten years ago, with my father and brother."

"Your father taught you well," said Bernard.

When they were back in the truck, Bernard didn't immediately switch on the engine. He turned to Jakób and said, "Jakób, we realize you don't want to say anything behind Grietjie's back and we respect you for it, but we have no idea how things fit together."

He wished he could tell this man with the open face the whole truth—he knew it wouldn't make the least difference to his love for his daughter. "I found Grietjie after her family died," he said, "and I took her to my parents' home in Poland."

He knew the other man was waiting for an explanation, but he did not elaborate.

"And then?"

"She stayed with us until I took her back to Germany, to an orphanage. From there she came to South Africa."

Bernard shook his head in disbelief.

"I'm sorry, I can't tell you anything more."

In the late afternoon Grietjie joined the family on the veranda—Grandpa John with his whiskey, Kate with a glass of sherry, Bernard with a cup of coffee, Kobus with a beer.

"Can I get you a beer?" he asked Jakób in Afrikaans.

"Yes, thanks," said Jakób.

"And some orange squash for you," Kobus said to his sister.

The beer was ice-cold and bitter on his tongue. He took a long sip—the first one was always the best, Stan had always said. That was why your first sip had to be a long one.

The sun went down behind the rugged mountain. The veld lay around them, golden, peaceful. Darkness began to descend and the first stars appeared. Unfamiliar stars.

"The bushveld is beautiful, don't you think?" Grietjie asked beside him.

"It's lovely, yes," he replied. "You must speak Afrikaans to me, or your family won't understand what we're saying."

"But will you understand?" she asked.

"Yes, I will."

"Jakób told me to speak Afrikaans so that you'll understand," she told the rest of the group.

"It would be a relief," said Kobus. "I've suspected all along that you were talking about me behind my back!"

"We were!" she said. "And you'll never know what we said."

"I can always choke it out of you," he threatened.

"Daddy won't allow it, because I'm sick. Isn't that right, Daddy?"

Bernard smiled and shook his head. "Don't be flippant," he said. "You've been very ill."

"Well, I'm better now," she said, smiling.

But shortly afterward Grietjie felt tired and returned to her room.

That night Jakób had his own bedroom. He was grateful, because his body ached from lack of sleep.

But when he looked in on Grietjie, she was wide-awake.

"I've had too much sleep," she said. "Will you come and talk to me?"

"I'm old, Grietjie. I must get to bed."

She laughed heartily. For the first time in a long while he heard her laugh again, and his heart melted. "Oh, come on, Jakób, you're not old!"

"You're always telling me I'm old," he reminded her and lowered himself onto the chair beside her bed.

"Only when you behave like an old man," she protested. "Like when you think anyone studies on a Friday night!"

He gave her a keen look—despite her scorched hair and pale face she was still the loveliest girl he had ever seen. He reached out to push a lock of hair behind her ear, but withdrew his hand. *Jakób*, he told himself, *get a grip!*

"Why are you looking at me like that?" she asked.

"Do you remember the explosion?"

Her blue eyes looked straight at him. "I lost my hair, Jakób Kowalski, not my mind."

"And the previous explosion, in the ghetto?"

She gave him a searching look. "Yes, Jakób, I remember," she admitted.

"You didn't remember it before?"

She closed her eyes. "No."

Should I continue? Jakób wondered. But he knew he had to. "Who was Jurgen, Grietjie?"

She took a deep breath before she whispered, "My little brother."

"Did he die in the explosion?"

"I remember his terrible screams."

"Where was your grandmother?"

"She and Elza weren't there."

"And your mother?"

"She tried to put out the fire with her hands, but the flames were too high."

He took her hand. He wished he could stop asking questions—he was bringing the terrible events into the room. But for her sake he had to continue.

"How did the fire start?"

"Mutti wanted to cook me some food. The Primus stove exploded."

His heart went out to the girl in the bed. He laid his hand on her cheek. "It's the fire of your dream, isn't it, Grietjie?"

"Yes. I know it now. It's my fire."

They sat in silence for a long time. The soft light of the oil lamp on the dressing table reached every corner of the room.

Grietjie lay back with her head against the pillow and closed her eyes. "I can't believe I didn't remember it, Jakób."

"You erased it from your memory, in order to survive," he said.

"I remember everything about the ghetto as well," she said. "I didn't want to remember it before."

"Tell me, Grietjie."

When Kate and Bernard came in to say good night, Grietjie's eyes were closed and she didn't seem to realize they were there. Jakób motioned for them to be quiet and sit. They sat down on the bench on the other side of the bed.

"We lived in one room, all of us. We cooked and washed and slept there. The rest of the house was also full of people. There were always children crying and screaming."

She lay against the white pillow, pale as wax.

"Keep talking, Grietjie."

"We were always hungry. Oma and I stood in long lines for our food rations. The streets were filthy."

She didn't know that they were present in the room. With an enormous effort she was traveling back in time, like someone walking through thick sand. She kept clinging to his hand, as if she wanted to take him with her. Anxiety etched her parents' faces.

"Speak Afrikaans," he said.

Immediately she switched to Afrikaans. "In winter it was bitterly cold, and we had nothing to warm ourselves with. When a windowpane broke, Oma stuffed a rag in the hole to keep out the wind. But our bathroom no longer worked, so we were forced to go outside.

"The streets were filthy. There were piles of garbage everywhere."

She stopped for a moment, then carried on. Her voice was dull and revealed no emotion. "I remember the smell. Oma gave us a handkerchief to hold to our noses. It didn't help, Jakób. The smell came through the hanky; it came through the rag in the window, into our room.

"Sometimes we didn't have water to drink. It was hard, because Jurgen was small. Have I told you about the explosion?"

"Tell me again, Grietjie."

He listened again to the incident, imagining it through the eyes of a five-year-old. She told him about the stove exploding, destroying the rickety table on which it had stood, and the bed and all their earthly possessions, including her coat. He saw Kate huddle against Bernard's chest; he saw him draw her closer.

"Then we no longer had a stove to cook on," said Grietjie. "And Jurgen burned to death, I know."

"Tell me more about the ghetto," he said.

Across the bed he saw the confusion on her parents' faces.

"There was barbed wire on top of the walls. We had to wait in line for food. But I've told you that, haven't I, Jakób?"

"It doesn't matter. Tell me everything again."

"We had green ration cards, different groups had different colors. The people stole each other's cards. Or took dead people's if their families weren't quick enough. Once a woman who had been standing in line behind Oma and me collapsed and died. The people stepped over her and stayed in line, because if you lost your place, you had to wait hours longer in the snow or rain for your food. Oma told me not to look."

He squeezed her thin hand and felt himself shrivel inside. When he had taken her to his parents' home in Częstochowa, he had paid her little heed, had hardly been aware of her existence. The realization gnawed at his insides.

"Oma shaved our heads so that we could see the lice more easily. But then we lost the blade, and we couldn't do that anymore."

Jakób looked up and saw the pain in Bernard's and Kate's eyes as well.

"At night the sirens went off, then the bombs came. But the sirens weren't as bad as the loudspeakers during the day: *'Achtung! Achtung! Tomorrow at eight o'clock sharp all Jews in Group 12 must report at gate five for deportation to volunteer labor camps! Arbeit macht frei!'*

"Jakób, I think the people knew they were going to be burned in those ovens like the ones they had at Auschwitz, remember?"

"Yes, Grietjie, I remember," he answered calmly.

From the corner of his eye he saw Bernard drop his head and crumple like a man shot through the heart.

"People died in the ghetto every day. Most of them died of hunger or disease or injuries, or of cold. The people left the bodies in the streets, and a cart came to remove them. The legs of the dead stuck out in every direction. When Uncle Janusz and Stan brought you home in the cart, I thought—"

"Don't worry, Grietjie, I'm fine." To this day he remembered her face when he opened his eyes.

"Sometimes the cart only came in the afternoon, when Oma and I were standing in line for our food rations. One day my friend who lived lower down the street . . ." Her eyes flew open.

"I'm here, Grietjie," he comforted her, stroking her hair. "Tell me about your friend."

She began to cry softly. "Jakób, the rats had begun to . . ."

Grietjie held out her arms to him. He bent over the bed and wrapped his arms around her. "Keep talking, Grietjie," he said.

She clung to him. "The loudspeakers said, *'Achtung! Alle Juden Achtung! From this moment all green ration cards are invalid!'* Then we knew we had no more food. So Oma packed our things, and we went on the train that would take us to the labor camp."

She talked and talked. After a while he gently laid her back against the pillows and sat down on the chair. He kept stroking her hair, holding her hand, pressing it to his face at times.

At one point he feared that he was drowning and he rested his head on the bed. He simply couldn't bear to listen anymore. Then he felt Bernard's hand on his shoulder. Comforting, strong. The hand stayed there.

In midsentence, Grietjie fell asleep.

Kate climbed into bed with her daughter and cradled her in her arms.

Jakób fled outside.

———

The veld lay wide and open around him. The moon was his lantern. He walked and walked. He stood at the stone wall and looked at the silent humps of the cattle inside the kraal. He walked down the road and looked at the white sand in the dry riverbed. He walked along the newly graded road and looked at the hundreds of pigs in their neat sties. He rubbed the trunk of a rough thorn tree, broke off pieces of sticky resin, rolled them between his fingers.

He didn't think.

Fragments of her story came back to him. He tried to chew and digest it. Bits and pieces surfaced in the road ahead of him, rose up among the cattle, stood written in the white sand. Harsh details. He brooded and tried to understand.

It was too much. And she had borne it alone for more than thirteen years.

He knelt on the hard surface of the road.

Mother of God, carry her, carry all of us. Carry me.

Eventually his agitation subsided.

When he returned to the homestead much later, Bernard was waiting on the veranda. "Jakób?" he asked.

"I'll be fine," Jakób replied.

"I don't think any of us will be fine for a long time to come," said Bernard. "Kate has made coffee, if you want some."

"Yes, thank you," said Jakób. *Coffee and people around me—ordinary people who spoke to each other and engaged in family devotions and worried about the drought; people who, despite everything, drank coffee and would be getting up early tomorrow morning to milk the cows.*

"Is she asleep?" he asked when they entered the house.

"Yes, she's fast asleep."

The comforting smell of fresh coffee drew Jakób to the kitchen. They sat at the table. Kate opened a tin of rusks. He dipped the long, narrow biscuit deep into his coffee. It melted in his mouth. He couldn't imagine a time when the taste had been unfamiliar to him.

"What's the time?" he asked.

"Almost two."

"Jakób, why do you think she never told us?" Kate asked.

"She didn't tell anyone these things. I believe she had well and truly forgotten them."

"You didn't know either?"

"I knew she was Jewish, or partly Jewish," he explained. "I should have known about the ghetto, but I . . ." He shrugged his shoulders. "I just didn't think."

"I think she tried to talk to me," said Bernard, "specifically about the Jews. But I trod all over her with my muddy paws."

His wife looked at him earnestly. "We never suspected anything, Bernard. You couldn't have known." She turned to Jakób. "How long did she live in Poland with you?"

He looked at her and answered, "Four years—from 1944 to 1948."

"Four years? Wasn't she in a German orphanage then?"

He sighed deeply and pushed his fingers through his black hair. "Let me tell you everything," he said. "I believe Grietjie will understand."

———

Jakób slept until after twelve, took a shower, shaved, and changed his clothes.

"You look brand-new." Kate smiled at him through her own tired eyes.

He nodded. "How's Grietjie?"

"She's awake. She's talking to her dad. She's talking, Jakób, for the first time she's talking." She pressed her fingers against her temples. "Heavens, if only we . . ."

"Don't, Kate," Jakób said seriously. "You offered her a safe, happy home. It's something she never had. You couldn't have known about all those things."

She sighed. "She won our hearts from the very first moment," she said.

"I know," he said. "I know exactly what you mean."

Her cheeks were still pale and she looked different with the shorter haircut, but by Thursday Grietjie was up and about.

"I want to show you the whole farm today, Jakób," she said at the breakfast table.

"Too late, sis," Kobus said. "He helped at the pigsties yesterday. And he gave me a brilliant idea."

"What?" she asked inquisitively.

"Wait and see," said her brother secretively.

She pouted. "Jakób will tell me, won't you, Jakób?"

"Men's affairs are men's affairs, Grietjie," he said, putting on a serious face.

She turned to her grandfather. "Grandpa John, tell Kobus—"

"Fight your own battles!" Her grandfather laughed and held up his hands. "I'm enjoying my stay."

"You might as well stay till Christmas, Daddy," said Kate.

Grandpa John smiled and shook his head. "Thank you, but I have to go back before the beginning of November."

Bernard got up. "I'm going to town. Does anyone need anything?"

"I think I should go along," said Jakób and got up as well. "I want to buy my train ticket. Thanks, Kate, breakfast was lovely."

"Buy your ticket for Tuesday," said Grietjie, "then you can go back with Nico and me."

But Jakób shook his head. "I've haven't been in my job long. I can't take any more leave."

"Then I should go back with Jakób on Sunday," said Grietjie. "It'll be much nicer than going with that drip Nico. And I'll have time to get my room ready before classes begin Wednesday. What do you think, Daddy?"

"Shouldn't you stay with us awhile longer and get a little stronger?"

"I'll be all right, Daddy. For the first time I think I'll be quite all right."

Grietjie used their last few days to show him every corner of the farm. They talked and talked. She spoke to everyone about everything—the ghetto, her dim recollections of the synagogue, her escape from the cattle car on their way to Auschwitz, her four years at the convent school, attending mass in the cathedral. She also told them how she sometimes longed for the soft green hills around Częstochowa. And the snow, especially at Christmas time.

"I still think of the green hills and the white Christmases of my childhood," Grandpa John admitted. "It's an inextricable part of who we are."

One evening Jakób and Bernard had a conversation that lasted well into the night about the two churches in which Grietjie had been raised. The two men tried hard to understand each other's viewpoint but were limited by old perceptions and interpretations.

Finally Jakób said, "Maybe we should just agree to accept and respect each other's viewpoint. You can't just change what you believe in."

"You're right, you can't."

Jakób found Kate to be a strong, mature woman who listened with a gentle ear. "I was never sure I'd made the right decision to let her go to Africa," he said. "And there was no way to find out."

"How old were you when you had to make that decision, Jakób?"

"I had just turned twenty-one when she became my responsibility. She was a pale, painfully skinny little thing of six. Nearly seven."

Kate smiled. "The day after she turned twelve she was nearly thirteen," she remembered. She regarded him seriously. "You were too young to have to take on the responsibility of a child."

"I neglected her, I realize it today," Jakób said. "Right from the start—the war and the Home Army's struggle for liberation from the Germans and the Russians were more important to me." He shook his head. "I didn't take any real notice of her. It was only later, when I got to know her . . ."

The time after he was wounded. When he had experienced for the first time the tender care of a woman. Even if she was only seven at the time.

"We all made mistakes," Kate said calmly.

He nodded. "I still haven't told you about my biggest mistake," he said.

"Maybe you should."

He hesitated a moment, then said, "I planted the bombs that blew up the train."

"The train in which her mother and grandmother died?"

"Yes, the train that was taking her mother and grandmother to Auschwitz. It was an unscheduled train. We were supposed to blow up a German troop train on its way back to Germany."

"You do know that it wasn't your fault?"

He laughed briefly. "Even if I were exonerated by the pope, I'd still be the one who did it."

On Sunday morning everyone went along to the station to see them off, after which the rest of the family would be going to church.

"Jakób, wait till you see the lovely picnic Maria has packed for us," Grietjie said. "It makes going away so much easier."

"Yes, if she allows you to eat anything," Kobus said under his breath, but loud enough for Grietjie to hear.

"If I didn't stop you, you would finish the food before we reached Warmbaths, with the entire Springbok Flats still ahead of us," she defended herself.

"Yes, Miss," he teased.

"When will the two of you grow up?" Bernard asked, smiling fondly.

"When Kobus is married," Grietjie retorted.

"When Grietjie stops thinking she's the queen of England."

At the station Kobus helped put the suitcases and cake tins on the luggage rack. "All of a sudden I miss Pretoria," he said.

Bernard embraced Grietjie and held her tightly. "Let us know if there's anything you need," he said again. "I wish you would stay just a little longer."

Just before they got into the train, Kate drew Jakób aside. "Jakób, please call if there's the slightest reason for worry."

"I will, Kate."

"Promise me you'll look after her?"

He smiled. "I'll look after her."

"As if she was your own little girl?" asked Kate.

He understood exactly how she felt. "I promise, Kate, I'll look after her as if she was my own little girl."

15

"The month of October isn't the most beautiful month after all," Grietjie complained as she took off her wet shoes.

"Who said it was?" Karin asked.

"Leipoldt."

"Who's he?"

"C. Louis Leipoldt."

"Don't know him," said Karin. "Is he your partner for the year-end ball?"

"Karin! Leipoldt is an Afrikaans poet."

Karin gave her a puzzled look. "Roomie, I have no idea what you're talking about."

"I'm talking about the stupid rain that's been falling for four straight days and the exam that starts in two weeks' time."

"Oh." Karin frowned uncomprehendingly and shook her head. "Who's your partner for the ball, then?"

Grietjie sighed. That too. "I wasn't speaking about the ball."

"Who?"

"Pieter."

"Pieter Leipoldt?"

"Oh, Karin, you never listen to a word I say. Leipoldt is the poet. Pieter Rossouw is a guy in my class. And before you ask, no, there's nothing between us. But I can't wear the brand-new ball gown that's been hanging in my closet all term without a man by my side."

"Can he dance?" Karin asked.

"I hope so."

"I'm still sorry it didn't work out between you and Francois," she said. "You were such a lovely couple."

"He and Hester are a lovely couple as well," said Grietjie. "Now I have to study, I'm writing German tomorrow."

On Thursday Jakób phoned. "How are you?" he asked.

"I have both oars in the water, thanks for asking."

"Pardon?"

"I'm playing with a full deck."

"Grietjie?"

"Don't worry, I don't have a single loose screw." She couldn't help teasing him.

"Grietjie, talk sense," he scolded.

She laughed. "You must get to know your idioms. It's what spices up a language, it's—"

"Grietjie!"

She laughed gleefully. "I'm very well, thank you. And you?"

"No more dreams?"

"None. And you?"

"I'm going to end the call if you don't stop being silly!" he threatened.

"No, Jakób!" she protested. "Please, please, please don't put the phone down, I don't have any coins to phone you back. Will you please, pretty please, fetch me on Saturday morning? I have to get something for the year-end ball in the city and I don't have money for the bus."

"How will you pay for whatever you need to buy?" he asked.

"I have money for that."

She heard him sigh at the other end. "What time?"

"Early. About ten?"

"Is that early?" He sounded surprised.

"Yes. What time do you consider early?"

"Eight o'clock."

"Only old people are up at eight on a Saturday." She laughed.

———·———

He double-parked in front of the Uniewinkels store. She rushed inside and emerged with a small packet. He thought it best not to ask what she had bought.

In his apartment she said, "I'll make the coffee and then I'll teach you to rock 'n' roll. I've brought a record."

"Grietjie . . ." But she had already vanished into the kitchen.

"You can't go through life without knowing how to rock 'n' roll," she said when she had switched the kettle on. "What if you go to Iscor's year-end function and everyone is rocking except you?" She put the record on the turntable. "It could spoil your chances of promotion." Carefully she lowered the needle onto the record. "I could never forgive myself if that happened to you."

"I doubt whether my advancement depends on my ability to rock 'n' roll," he said.

"Well, you never know, that's all," she said firmly. "Look carefully now. You put your feet down like this, then you step like this and rock your . . . Jakób, watch my feet!"

"I'm watching," he surrendered.

"Okay, those are the basic steps. You can use them in any combination. Easy, don't you think? Now you add the hands. Give me your hands. Feel the rhythm."

She grabbed his hand, rocked back, rolled into his arm, let go of his hand, bounced back, grabbed both his hands. She stretched and yanked and pranced in front of him, around him, behind him.

"Loosen up, Jakób!" she cried over the sound of the music. "Isn't it great?"

She jerked her head back and wiggled from head to toe. She squirmed and wriggled. Laughter and music filled the apartment.

He rocked for all he was worth. He grabbed and let go and swayed and stepped, but the rhythm just wouldn't grab him. *Kowalski, you've lost all your screws or whatever,* he thought.

Laughing, he fell on the sofa. "I'm too old for this, Grietjie."

She fell down beside him and snuggled under his arm. "But it's fun, isn't it?" she asked breathlessly.

Her warm body was too close. He got up. "Where's that promised coffee?"

"I'll bring it, sit," she said at once and hurried to the kitchen.

He sat down in one of the armchairs.

When they were each sitting with a cup of coffee and a ham sandwich, he said, "I won't be working at Iscor next year, Grietjie."

Her eyes widened. "Why not? Are you going back to Poland?"

He smiled reassuringly. "No, that's not possible. Mr. Woodroffe offered me a position at Rand Consolidated. Not Grandpa John, Mr. Peter Woodroffe."

"Have you met Uncle Peter?" she asked, surprised.

"Yes, I went for an interview."

"Jakób!" she said crossly. "Why didn't you tell me you were going? And why are you only telling me now that you got the job? When do you start? And will you get an apartment in Johannesburg?" She jumped up and knelt beside him, grabbed his hands. "You'll have to go there, won't you? I'll also be working there. Maybe you could come and live with Grandpa John as well!"

"You must learn not to ask so many questions, Grietjie. You've just asked five or six."

"I'm just excited, that's all. When do you start?"

"The first of November, in less than three weeks. I'm moving into an apartment in Hillbrow. One of my future colleagues at Rand Consolidated has just bought a house."

"Oh." She sounded disappointed. She sat down at his feet. "I want you to spend Christmas with us on the farm, Jakób. My parents invited you. Will you get leave?"

"I doubt it."

He noticed her disappointment. He didn't want her to be unhappy. "I could try, but I shouldn't think so."

"I won't enjoy it one bit if you're not there, Jakób," she said earnestly.

He couldn't resist her eyes.

He sighed and pushed his fingers through his hair.

His promise to Kate weighed heavily on him—*I'll look after her like my own little girl.* But he could no longer trust himself. He picked up the empty cups.

"Get your things and I'll take you back to res."

"But it's early," she protested.

"I'm sorry, I have work to do."

When he stopped in front of her residence, she didn't get out immediately. She turned to him. "Jakób, are you cross with me?" she asked.

"Not at all. But I have a lot of work to finish at Iscor before I can leave."

"Will you come and fetch me for mass tomorrow?" she asked.

He desperately wanted to. "No, Grietjie. Go to your own church."

He saw the confusion on her face. "It's better that way. You know it, don't you?" he said. "I'll phone you next Friday."

She didn't wave as she always did before she vanished through the big door.

———

Her parents always phoned on a Sunday evening, but nowadays they were phoning in the middle of the week as well. Grietjie understood. They were worried about her. She tried to put their minds at rest.

"I'm really fine, Mommy, I promise."

"Have you dreamed again?"

"Yes, Mommy, I have. But I know now what the fire was, what caused it, what happened, so I don't have to wonder about it anymore. I don't fear the fire anymore. And when I wake up after I've had the dream, it doesn't stay in the room, because I know that it's something that happened a long time ago."

"I hope the nightmares will go away completely in time, my love."

"They will, Mommy. I know they will."

Friday was a catastrophic day. It began early in the morning when Grietjie lost her grip on her new bottle of shampoo and it shattered on the floor. The glass splinters flew in every direction and the thick shampoo spread, making the floor slippery.

"Wait, let me pass you your shoes, you'll cut your feet," said Karin and bent down to pick up the shoes. But as she straightened up, she spilled her coffee all over her assignment, the one she had been working on all night and had to deliver in an hour's time. She burst into tears.

Grietjie grabbed a handful of tissues and began to mop up the coffee. "It's no use crying," she said strictly. "Mop the floor before we slip and fall. I'll save your assignment."

"It's because it's Friday the thirteenth," Karin sniffled. "And bad things always happen in threes. You'll see, another calamity is going to strike."

"Don't talk like that, it's a sin to be superstitious. Just be careful of the broken glass."

In the evening Karin said, "Well, it's been an awful day, but at least there wasn't a third catastrophe, knock on wood."

A first-year knocked and peered around the door. "Telephone for Miss Grietjie," she said and disappeared.

"Uh-oh," said Karin, rolling her eyes. "I spoke too soon."

"You're a real prophet of doom, Karin! It's only Jakób to hear whether I still have my marbles," said Grietjie before hurrying to the phone.

But it wasn't Jakób. It was Pieter with the news that he had German measles.

"My knight in shining armor is covered in spots from head to toe," Grietjie announced dramatically when she returned to their room. She fell down on the bed, a picture of dejection. "He's no longer fit for a ball."

Karin gave her a puzzled look. "What are you talking about?"

"Pieter, German measles. I'm done for, roomie, dead! I have to find another date."

"Impossible," said Karin, "unless you want to drag along a first-year. What about that Nico fellow who . . ."

"Out of the question," said Grietjie. "I'd rather go alone."

"It would be weird," Karin said.

Jakób didn't phone that night. She stayed up until after midnight, waiting. He'd promised, and he never broke a promise. Maybe something had happened. Or he was annoyed with her—she just couldn't think why.

Maybe Karin was right after all, maybe Friday the thirteenth was an unlucky day.

———·———

The next morning she was lying in bed reading, as she often did on Saturdays, when a first-year knocked. "A visitor, Miss Grietjie."

"Who on earth can it be this early?" she complained.

"It's that tall man," said the first-year.

She flew out of bed. "Jakób! Tell him I'm coming, I'm just getting dressed."

She pulled a dress over her head and dragged a comb through her hair.

He was standing in the garden with his back to the front door. His dark-blue shirt was taut across his broad shoulders, and his dark hair curled over the collar. Aunt Anastarja would tell him to get a haircut if she could see him now, Grietjie thought.

She longed to put her arms around him from behind but she didn't. Something between them had changed. In the train on their way here he had been reserved, not the Jakób she knew. And she had seen him only once since their return—last Saturday, when he brought her back to the residence so early.

"Hello, Jakób Kowalski," she said.

He turned. She stood in front of him in her cool summer frock, barefoot, the curly blonde hair framing her face, the blush back in her cheeks. He reached out to draw her closer, but put his hands in his pockets instead.

"I'm sorry I couldn't phone yesterday," he said. "My phone is out of order."

"I was afraid you're still cross with me," she said. Her eyes were impossibly blue.

He looked away. "I'm not cross, Grietjie. How was your week?"

"Wonderful. Until yesterday." They sat down on a bench. "Yesterday everything, just everything went wrong. First I dropped my shampoo— my new bottle!—and then Karin spilled her mug of coffee over her assignment. And, Jakób, last night a terrible thing happened."

He frowned. He hoped it wasn't another of her dreams.

"My date for tonight has German measles! Tonight! He's covered in spots, and now I have to go to the year-end ball on my own. Can you believe it? Alone! It's the biggest catastrophe that could befall a girl. And it's my very last ball at campus. I even had a new dress made."

"I'm sure there's someone else you can ask."

Her face lit up.

No.

"Jakób, you could . . ."

No! no!

". . . go with me! It would be wonderful! It would be so much nicer than—"

"No, Grietjie. I'm too—"

"Don't say you're too old!"

He gave a guilty smile and put his hands up. "Too busy?"

"No, that's a feeble excuse. Jakób, you don't know what fun—"

"I don't have a suit." That was a good excuse.

"—our year-end ball always is. You can rent a suit."

"Where?" he asked.

"In the big hall, here on campus. You can pick me up at seven."

"I was talking about the suit."

"Oh, that. Dippenaar's, in the city." She flung her arms around his neck. "I'm so happy. I'm looking forward to the ball twice as much as before. Thank you, thank you, Jakób!" She hugged him tightly.

Slowly he extricated himself and got up. "I'm glad you're so happy. I'm going now, I have work to finish," he said, smiling, "seeing that I'm going to be kept out of work tonight."

"You won't regret it, I promise," she said as she turned to go back inside. In the doorway she looked over her shoulder. "Thanks, Jakób!" She gave him a cheerful wave and vanished.

I regret it already, he thought.

———•———

Grietjie couldn't imagine that she'd ever looked forward to anything quite as much as this ball.

"I have a date!" she sang, dancing into the room.

Karin looked up from her desk, astonished. "Who?"

"Jakób!"

"Of course!" Karin cried. "Why didn't you think of him before?"

"Because he's Jakób. He can't really be a date, if you know what I mean."

Karin laughed. "You sound like Kobus. I'm just glad you're not going alone."

They ran their baths early, with plenty of bubbles, while there was still hot water. They sliced cucumber for their eyelids and painted their nails and did each other's hair. At six they began to get dressed.

"You look lovely, Karin!" Grietjie said sincerely. "Tonight you're going to sweep Heinrich off his feet!"

"And you look breathtaking," Karin said with admiration. "You're going to sweep all the men in the hall off their feet!"

They laughed. Karin was picked up first. "Keep seats for us at your table, will you?" Grietjie called after her.

When the first-year came to fetch Grietjie, she took a last look in the mirror. She knew she looked good. Karin had done her hair up in loose curls so the spot at the back that had caught fire was invisible. Her gown was a dark greenish-blue silk taffeta—*like the feathers of a glossy starling in the sunlight*, Aunt Bettie had said. The gown had a simple neckline and a cinched waist, flaring gently to the hemline.

She turned slightly to look at the low-cut back. She felt a thrill of excitement.

Over the years there had been so many occasions when she had wished Jakób could see her—in her Voortrekker dress, at her confirmation in church, at her matric dance. Tonight Jakób would see her all dressed up for the first time.

She walked to the top of the stairs and looked down.

He was standing near the door, leaning with one shoulder against a pillar, one ankle crossed over the other. He hadn't seen her yet, but she knew—at the foot of this staircase Jakób Kowalski was waiting for her, Grietjie Neethling.

She stood very still and gazed at him.

His dark suit was snug across his shoulders. It fitted his tall body perfectly. His suntanned skin contrasted with his snow-white shirt, and his thick, dark, curly hair was slicked back, except for a few strands that fell over his forehead.

She felt a strange twitch in the pit of her stomach. She had never imagined Jakób could look like this.

He looked up. Across the length of the staircase they looked into each other's eyes. She smiled and slowly began to descend. He felt his insides contract painfully. He was unashamedly staring.

The other people in the foyer faded.

He watched as she slowly came down the steps, the slim feet in the delicate sandals almost uncertainly feeling for the next step, the fabric softly hugging the curve of her hips, a suggestion of femininity under the tailored bodice.

He couldn't imagine ever having seen anything more beautiful.

Mother of God, he pleaded, *be merciful to me, a sinner.*

He stepped forward, held out his hand, and said as neutrally as possible, "You look lovely, Grietjie."

They drove to the hall in an uneasy silence. *I hope Jakób isn't having second thoughts,* Grietjie thought anxiously. *What if he doesn't feel like spending the evening with a bunch of silly students? What if he doesn't like my friends? What if . . .*

She reached out and touched his arm. "Is everything all right, Jakób?"

He smiled at her reassuringly. "Everything is fine."

"Are you looking forward to the evening?"

"Yes, I am. Though I'm still not sure I know how to dance."

"Is that why you're so quiet? Don't worry, I don't dance very well either. We can just sit and talk if you want to."

He kept his eyes on the road and said nothing.

"Jakób?"

"It's going to be a lovely evening, Grietjie. And we're going to dance, I promise."

The hall was decorated with greenery and hundreds of candles that cast a soft glow. The background music was barely audible over the hum of voices. She led the way to the table where Karin and a few of their friends were already seated and introduced Jakób. She noticed the inquiring looks.

"Karin is my roommate, Jakób. You'll be sitting next to her."

The conversation was rather awkward at first. Jakób wasn't completely fluent in Afrikaans, and he was the only one who didn't know any of the others. *It was a mistake to invite him*, Grietjie thought anxiously. But things improved when Heinrich, an engineering student in his final year, leaned over to talk to Jakób about his work.

After the appetizer had been served, the chairman of the student council and the rag queen opened the dance floor with their respective partners. The rest of the table got up to join the dancers, while Jakób and Heinrich continued their conversation.

When the band struck up with the second tune, Karin said, "For Pete's sake, are you two men going to spend all night talking?"

Heinrich gave an embarrassed laugh and got up. "Shall we dance?" he asked with an exaggerated bow and held out his hand to Karin. She laughed and got up.

Grietjie watched them as they stepped onto the dance floor. She wasn't sure what to do next.

She felt Jakób's light touch on her cheek. "Will you dance with me?" he asked in his deep voice.

She got up slowly and lifted her chin, suddenly struggling to keep her composure. The touch of Jakób's hand on her bare back felt utterly strange. On the floor Jakób tucked her into the crook of his elbow. His other hand gripped hers.

Everything felt unreal. She had known this hand for years and years. She had grown up with her hand in his, but tonight it was an unfamiliar hand. She knew exactly what Jakób smelled like, what he felt like, but tonight everything was different. She could never stop chattering when she was with him, but tonight she couldn't think of a single thing to say. She knew that the circle of his arms offered shelter, but tonight it made her inexplicably nervous. She felt the rhythm of the music flow through her body. She knew she was a good dancer, but tonight she was falling over her feet.

Jakób's strong arms held her more tightly. He bent his head and said in her ear, "Relax, Gretchen."

His voice was familiar, wonderfully familiar, safe. She felt his tall body move against hers, sensed that he knew what he was doing. She began to relax, easily following where he led. *I've never been this close to a man*, she thought, *though I've danced with scores of men before.*

The same strange excitement she had felt earlier was growing steadily inside her. She took a deep breath but felt as if she wasn't getting enough air.

Her heart was pounding.

Jakób held her close.

She swallowed. Her mouth was dry.

She nestled under his arm. He drew her even closer.

They danced around the floor effortlessly, around and around, floating somewhere in space, in a bubble that could burst at any moment.

At the end of the fourth dance he stepped back. "You're a very good dancer, Gretz. Who taught you?"

She was afraid to look up into his eyes. What if he could see what she had been thinking?

Heading back to their table, she answered, "When you grow up on a farm, you learn to dance in the barn at a young age—at weddings or New Year's parties or birthdays. My brother and my dad taught me. We call it sakkie-sakkie."

Her hands were trembling. She didn't know what to talk about next. What if . . .

Fortunately it was time for the main course to be served.

"You're from Poland, aren't you?" asked Stefan, who was sitting opposite Jakób. He was doing a master's degree in history. "Were you in the war?"

"Yes, but not at the front," Jakób answered. "I was part of the Home Army, the Polish resistance."

"The Home Army!" Francois exclaimed, moving closer. "My dad told us how they used to drop weapons and supplies for the Home Army at night."

"Was your father a member of the South African Air Force?" Jakób asked, surprised.

The men gave Jakób their full attention. They were all too young to have been part of that war or the Afrikaners' own resistance movement.

"I'm going to powder my nose," Karin announced and the other girls tagged along.

"Heavens, Grietjie, he's the best-looking man I've ever seen!" one of their friends exclaimed. "Where did you find him?"

"He's just Jakób," she protested.

But she didn't know whether she believed herself anymore.

———

When he stopped the car back at her residence, the glow of the street-light lit up her hands, but her head was in shadow. She leaned over and rested her head on his shoulder. He felt her hair against his cheek. He drew a deep breath, inhaling the fine scent of her perfume.

Gretchen! His heart lurched.

He turned sideways in the seat and took her face into his hands. "You were the most beautiful girl in the entire hall tonight," he said softly.

He bent down and gently kissed her soft lips, just a moment.

With an enormous effort he raised his head and opened the door. "Come, Grietjie," he said.

———

She watched through the window as he walked back to the Volksie, took the keys from his pocket, bent to unlock the door, and got in.

But he didn't pull away. In the dim light he lowered his head onto the steering wheel. He sat like that for a long time before he switched on the car and drove away.

She watched until she could no longer see the red taillights of the Volksie.

—·—

The next morning the chauffeur came for her early, before church. She hugged Grandpa John for a long time when he came out to greet her.

They had tea in his study. They walked in the garden and had a glass of sherry before lunch. They sat at the long table, just the two of them, and ate Aunt Nellie's delicious meal using the polished silver cutlery. After lunch Grandpa John lay down for a while. Grietjie found a book in the study, put on some soft music, and curled up in the leather chair.

At four Grandpa John came down. She sat beside him on the sofa. "You loved Ouma Susan, didn't you?"

Grandpa nodded. "I loved her more than you can ever imagine."

"What does it feel like to be in love, Grandpa?"

He smiled at her. "You're testing an old man's memory!"

"It's a good thing you're so smart." She smiled back.

"Well, I don't know about being smart, but I do know what it's like to love." He thought for a while. "Falling in love is like an explosion inside you. You temporarily lose contact with the world. You're floating somewhere in space. You're larger than life itself and smaller than a grain of sand."

In that case I'm in love, Grietjie thought. *Hopelessly in love.*

She was silent for a while. "But what is the difference between being in love and truly loving someone? How do you know you really love someone, Grandpa?"

He got up slowly, took a cigar from the top drawer, cut off the end, and sat down next to Grietjie again. "When the dust settles after the explosion, you look at the pieces that remain. Then you have to decide whether your lives have become so entangled that you can no longer live without each other." He struck a match and lit his cigar. The flame burned high, smoke billowed. "Grietjie, love is not about excitement and physical desire and attraction. Those things are important, of course. But true love is the core that remains after the infatuation has burned out."

She listened carefully to his words, considered the ideas, visualized the images—the explosion inside her, the fire that is a crucible, the flames that burn away every impurity until a pure, mutual love shines through.

"Grandpa John?"

"Yes, Grietjie?"

"I'm in love with Jakób."

Her grandpa looked neither upset nor surprised. He nodded slowly and puffed at his cigar.

"Not only in love," she said, "I think I love him."

"I saw it coming," Grandpa John said calmly.

She breathed in the soothing aroma of Grandpa John's cigar. "Do you think he's too old for me?" she asked. Her life depended on Grandpa John's reply.

"I was more than eleven years older than Susan," Grandpa John answered. "I don't deny that sparks flew at times, but it was a marriage made in heaven." He paused, then said, "Your father won't be impressed."

She snuggled under his arm. "But do you think the relationship could work?" she asked after a while.

"That's something only you can decide," said Grandpa John. "But I should think it's worth a try."

"Jakób doesn't know how I feel," she said. "I think he still sees me as the little girl he was responsible for, Grandpa. Or maybe just a silly student. He doesn't realize I'm a woman."

"I don't think Jakób is that blind," Grandpa John said and drew at his cigar.

"I'm scared to tell him. What if it doesn't work out? I don't want to lose his friendship—ever."

Grandpa John looked at her intently. Then he said, "You know, Grietjie, life is like a silver coin. You can spend it any way you wish, but you can only spend it once."

———

On Sunday evening she missed Jakób so badly that her heart ached.

When a first-year came to fetch her to take a telephone call, the longing almost tore her chest apart. She charged down the stairs two at a time, took a deep breath, and said, "Grietjie speaking."

Her parents were on the line. She told them about the ball and her gown and what she had done with her hair. She didn't tell them she had gone to the dance with Jakób, because she remembered Grandpa John's words: *Your father won't be impressed.* Besides, they didn't ask. Then she told them about her visit to Grandpa John. Her mother talked about the wedding preparations for Kobus and Salomé, and her father said they'd had good rains, the vines were looking good, and did she have enough money?

On Monday she struggled to focus in class. Jakób weighed heavily on her mind.

By Tuesday the longing filled her entire body. It hurt like a physical pain.

On Wednesday morning she knew he would phone. He always phoned on Wednesdays—at least, he usually did.

He didn't phone that Wednesday.

She woke in the middle of the night. Moonlight fell through the window. *Shine your light on Jakób, moon, and tell him there's a girl who's in love with him.* Later she got up, went to the bathroom, and drank some cold water. She looked at her watch. It was past midnight. She had to get some sleep for a test the next day.

Quietly she returned to her room, took her purse, and went to the phone booth.

She withdrew a shiny new silver coin. If she put it into that slot now, it would be gone forever.

Dear Lord, she prayed, *this is my only tickey.*

Resolutely she picked up the receiver.

———

Jakób sat up in bed and looked at his watch. Almost one in the morning! Who could be phoning at this hour?

He switched on the light in the living room. He hoped it wasn't a problem at the new plant. Surely it wasn't possible? He had tested the system thoroughly.

Her voice on the telephone was like a blow to his stomach.

"Grietjie?"

She gave an embarrassed laugh. "I just want to talk, Jakób."

"Have you been dreaming?" he asked worriedly.

"No. I studied until late. Then I couldn't stop thinking about you."

He sat down on the chair next to the phone and closed his eyes. Every moment of the past week he had been longing to hear her voice, her cheerful laughter. Every night he had missed her presence, her hands, her silky soft hair, her blue eyes.

"Fine," he said, "what do you want to talk about?"

"Nothing, I just missed you, so I phoned."

He sank deeper into the chair and stretched his legs in front of him. A warm feeling settled at the pit of his stomach. "I'm too old for this kind of thing," he said.

"What kind of thing?" He heard the playful tone in her voice.

"Too old for chitchat in the middle of the night."

"Did you miss me this week?" she asked. Her tone was light, almost teasing.

The warmth inside him solidified. *Careful, Jakób Kowalski!* he told himself. "Why aren't you asleep?"

She laughed. "You're not answering my question. I've already told you, I'm not asleep because I miss you."

"Get back into bed and go to sleep, Grietjie."

"Fine, but promise me something."

"What?" he asked cautiously.

"Dream of me?"

"Grietjie!" he warned.

He heard her laughter at the other end of the line before she replaced the receiver.

He managed to refrain from phoning her all weekend. He managed to sit at the table in his apartment on Saturday and finish his reports. He had supper in the city and didn't drive to Hatfield. He went to mass alone on Sunday. He made his own lunch and read a trade journal while he was eating. But when she phoned just before six, he couldn't resist her request.

"Yes, Grietjie, I'll fetch you," he said, running his fingers through his hair.

—·—

She watched as he strode to the front door, his sleeves rolled up, exposing his suntanned forearms. He was wearing shorts, and she watched the muscles in his thighs move as he walked.

Excitement bubbled up inside her. *I'm hopelessly in love with this man on his way to the door.*

But I also know the core, she thought, *the core that remains after the flames have died down. I have known that core since my childhood. He is a central part of my existence.*

The streets were quiet this Sunday evening.

In his Volksie she looked at the hands resting on the steering wheel: strong hands, broad fingers, square nails, fine black hairs on the back of the fingers. *It's strange*, she thought, *I've never looked at Jakób's hands like this.*

At his apartment she made coffee and carried it to the living room. He was standing with his back to her, searching among his records. He took one out of its sleeve and put it on the turntable. Carefully he lowered the needle and turned to face her.

"Here's your coffee," she said.

"Thanks, Grietjie." He sat down in one of the chairs.

She was on the sofa. "This is beautiful music," she said.

"Yes, it is."

They listened in silence.

"The coffee was very good, thank you," he said when he had emptied his cup. He put the cup on the table.

"Yes, it was."

Silence. What was there to talk about? The week's classes? The election of the new student council? He wouldn't be interested.

She felt tension mounting inside her. "How was your week?" she asked after a while.

"Busy, but good, thanks." He was quiet for a moment. "And yours?"

"Also good, thanks. Also busy."

She didn't understand this new awkwardness between them. She couldn't stand the strangeness that had crept in.

"We haven't spoken about the weather yet, Jakób."

He sighed. "Yes, Grietjie." He got up. "Maybe I should just take you back to res."

Her disappointment stuck in her throat. She felt almost humiliated. She shrugged in an offhand way.

"I think so too. You're so cranky not even the queen of England could talk to you."

He gazed at her for a moment, then turned and opened the door for her.

They drove back in silence. Her heart was weeping. What had happened?

At her residence he opened her car door. Side by side they walked to the entrance like strangers. Then he slowed down.

She sensed his hesitation, stopped, and turned to him. "Jakób, you're different, you're cold. Talk to me! We always talk."

"You're imagining it, Grietjie."

In the semidarkness she looked at him. "Don't sidestep the issue, Jakób. I know just as well as you do what this is about."

His black eyes looked into her own. Then he gave a deep sigh and turned his gaze to the front door. "I promised to look after you. More than once."

Did he still see her as a child? Even after the ball? Her misery changed into irrational fury. "I'm sick and tired of that old story!" she cried. "There's more than one way of looking after someone. You're not my father, Jakób. I've got a father, a big, strong, clever father, who has been looking after me for years—since the time you left me at the orphanage."

She saw his eyes. She knew she had gone too far.

"Then how do I fit into your perfect little picture?" His face was pale, his voice very soft and low.

She placed her hands on her warm cheeks. "Jakób, I'm sorry." She closed her eyes, shook her head. "I didn't mean it that way. You just make me so angry!"

"I'm asking, where do I fit in?" he asked coldly.

She felt her anger override her guilt. "I don't know how we fit together, Jakób! That's what I wanted to ask you! But you're always such a pain, so correct, so afraid to do anything that . . ."

She saw a muscle jump in his jaw, saw the intense emotion in his dark eyes. Her heart beat faster; she drew a sharp breath. The next moment his arms closed around her and his mouth came down hard on her own. Her blood rushed fiercely through her veins and into her bruised lips. Alarmed, she pulled away.

"Heavens, Grietjie, just go inside," he said in a choked voice.

She fled into the building. She saw nothing, understood nothing. She stuck her fingers in her ears and heard nothing.

She smothered her sobs in her pillow.

After a while she went to the bathroom to take a shower. Cold water poured over her face, her body, down her legs to the drain. The cold water washed away her tears, washed away the worst of her fright.

But the water didn't wash away the knowledge that it had been a man who had taken her into his arms and held her, the way a man holds a woman. Blood rushed to her cheeks.

Neither did it wash away the words: *You left me at the orphanage.* How could she? She, who knew better? She was aware of the hard knot in her stomach.

The feelings remained: confusion, an unfamiliar vulnerability, an excitement she had never experienced before.

She gazed at herself in the mirror, carefully touched her lips. She looked exactly the same. She felt completely different.

Back in her room she brushed her hair, switched on the immersion element in the enamel jug. Karin would soon be back.

Deep into the night it began to rain softly. She missed Jakób. She ached with longing for him.

She was not a crybaby, yet she cried all through the night.

———

Monday morning she got up with a thick head. Her body ached. Her heart was a heavy stone. She rinsed her face in cold water. She didn't go down to breakfast but drank a cup of black coffee, put on her raincoat, and walked to class in the soft drizzle.

He was waiting just outside the gate. She didn't see him before she was nearly next to him. There were fine raindrops in his thick black hair and on his face. His wet shirt clung to his skin.

Her heart pounded.

"Grietjie?"

He hadn't slept a wink, she knew, because he looked the way she felt.

She looked up into his black eyes. "I'm sorry, Jakób, I truly am. I never meant to—"

"Don't say anything, Gretchen," he said softly.

She looked at him, alarmed.

"I'm sorry about last night," he said. "I don't know what came over me. It will never happen again."

"And I'm sorry about what I said," she replied.

"It's settled, then. I'm off to work. You're on your way to class."

"Okay, Jakób."

Her eyes followed the blue Volksie as he drove away. When it had turned the corner, she walked on.

His words lay like a rock inside her: *It will never happen again.*

———

Monday night she didn't sleep at all.

"Roomie, are you sick?" Karin asked worriedly on Tuesday morning. "You look very pale."

"I must be coming down with something," Grietjie said.

"Why don't you stay in bed? It's cold and wet outside."

"I'll lie down after class this afternoon."

That afternoon she fell into a deep sleep. When she woke just before five, she sat up, confused. It was late afternoon, she realized, not morning. *And my heart aches*, she thought, *and my spirit is in turmoil.*

On their way to the dining room, Karin asked, "Isn't that Jakób's car?"

The blue Volksie was parked at the gate.

She stopped, drew a breath. The stone inside her crumbled to dust. Excitement took over, and infinite joy. *Jakób!*

She left Karin without a word and walked toward his car. Her heart, her stomach, and her breath all gathered in her throat.

She opened the door and got in. "Hello, Jakób."

His eyes were tired, but he smiled. "Don't you want to get your supper first?"

"No, I want to talk to you."

"I'll wait, Grietjie."

She shook her head and closed the door.

He sat quietly beside her. His hands lay on the wheel. He was very close to her. It felt strange.

She couldn't endure the strain a moment longer. She looked at him: dark hair, dark eyes and eyebrows, straight nose, strong jaw, a mouth that . . .

She mustn't look at his mouth.

This is Jakób, not a stranger.

"Jakób, what happened?" she asked earnestly. "We've never argued before."

"It's my fault," he said.

She waited quietly. The rain was a gray veil hiding the two of them inside the car.

He opened his arm. She nestled into her customary place against his broad chest, seeking comfort against the sadness and the confusion she was feeling. His other hand cradled her head.

They sat like that for a long time while peace spread over her and she soaked up the warmth of his body. When he spoke, his voice was gentle. Her ear was over his heart, and his words went through her ear and straight to her own heart.

"You baffle me, Grietjie," he said. "You're always on my mind."

Joy washed over her, warmed her cold body. She knew exactly how he felt. Slowly she sat up and met his gaze. "You're always in my heart," she said.

She saw the expression in his eyes before he looked away.

"Jakób, what has happened to us? It feels as if there's an explosion inside me every time you come near me, even if you just phone. Every time I'm called to the phone, I feel a surge of joy or hope or who-knows-what inside me, because it might be you on the line."

"I suppose we have to talk," he said.

"Yes, Jakób, we have to talk."

He switched on the Volksie. They drove to Sunnyside in silence. He stopped in front of his apartment.

Inside she waited a moment, then said, "I've told you how I feel, Jakób."

He pushed his fingers through his hair and avoided her eyes. "It's part of growing up," he said. "It's a natural reaction, it will pass."

She couldn't believe it! "Natural reaction, my foot!" she said firmly. "I know how I feel!"

"Heavens, Grietjie, you're a—"

"Don't tell me I'm a child, Jakób!"

"You're at least fourteen years my junior," he said.

"Thirteen and a half," she said. "I may not have your years of experience at this kind of thing, but I've come a long way in life."

He sat down at one end of the sofa. She sat at the other end, facing him. "We can feel any way we like and argue until we're blue in the face, the fact remains—I'm too old for you."

"Maybe it's not your fault; maybe I'm the one who's too young for you. But I'll get older, I promise."

"Grietjie, I'm serious. Heavens, you don't make it easy for a man!"

"No, Jakób, you're making a mountain out of a molehill. At a certain point age becomes irrelevant."

He looked at her for a long time, then shook his head.

She leaned across, reached out, and placed her palm against his cheek.

He groaned and turned away. "Don't, Grietjie."

"Why not, Jakób? You've always held me, you held me last month when I was ill. What has changed?"

"You know very well what has changed." His voice was raw.

She leaned back. Everything had changed, she knew it. It was what she had feared most. But at the same time she realized that things couldn't have stayed the same. And she knew that he knew it too.

"Jakób," she pleaded.

"Oh, Grietjie."

He opened his arm and drew her to him. She laid her head on his chest, heard the rhythmic beating of his heart, felt him stroke her hair with his free hand. Her heart was full, her throat was so tight that she could hardly speak. "I love being here with you, Jakób. I feel safe," she said after a while.

He sighed. "It's hard for me," he said and got up.

She shifted her weight and tucked her legs underneath her. "Why? What's so hard about loving me?"

He gazed through the window, his hands deep in his pockets.

"Jakób?"

He turned. "Heavens, Grietjie, it's not just a matter of loving you. You're a fire inside me, threatening to consume me entirely."

Her heart exploded with happiness.

He sat back down on the sofa, leaned forward, and lowered his head into his hands. "What have I allowed to happen, Grietjie?"

"You've lit a fire in me, too, but I'm not afraid," she said. "You asked me last Sunday night where you fit into my picture. I know now: You're Jakób, the man I love. You're the core that remains after all else has burned away."

"Don't. Please!"

"Do you love me, Jakób?"

He looked up, his black eyes very serious. "Yes, Grietjie, I love you." He shook his head. "I'm sorry."

"Don't be sorry, Jakób! Be happy! Be glad!"

But he kept shaking his head. "It's not that simple, Gretchen. It could never work."

"But it's worth a try," she pleaded.

"And if it doesn't work?" he asked with a grave expression. He took her hands into his own. "You're a part of me, I can't ever lose you again." He was silent for a moment, then shook his head. "No, the risk is too great."

She took a long time to answer. "We'll always be part of each other, you and me. You remained a part of me during the nine years I've spent here. If a relationship between us doesn't work out, that part won't change. It's irreversible."

He let go of her hands, leaned his head back, and closed his eyes.

She knew him so well. She climbed into his lap and put her arms around his neck. "Jakób?"

He wrapped her in his arms, held her against him, hugged her so tightly that it almost hurt. She wished he could hold her even closer. His hand slid over her arm, moved over the curve of her hip.

Then he bent his head. She closed her eyes. She heard him breathe, felt his lips on her own. Her lips parted slightly. Desire welled up from deep inside her. His arms tightened around her as he drew her against his strong body. Her pulse was racing, his lips were searching her neck, scorching her skin. Her breath caught in her throat. She was frightened by the intensity of her own desire.

"Jakób?" she whispered.

He let go of her at once. "Heavens, Grietjie!" he said.

She smiled at him, wrapped her arms more tightly around his neck, pulled his head toward hers. He groaned softly. His lips caressed her face, her jaw. He kissed her eyes, cupped his hands around her face. His mouth rested on hers—softly, searchingly at first, then harder, more hungrily. Deep in her a joy was growing that she had never felt before.

"Grietjie?" he asked softly.

She read her own emotion in his eyes—the God-given desire between a man and a woman.

Late that night, curled up in her bed, her happiness wrapped around her like a comfort blanky, a tiny black bug gnawed at her mind: *Your father won't be impressed . . .*

Exams were starting in two weeks. Grietjie was studying hard. Her schedule was a nightmare.

"It's because you have so many majors," said Karin. "I said right from the start you should have your head examined."

Jakób phoned every day. On Friday evening she begged, "Come over tomorrow, please?"

"You have to study, Grietjie."

"I take a break sometimes! Come and fetch me and I'll study at your apartment."

"The minute you walk into this apartment there won't be much studying going on!" he predicted.

She laughed happily. "And if I promise to study?"

"I have to pack. The movers are coming next week," he said.

"I'll help you pack," she suggested.

"Out of the question. You have to study." He was unyielding.

She told Karin, "Jakób takes life too seriously. I'll have to work on that."

Karin laughed. "It's your own fault for choosing an old man."

"He's not old! He's perfect!" Grietjie protested.

On Saturday afternoon he turned up after all. He stood in the foyer, looking almost guilty. "I missed you too much," he said.

"Don't tell me the Pole is melting," she teased. "I'll bring my books, Jakób, and you'll see for yourself—I *can* be with you and study!"

They had coffee and ham sandwiches he had made. He paged though her German poems while she studied French literary history. He stretched out on the sofa and read some of her English short stories while she wrestled with *Hamlet*.

At eleven she pushed her books aside. "My head is like cotton wool," she said, stretching.

He put down the book he was reading and looked up. "Well, come and sit here so that I can show you what this Pole is made of."

In two strides she was on the sofa. "This Pole appears to be burning up," she joked, curling up beside him.

"This fiery Pole," he said, "has only half an hour before he has to return the most beautiful princess on the planet to the Dragon's den."

She spent all of Sunday studying at his apartment, achieving more than in the entire chaotic previous week. They talked during her study breaks, because there wasn't much time to say what needed to be said. She was starting her exams, and he was moving to Johannesburg. They had the serious conversations of two people who knew that an uphill road lay ahead.

"Tell me about Mischka," she said on Monday evening when she had moved her books aside and they were taking a coffee break.

"Sit with me on the sofa," he said, putting down the magazine he'd been reading. He couldn't stop looking at her, and he struggled to keep his hands to himself.

She sat down beside him, tucking her legs underneath her. "Tell me, Jakób," she said. There was a vulnerable look in her eyes.

"Mischka is a doctor who worked in the same hospital as Haneczka," he said, stroking her hair. "She's gone back to her native country, Hungary."

"Is she pretty?"

"Yes, Grietjie, she's very pretty. She's tall and dark and very elegant."

"Did you love her a lot?"

He knew Grietjie wouldn't stop before she knew exactly where she stood.

"I loved her enough to want to marry her," he answered honestly. "But I never forgot you. I thought of you sometimes, even when I was with her." He gave a slight laugh. "In my mind you were still the ten-year-old with the broad smile and the bow in her hair. Do you remember that newspaper cutting you sent me just before you left Germany?"

She sat up excitedly. "Did you get it, Jakób?" she asked.

"I kept it all the years, but when I fled, I had to leave it behind."

"It doesn't matter, because now you've got me."

"Yes, Grietjie, now I've got you." *Mother of God*, he prayed, *be merciful to us, because the road ahead is dark.* He never wanted to put her in a position where she had to choose between him and her adoptive parents. But the conversation he had had with Bernard one late night at the kitchen table flashed inside him like a red light.

"I still have the little wooden cross you gave me just before you left," she said. "I held it in my hand at night, when the dreams scared me. All through my school years." She looked up at him. "But now I've got you."

She curled up contentedly beside him.

They sat like that for a long time. He didn't want to spoil the atmosphere, but he knew he had to speak. "There's something I have to tell you," he said evenly.

"Mm?" She snuggled under his arm.

He sighed. "This is hard," he said.

"Mm?"

"Grietjie, are you listening?"

"I'm listening, Jakób, I'm sitting close to you because next week you'll be gone. But you can speak, I'm listening."

"The train . . . the one the resistance blew up, the one . . ." How was he going to tell her?

"The one with Oma and Mutti?"

"Yes, that one." He drew a deep breath. "That train was unscheduled. We were supposed to blow up a troop train that would come past later. Grietjie, I planted the bomb that blew up that train."

She was still for a while. Then her arm crept around his waist. "Why didn't you tell me this long ago, Jakób?" she asked against his chest. "It must have been so hard for you to have known it all these years."

He held her against him. "It was harder to say the words," he said.

"It wasn't your fault, Jakób."

"I'm still the one who planted the bombs, Grietjie."

He felt her nod against his chest. "I understand." She sat up straight and looked into his eyes. Her eyes were impossibly blue. "But now you know that I'm the woman who loves you, the one you can talk to about anything, no matter how hard."

He pushed her hair back, cupped his hands around her face. "We're so lucky, you and I," he said.

"Things will work out between us, won't they?"

"There are no guarantees, Grietjie. We'll see. We'll take it step by step. And remember, if it doesn't . . ."

She stuck her fingers in her ears. "Don't say it, I know," she protested.

"I love you."

She laughed happily. "I know, Jakób Kowalski. I know."

On the last Wednesday in November she wrote her last exam. That evening Jakób drove all the way from Johannesburg to say good-bye. On Thursday she and Grandpa John would go to the farm, and the week before Christmas Kobus and Salomé would marry.

Jakób and Grietjie went for a meal at Janina's again. He drew out a chair for her, ordered a bottle of wine. His eyes were drinking her in.

"I'm going to miss you terribly, Grietjie. The farm is very far away. Four weeks is a long time."

"But you'll try to come for Christmas, won't you, Jakób?"

"I'll try," he said. "On one condition."

"Your wish is my command, noble lord."

He smiled briefly. "Until I have spoken to your father, I'll be there as a friend of the family, because that's how I was invited. I won't be coming as your special guest."

Her eyes twinkled. "You mean I'm not allowed to hug and kiss you?"

He kept a straight face. "That's exactly what I mean."

"At least not in the presence of my family?"

"Nowhere. I'm serious, Grietjie. If we embark on a relationship, I want to clear it with your father first."

"We've already embarked on a relationship," she said. "Besides, you don't speak to the parents unless you want to get married."

"In our case it's different, and you know it."

Maybe that was what made her happiest—that he was Jakób, the perfectionist. "Yes, I know, you're right. However"—a thousand sprites danced in her eyes—"*I* might manage to behave, because I have an iron will and incredible self-control. But how *you're* going to resist me, I don't know."

"You'll be surprised, Miss Neethling," he said, putting on a long face.

"Will you at least kiss me on Christmas Day?"

The long face remained. "I doubt it, Miss Neethling, I doubt it very much."

She laughed, but the rough little claws of the black bug kept scratching at her mind: *Your father won't be impressed . . .*

16

She had told him not to phone, because the farm lines weren't private. "Everyone listens in, Jakób. You have no idea how much gossip it leads to."

But four weeks was a very long time—much longer than she had imagined. She missed him when she woke in the mornings and when she went to sleep at night, when she helped her mother with the household chores or talked to Grandpa John or heard her father's pickup outside.

And now that she was home again, she became more and more anxious about how her parents would react, especially her father. He liked Jakób, she knew. But Jakób was a foreigner. He didn't speak fluent Afrikaans, he didn't know the country's traditions and customs, he was years older than she was. And he was Catholic. That would never change. She knew it, because she knew Jakób.

The week before Kobus and Salomé's wedding, the farm was a hive of activity. Grietjie was grateful for the distraction. She lent a hand with the final preparations, she put on a beautiful dress, and she kept her smile in place all day. It was a wonderful wedding.

But that evening she sat alone on the veranda and looked out over the veld. She missed Jakób with all her heart.

And she was afraid.

A few days later her mother asked, "Grietjie, is something bothering you?"

"No, Mommy. I'm just lazy after the exams and the wedding and everything. And would you believe it? In ten more days I'll be a working girl!"

"But you'll tell me if something is bothering you?" her mother persisted.

"I will, Mommy, I promise."

It was going to be a strange Christmas, Grietjie thought, with only herself, her parents, and Grandpa John. And of course Jakób, who was coming on Friday. The closer it came to his arrival, the more Grietjie felt as if the black bug had got hold of a screwdriver, inserted it in her navel, and began twisting.

At breakfast on Thursday morning she couldn't eat a slice of toast, no matter how hard she tried. "Grietjie," her mother said worriedly, "you look pale. Don't you feel well?"

"I'm okay, Mommy. I'm just not hungry. It must be the heat."

But when her father had left to tend Kobus's pigsties and Grandpa John was sitting in his favorite place in the garden, Grietjie went to the pantry where her mother was busy.

"I want to talk, Mommy."

Her mother turned at once and gave her a look. "Let's go to your room," she said.

Now I've made a mistake, Grietjie thought as they walked down the passage. *I was stupid to have said anything.*

"What's the matter, Grietjie?" her mother asked when they reached her bedroom.

"Jakób and I are in love, Mommy."

She saw the astonishment on her mother's face, saw her frown, then turn pale. "Jakób?"

"Yes, Mommy, Jakób Kowalski."

"You mean . . . ?"

She should never have said anything. It's always better to say nothing. She had to stop Jakób in time so that he didn't speak. She had to—

"Grietjie?"

"Yes, Mommy. I mean Jakób and I have fallen in love."

"But, Grietjie," her mother exclaimed, "you can't! He's years older than you!"

"Yes, Mommy, thirteen and a half years," she said.

Her mother stared at her in disbelief.

She played her first trump card. "Grandpa John was almost twelve years older than Ouma Susan."

Her mother ran her hand over her face. "But . . ." She shook her head. "Jakób? He's from a different culture."

If her mother reacted like this, what would her father say? She had known it would be difficult, but she hadn't realized it would be this hard.

"You were English, yet you and Daddy got married. And you were raised in Grandpa John's wealthy household. Daddy was very poor, wasn't he?"

Her mother nodded slowly, still bewildered. "He was, yes."

Grietjie thought of something else. "And remember, I came here from Eastern Europe. We actually have the same roots, Jakób and I."

Her mother shook her head. "You speak Polish to each other. You'll always be strangers in South Africa. You'll find it hard to make friends. If you have children . . . gracious, Grietjie! The relationship could never work!"

"It could, Mommy! What exactly is my mother tongue? German? Polish? Afrikaans? Understanding each other is about much more than the words we speak. Yes, we still speak Polish and sometimes German, because Jakób has been in the country for less than a year. But he's learning fast; he spoke Afrikaans to Daddy when he was here in October." She paused for a moment. "Jakób and I understand each other no matter what language we speak."

Her mother lowered her head in her hands. "It's so sudden, Grietjie." She looked up, her eyes filled with concern. "He's Catholic, isn't he?"

Grietjie nodded. "Yes, Mommy, he is. And that's not going to change."

Her mother took a deep breath and shook her head. "Good heavens, child! I never thought . . . I trusted Jakób . . ."

"Jakób did nothing wrong," Grietjie cried. "He kept sending me away." She grabbed her mother's hands. "Mommy, I'm the one who convinced him we should try, at least try. And if it doesn't work out, we'll still be friends. But we love each other, Mommy!"

Her mother gently stroked her cheek. Then she asked earnestly, "Why are you so sure that you love him, Grietjie? Isn't he just an anchor to you? A piece of your past that you've rediscovered and don't want to lose again? A father figure?"

"Daddy is my father figure, Mommy. He's the best father in the world, that I know," Grietjie said firmly. After a moment she continued, "I don't know for sure what it means to love a man, Mommy. But one thing I do know: I want to be with Jakób, all the time. I'm happy when I'm with him. Maybe you're right. For a long time he was the anchor in my life. And now he has become my anchor again, and I don't want it otherwise."

"I understand," her mother said slowly.

"Because that's how you felt about Daddy too, didn't you?"

"Yes," said her mother, "that's how I felt about Bernard Neethling."

"And look how happy you are," said Grietjie.

Her mother gave her a keen look. "Oh, my darling, you're so young."

"But I've come a long way, Mommy."

Her mother nodded. "Yes, you have." She frowned and said, "Do you want me to speak to Daddy?"

"No, please don't. I should never have spoken to you. Jakób wanted to do it himself. It's just that I'm so afraid of how Daddy will react."

Her mother took her hand. "It's a good thing that you told me, Grietjie," she said. "It would be better to warn your father before Jakób speaks to him. He and I will want to discuss the matter, pray about it."

Grietjie nodded. "You're probably right," she said reluctantly. She shook her head. "I really don't know what Daddy will say."

Her mother got up and gave her a searching look. "Your father won't be happy," she said.

"I know, Mommy. I know."

When her father appeared in the door of the living room just before noon, she saw it in his face. "Can we talk, Grietjie?" he asked. Her heart sank.

They walked out to the kraal. Her mouth was dry, an iron fist gripped her throat, the stone was back in her tummy.

He sat down on the flat rock behind the kraal and she sat down on her own rock, where the two of them had had so many discussions in the past. The sunlight fell through the leaves of the thorn tree and made lacy patterns on the ground. Downy yellow blossoms lay at her feet.

Her nails cut into her palms.

"I don't want to argue with you, Grietjie," said her father's beloved voice.

She tried, but she couldn't stop the tears from pouring down her cheeks.

Her father handed her his handkerchief. "Calm down first," he said. "I just want to talk." He bent down, picked up a stone, and rubbed it between his thumb and forefinger.

She blew her nose hard. The handkerchief smelled of her father, of the farm.

"I know," she sniffed, "you just want what's best for me. And I want to be the best daughter for you. And I know you don't want Jakób, but I love him!" It sounded as if she was pleading and it was not what she had intended to do!

Her father placed his big hand on top of hers. "Come now, Grietjie," he said calmly. "We can't talk while you're being so emotional. I just want to discuss the matter with you—I'm not going to run Jakób off the farm."

She closed her eyes for a moment. "I'm sorry, Daddy. I'm just so terribly afraid."

"What of?"

She thought for a moment. What was she afraid of? "Of what you'll say."

"And what do you think I'll say?"

She sighed. "That Jakób is too old for me."

"And do you think he is?" asked her father.

She turned her head and met her father's gaze. "He's much older. But the relationship could work, depending on how we handle it." Suddenly she felt calm, collected. "Grandpa John was almost twelve years older than Ouma Susan."

Her father nodded slowly, but his face betrayed nothing. "What else are you afraid of?" he asked after a while.

She picked up one of the yellow blossoms. She considered her answer. "That you're going to say he's a Pole, he speaks Polish, and he's an outsider."

"And then you'll say Grandpa John was more than just an outsider, he was the enemy?" replied her father.

"Yes. And weren't you also an outsider in Grandpa John's home at the beginning?"

"Very much so, Grietjie," her father agreed.

A ring-necked dove called from a tree. *This is the Lim-po-po, this is the Lim-po-po*. Her father asked, "What else will I say?"

She took a deep breath and looked straight into his blue eyes. *How strange, there are tiny brown specks in his blue eyes*, she thought.

"That he's Roman Catholic, Daddy."

Her father nodded. "Yes, Grietjie."

She waited. Her father remained silent.

"He's not going to change, Daddy."

"I know."

They sat in silence again. *It feels as if a big bat has landed on my head*, Grietjie thought.

"I don't know what else to say, Daddy."

"What will you do, Grietjie? If the relationship works out, where will you stand?"

She looked at him fearlessly. "I'm a Protestant, Daddy. I don't feel ill at ease in the Catholic Church, because it's so familiar to me. But I was confirmed in the Protestant church and that's where I belong. Jakób has been to church with me. He likes the simplicity; he says our church is stripped of pretense. I'll probably attend his church sometimes, and sometimes he'll attend mine."

Her father gave her a searching look. "You realize that's not a solution, don't you?"

She looked down at the blossom that had wilted in her hand. Then she looked up. "It's the only solution we can think of, Daddy."

Her father nodded slowly. "We like Jakób, Grietjie," he said, "you don't have to doubt that. He's a strong, reliable man, and I believe he'll be a good husband to his wife. He's too old for you, yes, and he's an outsider, but two people who love each other should be able to bridge that divide."

She knew it was no good taking courage. She heard it in her father's tone of voice. "But?"

Her father nodded. "But I consider the issue of his faith insurmountable, Grietjie."

"Surely that's for me and Jakób to decide!" she cried. "You said you wouldn't run him off the farm!"

"I won't, Grietjie. Your great-grandfather did it with Grandpa John almost fifty years ago, and it led to thirty years of heartache. I don't want that." He looked at her earnestly. "But I'm going to implore Jakób to break off all contact with you."

"Daddy!"

"Allow me to finish, Grietjie," said her father. The pebble fell from his hand—it was shiny and clean, polished between his fingers. "I'm going to ask him to have no contact with you at all until you're at least twenty-one. Your mother and I feel that you need time. You're young, Grietjie, you know very little about adult life and its demands. We realize Jakób is an anchor to you, but marriage is far more than—"

"And then? When I'm twenty-one?" She put her fingers in her ears. "Then you'll have another excuse! You're taking away my only chance of happiness! I hate you! I wish I never—"

"Grietjie, pull yourself together!" her father said sternly. "You're behaving like a teenager. Don't say things you might regret."

She threw her head back and kept her eyes closed. "Sorry, Daddy," she said deliberately.

She got up and walked blindly into the veld.

Hours later she heard the pickup approach. She was exhausted, empty. She no longer knew why she was crying. Because she couldn't see Jakób for nine months? Surely that didn't mean it was the end of the road for them. Because she had argued with her father? They had disagreed before, especially during her teenage years. Because she had behaved childishly? It only proved that her father was right.

She was relieved to hear the pickup. Her father had come to fetch her before dark.

She went to meet him. He opened the door from the inside. She got in. "Thank you for coming to fetch me, Daddy," she said.

"No problem, Grietjie."

They drove back in silence. The pickup bounced along the rocky track down the mountainside.

When they were almost home, she asked in a choked voice, "Can Jakób still come for Christmas, Daddy?"

Her father's big hands lay calmly on the wheel. "I've already spoken to him on the phone," he said. "He respects my request."

Sorrow made the words stick in her throat. "So he's not coming?"

"No, Grietjie, he won't be here for Christmas."

Her heart ached, her entire being contracted with longing for him.

It was his first Christmas in this barren southern country. And he would be spending it alone.

She wanted to rant against her father; she wanted to rush at him and shake his shoulders and hammer with her fists on his chest so that he would understand.

But she knew him well enough to know that he would stand by his decision.

"Did you quarrel with him, Daddy?" Her tears were just below the surface.

Her father drew up next to the house and switched off the engine before turning to her. "Do you know me as someone who quarrels?"

She sighed. "No. I know you as someone who says what's going to happen and then it happens."

———

Early on New Year's day she drove back to Johannesburg with Grandpa John. They picked up Aunt Nellie at her sister's house in town and she sat in the front seat with the chauffeur.

"You always stay in the bushveld until the end of January," Grietjie protested feebly.

Grandpa John smiled. "I would never let you start a new life in Johannesburg on your own," he said.

She unpacked her things in the closet in her mother's former bedroom. It was hers now.

She took out the photograph taken of her and Jakób at the ball. It was the only one she had of him. She put it on the bedside table, next to her wooden cross.

If only Daddy understood the way Grandpa John does, she thought. The longing got worse every day.

The next morning she started work at *Die Transvaler*. The first week was a nightmare. She got lost, she forgot things, she translated texts without comprehending their content.

"It's just politics!" she told Grandpa John one evening. "International politics and economic terms I don't really understand."

"It must be interesting," he said.

"It might be interesting if I could make heads or tails of it," she said skeptically. "Why is the market sometimes a bull and at other times a bear, for instance?"

Grandpa John laughed. "Sit here, and I'll explain it to you," he said and sat down behind his desk.

She missed Jakób every day. She missed him so much that it hurt. She wanted to tell him things. She wanted to ask him questions and share her fears and her excitement with him, because a new world was slowly opening up to her. She wanted to tell him how strange it was to receive reports directly from Germany and the Netherlands and France, to read articles written there about South Africa, about apartheid, or tourism, even agriculture. He would understand how a phrase or a name, even of a village or a district she had known long ago, could open old wounds.

She began to develop an interest in European politics. She came to realize how deep her European roots went.

After a month she began to get the hang of things. The days at the office were full. She buried herself in her work. "You're doing a good job," the news editor complimented her.

At the end of January the first Polish article landed on her desk. It was just a short report about the struggle of the church against the Communist regime. While she was translating it, her heart went out to the people she had known there—Sister Zofia with her doe eyes behind thick lenses, Sister Margaret all the way from Ireland to bring Polish children to the Lord, Aunt Anastarja attending every mass she possibly could, old Mrs. Sobieski knitting warm socks for her, even Jakób's old professor with his broken glasses. In her mind's eye she saw them all with their crosses around their necks.

Daddy, she argued with her father in her imagination, *these people are Christians, good Christians, devoted to their way of worship, which may be strange to you but is part of their ancient culture.*

Part of Jakób's culture.

Maybe she should write her father a letter, explain it to him. Maybe include the article she had translated.

The article didn't make it into the newspaper. "Poland is a long way from South Africa," the news editor explained. "And it's a Communist country."

Her days consisted of words, sentences, and phrases translated from European languages into Afrikaans and typed on paper.

But her nights were a dark abyss of longing. Wave upon wave broke over her head and knocked her flat. Or washed over her, the water closing over her head and leaving her gasping for breath.

———•———

"It's no good to sit at home pining, Grietjie," said Grandpa John about six weeks after she had started to work in Johannesburg. "It's good for you to get out and meet new people, get to know them. You're young and you're lovely. You must go out, dance, mingle, go to the movies, or whatever you youngsters are doing nowadays."

"I don't want to do it without Jakób, Grandpa," she said.

"That's not a mature argument," Grandpa John said earnestly. "You might as well put these months to good use. In the process you can make certain he's the right man for you. You're too young to be so somber, Grietjie."

"I know, Grandpa, but I love Jakób."

"Do you think going out with other people will have an adverse effect on your love for Jakób?"

"No, never, Grandpa. I just don't feel like going out."

Grandpa John gave her a sidelong glance. "So you want to crawl into a hole and waste away?"

She thought for a moment and smiled. "No, you're right. I'll try to go out. Maybe I'll even enjoy it."

But she didn't believe she would.

Early in March, the fellow with the messy desk opposite her own was appointed European correspondent in London. Hein was beside himself with excitement. "Let's celebrate tonight, Grietjie," he said on the spur of the moment.

She put on her black evening gown. Not the dark greenish-blue silk taffeta, the color of a glossy starling in the sunlight.

They talked and ate and drank wine. They laughed and danced until they nearly dropped. They celebrated Hein's appointment with gusto—it was his dream come true.

In the early hours he took her back to Grandpa John's house in Parktown. Just before he got out to open the door for her, he turned to her and said, "Grietjie, you're so lovely, why isn't there a man in your life?"

She told him about Jakób. Everything. It felt good to tell a stranger.

When she had finished Hein said, "He must be a remarkable man to win the heart of someone like you."

"He *is* a remarkable person," Grietjie said.

Hein nodded slowly. "My parents would also have a hard time accepting a Catholic daughter-in-law," he said. "Maybe you should get yourself a good Afrikaner boy. You know, one who votes for the right party, shouts for the right team, sings in the right church choir?"

"Yes," she replied, trying to keep the conversation light, "maybe I should. A pity you're going to London for three years."

He laughed out loud. "You're the first person to mistake me for a good Afrikaner boy!" he said.

On a Saturday night in April Kobus came to spend the night with Grandpa John on his way to Estcourt. Grietjie sat with the men at the supper table like in the old days, and later around the fireplace in the study.

They laughed and chatted as if Jakób weren't so near, and yet so far.

On Sunday Uncle Peter and Diana came for lunch. The conversation turned to Kobus's pig farming.

"It's a good thing you diversified," said Uncle Peter. "I think you struck gold with your plan to supply bacon pigs to the factory in Estcourt."

"It's going well," said Kobus. "I'm on the point of signing a second contract with them. Next year I want to start exhibiting as well, at all the big agricultural shows, like the Rand Easter Show and the Royal Show in Pietermaritzburg. I want to make a name for myself as a pig farmer."

She enjoyed listening to her brother. She was proud of him.

"We also plan to diversify," said Uncle Peter. "We want to expand into the coal industry. Black gold, they call it."

Kobus leaned forward. "That's interesting," he said. "But won't it be a very costly exercise? Surely it requires different equipment?" He laughed. "Not that I know much about that kind of thing."

"We're thinking of collaborating with a German company," Grandpa John said.

"And Iscor is also interested in entering into an agreement with us," Uncle Peter continued. "It was actually Jakób's idea, he . . ."

Grietjie's mouth went dry. *Jakób!* She pressed her cold hands to her hot face. *Jakób!*

". . . with the negotiations," she heard Uncle Peter's voice again.

"Grietjie, will you go and see what's happened to the coffee?" Grandpa John asked calmly.

He could have rung the bell, but she got up. "Yes, Grandpa," she said.

". . . brilliant fellow, he's acting as . . . ," she heard Uncle Peter say just before she entered the kitchen.

When she returned seconds later, the conversation had moved on to something else. Jakób's name wasn't mentioned again.

That night she couldn't sleep. She stood looking at the moon. Jakób was in this city, not in distant Poland. He worked with Uncle Peter every day. She knew Grandpa John regularly spoke to him. But when she had reentered the room, his presence had been erased from the conversation. Deliberately, she knew.

The next morning Kobus left early. Grandpa John was still asleep, but she filled Kobus's flask with coffee and gave him the food Aunt Nellie had packed for him.

"How are you really, Grietjie?" he asked just before he got into his pickup.

"I miss Jakób terribly," she said honestly.

"You haven't seen him again?"

"Not at all, nor spoken to him. Kobus, nine months is a very long time. I'm sick with longing for him."

Kobus looked at her seriously. "Go out with other men, Grietjie," he said. "It's no good wishing the nine months were over. I can't see Dad ever accepting Jakób's Catholic faith. I don't want you to get to a point where you have to choose between him and us."

She was aware again of the knot in her tummy. "Do you think it's that serious?" she asked.

He nodded. "I do, Griet. I'm afraid so."

Jakób strode down Market Street, past Corner House to Barclays Bank. He pushed open the door, caught a glimpse of the long lines at the tellers, and sighed. He pushed his fingers through his thick black hair and considered returning later. But later he wouldn't have time either, he thought, and joined the shortest queue.

Only then did he glance at the people around him.

She was standing in an adjacent line, slightly ahead of him. His heart leaped into his mouth. He stared, transfixed.

She was beautiful. He could see only her profile—the pert, turned-up nose, the full lips, the blonde curls in a new, modern hairstyle. She was dressed in a dark-red suit, the jacket emphasizing her feminine curves, the skirt showing just enough of her shapely legs.

She was studying the statements in her hand. If she turned her head, she would see him.

His licked his dry lips.

His entire being cried out to her.

She was so close, he could have reached out and touched her.

Quietly he turned and left the building.

"A man called Francois phoned," Grandpa John said late one afternoon when she came home.

"Francois!" Grietjie said, surprised. "He's my roommate's brother, remember? He lectures at Pretoria University now, and he's studying for another degree or something. Did he leave a number?"

"He did. And he said his sister would be in Pretoria this weekend. They want you to come over."

"Grandpa, that's the best news! I'd love to see Karin again. And Francois as well. We're such good friends." She took the note with the phone number and went straight to the telephone.

It was wonderful to hear Francois' voice. She asked about Karin and promised to catch an early train to Lyttelton on Saturday. She asked about Hester and the university and his studies. She told him about her new job, how much she was learning, how interesting she was finding it.

"And Jakób, Grietjie?" he asked after a while.

"Karin probably told you I'm not allowed to see him before my birthday," she said.

"She did, yes."

"I miss him terribly, Francois."

He was quiet for a while. "What will change when you're twenty-one, Grietjie?"

"Nothing," she said. "Nothing."

She could imagine him nodding at the other end. "What are you doing the weekend after this one?" he asked casually.

"Why?"

"A group of us are going over to Lourenço Marques. We're putting in leave for Friday and we're leaving on Thursday night. There's room in my car if you feel like coming."

She smiled. "Besides you, Hester, and me, who else will be in your car?"

He gave an embarrassed laugh. "A friend of mine, Hermann Grové."

"Also a shrink?"

"No, another kind of doctor. A vet."

"Mm. I'll decide this weekend."

That evening Grandpa John said, "Sounds like an excellent idea, Grietjie."

"What? Seeing my friends over the weekend, or the trip to the coast?" she asked.

"Both," he said, looking amused. "Just do it, my dear."

"Why don't you write that book you always talked about?" Karin suggested on Saturday afternoon. "It would take your mind off things."

They were sunbathing in the feeble sunlight, just as they had often done when they were students. *It feels like such a long time ago*, Grietjie thought. Now Karin had an engagement ring on her finger. And Grietjie had a great longing in her heart. Even worse was the fear that was gradually consuming her.

The fear that nine months wouldn't change a thing.

"You must have a story before you can write a book," she said.

"Why don't you tell your own story?" Karin suggested, pushing her cat's-eye sunglasses up the bridge of her nose. "Not everybody has such an interesting one."

"I've considered it. I've even thought of a title," she admitted. "But I can't write a book with such a miserable ending. My dad will never accept Jakób, Karin. I realize it more every day. No one will want to read a story that ends like that."

"Well, make up your own ending." Karin shrugged. "It's your story, after all, you can do with it as you please."

Grietjie smiled slowly. "You're right. You're quite right. It's my story, I can do as I please."

Just before they went inside, Karin asked, "What's the title you thought of?"

Grietjie hesitated for a moment, then replied, "'The Girl from the Train.'"

"Grietjie!" the news editor called one Wednesday morning. "The boss wants to see you in the glass case!"

Surely I couldn't have done something wrong, she worried as she went up the stairs to the dreaded office lined with windows. She lifted her chin, knocked once, and pushed open the editor's door.

"You're Grietjie Neethling, aren't you?" the editor asked, peering at her over the top of his spectacles.

"That's right, sir." She stood up straight and met his gaze. She hoped she looked businesslike, professional.

"Yes, well, I believe you speak German?"

"That's right, sir. I do."

"Well, good. I want you to come along with me this afternoon. We're entertaining the editorial team of the *Frankfürter Allgemeine Zeitung*." He rifled through the papers on his chaotic desk. "It's a German newspaper," he said, then looked up at her over his spectacles again.

"I know the paper, sir," she said. "What exactly do you want me to do, sir?" she asked.

He looked up, surprised. Or maybe the thick lenses gave him the surprised look. "Translate," he said. "Interpret. Speak when we get stuck. Some of us know basic German; others don't understand a word. And I believe their English isn't up to much either."

"Fine, sir, I'll come." She smiled.

"We're leaving in half an hour. We're meeting them at the German Club in Pretoria at noon," he said. "You're going with that photographer with the greasy hair—what's his name again?"

It could be any of the young photographers. "Juan?" she ventured.

But the editor had already moved on to something else.

The German Club was an unimpressive pre-war building on the corner of Paul Kruger and Vermeulen Streets. She and Pierre—not Juan after all—walked up the wide steps hollowed out over the years by a multitude of feet. When they reached the door, he produced a comb from his sock, combed his hair back, slicked down his sideburns with his fingers, and said, "Let's go for it, Grietjie, girl."

The German visitors were late. The editor paced up and down, gave a few last-minute instructions, kept an eye on the door.

When the visitors arrived, the manager of the German Club stepped forward and welcomed them in eloquent German. The editor delivered the speech Grietjie had helped him prepare. Everyone got acquainted with everyone else.

Their party of nine was shown into a private dining room—Pierre wouldn't be joining them, as he had already taken his photos and completed his assignment.

Grietjie followed the men, who were engaged in animated conversation. Her services didn't appear to be required after all.

In passing, she glanced into one of the other rooms. She recognized Uncle Peter and stopped to take a second look. Jakób was in an armchair, facing the door. He was leaning forward, engaged in conversation, a serious expression on his face.

She drew a deep breath.

He was here, yards away from her. His pitch-black hair gleamed in the lamplight. He waved his big hands as he spoke, and her ears picked up the soft tone that belonged to his voice.

"Will you be coming inside, Miss?" asked the waiter who was holding the door of the adjacent room for her.

She took a last look. If only he would look up . . . If she could just give him a smile . . .

But he didn't look up.

She followed the waiter. Her hands were trembling, her heart was pounding, hot blood was pumping through her body, yet she felt ice-cold.

The waiter closed the door behind her.

———

"I saw Jakób today," she said at supper that night.

Grandpa John frowned. "Jakób? I thought they were in Pretoria today."

"They were, he and Uncle Peter and three other men. In the German Club. I was there too."

"Why was that?" Grandpa John was still frowning.

"My editor had a meeting with some people from the *Frankfürter Allgemeine Zeitung*—the German newspaper. I was asked to interpret. I saw Jakób in one of the lounges, but he didn't see me."

"And now?" asked Grandpa John.

"Now my heart aches, Grandpa. If my parents phone tonight, I won't be able to speak to Daddy. It hurts too much. I miss Jakób terribly, Grandpa."

"But you didn't go to him?" he asked.

"I would have, Grandpa, if he had looked up and seen me. But he was deep in conversation."

"It's better that way," said Grandpa John.

She leaned across the table and took his hand. "Grandpa, please tell me about Jakób," she pleaded. "Just tonight, Grandpa, I won't ask again. But I'm desperate to know how he is, what he's doing, whether he's happy. You see him every week. Please, Grandpa?"

Her grandfather shook his head. "I really shouldn't," he said.

"Just this once, for me? Please, Grandpa John?" she insisted.

He gave a slight smile. "Just this once," he conceded. "Bring the coffee to my study—it will be warmer by the fire."

He told her how well Jakób had settled in at the company, how he had come with innovative ideas, how he was the mastermind behind the new coal mine project and the collaboration with the German company and Iscor.

"He's very clever, isn't he, Grandpa?" she asked.

"He is, Grietjie. Not only in his field, but also as a businessman. And he has the necessary experience. He has specific, specialized expertise that's still new to us here in South Africa. We're very lucky to have him in our company." He paused. "We're going to offer him a full partnership as soon as the new project is off the ground," he added.

"And when you see him . . . does he ever ask about me, Grandpa?"

Her grandfather gave her a long look, then sighed. "Yes, Grietjie. He asks about you. Every single week."

Winter came. In the mornings the windows were steamed up. A thick blanket of fog hung over the city, and the grass was covered with a stiff, white ice blanket. The streets were full of people snugly wrapped in boots and coats. The cars drove with their headlights on in the mornings, their exhaust fumes trailing behind them in dirty white clouds.

This year, the cold winter nights were more than just a dark abyss. At the bottom lay a longing that held her in its grip, a loneliness that kept her in chains. She stood at her bedroom window and looked out over Johannesburg. Lights were moving in the distance, people were moving.

Somewhere among them was Jakób. The night sky was overcast. It looked as if the moon would never break through again.

One Sunday night at the beginning of August she heard the sound of Grandpa's favorite music coming from the study: Galli-Curci's *Il dolce suono*, Caruso's *La donna è mobile*. She went downstairs and slowly pushed open the door. Grandpa John sat deep in his soft leather chair, his legs stretched in front of him, his eyes closed, a slight smile on his lips. His whiskey glass was on the table next to him, and the sweet smell of a Cuban cigar hung in the air. Softly she closed the door behind her and sat down in the other leather chair.

The music and the nostalgic atmosphere of a cold Sunday night at the fireside enveloped her.

"Beautiful?" asked Grandpa John when the last notes had faded.

She nodded. "*Sehr schön,*" she said.

She got up and picked another record from the shelf. She stooped and carefully lowered the needle onto the vinyl disc before she sat down again.

A male voice began to sing *"Das Zauberlied."*

"*Das ist Deutsch*," Grietjie said with a smile.

Grandpa John smiled and nodded. "Josef Schmidt," he said. "You have a good memory. Sit here with me?" He opened his arm and Grietjie nestled into the familiar space. He held her against him. Together they listened to the German music.

"Do you still miss Ouma Susan?" she asked when the music ended.

He nodded. "At times it's very bad."

"I miss Jakób all the time, Grandpa," she said.

"I know you miss him," he said. "I know you've tried going out with friends. I can see it doesn't help."

"Grandpa, I don't know how we're going to get past my dad," she said softly.

He pressed her head to his shoulder. She felt him sigh. "Wait for September," he said. "Time will tell."

But Grandpa John didn't sound very positive.

———

Grandpa John had planned a birthday party at the elegant Rand Club for her coming of age. Her parents and Kobus and Salomé were coming to Johannesburg on Saturday morning. A group of friends and relatives had been invited: Uncle Peter and Diana, Britney and Sarah and their husbands, Karin and Heinrich, Francois and Hester. At the last minute she had invited Hermann Grové as well. He was a good friend and at least she'd have someone to dance with. But she knew in advance that the pain would be worse that evening—she was desperately missing Jakób.

Sometime after her birthday she would see him again. And sometime after her birthday they would have to talk to her father again.

On Friday night she and Grandpa John sat beside the fireplace in his study, reading. At half past seven Grandpa John got to his feet. "I'm going to bed. Tomorrow promises to be a long day," he said, rubbing his cold hands together. "I hope Nellie has remembered to put a hot-water bottle in my bed."

"She always does, Grandpa. I think I'm going to read in my bed as well."

But he shook his head. "Stay for a while," he said. "You always enjoy the fire, don't you?"

"I do, Grandpa, and it *is* very early." She laughed. "You're going to bed with the birds tonight," she teased him.

She heard him go through to the kitchen. She tucked her legs underneath her, curled up in the soft leather chair, and sat staring at the flames for a while. Even the fire seemed to be feeling the cold. On the farm they used leadwood, and the fire burned all through the night. *The wood you buy in the city is like paper,* Kobus always said. *It doesn't make proper coals.*

"Gretchen?"

He spoke very softly so that she wouldn't be alarmed.

At the sound of his voice she turned her head.

He was standing at the door of the study. He filled the entire doorway. He was wearing a white shirt and a chunky dark-blue sweater. His broad shoulders were square in the doorframe. His suntanned face looked dark against the white shirt collar. His curly black hair was slightly tousled and fell over his forehead.

She gazed at the man she loved.

He smiled at her across the room and made a slight movement with his hands.

In two strides she was in his arms.

His arms closed around her. She pressed her head against his chest, she smelled him, heard his heart pounding, felt him against her.

"Jakób," she said.

He ran his hand over her hair, her neck, her back, and the curve of her hips while his other arm held her close.

"I know it's two days before your birthday, but I couldn't wait any longer."

They moved to sit on the soft leather couch.

She stroked and stroked his hand, his broad fingers with the square nails and the fine black hairs. "How did you get in?" she asked dreamily.

"Grandpa John left the front door open for me."

He kept touching her, stroking her hair, her neck, pressing her hand to his lips, kissing her fingers one by one.

"Good heavens, Grietjie, I missed you," he said over and over.

She turned to him, traced the familiar lines of his face with her finger, leaned over, and gently kissed his eyes.

"I love you too, Jakób Kowalski," she said. "I want to stay with you forever."

When he left late that night, she had no desire to sleep. The fire was dead. She lit a candle on the mantelpiece, put the record she and Grandpa John had listened to earlier back on the turntable, and curled up in the soft leather chair.

She heard Grandpa John come down the stairs. She realized he hadn't been asleep. She hoped the following day would not be too much for him.

He pushed open the door, entered without speaking, and poured them each a glass of brandy. Then he turned to his desk and opened the wooden box with the Cuban cigars. He took the cigar cutter from the top drawer of his desk and carefully snipped off the end of the cigar. Pensively he tapped the cigar against his left thumbnail.

"Grandpa, if I have to choose between my parents and the man I love, there's only one option. I'd choose the same way you and Ouma Susan did."

He nodded slowly. "I see." He struck a match and lit his cigar. Like so many times before, the rich aroma filled the room. "It's a sad path to choose, Grietjie."

"I know," she said, "but there's no other way."

"No," he said, puffing at his cigar, "there's no other way."

Her parents, Kobus, and Salomé arrived just before lunch. She was happy to see them all. Her mother embraced her and touched her hair, laughing happily because they were all together again. Her father hugged her to his chest. "My little city girl," he teased.

She laughed. "It's too cold, or I would have been barefoot," she said.

They had coffee and talked about the farm and her job at the paper and Grandpa John's company.

They acted as if there were no Jakób waiting in the wings. But she knew they also knew. The meeting was unavoidable.

On Saturday night they formally celebrated her coming of age with toasts and champagne, a delicious meal, and heaps of fun.

On Sunday, the morning of her actual birthday, her mother brought her coffee in bed. Her father and Grandpa John joined them, and after a while so did Kobus and a sleepy Salomé. Even Aunt Nellie popped in. Grietjie opened her gifts: gold earrings from her parents—"so delicate, so lovely!"—Etienne Leroux's latest novel from Kobus and Salomé—"daring, aren't you?"—a crocheted doily from Aunt Nellie—"did you really make it specially for me?"

"My gift is outside," said Grandpa John.

"Can I take a look?" Grietjie asked excitedly.

"Wait, let's get dressed first, then we'll all go out together," said her mother.

She put on her lovely new birthday outfit. She wished Jakób could be there.

And yet, maybe not, because she didn't want her bubble of happiness to burst.

They waited for Grandpa John to get dressed. He came walking through the entrance hall and past the study. He opened the front door and stepped back.

Parked in the driveway was a brand-new DKW. Someone had tied a red ribbon around it, with an enormous bow on the roof.

Grietjie stared, astounded. She turned to him. "Grandpa John?"

He smiled and held out the keys.

She looked at the people around her. Their smiles reflected their joy; their eyes radiated their love for her. They were her family. They had welcomed her when she'd been homeless, abandoned, completely alone, and to this day they cherished her as their own little girl.

She could never turn her back on them. Not even . . .

She took the car keys from Grandpa John and unlocked the door of her very first car. One by one she took them for a spin around the block.

After Aunt Nellie's enormous lunch—even better than the previous night's sumptuous feast, they all agreed—everyone lay down for an afternoon nap.

Grietjie's heart was full and heavy. Her thoughts were a thick, sandy footpath that was holding her down and sucking her in so that she could hardly move. She couldn't renounce Jakób.

The house was quiet. Everyone was asleep.

Eventually she got up and rinsed her face. For a long time she stood looking at the city lying so peacefully beneath her. Somewhere in the city was Jakób.

When at last she went downstairs, her mother was sitting on the veranda in the weak early-spring sunshine. A book lay open in her lap but she wasn't reading. "Shall I make coffee?" Grietjie asked. "Or is Daddy still asleep?"

Her mother looked up, her eyes strangely veiled. "Daddy is in the study, Grietjie. He and Grandpa John are talking."

Grietjie drew a slow breath. "Mommy? Since after lunch?"

Her mother nodded.

"It's . . . almost five."

"Six minutes to five," her mother said without looking at her watch. "Make the coffee, Grietjie."

———•———

On Monday morning she got into her brand-new car and drove to work with a heavy heart. No one had said a word about the conversation in the study.

On her desk lay a bunch of flowers from her colleagues. Grietjie clapped her hands. "It's lovely!" she cried, surprised. "How did you know it was my birthday?"

At ten a bouquet of red roses was delivered at the office. Twenty-one red roses. "I love you, Gretchen," the card read.

But he didn't phone.

At five she drove home. *He mustn't come tonight,* she thought. *Not yet. I simply can't!*

When she drove through the big gate, his car was in the driveway. Not the old blue Volksie, but his new fiery-red Alfa Spider convertible.

She sat in her car for a long time, too afraid to go inside.

After a while he came out, opened the door of her new car, and sat down in the passenger's seat. He seemed to fill the entire car. "Happy birthday, my darling," he said and kissed her tenderly.

"Jakób?" She could hardly get the words out. "When did you come?"

"Earlier," he said vaguely, brushing the curls out of her face. "Do you like your car?"

"My dad?" Her voice stuck in her dry throat.

"He's waiting to speak to us, Grietjie."

"But have you spoken to him?"

"Yes, we've spoken. We had a long conversation."

"What did he say, Jakób?" she pleaded.

"He wants to speak to the two of us."

"Jakób, I . . ."

Gently he touched her cheek and opened the door. "Come, Gretchen, your father is waiting."

The house was quiet, holding its breath.

Her parents were in the dining room. They were seated at the table, the fresh coffee and Aunt Nellie's scones untouched.

She felt Jakób's hand on her back, a reminder he was there.

He pulled out a chair for her and she sat down, facing her father. Jakób sat down next to her. She took a deep breath. She couldn't think anymore, so she spoke from her heart.

"Daddy, Mommy, you took me in when I was an orphaned waif. You said I was perfect and lovely, you loved me like your own daughter, you gave me a home and security and a wonderful education and my own identity. You're the best parents any child could ask for. I love you dearly. I'm so grateful that God brought me to your home here at the southern tip of Africa."

Under the table her hand reached for Jakób's. He took it, as always, and held it tightly, as always.

"But I love Jakób. This past year has made me even more certain of it. I could never give him up."

She looked at her mother. Her mother nodded slowly, her expression tender. *She understands*, Grietjie thought.

She clung to Jakób's hand. Then she looked at her father.

His blue eyes looked back at her. She waited.

"Jakób and I had a long conversation today," he said calmly. "I would have preferred a different partner for you, someone . . . of your own faith . . ." He thought for a moment. "But it didn't work out that way. I understand how you feel. I believe you've had enough time to reflect during the past months."

He looked at his wife, took her hand. "Grietjie," he said, "I want you to be happy, truly happy."

She nodded. She couldn't speak.

Her father turned to Jakób. "My wish for Grietjie is to know the happiness her mother and I have been blessed with," he said.

Jakób nodded. "I pray that we will have it too," he said seriously.

Her father looked at her. "Grietjie?"

"Jakób makes me happy, Daddy. He always has. And . . . you're right, I've had a lot of time to reflect during the past year. I'm certain that I want to be with him, always."

Her father got up and offered Jakób his hand across the table. Jakób got up and shook his hand.

"Look after my little lamb," her father said hoarsely.

"I will, Bernard," said Jakób. "I'll guard her with my life."

Her father was still looking at Jakób. He hadn't let go of his hand. "And from now on," he said, "you're part of this family. We're leaving the past behind us."

"Thank you, Bernard," said Jakób. "It would be an honor for me to be part of your family."

Her father turned to her with a slight smile.

"Daddy?" she said. Her voice was small.

He held out his arms and she went to him. He held her close. He didn't speak. After a while he reached out with one arm and her mother joined the small, strong circle.

She turned her head and looked at Jakób across the table. His black eyes held her gaze. He was waiting for her. She smiled broadly. He opened his arms wide.

Gently she extricated herself from her father's embrace and stepped into Jakób's arms.

———————

That year they celebrated Christmas at the farm as usual, except that she was sitting next to Jakób now instead of her father.

Late Christmas Eve she and Jakób stepped out on the veranda. "Let's walk to the stream," she said.

He laced his fingers through hers as they walked along the sandy path. Her hand lay securely in his. Around them the veld was asleep. "When I was a child, I always thought this must be what the open fields of Bethlehem had looked like when the shepherds heard the angels sing and the *Drei Heilige Könige* saw the star," she said.

The moon was full, bathing the path and the grass and the yellow blossoms of the thorn trees in its soft light. "The moon has come a long way since earlier this evening," said Jakób.

"In Poland the fields are covered with snow now. The moon over there is silver, not gold," she said.

"And the people are on their way to midnight mass," he said.

"Yes," she said, "the cathedral will be full of candles, the organ will be playing beautiful music." She stopped and turned to him. "We can go to midnight mass at Christmas sometimes, if you want to, Jakób."

He smiled at her. "A white Christmas belongs to Poland, Grietjie," he said. "I think we'll always come to the farm—that's how one should celebrate Christmas in this southern land."

Under the big bushy willow they paused. The moon shone up at them from the water.

"I'm so glad you're here with me, Jakób," she said. "I've missed you for so long."

"Grietjie." He put his arms around her, pressed her head to his chest, stroked her hair. "I love you."

———•———

When they came back later, Grandpa John was sitting on the veranda of the old homestead.

"I've always gone to Grandpa John on Christmas Eve," she told Jakób, "ever since my first Christmas here."

"Then you should go to him now," said Jakób.

"Come with me," she said.

They walked along the concrete path and up the steps. Jakób sat down on the top step and leaned his back against a pillar while she knelt beside her grandpa.

Grandpa John put his arm around her shoulders.

"Are you very sad tonight?" she asked, stroking his gray hair.

"Not really, Grietjie, not really," the old man said slowly. "All my memories are happy ones tonight. I had a love of my own."

Epilogue

ONE YEAR LATER

The bubbles clung to the glass for as long as they could. Then they let go, rose to the surface, and burst. The soft candlelight flickered on the crystal glasses and the snow-white linen. If she turned her hand slightly, the candlelight struck brilliant sparks from the big diamond on her finger.

She looked up. Outside a full moon was shining over the bare veld. The plains of the Free State were bathed in gold. The wheels went *clickety-clack* on the tracks.

The train gave a long whistle. She turned her head and looked into his dark eyes.

"I can't believe we're honeymooning on a train!"

"Not just any old train, I'll have you know, Mrs. Kowalski," Jakób said reprovingly, his black eyes twinkling. "The world-renowned Blue Train!"

Grietjie threw back her head and laughed. "It sounds marvellous—Mrs. Grietjie Kowalski. I've had a number of names: Gretl Schmidt, Gretz Kowalski, Grietjie Neethling. But this is the best one by far—Grietjie Kowalski. Let's have another glass of champagne, Jakób."

"Oh no," he said, drawing her to him. "The champagne is on ice. It can wait until later. Much later."

———

As they stood looking through the train window at the Du Toits Kloof Mountains the next morning, Grietjie asked, "When will we get there?"

"We'll be in Cape Town just after twelve," Jakób replied. He cradled her face in his hands, stroking her cheek with his thumb. "But you and me, Gretchen, we reached our destination yesterday."

She looked up into his dark eyes. "Yes, Jakób Kowalski, we did. And it has made our journey worthwhile." She took a deep breath and said, "Our long, long journey."

A Letter from Gretl to Jakób

18 July 1948

Lieber Jakób,

I am writing you this letter because you told me to let you know
what is happening to me. But the news is not very good, I am sorry to
tell you.

Today the people from Südafrika came to see which of the children
are good enough to go with them. I made myself look neat, but my hair
was a bit wild. So Elke, she's a big girl who sleeps in the bed next to mine,
helped me to tie a ribbon in it.

We didn't go to school. Two people from Südafrika came. One is
Onkel Schalk Botha. He is the head of the people who gave the money to
fetch the children. Jakób, I could see he is a rich man. He is fat and he was
dressed in smart black clothes and he wore round glasses.

The other person is Doctor Vera Bührmann. She is going to make
sure the children are healthy. She did not say anything to us.

Onkel Schalk doesn't speak very good German but I understood
that he wants to take us to a very good country where a good mommy
and daddy are waiting for us. We'll have a very good life. He kept saying
"sehr gut" but he couldn't say it properly in German.

He said we have to know it's for ever, we are never coming back to
Germany. But I know that already because you told me so.

Then we had to go to our rooms. Elke began to cry and she won't
stop crying. Do you know why, Jakób? It is because they only want children who are eight years or younger.

I wanted to cry too. I am very, very sad because I am ten. But crying
doesn't make your heart feel better and it makes your head hurt so now

I am writing to you. My tummy hurts too because of the lump, Jakób, I have to tell you. And my throat hurts too because I want to cry, see?

I won't mail the letter now, because I have only this one envelope and stamp that you gave me.

20 July, Early morning

Lieber Jakób

Do you think it could work if I just go to the doctor lady and tell her how healthy I am? I am Aryan and a full orphan and everything, and I don't look ten, I look younger than eight so I'm going to do it. You must ask the Mother of God to help me, Jakób, I'll ask God. Thank you, Jakób.

Evening

I went to see the doctor lady this afternoon, Jakób. I did my best but I don't think I have good news.

Before I went to see her I read the newspaper story about what they are looking for over and over again. I know it by heart now. I tried to tie my ribbon but it was too difficult. Then I went to the office where the doctor lady is.

A child was crying in the office. His mommy brought him to be adopted but he wouldn't let go of her. She cried a lot when she came out.

I remembered your words, Jakób. You said: I made a promise to the Holy Mother of God to do the best I can for you, to do what I believe is best for you.

I wanted to say those words to the mommy because they are good words, but she was already gone.

I went in and said: I must be examined to go to Südafrika.

The doctor lady asked my name and I said Gretl Schmidt. I stood up very straight, Jakób, so I would look neat.

She could not find my file because it wasn't on the table because I'm too old, you understand? Then she asked: How old are you?

I looked the lady in the eye and said the words I practiced: I am ten, but I look eight. I am a Protestant orphan, I have a certificate of baptism that says Pfarrer Helmut Friedrich baptized me Gretl Christina Schmidt in the Deutsche Luthersche Kirche on 18 December 1937. My father was Herr Peter Schmidt, a fallen SS soldier. Here is a photo of him in his SS uniform. I have an official letter the government sent my mother to say he was a hero.

The doctor lady looked at me but she did not say anything.

So I went on: I am a full orphan, because my mother died in an explosion, my mother and my grandmother. And my sister also died so I became a Findelkind. And I am Aryan.

Jakób, that is the most important thing, and I nearly forgot to tell her.

Then the doctor lady examined me. I was afraid she would think there's something wrong with my heart because it beat so fast. I had to open my mouth very wide and say "aah" and then I could put my dress back on.

But, Jakób, then she said I am too old and she is bound by the rules of the German Children's Fund committee. Because they are giving the money, see? And the new mommies and daddies prefer younger children. But she said if they can't find enough children who are younger than eight, maybe they'll take older children. But only maybe.

Lieber Jakób, at first I didn't want to tell you tonight because then your heart will hurt as much as mine. But now I did. I don't want to make you sad, understand? I just wanted to tell you.

16 August

Lieber Jakób

I have been chosen to go to Südafrika. We are leaving at once on a bus to Lübeck-Brandenbaum. I don't have a lot of time, I have to pack so I'll tell you more later. Jakób, I'm so very happy. I can't believe it, I'm so happy!

Red Cross Orphanage
Lübeck-Brandenbaum

18 August

We are at the Red Cross Orphanage now. Today we were given clothes, first the shoes and socks, then we had to see which of the dresses fit. I got two pairs of underpants, a dress with yellow flowers, a little too big, a navy blue skirt and a red blouse. The blouse is much too big, it's almost longer than the skirt when I tuck it in. I didn't get a new sweater because I still have the one Mrs Sobieski made for me. And my red coat. Now you know what my new clothes look like, Jakób.

20 August 1948

Today we went to Hannover in a special bus. First the minister spoke for a long time. He said we are going to a new country now but we must remember the Germans are a proud nation, we will always have German blood in our veins and we must behave like true Germans.

In the bus the helper ladies gave us syrup sandwiches. It was messy and the boys didn't behave like true Germans at all, they got syrup all over themselves. I am really glad I'm not a boy, Jakób.

A man spoke to me in the bus. He said in Hannover I must speak to the journalists, they are people who write for the newspapers.

We will spend only one night at the Maschsee in Hannover. Then we are going to the Netherlands in an English train and across the sea to England in a ferryboat. We are going to have lunch now, then the journalists are coming. One of the helper ladies is going to tie a ribbon in my hair.

Evening

I must go to bed, I am writing quickly because I want to tell you. The journalists came and one man asked what we are going to do in South Africa. So I said: I am going to get a home and a family who wants me, and the journalist said it is a good answer. Some of the boys gave really stupid answers.

I said we will have to learn a new language, Afrikaans, so he asked me what it sounds like. I said: Goeiemore, goeienag, slaap lekker. Jakób, that's Guten Morgen, gute Nacht, schlaf gut. See, it's almost the same.

Then a man with a big camera took my photo. I gave a really big smile so that it would be a nice photo.

Tomorrow I have to mail the letter because there are German stamps on the envelope and tomorrow I am leaving Germany for good. My heart aches, Jakób, because after that I can never speak to you again.

Midnight

I can't sleep, Jakób. I really, really want to talk to you.

There is a broken moon in the sky tonight. Can you see it too, Jakób Kowalski?

From Gretl

Morning

Jakób, this morning the man with the camera came and gave me this newspaper cutting with my picture! It was in this morning's paper. You can keep it.

Scenes from the
Original Afrikaans Edition

Jakób Returns from Warsaw

She walked home very slowly.

At the house Stan carried Jakób to his bed. The woman stayed in the room, while Uncle Janusz and Stan went to the kitchen. Gretl remained on the porch.

She felt ice-cold.

When she saw Aunt Anastarja return from the cathedral, she ran to meet her. "Stan and Jakób are back," she said.

Aunt Anastarja turned round. "Then I have to go back and light candles to give thanks," she said and set off across the grass.

"I think Jakób is . . ." Gretl said to her departing figure. She couldn't bring herself to say "dead", she just couldn't. But Aunt Anastarja kept walking and it didn't seem as if she had heard.

In the kitchen the woman was drinking coffee with Uncle Janusz and Stan. Monicka had come from the bedroom—the baby was probably asleep—and was buttering bread. Gretl stood in the doorway.

"He's very weak," said the woman dressed like a man, "and the journey here didn't do him any good."

They were speaking about Jakób.

"Why didn't you leave him there in a hospital?" asked Monicka.

They were *really* speaking about Jakób.

"Because there is no hospital," said the woman. She sounded cross, impatient. "We took care of him, kept him alive for more than a month in the most primitive conditions imaginable. Until the situation became impossible. If he didn't have a constitution like an ox he would never have survived."

He couldn't be dead as well, he just couldn't be.

Jakób and Gretl in Germany and the Orphanage

Jakób found a place for them to sleep in a ruined building. The rain was coming down, but they managed to find a dry spot in a corner. Jakób gave her a piece of bread and some water from his bottle.

He didn't eat anything himself. "You eat, I'm not hungry," he said.

He drank a lot of water. Then he spread the blanket on the floor. "Put on your coat," he said.

"To sleep in?"

They talked until she was too sleepy to continue. He told her what he had read. There were Negroes and white people in South Africa, people who had lived in Holland and England and Germany long ago. They preferred to live in South Africa now, because it was far away from any war zone. And there were no Communists in South Africa. They didn't like the Communists at all.

He told her about the sun always shining and the milk and honey— the man who had been in hospital with him had said so.

He told her that according to the article in the paper good people would become her new mommy and daddy, people who wanted her so much that they had put their names on a special list for a little German girl.

Jakób was unable to sleep. Hunger was gnawing at his belly, but the doubt gnawing at his heart was much worse.

Was he doing the right thing?

South Africa? Africa?

He watched the sleeping face next to him in the feeble glow of the streetlight. He took off his jacket and covered her with it. He stroked and stroked her hair. A tight cord seemed to be tied around his neck.

God knows, it was the hardest thing he'd ever had to do.

Only ten of them shared a room now, and the older children had their own beds. Gretl was one of the older ones.

This time Onkel Schalk spoke only to the older children, who could understand him. He told them about the Union of South Africa, which was the full name of the country where they were going. He said the people really wanted them over there, especially the mommies and daddies who were waiting for them. He spoke about a place where the sun always shone and where there were plenty of oranges and bananas to eat. Gretl's thoughts began to wander.

I am really getting a new mommy and daddy, she thought, amazed. I don't remember my own father at all, and even Mutti's face and voice have faded. It's going to be strange having a new mother. And a home with piles of oranges and bananas, and plenty of milk and honey. But I'll have to learn a new language—two new languages, in fact.

I must remember I'm not Catholic, but German-Lutheran. The people in the Union must never know I once lived in southern Poland, she reminded herself, because they will want to know how I got there. And no one must ever ever know I have Jewish blood, that I'm not pure Aryan. And I mustn't say I learned Russian at school, because the Afrikaners hate the Russians, just as the Poles hate the Germans and the Germans hate the English.

The lump was back in her tummy.

Around her the children got up. She got up as well and stood in line. "Where are we going?" she asked the girl in front of her.

But they were already filing out to the dining hall, where piles of clothing were stacked on the tables: shoes, socks, blouses, dresses, sweaters. Even underpants. Two ladies stood behind the tables. The boys lined up on one side, the girls on the other.

"I'm Tante Hildegard Redecker," the lady on the girls' side said. "Onkel Schalk bought these clothes at Marks & Spencer's in London. I'm going to hand them out now."

All the children were talking at the same time. "No, no, this won't do," said the lady. "We'll hand out the shoes and socks first. Then we'll try on the dresses."

They walked up and down in their new shoes to see whether they fit.

GRETL'S JOURNEY TO SOUTH AFRICA

AT THE MASCHSEE IN HANNOVER THEY WERE EACH GIVEN A BED FOR ONE NIGHT ONLY. THE NEXT DAY THEY WOULD BE LEAVING FOR THE NETHERLANDS AND FROM THERE THEY WOULD TRAVEL TO ENGLAND ON A MILITARY TRAIN.

"There's a sea between the Netherlands and England," Gretl warned Onkel Schalk. A train can travel to many places, she knew, but not across a sea, because there are no tracks.

"You're right," he said and asked one of the helper ladies to show her the map. They would get off the train at Hoek van Holland in the Netherlands and cross the channel to England on a ferryboat. There they would catch another train that would take them to London. Gretl understood. She knew how an atlas worked.

When they got out at the station, the wind was gusting and the rain pelted down. They ran for the ferry. Gretl held Horst in her arms and told Ingeborg to hold on to her dress. She couldn't run, so all three of them were soaked and freezing when they reached the boat.

Inside Tante Hildegard took Horst from Gretl and gave her a towel. "Here, dry yourselves," she said. "We don't want sick children on the boat to South Africa."

At three in the morning the wind died down. Gretl did her best to clean up herself and Ingeborg before they both fell asleep.

The next morning was sunny and the boat lay motionless when

they woke up. They had already docked in Harwich. Gretl went up to the deck. Sunlight glittered like diamonds on the water and wavelets lapped against the boat. From the blue sky white birds dived into the water, making loud squawking sounds.

Some friendly ladies took them to a church to wash and have breakfast. Then they were taken to the Harwich station. Everyone spoke English, so Gretl didn't understand a word. The lump had shifted to her chest, because she knew the people in South Africa would be speaking English as well. It was completely different from German. "Can you speak English?" she asked Rita.

"No, only German," said Rita. "I took an extra sandwich, do you want a bite?"

The train took them to London, England's most important city. The station at London was called Liverpool, and more journalists were waiting for them there. "I won't be able to talk to them, because I can't speak English," Gretl told Tante Hildegard.

"Never mind, I think they'll speak to Onkel Schalk."

From Liverpool station they were taken to their hotel in a tall red bus. *Imperial Hotel*, Gretl read on the sign on the wall. It was a large building with many floors. They got off the bus and obediently filed to the front door.

Inside the hotel it was very smart. Smarter than a palace, Gretl thought. Ingeborg clung to her hand. Even Horst stopped to look around. The floor was shiny. The walls were hung with pictures and the stairs were carpeted.

But Onkel Schalk wasn't happy. The children's rooms were spread across all eight floors. "We won't sleep a wink tonight," Tante Hildegard said to one of the other ladies.

"I think the kids will sleep," said the other lady. "Last night has taken its toll on them."

Onkel Schalk had a surprise gift for each of the children: a toothbrush and a facecloth. They couldn't believe it.

"Das is meins, meins ganz alleine," they told each other.

"How do you say that in Afrikaans?" Gretl asked.

"Dis myne, net myne," said Tante Hildegard.

"I might be able to understand a little, but it's going to be really hard to speak the language," said Gretl, stroking the soft pink facecloth.

"You're clever; you'll soon pick it up," said Tante Hildegard. "Give Ingeborg a bath, I'll try to clean up Horst."

When Gretl woke the next morning, the sun shone cheerfully into their room.

In the dining room Tante Hildegard showed Gretl the newspaper.

"They've written about the South African Germans. See, here they talk about us. They say they were very impressed with the way eleven-year-old Eike Howaldt from Hamburg helped Miss Hildegard Redecker with the little ones in her group."

"What about me?" Gretl exclaimed indignantly. "I look after Horst! He's more trouble than five others!"

"You help me a lot," said Tante Hildegard. "They just didn't notice you. See what they say about the children: 'They all look fairly fit despite being very pale.'"

"I'd like to see the color of their faces after spending all night on that boat," Gretl said crossly. The English newspaper had upset her.

A bus took them back to Liverpool station, from where they were to catch a train to Southampton. "This is the last English station," Gretl told Rita. "The next time we arrive at a station we'll be in South Africa."

The first thing they had to do was learn what to do if the ship should sink. The children listened, wide-eyed. After the night on the ferryboat no one wanted to fall into the sea! Gretl made certain she knew where to find the boat she had to climb into if the ship sank. Tante Hildegard said she didn't have to worry about Ingeborg and Horst, the ladies and the crew would look after the toddlers. She was relieved. Ingeborg wouldn't be a problem, but Horst would never sit still on that small boat.

After supper the bigger children went to the games room, where Onkel Schalk spoke to them. "We must consider the other passengers," he said, "They are mostly British emigrants wanting to settle in the Union.

For the next three weeks you can't play wild games and make noise. But once we're in South Africa you'll have more than enough room to play."

Then he read to them from the German Bible and prayed in Afrikaans, because you speak to God in your own language, he said.

Gretl wondered in what language she was supposed to pray. If she wanted to speak to Lieber Herr Jesus, she prayed in German, and if she wanted to speak to the Holy Mother of God, she prayed in Polish, as the nuns had taught her.

"From tomorrow we're going to teach you a new Afrikaans hymn every evening," said Onkel Schalk. "Go to bed now, and I'll see you tomorrow."

"May I go up to the deck quickly?" Gretl asked Tante Irmgard.

"No, you must go to your cabins now. It's cold on deck. Why do you want to go there?"

"To look at the moon," Gretl said.

"Oh. We'll go another night, okay?" Tante Irmgard said and left.

In the evenings after supper Onkel Schalk and Mr. Johannes taught them Afrikaans songs: *Jan Pierewiet* and *Daar kom die wa* and *Ver in die wêreld, Kittie*. Tante Irmgard played the accordion. They also learned Afrikaans hymns: *O du fröhliche, o du selige*—which was now *O die vrolike, o die salige*—and *Kom kinders, kom juig nou, met vrolik geskal* and *Stille nag*. They were the same songs they had sung in the Deutsche Luthersche Kirche, but with Afrikaans words.

When they finished, it was too late to go on deck. Gretl wondered if the moon would be sailing all the way to South Africa with them.

What if no one wanted her? They might send her back to Germany. Then she could take the train to Poland. But it was no good thinking like that, she knew.

Or what if no one understood what she was saying? On the other hand, she understood a little Afrikaans, and she could say a few things, like: "It looks like rain in the west. It would be a relief." That was what you were supposed to say when there were clouds in the sky. But yesterday the sun had blazed all day.

What if the people who took her were awful? She wouldn't even think of that.

She didn't understand everything, but one thing she knew—no one must know that she had lived in Poland for four years, no one must know about her Jewish blood, and no one must know that she spoke Russian. And she had to be careful not to make the sign of the cross when someone prayed, because it was a sin.

The next morning there was a crowd to welcome them at the Pretoria station. Cameras flashed and there was a great commotion. Gretl's head throbbed. She was afraid it was going to explode. The big lump in her tummy ached, as if she had swallowed a stone.

The children were hurried along to a bus that drove them through a great many streets.

I hope I'll never have to smell a station again, she thought. For a moment she wondered what the smell of Jewish blood was like.

On the night of her eleventh birthday her tummy ached so badly that she couldn't sleep.

GRETL SETTLES INTO LIFE IN SOUTH AFRICA

THE LADY STROKED HER HAIR. "GO TO SLEEP THEN," SHE SAID.

They want me, Gretl told herself. They really want me, even though I'm eleven. It's what I wanted too. I've prayed for this night.

For weeks she had prayed—in orphanage rooms and on the ship and in jerking trains. But all she felt now was emptiness and a yearning for the familiar. The soil in this country was too hard and dry, the sun was too hot, the sky too blue.

When their father read from the Bible in the evenings, they all sat at the table. She sat next to her mommy and when they prayed, she held hands with her mommy and Kobus. When Kobus wasn't home, she sat in his chair next to her daddy and held hands with her mommy and daddy.

That day she had resolved to become a nun, like the dear sisters at school.

But now the synagogue and Częstochowa and Germany lay on the other side of a three-week ocean. And there was no one she could ask if the same God lives everywhere. And if he understands every language. So she decided simply to accept the fact that she had been blessed numerous times in her life.

A crowd of people came to the house after church. They ate the cake her mommy and Maria had baked and drank coffee and ginger beer. It was very hot, but she and Kobus weren't allowed to swim because it was a sin to swim on a Sunday. On Sundays you were allowed to read the Bible, but no storybooks. And the *Good News* magazine, which wasn't very interesting. Luckily her mother turned a blind eye to that rule.

In the late afternoon she and her father took Kobus back to boarding school. She was sad, because she had enjoyed having him home every day.

Suddenly she wasn't so sure any more about going to school the next day.

When she noticed a big fat spider watching her from a corner of her bedroom that night, she knew it didn't bode well for the following day.

That night her father prayed that Almighty God would be with her and give her strength because it wasn't easy at school. At bedtime, when she knelt beside her bed—just as Mutti had taught her when she was small—she pleaded with Lieber Herr Jesus in German to help her. Then she prayed to the Holy Virgin in Polish, just for good measure.

After that, some days at school were still very bad, but never as bad as that first day. When Kobus came home on Friday afternoon, he asked: "Did the children give you trouble?"

"Yes, but the teacher gave them hell."

Her father frowned. "Where did the child learn to speak like that?" he asked.

Her mother smiled. "Ask your son," she said.

She knew then that she could ask her father anything at all because, just like Jakób, he knew everything. Yet she couldn't ask him about the different Gods, because he could never know about the Jewish blood and the Catholic Threat.

"I'm not afraid of that eye anymore," she told Kobus the following Friday. "It's just God looking after me so that I don't burn."

"What are you talking about?"

"About the eye, in the picture in Auntie Lovey's house. And the fire that purifies me until I reflect the image of God."

He gave her a blank look. "You're silly, you know that?" he said. "The fire is in hell, and God isn't in hell. Don't talk like that; it's the devil's talk."

She shrugged. Maybe he didn't understand because she wasn't very good at explaining in Afrikaans. Or maybe he was just thick—boys were thick, after all.

"Ask Daddy," she said and walked away.

Before the schools closed for the summer vacation, Kobus told her that Grandpa John would be spending Christmas with them. He would be sleeping in the bedroom on the veranda of the old homestead. And Kobus would be sleeping there as well, in one of the inside bedrooms.

"Can I sleep there too?" asked Gretl. It sounded like fun.

"No, you're a girl," Kobus said firmly.

Kobus said he didn't like Englishmen, but he loved Grandpa John, because he wasn't like the rest of them. Well, maybe he was, but anyhow . . . did she understand? She didn't understand at all, but she said yes, she understood, so that Kobus wouldn't think she was a dumb girl.

A week later she and Grandpa John were having long conversations. They didn't always understand each other's words, but they understood each other nonetheless.

She was too excited to eat.

Tonight they were sitting at the Weihnachtsbaum in the living room to read the Bible. "Kersfeesboom," it was called in Afrikaans. She sat on her daddy's knee, and his arm was around her. Her mommy sat with Grandpa John, because he was her daddy. When she spoke to him, she called him Daddy. Kobus sat alone, because boys didn't like sitting with anyone.

They sang *Stille Nag* in Afrikaans. Then her mommy and Grandpa John sang *Silent Night* in English, then she and her mommy sang *Stille Nacht* in German.

Finally Kobus began to hand out the gifts.

When Jakób had come home, from Katowice, he had put his bag down and opened his arms.

He had brought her a white and a red ribbon, and warm shoes.

She looked at her new watch. It was almost eleven.

The cathedral would be full of candles tonight, now, at this moment. The organ would be playing beautiful music.

After the midnight mass they would walk home in the moonlight.

Jakób would remember her, she knew, because it was Christmas.

The date on the new *Brandwag* said 24 December, but it arrived by mail the week after Christmas. It was Kobus's turn to read it first, and after a few moments he shouted excitedly: "Grietjie, come and take a look! There's an article here on one of the German orphans!"

She grabbed the magazine from him and read:

Mr and Mrs L.I. Fouché of Florida had wanted a little boy. At the end of September Mr Fouché left for Pretoria to fetch his son.

"In Pretoria I paced up and down in front of the office where Dr Bührmann and Mr J.C. Combrink, chairman of the Fund's Allocation Committee were speaking to the various foster parents. After a while a little boy with red hair came running along. He was skinny, with thin legs and even thinner arms. His face was thin too, with a slight rosiness in the pale cheeks. His bare feet were obviously tender, because he was limping along the gravel path. I looked at him with interest and objectively I decided: Well, it would be fine if I got you.

"Not long afterwards I was facing Dr Bührmann and Mr Combrink across a desk. I was reminded again that the committee had allocated an excellent boy to me. Dr Bührmann briefly described the background of seven-year-old Heinz-Jochen Schulz from Nordrhein-Westfalen. Dr Bührmann left the room and when she returned, the big moment arrived. 'Er ist dein Vater,' she told Jochen.

"For a brief moment Jochen looked at me with his blue eyes. Then he jumped into my lap, grabbed me around the neck and pressed his cheek to mine, his small body trembling with excitement, a picture of contentment, as if he knew he had arrived at a safe haven after years of facing countless tribulations.

"While the documentation was being attended to, we fetched his few items of clothing—wrapped in brown paper and tied up with string. Full of confidence, his small hand clinging tightly to mine, he walked on those sharp stones until 'Vater' picked him up. Then the floodgates opened. "Do you have a car?" was the first question he asked. With great difficulty I dredged up my rusty German, which I hadn't spoken for thirteen years, and with much waving of hands and gesturing we got through his questions.

"When we reached home, he politely held out his hand and, bowing halfway to the ground and looking extremely pleased, he mumbled: 'Tag, Mutter.'"

Inquisitive and interested neighbors stayed up late that evening to meet the Fouchés' new German child.

What left a lasting impression on the Fouché couple was how undernourished Jochen was. "Thin, little more than skin and bone, with veins so blue so that you could count them as they criss-crossed the milky skin of the small back.

"In a matter of days he was quite at home. It's amazing how quickly Jochen has learned to speak Afrikaans."

Gretl smiled. She clearly remembered the red-headed Heinz-Jochen Schulz from Nordrhein-Westfalen. She was glad he was doing so well.

She wished she could find out what had happened to Ingeborg, and busy little Horst, and her friend Rita, who had always been hungry.

On 16 May 1952, three hundred years after Jan van Riebeeck had landed at the Cape, *Die Huisgenoot* published an article about the German orphans who had come to South Africa from Europe four years earlier. There was a photo of Gerti and Peter Jaensch and Joachim Taube doing volkspele. Gretl remembered them. The article mentioned how well the German orphans had been assimilated in the Afrikaner community, and what a credit they were to the Afrikaner people.

Jakób and Gretl reunited in South Africa

It was only when he was in his blue Volksie, on his way to his apartment that he found time to reflect. She'd had a fright, she was asking for him. Thank you, Holy Mother of God, that she's unharmed.

She had been frightened by an explosion, she wanted him on the farm. She had told her parents about him that was why Grandpa John had been able to find him.

On the other hand, Grandpa John had not known his last name. He had simply asked for a metallurgical engineer named Jakób.

He packed a few items of clothing and locked the door behind him.

The old man smiled. "Yes," he said, "that's what everyone calls me, even my daughter-in-law. And my very Afrikaans son-in-law, whom I hold in high regard."

The town was small, with only one tarred street straight through the middle. Jakób saw the church first, and then Cohen Crown's store, the Co-op and the coffee shop. The school was a red brick building with a long veranda and a row of classrooms, much like the school he had attended in Częstochowa as a boy.

When they had left the town behind, they crossed the railroad. "It's not too far now," said Grandpa John.

The land here is dry, even drier than in Thabazimbi, Jakób thought.

They drove along the foot of a rugged mountain strewn with big boulders, they crossed a dry, sandy riverbed, and drove past a kraal built of stones. "There's the homestead," said Grandpa John.

He looked at Grietjie's home in Darkest Africa, where he had sent her—the large sandstone house with the wide veranda which had become her entire world. If only he had known, all those years, how much light there was over here.

"It's beautiful here," he told Grandpa John, "very beautiful."

They stopped in front of the veranda. Two dogs came bounding around the corner, barking. When they recognized the car, they approached, tails wagging.

An attractive woman and a very tall man came up to the car. Grietjie was nowhere to be seen.

Jakób followed Grietjie's new mother—Grietjie's only mother. They crossed the veranda, walked through the elegant living room, through the dining room with its long table and many chairs, with enough room for a big family. "She's not doing well," said the woman and her eyes filled with tears again. "She doesn't speak. In fact, she hasn't said a word since the accident. She just lies there, her big blue eyes staring at the door. She doesn't sleep, she doesn't eat. When the doctor gives her an injection, she falls into a restless sleep, during which she mumbles and keeps calling your name. I'm sorry, but we didn't know who you were."

They walked past two bedrooms. Grietjie's mother pushed open the door of a third one.

"I knew it would be good for her to talk. I asked her. She just said her father had died on the battlefield, she'd never known him. And her mother and grandmother had died in an explosion, her sister of an illness."

He listened quietly, waited for her to continue. She stroked and stroked the blonde hair. "Jakób, my child is broken."

"I knew Grietjie when she was small," he said, "in Europe."

"You can speak English," said Grietjie's father.

"I'm learning Afrikaans. I'm from Poland."

"Poland?" the man asked, frowning.

At different times they were joined by Kate, or Grandpa John, or Bernard. Just before suppertime Grietjie opened her eyes. "Jakób?"

"I'm here, Gretz."

She smiled slightly, and seemed relieved. "I'm hungry," she said, still in Polish.

"What do you feel like eating?"

"Soup. Potato soup."

He translated for Kate, who stood by anxiously. "I'm glad she wants to eat," she said. "But potato soup?"

Grietjie fell asleep again. Kate brought Jakób a plate of food. "The soup isn't ready yet," she apologized.

"Don't worry, she's gone back to sleep," he said.

After supper the family gathered in the bedroom. Kobus fetched the big family Bible.

They took each other's hands. Grietjie was still clinging to his hand in her sleep. Kate took his other hand, Bernard leaned over and put his free hand on Grietjie's head.

Jakób looked up at Grietjie's father. "Thank you," he said in Afrikaans, "thank you for praying for me as well."

Bernard nodded and turned to Grietjie. "Is Daddy's little lamb awake now?" he asked tenderly.

She turned her head to him and smiled slightly. "Daddy," she said. Then she closed her eyes and promptly went back to sleep.

After a while she said: "Jakób, I'm very hungry."

"Your mother made soup, but it will be cold by now. Shall I heat it up for you?"

"No," she said, "stay with me. I'll eat cold soup."

He didn't ask about the explosion or the fire or who Jurgen was. He helped her eat the soup and spoke about everyday things.

Suddenly she frowned. "Jakób, how did you get here?"

"I came with Grandpa John," he answered as simply as possible.

"Do you know Grandpa John then?"

"I know him now. He's a remarkable person."

"He is, yes," she said and fell asleep again.

Jakób woke when Kate touched his shoulder. The sun wasn't up yet but it was starting to get light outside. "Don't you want to lie down for a while?" she asked. "I'll sit with her and call you when she wakes up."

Jakób straightened his spine and stretched his neck. "Thanks, Kate, but I promised I'd stay with her."

"Shall I bring you some coffee?" she asked.

"Coffee would be wonderful, thanks."

Jakób asked: "Don't you feel like getting up and sitting on the veranda?"

"Yes," said Grietjie, "I'll get up. They'll be having coffee now, or orange squash, and Grandpa John his whiskey."

"Put on your bathrobe and your slippers. Shall I help you?"

She shook her head. "No, I'll manage. Don't go without me."

But when she got out of bed, she was suddenly light-headed. "Goodness," she said, "I'm drunk!"

"From Grandpa John's whiskey?" he teased.

"No, Jakób Kowalski! From too much sleep, I suppose."

"Shall I carry you?"

"No, I'm not sick. Just hold my arm."

Her parents took her to her room. Jakób remained on the veranda. "I'd like to see your pigs tomorrow," he told Kobus.

"I'd be happy to show you," said Kobus. "You can tell me about your farming methods in Poland."

Everyone was waiting for him to say something, Jakób realized, but no one asked. As soon as Grietjie was strong enough, they'd have to talk. And they couldn't put it off for too long, because he couldn't take more than a week's leave. Even if Grandpa John was a personal friend of Mr Meyer's.

But first, he thought, I must try and figure out who Jurgen is and what happened to him.

She was quiet for a moment. Her eyes remained closed. "Oma didn't want to tell me where Jurgen was, but I remember he was on the bed. I think he got burned, Jakób."

"Yes, I think so too, Grietjie," Jakób answered evenly.

Kobus found them like that early the next morning. "Don't tell me I'm getting coffee I didn't make myself this morning!" he said cheerfully.

Then he frowned. "Is Grietjie okay?"

"I think she will be," answered his mother and got up. "I pray she'll get better now. I'm going to see if she's still asleep."

"Dad," Kobus said worriedly, "what's going on?"

"We put out the fire," Bernard answered and followed his wife.

Kobus turned to Jakób. "Are they okay?"

"Yes, but it's been a long night," Jakób said. "And I'm much too tired to explain."

DISCUSSION QUESTIONS

1. What are the key influencers of Gretl's early identity, and how do they shape her perception of the world and of herself? What words would you use to describe her character when we first meet her and then as she begins to face the difficult realities of the life ahead of her? Would you say that Gretl experiences an identity crisis at any point in the story?

2. In spite of her early life of deprivation and displacement, Gretl still maintains the ability to connect meaningfully with the people she encounters along her journey. What are the core aspects of Gretl's character that allow her not only to survive but to thrive in such uncertain circumstances?

3. Why is Jakób able to extend himself beyond the limitations of his circumstances to care for Gretl? What are his motivations—guilt, human kindness, an unusual sense of connection to Gretl?

4. Discuss the progression of Gretl's relationship with Jakób from father figure to romantic figure.

5. Compare and contrast Gretl's character development—her gradual growth to maturity—with Jakób's very different journey. How are their perspectives different, and what allows them to find a common place to inhabit together?

6. Describe and discuss Gretl's religious journey throughout the story. How does she ultimately make a specific belief system her own? Did this embracing of her Protestant identity feel authentic to you? Why or why not? What about her embracing of religious tolerance and her acceptance of Jakób's Catholic faith?

7. Does Gretl ever experience a sense of shame of her true identity? If so, when, and if not, why not?

8. What are the core themes of the novel, and how are they treated through Gretl's character development and her journey? How are these themes relevant today?

9. Discuss the thematic imagery around trains in the story. How does the image of the train evolve throughout the course of the novel?

10. Discuss the role of fairy tales in the story (dragons, Hansel and Gretel, Witch, Heidi, Ugly Duckling, Cinderella). How does Gretl try to write her own happy ending to her story?

11. Discuss the role of Old Testament stories in the narrative.

12. Discuss the recurrence of explosions and fire in the story and their relevance to Gretl's evolution.

13. Discuss the symbolism of the moon in the story.

To enhance your reading and book club experience, visit GirlFromTheTrain.com in order to access more exclusive bonus features.

ACKNOWLEDGMENTS

If I have talent, it's by God's grace—my thanks go to my Heavenly Father.

Thank you to the following people: my cousin Jackie Grobler and my son Jan-Jan for managing to find unobtainable books; my brother Johan Moerdyk for his knowledge of the armament and battle strategies of World War II; Jan-Jan for touring through Eastern Europe and braving Auschwitz with me; my friend Werner Schellack (Van der Merwe) for his wonderful book on the German orphans; Elize, Helene, Madeleine, and Jan-Jan for polishing my manuscript.

A special thanks to my family and my Meintjes friends, who put up with my writing, even during our vacation, and to my mother, Alida Moerdyk, who, ever since my childhood, has made me believe that I can write. And a big thank-you to my husband, Jan, who supports and encourages me. And loves me.

Sources

Bethell, Nicholas. *Gomulka, His Poland and His Communism.* Longmans, 1969.

Bór-Komorowski, General. *The Secret Army.* (This book was apparently published in 1945 and is out of print. The writer used photocopies of the relevant parts sent to her from Poland. Attempts to trace the publisher and date of publication have been unsuccessful. The material provides inside information about the Polish resistance movement.)

Dziewanowski, D. K. *Poland in the Twentieth Century.* Columbia University Press, 1977.

Karski, Jan. *Story of a Secret State.* Simon Publications, 2001.

Mikolajczyk, Stanislaw. *The Rape of Poland: Pattern of Soviet Aggression.* Whittlesey House, McGraw-Hill Book Company. (The page showing the publication date had been removed.)

Syrop, Konrad. *Spring in October: The Story of the Polish Revolution, 1956.* Frederick A. Praeger Publishers, New York, 1957.

Van der Merwe, Werner. *Vir 'n "Blanke Volk": Die verhaal van die Duitse weeskinders van 1948.* Perskor, 1988.

About the Author

International bestselling author Irma Joubert lives and works in South Africa and writes in her native Afrikaans. A teacher for thirty-five years, Irma began to write after her retirement. She is the author of eight novels and is a regular fixture on bestseller lists in both South Africa and The Netherlands. Irma and her husband Jan have been married for forty-five years, and they have three sons and a daughter, two daughters-in-law, a son-in-law, and three grandchildren. *The Girl From the Train* is her first novel to be translated into English.